The Day of the Labyrinth

The Blind Seer and the Gift of Love:
A Novel

The Day of the Labyrinth

The Blind Seer and the Gift of Love:
A Novel

Roger Haydon Mitchell

**TOP HAT
BOOKS**

Winchester, UK
Washington, USA

JOHN HUNT PUBLISHING

First published by Top Hat Books, 2023
Top Hat Books is an imprint of John Hunt Publishing Ltd., No. 3 East St., Alresford,
Hampshire SO24 9EE, UK
office@jhpbooks.com
www.johnhuntpublishing.com
www.tophat-books.com

For distributor details and how to order please visit the 'Ordering' section on our website.

Design: Lapiz Digital Serivices

UK: Printed and bound by CPI Group (UK) Ltd, Croydon, CR0 4YY
US: Printed and bound by Thomson-Shore, 7300 West Joy Road, Dexter, MI 48130

We operate a distinctive and ethical publishing philosophy in
all areas of our business, from our global network of authors to
production and worldwide distribution.

Contents

This novel choreographs the compelling journey of a diverse group of companions in their attempt to subvert the Roman Empire with justice and love. Grappling with the political realities of war, violence and selfish ambition as they interface with peace, friendship and belonging, it investigates the potential of love as an alternative way of being. The narrative is rooted in the first episode of the author's doctoral research which investigated a proposed fourth-century fall of the church and is published under the title *Church, Gospel and Empire: How the Politics of Sovereignty Impregnated the West* (Eugene, Oregon: Wipf & Stock, 2011). The story uses the disturbing and challenging research findings about Constantine the Great and Eusebius of Caesarea alongside the popular French legend of Saint Quentin and Eusébie to develop a mainly fictional or "fantastic" history. The result provides a further window on the relationship of church and empire. It is intended as the first of four such fantastic narratives!

For the coming generation and all who love them. Especially my grandchildren Jasper, Imogen, Emilia, Wanda and the unexpected addition of Ben, Chloe, Avellana and Bertie!

Glossary

amicus, amici (plural): friend

atrium: the main central living space of a Roman Villa, open to the sky

Ambianum: Amiens

Arretium: Arezzo

Augusta Veromanduorum: original Roman name of the French Town of St Quentin near the source of the Somme

Augusta Treverorum: Trier

Augusta Taurinorum: Turin

aurochs: The aurochs is an extinct cattle species, considered to be the wild ancestor of modern domestic cattle. With a shoulder height of up to 180cm in bulls and 155cm in cows, it was one of the largest herbivores in the Holocene; it had massive elongated and broad horns that reached 80cm in length

auxilia: Roman army troops who were non-citizens

aviae: grandmother

caput capitis: expletive, knob head

carpentum: pl. carpenta: the bus or limousine of wealthier Romans. For four or more passengers. It had four wheels, a wooden arched rooftop and was pretty comfortable, spacious and nicely decorated inside. Pulled by two or four horses

carruca: pl. carrucas: like a smaller carpentum. Again it was usually used by wealthier Romans and could accommodate two passengers. It had four wheels and was usually pulled by two horses

carrus clabularis: a large, open wagon, with sides of wicker work, used in transporting soldiers

castrum, castra: the singular form castrum meant "fort", while the plural form castra meant "camp"

Cataractonium: Catterick

cena: main meal of the day, eaten at midday or early afternoon

centuria: originally the basic tactical unit of the legion in the Roman army. Initially, it had a hundred soldiers (centum means "one hundred") commanded by a centurion (centurio). In the fourth century BCE, a new tactical unit consisting of two centuries was created

Christos: Christ

Clusium: ancient Etruscan town on the site of modern Chiusi, in Tuscany the region, north-central Italy

Colonia Agrippina: Cologne

comēs rei militaris: titled military advisers to the emperor

Constantinus invictus: Constantine invincible

Coria: Corbridge

decurio: originally the head of a group of ten men, by late Roman times was the leader of a turma

domus: substantial town house

Eboracum: York

ecclesia: Greek word for the elders responsible for a Greek city such as Athens. Taken up by Jesus to refer to the body of his followers cf. Mtt 16: 18

essedum: a fast two-horse chariot

Fiano Romano: a town 25 miles north of Rome on the Via Tiberina

Florentia: Florence

Frumentarii: Roman secret service

Gesoriacum: Boulogne-Sur-Mer

homoousios: from Ancient Greek: ὁμοούσιον, lit. "same in being, same in essence", from ὁμός, homós, "same" and οὐσία, ousía, "being" or "essence." It became a Christian theological term, most notably used in the Nicene Creed for describing Jesus (God the Son) as "same in being" or "same in essence" with God the Father

ientaculum: breakfast

impluvium: A low basin in the centre of a household atrium, into which rainwater flowed down from the roof in hoc signo vinces: in this sign you will conquer

labarum: a banner or flag bearing symbolic motifs, which came to be identified historically with the Tau and Chi Rho symbols of the cross on the banners of Constantine's army

Latanculi: Roman board game

legatum legionis: legion commander

Lindum: Lincoln

mansiones: service station situated at similar distances on the Roman Road as today's motorway services

mare clausum: used to refer to sea officially closed to navigation in winter

Mediolanum: Milan

meretrix: female prostitute

Pax Romana: political term for the established and settled mid-to-late Roman Empire, under threat by the time of Constantine the Great

pecunia: money

paenulae: a long sleeveless cloak of ancient Rome usually having a hood and sometimes a front opening

peristyle: a continuous porch formed by a row of columns surrounding the perimeter of a building or courtyard

praefectus: high administrative official or chief officer

proavia: great grandmother

procurator: imperial governor of a minor Roman province

quadriga: chariot drawn by four horses abreast and favoured for chariot racing

quid mirum: what a surprise

Rho: the Greek letter "r", which written as a capital is somewhat confusingly for the uninitiated written as "P" and often combined with X as the sign Chi Rho as in Christos

sacerdos: Roman official authorised to lead the sacred rituals of a religion

sagum: a square or rectangular cloak made of coarse wool, fastened usually on the right shoulder, worn by soldiers

Scholai Palatinae: an elite military guard unit operating as the cavalry arm of the Praetorian Guard

servus corporis: personal attendant or body slave

tabernae: a single-room shop for the sale of goods and services

Tad: Pictish for Dad

Tau: the Greek letter "T"

Trimontium: Melrose

turma, turmae (plural): approximately 30 cavalrymen in the late Roman army

Vagharshapat: ancient capital of Armenia

vesperna: supper, lighter meal than the midday or early afternoon cena

vestibulum: a spacious entrance hall

villa: substantial country or suburban house

Volusii Saturnini: The Villa dei Volusii Saturnini is an archaeological site located in the municipality of Fiano Romano

Part One

Prelude

She sat at the source of the river in the shade of the oaks and breathed out gently across the surface of the pool. At first almost imperceptibly, but then with gathering momentum, the water troubled, stirred, opened, and the angel of the Somme gradually emerged, first kneeling, then standing fully upright into the evening sunshine. Beatrice watched in delight as the lissom spectre shook themself in the gentle breeze and, lifting their head, began to sing. Softly at first and then with burgeoning splendour, the love song of the land filled the evening air. Extemporaneously, after a few moments, she joined in. Tenderly, the angel held her gaze and then, harmonising together in clarion refrain, their song resounded out over the verdant meadows, calling for tribes of humanity to come in unity and make their home in joyful partnership with the coastlands and islands of Gaul and Britannia. As the breeze gathered strength, the vegetation and trees joined the chorus, their rustling leaves and sweeping limbs giving orchestral accompaniment as the song rolled on across the surrounding countryside and away over the distant horizon.

Chapter One

Minotaur and Angel

As the day progressed, the palm tree cast its shadow across the mosaic floor of the *atrium* like the gnomon on a sundial. Eusébie watched its relentless approach towards the imprisoned Minotaur, as she had done every summer day for as long as she could remember. Other eyes had watched its progress similarly for a century and more, but none more avidly than hers. "Would the inner walls of the labyrinth prison break open at last?" She longed for her father Julius to return. Then order would come again to the household and the physician would return with more salve for her eyes. She knew her sight was deteriorating. She could still see the sharpness of the sunlight and the precise line cast by the tree's trunk but the distinction between the white and black tiles of the mosaic blurred more and more as her birthday drew closer. She could hear the clatter of bronze pots and kettles and knew the slave girl would soon bring the evening meal.

"Abaskantis! Is it nearly time for *vesperna*? Will mother be home tonight? Is there news of father? Have we heard from Uncle Quentin and is Valeria coming to see me?"

Abaskantis was a secret listener to many conversations as she went about her daily household tasks in the *villa*, catering and cleaning. If there were news from the senate, the battlefront, or the mission, she would soon know and willingly spill all to her young charge. She was, to be honest, uneasy about Valeria's pride of place in Eusébie's affections, so that was the one question she would not be answering if she could help it. Valeria was Eusébie's aunt and Quentin's sister, but two less alike you could hardly imagine. The latter strong but gentle, quietly attentive to all around him, while fully intent on living out his radical faith. His sister, on the other hand, was a carefree, excitable enthusiast able to make everything an adventure, even her niece's encroaching blindness. She was furious when her father forbade her to travel with Quentin and his companions on their return to Gaul the previous summer. Then she was only eighteen and about to be married off, as she accurately feared, and still much too young to be a countercultural heretic in the eyes of her senator father.

By now, the tree's shadow was cutting through the Minotaur's bullish neck, severing head from body as the mealtime approached. These days the remaining bold outlines of the story enacted on the floor of the atrium tended to encourage Eusébie to believe that the battles really would soon bring peace to Villa Metilia.

"Abaskantis," she called, "can you hear me? I want the battle to be over!" In the past when Eusébie's sight was clearer, the gnomon broke first the wall of tiles that framed the Minotaur's gaol and darkened her later dreams with images of the beast's escape from the labyrinth and the ancient tales of Europe's origins with which her young aunt delighted to scare her.

"A young noble woman is never too small to beware the predatory intentions of Roman generals and their minions," was Valeria's excuse when Eusébie begged her to stop.

Abaskantis emerged with a tray laden with goodies, which she spread out on the low table. From the quantity, it was obvious that this was not going to be a solitary meal.

"Your mother may be home later, I'm not sure, but in the meantime you eat, and I will tell you the news from the battlefront." Eusébie carefully selected a large piece of her favourite honey sweetened cake and patted the seat next to her on the couch.

"So tell me, tell me, Abaskantis, what have you heard?" The slave girl seated herself gratefully, not something she would have dreamt of doing had her mistress been present, and began.

4

"Well, the empire's not going to collapse after all! The new emperor has what it takes and the borders are being won back everywhere. They will make the barbarians pay, you can be sure of that. As for your father, the news is that he is only days away from Rome and on his return from victory over the Samartians at last! But the story spreading everywhere is that Diocletian says we must return to the old gods if the victory is to hold!" Eusébie paled visibly on hearing this.

"I'm sure that's what grandfather really thinks, maybe father too." Seeing her reaction Abaskantis set about reassuring the young girl,

"Now don't you go worrying about that uncle of yours..."

The sound of a *carruca* sweeping into the courtyard outside, with its doors banging and shouts of laughter erupting, halted the slave girl midstream. Valeria, her long brown hair gathered at the neck but flowing in the evening breeze, swept into the atrium announcing herself with, "Hey there, gorgeous girl, leave some for me!"

At her appearance, Abaskantis quickly retrieved the empty tray and retreated, while Eusébie leapt to her feet and flung herself on her aunt.

"I knew you would come! Have you heard the news? The battles are won, and father is only days away. Oh, Valeria, the emperor says now we must go back to the horrid old worship!" Valeria hugged her niece tightly, swinging her full circle and tumbling them together onto the couch.

"Come on, Eusébie, have some more of this delicious cake. Your uncle's love for friend and enemy alike will disarm them all in the end, you see if it won't, whatever Diocletian and Maximian have to say about it."

Eusébie was lost in her thoughts for a moment, remembering the months when, as a six- and seven-year-old, she had spent delicious days with her uncle on his return to Rome during his mother's, and her grandmother's, sickness and death. The unusual closeness of the three of them in those months had transformed the child's usually isolated existence, mainly alone with Abaskantis. Until then her grandmother was always busy with the duties and responsibilities of patrician life and had seemed a somewhat aloof, imperious woman, despite her faith. However, the return of her older son and his insistence on weaving Eusébie into the routine of warmth and love with which he surrounded his ailing mother meant that despite the sadness and subsequent mourning, it had been the best of times for the child.

"Hey, where have you gone, little one?" Valeria asked, wrapping her arms around her once again and quite literally pulling her back into the present.

"I'm remembering Uncle Quentin's stories! How they spent whole days praying and even though his chubby friend kept dropping off to sleep, they'd go out among the crowds and when he made the sign of the cross, the blind saw, the deaf heard and the lame walked, just like in the Jesus story!"

"Yes," chimed in Valeria, "and how he told us that the great villas like ours here on the Janiculan Hill were built on the reclaimed ground where they used to throw the crucified corpses of the slaves and the poor. Then the cross was the symbol of Rome's bloodiest oppressions. Now it's the love sign to conquer war and pain!"

Later that evening, long after their reminiscences had ended and Valeria had helped settle her niece to sleep, Eusébie's mother Claudia and the senator returned. Zeno was more and more exhausted of late, well into his seventies and still carrying a huge sense of responsibility for the city and empire. The impact of Diocletian's reforms, while greatly improving the security of Rome and its empire as a whole, had weakened the authority of the senate. One such reform asserted the right of the emperor to take power without the consent of the senate at all, thus depriving it of its status as the ultimate depository of supreme authority.

Responsibility without power weighed heavily on Zeno, and the waning of the transcendent impact of the old religion added to his sense of impotency in the face of the future. It was this, perhaps, that explained his ambivalence towards the counter-politics of his eldest son and his influence over their household, and why his soldiering younger son brought him such reassurance. His daughter-in-law did all she could to lighten the load of his days, and he was grateful. Now she took his arm and led him across to the dining area where Abaskantis was hurriedly adding fresh supplies to the table.

"Sit down and eat, Pater, don't go hungry to bed". The business of the day had been outside the city, they had eaten nothing since *cena*, which had been a disappointing stop-off at a *mansiones* that had seen better days. Zeno seated himself, wearily, but then a smile broke through the worry lines etched into his once handsome face.

"Julius is less than a week away by now. He should be here in time for Eusébie's birthday. And it may be the last time she sees him with her own eyes, so we need to make this one to remember!"

Claudia was both excited and apprehensive at the thought of Julius' return. He had been gone now almost as long as his brother. His return would bring a welcome order back to the villa, no doubt. He was ever the organiser, the problem solver, the deviser of new plans and positions. He would put the slaves to work on the farm with new vigour and the house would become again a place of hospitality and convocation for the rising generation of patricians. Maybe even Diocletian himself or at least his victorious lieutenants would visit to reflect on the hard won successes and talk consolidation of power. She had enjoyed supporting Zeno in her mother-in-law's place on his continual round of visits and appointments. That would have to stop, she reflected, and her much more demanding husband would take centre stage.

"He will have remembered the birthday, Pater, won't he? He will have so much else on his mind." Zeno passed a weary hand over his drooping eyes.

"He'll not forget, Claudia. He loves the child. Now I will leave you to your thoughts, my dear. I need my bed." He rose and crossed the atrium to his room and Claudia, after looking in on Eusébie, made her way to her own bedroom.

Her daughter appeared to be sound asleep, but actually, she was dreaming. She was in the atrium and the shadow of the palm tree was moving across the mosaic as on a typical day. Yet something was awry. The Minotaur had gone! Eusébie stepped gingerly along the tiled maze of the labyrinth, all the way to its centre, something she had never before dared to do, until she reached the now empty middle square. Suddenly, the floor opened beneath her and she felt herself falling, falling, way down through darkness, but then landing on both feet, shaken but unhurt, on the floor of a great hall. In the dream, she could still see with a clarity unavailable to her in real life. Shadows surrounded the walls and gave off a silvery light. She knew instinctively that they were ghosts, shades of the empire's crucified slaves and prisoners of war. Then, as she adjusted to the light, she saw that in the middle of the hall was an enormous bed, and lying on it, a beautiful young woman—

"Is it Valeria?" But no, it was similar to her, but it was a woman from the olden days, like a Greek princess, almost a goddess. Although Eusébie knew, she was human nonetheless. Then, from the very far end of the hall, there emerged a huge creature.

She could hear its footfall, not hard or harsh, but firm and relentless in its progress. The beast was beautiful, like an enormous pet, its white, soft coat shimmering in the ghostly light. Then she saw, trembling now for the woman on the bed, that it was a huge, white bull. It came to the bed, climbed in, and nestled up to the woman, who was unresisting at first. But after that, suddenly and with brutal ferocity, it thrust its huge bulk on top of her! Eusébie tried to cry out, but found herself altogether rigid with shock, her tongue clinging to the roof of her mouth. And then, all at once, she was awake, gasping for breath, horrified at what she had witnessed, wanting to call out, but still unable to do so. Eventually she found that she was able to slip out from beneath the bedclothes and make her way over to the washstand where Abaskantis placed fresh water each evening, and began to gulp it down thirstily. Gradually she calmed down and made her way back to bed. Then, with a mental note to ask Valeria about what she had seen, she fell back to sleep.

***

Quentin braced himself against the vibration of the metal rims of the carruca on the unyielding surface of the road. The journey from *Augusta Veromanduorum* had impressed itself on his sciatic nerve for several days. Now the return to *Ambianum* threatened to set it off again. He reflected on how much better the road was than since he first arrived in Gaul. Not that the improvements in the security and prosperity of the empire since Diocletian and Maximian got a grip on things had been positive for him and his companions. The increasing anarchy and near collapse of the empire in the previous decades had left the first years of their mission work in Ambianum comparatively unhindered by the authorities such as there were. With its roads radiating out like the sun's rays and providing easy communication for the message of light despite their decaying condition, it made for a near perfect hub from which to operate strategically throughout the region. A veritable Gaulish Antioch just as they had planned. That is, until Maximian's new *procurator* had arrived on the scene. Now there was nowhere to hide from the newly reordered administration and its determination to reassert the grip of Rome.

Quentin looked amusedly across at Fuscian, sleeping soundly on the opposite side of the carruca, the very picture of cherubic contentment despite everything. His face and body bore the scars from the beatings and torture inflicted on them both earlier in the year by the said procurator, Rictiovarus. A hard enemy to love, that one. Quentin had tried to honour him by succumbing at first to his insistence that they joined him in making offerings to the old gods. The apostle Paul had advised on being subject to the imperial rulers as far as possible, and he had tried to see their worship as after all meaningless, simply participating in the culture of the time for the sake of the peace. Now he knew it was more than that. This was not just some old Roman ceremony; this was agreeing that the whole of the political crisis of the last half century was at root a fault, a curse, brought about by the followers of Jesus of Nazareth. Whereas it was his peaceable kingdom which might actually end oppression and make wars cease. This reassertion of imperial power was something that love simply had to oppose, even if martyrdom were the outcome. After all, martyr was Greek for witness, and they were all only witnesses to a better way, neither more nor less.

A harder than usual rut in the gravel surface of the road jerked Fuscian from his slumbers. "What? Where in the name of the apostle are we? Huh! Thought they'd been repairing this road!"

"It's alright, sleepy head," responded Quentin, "I think that ale was more potent than you reckoned for! Anyway, it was a good few weeks' work tending the empire of love. Sleep the sleep of the just while you can. We can't duck the procurator's ire for much longer I fear." Fuscian leant his head out of the window and drew it back in again.

"No point trying to sleep now, we are nearly there. How long before he arrests us again do you think? Has he nothing better to do?" Quentin gazed thoughtfully at his friend.

"I don't think he can bear the idea of any alternative power. Not even the power of love. It eats away at him. He has to confront it." Almost on cue, the carruca drew up at their villa, and a cohort of soldiers crowded around their vehicle, opening the doors and pulling them unceremoniously out onto the rough flagstones. The soldiers thrust them forward as Rictiovarus strode up to them.

"Deluding the natives again, are we? Where has it been this time, Augusta Veromanduorum? Have you no shame? Well, now is the time for the worms, cancer and maggots to penetrate unless you offer to the real gods. Come with us."

There was no point in resisting. There were too many of them and in any case, Rictiovarus had his men all over the city, now firmly secured as a Roman bastion once more.

"Well, someone got out of bed on the wrong side", observed Quentin, nonchalantly, as if to Fuscian, but loud enough for the procurator to hear. "No peaceful vesperna with the comrades tonight then."

"You'll be less cocksure when I've finished with you," retorted the procurator, his face reddening with anger. The cohort led them away across the main street and down towards the Somme Bridge where the main garrison was situated. "You will offer your vesperna tonight to the gods, or if you refuse, you will both be in solitary!" Rictiovarus declared angrily. "Well, we've been thinking, and there's an easy answer to that. Ambianum needs the message of love, not Zeus and his fellow rapists. So we'll not be making any more offerings to them," responded Quentin matter-of-factly.

"Amen to that," replied Fuscian. Rictiovarus struck the corpulent votary hard across the belly with the flat of his sword and sent him sprawling backwards into Quentin's arms.

"To the slammers with them both," he commanded his men. "Tomorrow you will give me the names and locations of all

11

your comrades throughout Gaul. Otherwise it will be the rack for the both of you until I get them."

The men manoeuvred Quentin and Fuscian roughly into separate but adjacent isolation cells on the side of the wharf on which the barracks stood. These were stone cells approximately two by four metres in dimension. Each had short chains from the rear walls with ankle manacles attached and rough pallets on the floor. The manacles secured the ankles so that it was just possible to shuffle on and off the pallet, and to use the slop bucket already stinking from the detritus of the previous occupant. While the cells were of stone on three sides, the whole of the front was a door consisting of thick wooden palisades. These were very strong and securely fixed together, but rough and with narrow gaps, which provided the only light within. Quentin and Fuscian soon found themselves manacled securely to the rear walls and while their hands were free, it was impossible to reach the wooden door, and the iron manacles were completely impossible to loosen, let alone remove. It was also useless to attempt to communicate through the thick stone walls although it would have been just about possible to hear one another if they had shouted, because of the wooden doors. However, shouting would have simply brought the cohort, so there was really nothing for it but to attempt to settle down on the pallets, pray and contemplate the trials of tomorrow.

It was a little after midnight when the music started. Someone was singing, but it was no ordinary singing. Reed like, almost bird song, so quiet at first that Quentin could barely hear it, although he was wide-awake. While there were no distinct words that he could make out, without doubt he knew it to be a love song. It gradually swelled in strength, and at the same time, light began to penetrate brightly through the gaps in the palisade. He managed to manoeuvre himself as far forward as he could and, propping himself up on one elbow, obtained a line of sight through one of the apertures. Revealed in the shaft of light was a stunning spectacle. A spectral being – a man, or was it a woman? – clothed in shimmering garments, was balancing on the surface of the river and seemingly travelling down the shaft of light towards him. As they came up to the gap between the shafts of the palisade, the aperture grew and grew until it was an opening wide enough for a person to pass through. Quentin drew back in amazement; however, the angel, for such it was, reached out and took his hand, and even as they touched, the manacles around his ankles sprang open and he stood up and followed the angel back out through the gap. Then he saw that in the case of Fuscian it had been a gap big enough for even his rotund body to exit his cell through. There was neither sight nor sound of the cohort, nor any longer of the angel, and Quentin and Fuscian simply walked back home to their villa, apparently unseen and unmolested.

Dazed but elated by their experience, the two friends talked long into the night about what had happened and what they should do next. Clearly, the Trinity was with them and they could collaborate strategically. Before daybreak, they were agreed. Fuscian would take one of the companions and return immediately to Rome, and let the brothers and sisters there know what had taken place. Quentin would gather the rest of the company, pray, and plan for their future, whatever ultimately happened to him. Fuscian had resisted this idea at first.

"But Quentin, Rictiovarus might take a day or two to recover from the shock of our miraculous escape, but as you say, he can't bear the thought of any alternative power, not even love. He'll be back and the next time he won't leave room even for divine intervention!"

"That's why you need to get away and tell the story in Rome, and why I need to encourage the brothers and sisters here that God is with us whatever happens!" retorted Quentin.

By the time the sun rose, Fuscian and his companion were on the road to Rome, some thirty days away, and Quentin had sent the message out to the rest of the company to meet together that evening at the villa.

***

Back in Rome, Villa Metilia was a hive of activity. As expected, Julius' victorious return set in motion all manner of preparations for celebrations, the first of which was Eusébie's ninth birthday. Truth to tell, when the news of his arrival reached her, Eusébie was fearful that she might not recognise her father, after nearly two years away. She was aware that it was not only time's passing that was the problem, however. She knew for sure by now that she could no longer distinguish people's features at all clearly and went more by familiar shapes, scents and sounds or by their voices and position in the room. However, to her relief, the moment Julius entered the atrium she knew it was him. His familiar posture, the shake of his mane of hair, and his gravelly voice, hoarse from constant shouting of instructions, were unmistakeable. Yet she held back at first, uncertain of what a nearly nine-year-old might expect from a victorious general in the flush of his Parousia. Julius also stood still for a moment, appraising her from head to toe.

"Here's my girl!" he cried, lifting her up so that his gaze was level with hers. He held her there, suspended, as if to plumb the depth of his daughter, but also to examine the condition of her sight. Then he wrapped his arms around her and she snuggled into his embrace with a long sigh of contentment and relief. Her father was home, and for the time being, it was all that mattered.

That night, Eusébie dreamt again. As before, she was in the atrium, but this time the Minotaur was still in the centre square. Something else was different too. As she made as if to enter the labyrinth herself, as she had done in the previous dream, and stepped onto the first tile of the maze, she found herself caught up, suspended above an island with a literal labyrinth stretched out beneath her. Below her, at the entrance to the maze, a princely knight stood, sword at the ready. Was it her father? Yet once again, it appeared to be someone from the olden days. From her vantage point, she could see behind him a harbour where a ship lay moored. In one hand, he had a ball of string, which he began to unwind and thread around the foliage of the labyrinth to his left-hand side as he slowly and soundlessly entered the maze.

Eusébie held her breath, as the knight progressed around the complex circuit, heading all the time inexorably towards its centre and the Minotaur. As she looked, she could see the part-human creature stirring, his bull head cocked inquiringly while his human arms and legs raised him to his feet. As the knight approached, sword drawn at the ready, the Minotaur charged, huge muscular bull's shoulders powering his horns down on the knight and sending his sword spinning away beneath the foliage. Before the knight could recover, the Minotaur swiftly manoeuvred his opponent down into a body lock and knelt with his full weight onto the neck of the now disarmed prince.

"You thought to kill me. Instead, you will lead me out of this maze and I will make of you a great king, a father of empires. For as soon as I leave this place I can take whatever shape I will. Just as I have been at the heart of this labyrinth, I will inhabit the heart of your kingdom and defend it as I have defended myself from you this day."

As Eusébie continued to watch, spell bound, the Minotaur raised his knee from the knight's neck and simultaneously drew the sword from where it had lain hidden under the foliage. With its point resting into the small of his back, the knight struggled gingerly to his feet. Then, contemplating the creature's words, he began slowly but surely to lead the way back through the labyrinth, following the string as he went. As soon as they reached the entrance, the Minotaur vanished from view. Free from the pressure of the sword, the knight straightened up and looked around him. The Minotaur was nowhere to be seen. Breaking into a run, the prince headed down towards the ship in the harbour. At the same time, flying towards her in the sky above the dreamscape, Eusébie saw a huge eagle, wings outstretched, head lowered and its beak poised to strike. It was coming for her! She tried to cry out, to fend off the great bird, but rigid with shock just as before, she could neither move nor speak. Then, all at once, she was awake again, gasping for breath, wanting to call out but unable to do so. This time she calmed more quickly than at first and made her way over to the washstand and back to bed. Then, sure that the dreams belonged together, and wishing that her uncle was there to talk to about them, but knowing that Valeria would have to do instead, she went back to sleep.

Chapter Two

Eagle and Ecclesia

It was Eusébie's birthday, and from experience, Abaskantis expected her to be awake bright and early. However, with the new regime in place to serve Julius' constant stream of visitors, it was well past Eusébie's usual breakfast time before she looked in on her room, only to find her still fast asleep. The excitement of her father's return and the visions of the night had quite worn her out. Abaskantis hardly had time to wake her before Julius' gravelly voice announced the visit of the military physician who travelled with the legion and with whom he consulted over his daughter's sight. Eusébie had good memories of the sensitive warrior-doctor from when her father was last home two years previously. She tumbled out of bed and with the slave girl's help quickly changed into her day clothes, brushed her hair and emerged into the atrium where the two men were standing waiting. She knew without doubt which was her father, but would not have been able to identify the physician without Julius' introduction. She stood before them, unaware of the striking picture she presented. She was tall and lithe for her age; white albino-blond hair framed her oval face, with its typically aquiline nose. Most striking of all were her violet eyes, wide, wide open as if to take in every parameter of sight that remained.

"May I take a look?" The doctor stepped forward and gently lifted her chin, gazing into the near blind eyes. "You will have to regard it as a downside to your beauty, young lady. I am sorry, but there is no cure. I will not deceive you. I can prescribe more salve and let your mother know where to purchase it. It is made from a herb of natural origin and the slave girl may well know where it grows and how to prepare it for you. Yet be encouraged, you will develop senses that others do not have; I have seen it many times. I believe that you are experiencing it already. Your father will provide for your needs in every possible way, I am sure. You are his only child and he loves you dearly." Julius took his daughter's hand and drew her close.

"Not the best birthday present, my sweet one. I had hoped for better news." Eusébie squeezed his hand tightly. She wiped the tears from her eyes.

"It is well, father. The doctor is right; I think I really am beginning to see in other ways." Julius kissed her on both cheeks and stepped away, blinking back his own tears. "You are an extraordinary one and no mistake. I will see you at cena. It will be later and greater than usual because I have invited special birthday guests I want to show you off to." With that, the two men left, and Abaskantis appeared with a late *ientaculum* of wheat pancakes, dates and honey. Eusébie was more than ready for it.

That evening there was a splendid party of patricians and their progeny reclining in the dining area of Villa Metilia. It was the largest crowd of friends and family that Eusébie could ever remember. Her father had seated her at the head of the table between himself and her mother. Grandfather Zeno was at her father's left and Valeria was to her mother's right, next to her husband Lucius, also back from the Samartian victory. Around the table were other relatives and colleagues of her father and grandfather whose features she could not make out. Slaves, ones who Eusébie was less familiar with, had joined Abaskantis in order to take care of the demands of them all. She thought she could just about make out the features of Melissa, Abaskantis' mother who supervised the catering but rarely showed her face in the villa at normal times.

Eusébie contented herself with surreptitiously peering across at Valeria's husband of eighteen months. Lucius was older than her own father, something that horrified her, although quite customary in patrician society. Fully twenty years older than his wife, Lucius had been an older comrade in arms with her brother. He was an heir of the famous Illyrian family Chlorus, and the younger brother of Constantius, who, rumour had it, would be one of the new Caesar tetrarchs that Diocletian planned to put in place to consolidate his power. Now he rented a splendid *domus* in Rome where he had established himself and his new bride. Actually, Eusébie reflected, Valeria was pleased as punch to bask in the glory of such an illustrious patriarch who seemed to let her do whatever she wanted, and was in any case no more often in Rome since their marriage than her father. Eusébie did not like what she could see of him and hoped very much that once the meal was over, the men and women would separate out as was mostly customary, and she could siphon Valeria off to herself as the evening progressed.

That, as it happened, was the way things turned out.

"So how are you planning to spend the last hours of your birthday, favourite niece?" asked Valeria, as the men departed the room to talk war and politics or whatever it was that filled their food and wine infused conversations. The women might have had some more interesting matters to discuss, Valeria reflected, but it was her niece's birthday after all, and she would need cheering up. She had heard already from Claudia of the physician's visit and prognosis and was as ever indefatigably sure of her ability to turn even that dire news into an adventure. What she did not yet realise was just how much of a story Eusébie already had in wait for her.

"I plan to spend them with you if you let me, Valeria; I've got such a story to tell. Can you come to my bedroom, then I can get ready for bed, and maybe Abaskantis can bring us some desserts left over from cena – maybe candies, doughnuts or even cheesecake and more wine for you of course!" They soon enlisted Abaskantis' help, and before long, they had settled themselves comfortably in Eusébie's room.

"Now, Eusébie," Valeria began. "Listen to me; I know the news from the doctor is not good, but things will work out, you'll see. We are not about to abandon you to Abaskantis. You are getting more grown up by the minute. Well look at you, you are quite the young lady in her boudoir already and you know it! Your mother tells me that the doctor thinks that you will develop senses others don't have, and that you said it may be happening already!"

"Well," Eusébie began, "I have been dreaming, and I don't think they are ordinary dreams. If Uncle Quentin were here, he might know what they mean, but he's not, and you are next best!"

"You are very cheeky, Eusébie Metilia. But you are right of course, and to be second to Quentin has to be a compliment I suppose! So come on, tell me the dreams." Eusébie found that both dreams were still vivid in her memory, and she gave her aunt an animated account of them, beginning with the first. Valeria felt herself drawn into the narrative almost as if they had been her dreams too. When her niece had finished, Valeria was pensive for a long while. "Your dreams are very like two old Greek myths. I used to scare you with some of those when you were younger. Yet they are different to the originals in quite important ways. To begin with, did you really think the woman on the bed was me? Because the story is like the story of the rape of Europa by Zeus. She was deceived by her desire for money and power, and lay with a bull. Maybe Lucius is like the bull." She broke off, horrified. "But he's my husband..."

"But it wasn't really you," Eusébie interrupted reassuringly, "perhaps it's some kind of warning, do you think?"

"And in the second dream," Valeria continued, "you thought the knight was your father at first. So maybe that is a warning too. All the same, the story is different to the old myth of the Minotaur. In that story, the knight killed the Minotaur and returned home supposedly forgetting to change the sails of his ship so that his father the king killed himself and he became king of Athens instead, one of the greatest Greek kings that made way for their empire."

"But that does seem to fulfil the Minotaur's promise," said Eusébie. "What if the Minotaur is not dead and he's somehow after father?"

"This is heavy stuff for a nine-year-old," responded Valeria. "I'm going to have to think hard as to whether there's someone else we can share it with." The two of them sat silently together wondering. "I guess it's time for your bed. Are you sure you can sleep after all this?" Eusébie gave her aunt a hug.

"Don't worry, Valeria, two more candies, a doughnut and a sip of your wine and I'll be alright!"

***

In the meantime, Fuscian and his companion were bearing the joyful news of the intervention by the angel of the Somme on their travels across northern and central Europe, firstly along the Via Belgica to *Colonia Agrippina* and from there right the way down the Via Solemnis through the Alps to Rome. While making progress as swiftly as they could, it was still necessary to break their journey at nightfall each day to rest their horses and their own weary bodies. As far as possible, they did this at the centres of activity that the companions of love had seeded along the Roman roads during the previous two hundred years. Here they shared their story and were heard gladly. The news of the intervention of the angel was a massive encouragement to the increasingly threatened outposts of counter-political influence.

"Come on, have some more ale, tell us more!" was the almost nightly refrain. Unknown to them all, and a week behind, a second team of messengers was carrying much more disturbing news. The angel's work had been to prepare them all for the excruciating costs of inseminating love into the dominating structures of empire. Something rooted from the beginning at the heart of their alternative empire that remained endemically hard to grasp.

More than three weeks elapsed before Valeria and Eusébie were together alone again, despite her aunt's assurances not to abandon her. Fortunately, Abaskantis' company had never been any kind of abandonment for Eusébie. Slaves were taken for granted and treated like chattels in the Roman Empire, but that did not mean they acted as such! In fact, patrician life was completely dependent on them. As it happened, this was even more the case than usual in Villa Metilia. Roman patricians who made up the bulk of the senatorial class were generally rich landowners. They would often have a house in the city and a villa in the country run by slaves. In the Metilia's case, their villa on the Janiculan Hill was a combination of the two. It was far enough outside the city to have land run by slaves, but was the chief residence of the family. This enabled a more than usually collaborative relationship between the family and its slaves. The family could see how much their servants did for them, while their slaves in turn saw and shared the ins and outs of their owners' lives, as some members of the slave families worked the house while others worked the land. This arrangement had been in place for well over a hundred years, and an extensive family of slaves were born, who worked and died in slavery on the estate.

However, some thirty years previously an event took place that substantially increased the collaboration between the Metilias and their slaves. Zeno had been a naval general, and while engaging and sinking nine vessels off Carthage during the Battle of Tyndaris, had caught sight of two sailors struggling in the water as their ship went down. Moved with compassion, Zeno had his men rescue them from the water, brought them back, and added them to his stock of slaves. As it turned out, they were both disciples of Cyprian, the bishop of Carthage. They viewed their rescue as divine intervention, and set about becoming exemplary slaves, following along the lines of the apostle Paul's admonition, "Slaves be obedient to your masters, as unto the Lord," while knowing themselves to be at heart free men. Within a few years of their arrival at the villa on the Janiculan Hill, most of the slaves had become Christians and a thriving slave *ecclesia* grew up on the estate. What made the relationships between the Metilias and their slaves particularly close was that before long, Zeno's wife and her eldest son, Quentin, himself then then just nine years old, embraced the Christian faith and became part of the ecclesia.

All this being the case, as Valeria turned over Eusébie's dreams in her mind it was unsurprising that she kept thinking of Melissa. Abaskantis' mother, and in overall charge of all the catering at Villa Metilia, Melissa was a recognised prophet and leader in the slave ecclesia with a known gift of dream interpretation. Notwithstanding the unusual relationships that pertained between the patrician owners and their slaves at Villa Metilia, it was still a slightly awkward matter to arrange a private meeting between Melissa and her owner's daughter and granddaughter. This was particularly so in the context of all the unusual demands for hospitality. On the one hand, Melissa was unbelievably busy, on the other so many more patricians were in and out of the villa that it made meeting on an equal footing such as the ecclesial protocol required, harder to achieve than usual.

In the end, the demands of the empire intervened when Julius was called away to a key military convocation to discuss the next steps to consolidate the Western borders. The villa was all but deserted and Valeria quickly grasped the opportunity to visit the slave quarters and suggested to Eusébie that she send a message from Valeria to Melissa via Abaskantis to arrange a meeting that afternoon. It thus came about that Valeria and Eusébie were sitting together with Melissa in her rather rickety property in the slave quarters below the main villa on the Janiculan Hill pouring out the dreams, when the sound of horses descending on the slave quarters disturbed them. It was Fuscian and his companion, pell-mell from Gaul with the story of the angel's visit to free Quentin and Fuscian from their prison cells.

Melissa sent word for food and hospitality for Fuscian and his companion and after calling folk for a gathering of the ecclesia that evening she turned back quickly to Eusébie and Valeria.

"You are right, your dreams are warnings, but more, they are commissions. Eusébie, you may be only a child, but you have an important part to play in turning back the beast and his empire. Can you come back tonight and hear Fuscian's story in full? I think it will give us further light on all this."

Eusébie and Valeria made their way back to the still empty villa pondering Melissa's words. Abaskantis had set out cold food for the two of them for cena and was now back with her mother preparing the slave ecclesia's reception for Fuscian and his companion. While Valeria and Eusébie ate, they considered the advisability of heading back down for the meeting. The relationship between the house and the slave ecclesia was one of cautious acceptance. Neither Zeno nor Julius really approved of the connection, but the history of close relationships with their wife and mother and their grudging respect for Quentin meant that they tolerated it. It was in any case their only point of contact with Quentin's mission and wellbeing. Eventually Valeria decided that the cena at the garrison would continue well into the evening and that they could be with the ecclesia and return before the others.

So it was that Eusébie and Valeria made their way down to the slave quarters for the second time that day. The still hot sun of the sultry July evening shone on slave and free alike as they gathered in the open courtyard in front of the main storage barn. They stood around in groups, waiting for one another to return from their various duties and chores in villa and farm, as well as attending to the needs of their own children, the elderly and the infirm. In the summer, they invariably met in this open courtyard. In winter time or if the weather was bad, gatherings of the ecclesia would move inside, sharing the space with the stores and sitting on rough wooden benches made of timbers propped on hay bales. The waking life of slave and free generally took place between sunset and sunrise, and although there were some lanterns available both internally and externally, generally meetings were held shortly after dawn or in the latter half of the evening before dusk, as on this occasion. In any case, their slave duties filled the rest of their waking hours. Some meetings were regular events, or as with this, called in response to special happenings or news. When it became obvious that most had arrived, the gentle hubbub of voices gradually coalesced into plainsong and Mary's revolutionary hymn reverberated around the courtyard.

"My soul exalts the Lord, and my spirit rejoices in God my Saviour.

He has regarded the humble state of his bond slave; behold, from this time on all generations will count me blessed.

For the Mighty One has done great things for me; holy is his name.

His mercy is on generation after generation toward those who run to him.

He has done mighty deeds with his arm; he has scattered those who were proud in the imaginations of their heart.

He has brought down rulers from their thrones, and exalted those who were humble.

He has filled the hungry with good things; and sent the rich empty-handed away."

As the singing ceased, Fuscian stepped forward, his ample frame and beaming visage seemingly embracing the ecclesia drawn around him and savouring the story that he was about to tell them. He began with his and Quentin's arrival at their Ambianum villa after the journey from Augusta Veromanduorum. The "Oh no!", "Ouch!" and "Wow!" exclamations of his audience punctuated the story as he described their ill treatment and imprisonment. When he arrived at the point when the music began, however, a tangible stillness descended on Eusébie, Valeria and the gathered slaves. They hung on his every word and all of them embraced the story as if it were happening to them, right now. As he reached the climax of their release, the silence deepened into revelation. For the slaves, this was living myth that penetrated mind and heart, transfiguring their identity into partners of the transcendent Trinitarian realm. For Eusébie and Valeria, it was as if all false consciousness fell away and there they were, equal human beings with their slaves, raised by the angelic intervention out from the hierarchical bondage into which the institutions of empire locked them. Afterwards they reluctantly took their leave of Fuscian and his companion and made their way back to the still deserted villa.

The following morning, news that the convocation had agreed an immediate resumption of hostilities reverberated through Villa Metilia and the Chlorus domus in the city. This time it was to be in response to threats from the North Western borders in Gaul and Britain. Julius and his legion were to leave in only two days' time accompanied by the legions commanded by Lucius and his brother, Constantius. Valeria straightaway embarked on a whirlwind of work to complete all the necessary arrangements and preparations for her husband's departure. Villa Metilia was likewise a hive of activity. Eusébie, left to herself again, had no problem with that at all. She had so much to think about given the dreams and Melissa's words still fresh in her mind, together with the extraordinary news of the intervention of the angel of the Somme. Nonetheless, the prospect of another long period of separation from her father troubled her. Why did Rome need to fight so much? Could it not make friends with its enemies? She knew that he would make time to come and say a proper goodbye, and resolved to ask him. She might even attempt to tell him her dream of the Minotaur and warn him. Yet what would she warn him about exactly, and how would he take it?

Later that night before she retired to bed, the familiar form of her father entered the atrium and she immediately ran into his arms.

"Must you go father? What would happen if we tried to make friends of our enemies instead of meeting them in battle?" Julius shook his mane of hair and contemplated his daughter. "Where do you get these ideas from with your Uncle Quentin away? I hear that his friend Fuscian is here with some impossible story of an angel setting them free from gaol! Have you been with the slave ecclesia?" Eusébie focused her wide-open violet eyes on his as fully as she was able, as if to penetrate the depths of who he was. Julius recognised intently that for all his daughter's lack of physical sight, here was undoubted spiritual sight.

"It was grandmother's safe place, she used to tell me, and yes, I was there last night listening to Fuscian tell the story. I felt completely one with everybody in the whole universe while I was listening, and although I know nothing about them, when I heard that you were going to fight our enemies, I felt that they must belong together with us too. Why must we always fight?"

"How can I be having this conversation with a nine-year-old child?" retorted her father, challenged, but unwilling to give way to the anger that was not far below the surface. "Don't you understand that the *Pax Romana* is what civilises the world and protects everyone, slave and free alike? Love our enemies and treat everyone as equals? Just think where that got your Uncle Quentin. Today may bring an angel story, but mark my words soon it will be a different story. Then you will be glad you have a patrician soldier father to protect you."

***

Back in Ambianum, after the apparently miraculous escape of his prisoners, the Roman procurator brooded angrily for several days. He was at a loss to explain it. He assumed that someone must have bribed one of the garrison guards, as the unlocked manacles required someone with access to the key. He beat several of them severely but it failed to extract any such admission and once Quentin had gathered his companions and told his story, it spread like wild fire among the Christians and their contacts. For Rictiovarus this was intolerable. He concluded that the only remedy was to put a stop to it altogether. However, the maturity and reach of the companions in Ambianum was problematic. For if he arrested and killed Quentin among them there, he risked a riot, particularly with the superstition, as he saw it, surrounding the angel visitation now rife among the people. He decided that the best move would be to take Quentin captive to Augusta Veromanduorum. There the comparatively few followers of the companions would perhaps not yet have heard the story of the angel. If he publicly tortured and killed the recalcitrant patrician in front of them and the rest of the townsfolk, he would, hopefully, put an end to the influence of the superstitious troublemakers once and for all.

Early on the third morning after Quentin's escape, the procurator arrived at his villa with a cohort of soldiers. Breaking down the door and summarily overcoming his two companions, they dragged Quentin from his bed, bound his arms and legs securely and threw him into the back of a *carrus clabularis*. The procurator and his cohort then climbed in too and set out immediately for Augusta Veromanduorum, some two days distant. The military vehicle was uncomfortable even for Rictiovarus and his men, but they at least had fixed seats and could hold onto the sides if they needed to as they rumbled along. For Quentin, his sciatic nerve bumping along the rough wooden floor for stadia after stadia, it was an almost unbearable prelude to the coming torture. However, bear it he had to, and as the hours rolled by he began to treat it as an opportunity to work out how to endure prolonged pain. Praying for his captors was a great help in taking his mind off the discomfort and the silent gift of tongues was a wonderful resource, with its facility to dissociate from the immediacy of his physical senses for sustained periods at a time. Nevertheless, he was under no illusions, he was going to his death, a fate long expected, processed and embraced as witness to the kingdom of love. The miracle of his angelic reprieve had simply served to strengthen his resolve and expectation of transcendent support when the ultimate test eventually came.

That evening they overnighted at a mansiones much frequented by Rictiovarus and his soldiers, where good food and drink was readily available together with *meretrix* well known to them from previous visits. They simply left Quentin bound on the floor of the military transporter while the oxen were led away for the night. Apart from a brief drink from a bottle supplied by one of the cohort, he had nothing, and in any case, he was not keen to eat or drink given that his captors had not allowed him any opportunity to relieve himself and he was already unavoidably wet and uncomfortable as a result. Nevertheless, he did finally manage to doze fitfully. As the sun rose the following day, the prosecutor and his cohort reappeared, reunited the oxen with the vehicle and the excruciating experience of the previous day recommenced. Once again, as the hours rumbled painfully by, Quentin found respite in prayer and tongues. Finally, as they drew near to their destination, Rictiovarus began to taunt him with a stream of vitriol, working himself up into a near frenzy as if in preparation for the torture, beatings and execution to come.

"I warned you, and now the time has come, you pretentious bastard," he pronounced, whacking Quentin about the face with the backs of his hands. The prosecutor's expletives of the previous week were about to be consummated. It was time for the worms, cancer and maggots to penetrate.

Situated at the side of a stone-flagged square bordered by the river and the wharf, the Roman garrison at Augusta Veromanduorum had the same aspect as the one at Ambianum. On their arrival, the procurator shouted for his men to wheel out the rack from an adjacent warehouse. The news of their coming and the expectation of a public execution soon drew a crowd. As Rictiovarus hoped, some of these were the same peasants and townsfolk who Quentin and Fuscian had been working among, including new adherents to the companions of love. As the people gathered, an ominous hush descended and the dying late afternoon sun cast its shadow across the square, starkly silhouetting a single huge eagle perched on the garrison roof. It watched menacingly as the procurator's men pulled Quentin from the clabularis. Stripping him of his clothes, they hoisted him onto the rack.

"Form a ring around it and don't let anyone through!" commanded the procurator. Nevertheless, as he intended, the crowd could still see Quentin's torture and hear his cries, as the rack was a tall wooden frame on which he was strapped and hung vertically.

The torturers attached him to the rack by wires that pierced his flesh from the shoulders to the thighs, and secured him by iron nails that penetrated his hands and feet. However, the ring of soldiers from the garrison made sure that any attempts at retaliation or rescue by the companions of love would be futile. Finally, the executioner's axe swung and Quentin's head dropped from his decapitated body. Instantly, a tousle-haired youth by the name of Acco, overwhelmed with anguish at the treatment of his newfound friend, was hardly restrained by his fellows as he leapt onto the backs of the ring of soldiers, crying out to the procurator's surprise and perplexity,

"Father, forgive them," and "Jesus, lay not this sin to their charge." Then, even as the words of the martyr Stephen rang out, the shape-shifting eagle took flight, its shadow falling across the crowd and then chased away by the evening sun.

A shocked ease settled on the square, as gradually the crowds dispersed and twilight dipped towards night. Acco and his fellow companions dropped back under the cover of an outhouse alongside the garrison walls to see what might happen next. If they could, they would take Quentin's remains and give him an honourable burial. That, of course, was the last thing Rictiovarus was about to allow. Instead, he instructed his men to remove the body from the rack, and together with the head, they deposited it into an empty grain sack. Then, dragging it unceremoniously across the flagstones, they removed it into the garrison. Although Quentin's friends watched, it was clear that they would have no opportunity to honour their friend further, so they eventually headed sorrowfully back into the town. Much later that night under cover of darkness, the procurator supervised his men as they stowed the body onto a ferry and paddled out to the middle of the Somme where, adding several rocks to the sack as ballast, they threw it overboard into the deepest part of the river.

Early the following morning some of the companions of love met together to commiserate and pray.

"What do you think we should do?" Acco asked. "Will the angel that rescued him before do anything now?" he wondered.

"The apostle Paul himself was standing by consenting to his death when Stephen died, and that began to change everything for the companions, so who knows where this will lead?" one of the friends replied. Others surmised correctly that Quentin's remains might well be in the river by now.

"Well, let's have one good try and see if we can find that sack if this is what has happened," replied Acco, heading for the river and removing most of his clothes. Several others joined him but the river was wide at that point and had many hidden channels so, although they waded and dived, they never managed to find it. Instead, with many tears, they eventually entrusted their friend's remains to the angel who had emerged from the river to rescue him at Ambianum less than a week previously. Then, holding onto one another both literally and metaphorically, they promised themselves to live out his example in the days to come. "We must tell the brothers and sisters in Ambianum what's happened," declared Acco as they made their way back from the river, contemplating together all that had taken place and facing the return to what now seemed like very ordinary daily lives.

"It will take days to get there and back," responded Manus, Acco's father, with the murmured assent of the others.

"Well, I could go, as long as you could do without me father," retorted Acco. Manus looked reflectively at his son. Then he replied,

"I guess I can manage the smithy for a bit, it's only these last few months you've begun to be able to pull your weight anyway." Manus hesitated. "But not on your own, son, it's too risky." He ran his eyes over the group, the majority of whom had children to take care of, or bread to win for dependents. One man stood out from the rest in more ways than one. Dunnius was huge, a black Gaul of African descent, who like his father and grandfather before him had served in the Roman army. He was recuperating from battle injuries, and supplied occasional labour whenever a good arm, and sheer weight, were all that was required. "How about you, Dunnius, are you sufficiently recovered? Could you go?" Manus asked.

"All the way to Rome if necessary," was the gruff reply. And so it was, provided with an elderly carruca and horses from the stables of the one Gaulish patrician family among the new companions of love in Augusta Veromanduorum, the youngster and the warrior, clad in travelling cloaks and loaded with food, drink, and a change of clothes for the journey, set out for Ambianum that very afternoon.

Chapter Three

Friendship and Empire

Despite the brutality of the event they had witnessed, Acco found himself inspired and elated with something of the same ardour that had propelled him onto the backs of the soldiers to declare the martyr Stephen's words on Quentin's behalf. It was this, it transpired, that had moved Dunnius to cast his lot in with the youngster.

"Quentin's face was like the face of an angel," mused the big man as the carruca rumbled along the road to Ambianum. "And our friend was right to wonder where this will lead."

"Life, not death is what's coming, I'm sure of that. And the Trinity are with us and we are their messengers!" responded Acco. The vehicle was elderly but sound and the horses were on good form, so the companions made excellent time and by dusk were well on their way. Nevertheless, they were aware that they made a disparate pair and so as not to draw attention to themselves they simply drew the carruca off the road beneath the cover of a spinney before night fell. Then, while there was still enough light to see what they were doing, they released the horses from the shafts and tethered them lightly. The animals fed and watered, they tucked in to bread and the traditional diluted wine. Finally, as darkness fell, they covered themselves with their cloaks and made themselves as comfortable as they could. Dunnius stretched himself awkwardly in the carruca while Acco laid down partly hidden beneath it. Dunnius felt protective towards the youngster and was more at ease with this arrangement, which would become their normal practice as their journey extended across the continent, which deep down both suspected it would from the very start.

They arrived in Ambianum as the sun was setting on the second day and drew into the yard of Quentin's villa. They had feared that the procurator might have already commandeered the place and arrested all or some of the remaining companions and their household. However, it was still bustling with activity as usual with the various poor, homeless and sick folk for whom it was a place of refuge and support. Truth to tell, Rictiovarus had overreached himself beyond his expectations, and was pacing the yard of his own villa at that very moment. He had been greatly disturbed on his return to Ambianum some hours earlier to find that an eagle appeared to have stationed itself on the roof of his stables. Furthermore, he was unable to resolve an angry debate within himself between exhilaration at having destroyed his perceived enemy, and regret that he had been capable of brutally executing an obviously good and brave man. An internal conversation that was destined to dog his waking hours and consume his dreams for months to come.

The remaining companions of love received the messengers with open arms. Quentin had prepared them for his death, and frankly, they were expecting the news. Acco related the whole story in a mixture of tears and elation. As his and their tears flowed, the small crowd of needy guests clamoured for details and visibly warmed to the ultimate gift of Quentin's life, a fellow human who they knew to represent the unconditional love they were right now receiving. Then Dunnius interposed with his account of Acco's great leap onto the soldiers' backs and his shout of "Father forgive them," and "Jesus, lay not this sin to their charge!" At this the listeners burst into spontaneous applause and Mama Junia, the eldest of the companions and one of the first to join the company when Quentin and Fuscian began the work, kissed him on both cheeks while others slapped him on the back and he, red faced, assured them that he couldn't help but do it! Then without more ado, the companions and their guests declared that the pair must eat, drink and sleep before setting out on the four-week journey to Rome the following day, insisting that Quentin's friends and family needed to have this news first hand and they were the obvious ones to bring it.

Acco and Dunnius travelled down the same Roman roads and through the same cities as those that Fuscian and his companion had passed by on their recent journey. Some of those who heard their news were dismayed and confused at the apparent reversal of the previous exciting story. For others, the account of Quentin's willing martyrdom only served to strengthen their determination to displace empire with love. The centres where the companions of love thrived supplied them with food along the way, and found new horses to relieve their tiring steeds. For Acco the journey thrilled with sights and sounds that he had only heard and dreamt. Dunnius, on the other hand, had been this way before, both as a military child and as a soldier. He delighted in pointing out the compelling sights, telling the associated stories and attempting to answer Acco's penetrating questions.

The sheer size and scope of the empire revealed by the extent of the Via Belgica and the realisation, when at last after a full week's journey they reached Colonia Agrippina, that they were barely a quarter of the way, was almost overwhelming to Acco.

"How can the empire possibly be so big?" he mused to Dunnius. "Why do the Romans want to be in charge everywhere?" Dunnius was silent awhile before responding.

"It's the way it's been for time immemorial, and it's soldiers like me, my father and grandfather before me, who made it this way and keep it so at the cost of their own bodies and all that stand in the way."

"Why do they go on doing it, they're not the ones who benefit, are they?" Acco enquired. Dunnius again quietly pondered before he replied.

"Well, this one won't be doing it any longer, my body will never be up to it now, but more's the point, we've found another way, thanks to Quentin and the companions!"

At that stage in the journey, the Eifel Aqueduct confronted them. Stretching for ninety-five kilometres it brought water to the city from the surrounding countryside. Unlike the roads, Acco reflected, that at least had a two-way flow, this was a one-way supply. Yet it was evidence of the underlying reality. In the end, everything in the empire went from the country to the city and from the city to Rome.

"Why was Rome the centre of the world, pulling everything towards it?" The question imposed itself on Acco with ever-greater insistence. They rested a day in Colonia. They needed it and were grateful to the companions there for the opportunity to wash their clothes and refresh the horses. Some ten days further saw them in the foothills of the Alpine Mountains. The highway stretched on before them up to the Reschen Pass high above. For a lowlander like Acco, the magnificence and magnitude of the mountains brought a further new perspective to his musings, still haunted by scenes of the violence inflicted on Quentin by Rome's Gaulish procurator.

"These peaks were here before the power of Rome, Dunnius, and they will outlast it. I feel held by them, secure in them."

Over the next few days, as the Via Solemnis cut through the Alpine passes, the temperature fell and the night times were extremely cold. For several nights, the youngster and the big man slept in the shelter of a cluster of firs or a rocky overhang by the roadside, propped upright together in the carruca with their cloaks doubled over themselves for warmth. The horses, unhitched, slumped likewise alongside each other. The nights at the farms or occasional villas along the way where the companions of love welcomed them and provided, if not a bed, at least a straw pallet in barns or stables, were a relief to their weary, travel-worn bodies. However, while water to wash in and fresh stocks of supplies were most welcome, both on the journey out and the journey back, it was these nights on the mountains that remained impressed indelibly in Acco's and Dunnius' memory in the months and years to come. They belonged to a new humanity in contrast to the denizens of empire, where big and small, youth and adult, black Gaul and white Gaul, were brought together in the cause of an entirely different kind of power to that which the empire's roads facilitated. They lived, breathed and carried what they increasingly knew to be the presence of an entirely different kind of government.

***

Back at Villa Metilia, Fuscian was waiting patiently. He had little doubt that the dreaded news would come before many days were out. While building up the already mature faith and resilience of the slave ecclesia with stories of angels and agonies, divine and demonic manifestations from the Acts of the Apostles and Paul's writings, he made sure that they were prepared for the disturbing news that was coming. When it did come, he was telling the story of Stephen's martyrdom to those gathered at an evening meeting of the slave ecclesia. It was barely a week since his arrival with the extraordinary story of the intervention of the angel of the Somme when the messengers from Ambianum drove into the courtyard. All eyes were on Acco and Dunnius as they clambered from the carruca. Fuscian recognised them at once from his visits with Quentin to Augusta Veromanduorum, and from the demeanour of the emerging pair and his own spiritual sense, he knew what news they brought.

With the departure of Julius and Lucius and their legions for the Western front, all was quiet again at Villa Metilia and Valeria and Eusébie were among those assembled. Eusébie, too, although unable to see more than the outlines of the youth and the big man, shivered in certain anticipation of what they were about to hear. As their combined presentiment spread throughout the gathered ecclesia, Fuscian began to sing boldly from his favourite psalm. "Redeem me from the oppression of man, that I may keep your precepts.

Make your face shine upon your servant, and teach me your statutes.

My eyes shed streams of tears because they do not keep your law."

As he sang, the whole company rose as one and made a way through their midst for the two witnesses from Gaul.

Fuscian motioned for Dunnius to speak. However, instead, the big man placed his hands on Acco's shoulders and gently positioned the youth in front of him, facing the ecclesia.

"Acco will speak," he said, "and I will support him."

For several moments Acco simply stood, tears streaming down his face. Then, running his hands through his customarily tousled locks, he began, "I don't know how to tell you. The procurator and his men murdered Quentin, your friend and mine. They stripped him and fixed him on a ghastly rack with nails driven into his hands and feet and wires pierced through his body. How he cried out with pain! And after stretching him there they cut off his head and just let it drop to the ground!"

Eusébie's attention was riveted on Acco, even though she could not clearly see him. Quentin's pain was her pain too, as it was Acco's. As he paused, accompanying sobbing rose and fell from the ecclesia. Running his hands once more through his hair, he continued, but this time with a smile breaking through his tears.

"Let me tell you, we didn't need an angel this time! While he was hanging there, he was our angel, like Stephen in the Acts! Then when they cut his head off, I just could not stop myself. I leapt up on the backs of the soldiers who were protecting the rack and I shouted at the top of my voice, 'Father forgive them for they know what they do!' and 'Jesus, lay not this sin to their charge!' Now here we are, Dunnius and I, sent by the companions to bring you the love that can never die!"

At this, the ecclesia thronged them both, kissing them, embracing them and plying them with questions. "What happened next?" and "How are the companions?" and "What did they do with the body?" Then Melissa stepped forward and her reassuring presence quieted the hubbub. "These two are carrying the very substance of Quentin's love to us. Let them answer peaceably and what they have witnessed will be ours as well." Then the two messengers answered the questions as well as they were able, describing the brutal way that the soldiers had simply bundled Quentin's body and head into a grain sack and summarily dragged it away into the barracks. Dunnius described Acco's insistence on returning the following morning and leading the companions in diving bravely and repeatedly under the waters of the Somme in case the procurator and his men had dumped the body there during the hours of darkness, but to no avail.

Later that evening Valeria, at Eusébie's insistence, took it on herself to bring Acco and Dunnius back to the villa where they were installed in a guest room and supplied by Abaskantis with fresh robes and towels so that they could use the villa's bath. Valeria judged that Eusébie was right when she said that Claudia and Zeno would approve all this, even if grudgingly at first, once they realised that they brought news of Quentin. For all their doubts surrounding his mission, their love for him and respect for his and his mother's faith ran deep. The messengers were glad of the hospitality and soon headed for the bath to wash away the effects of the last days of the journey. Claudia and Zeno returned at that point, and Valeria explained all that had happened. Zeno was utterly distraught at the news of his son's death, and Claudia did her best to calm and care for him. He was seemingly inconsolable, but the demeanour of the huge black Gaul and the diminutive youth as they reappeared wrapped in their towels calmed and constrained him. Eusébie was determined that they would hear Acco's testimony first hand, once they had returned to their room and dressed, and to Claudia's relief it was balm to the ageing senator. He listened with attention to every detail that Acco and Dunnius related with great sensitivity, their tears flowing freely. Eventually sensing that their task was complete, Acco and Dunnius headed gratefully back to their beds, deciding together before the much-needed sleep overtook them that their primary work was finished. Acco, while wanting to see something of the city, made clear his desire to embark on the return journey within a day or two. He was concerned that his own ageing father would be feeling by now the absence of his son's developing muscles.

Valeria stayed that night at the villa, and in the morning, she and Eusébie were up early in hope of engaging the two messengers in further conversation. Eusébie had sensed an immediate connection with them both. She was sure that they had answers to her questions about the two empires represented by her father and her uncle. She was eager to tell them about her dreams of the Minotaur. However, the obvious status gap between the patricians and the messengers was stark, once back in the villa away from the slave ecclesia. Despite the importance of their news, Dunnius and Acco could not stay there for long. Aunt and niece sensed this intuitively, hence their early rise. In any case, conversation would be more difficult once Claudia and Zeno rose. As it happened, Claudia and Zeno had senate business to attend to, and were up already. They were both feeling responsibility for and uncertainty about providing hospitality at the villa for the two messengers. However, on discovering their intention of returning to Gaul in only a day or two, they were happy to request that Valeria remained until their departure and leave it at that. Thus, it was that Acco and Dunnius settled down to ientaculum with Eusébie and Valeria while Abaskantis, having laden the table with pancakes, dates and honey, lingered in the background.

Eusébie's hoped-for conversation began almost immediately when Acco's attention was drawn to the Minotaur in the centre of the mosaic floor.

"What's this about?" he inquired curiously. With a cautious glance towards Valeria, Eusébie began her tale.

"It's a Minotaur, and I've been dreaming about it and would like to tell you my dreams and then hear what you think about them." Dunnius had some sketchy memory of the myth from his military past, but it was completely new for Acco who listened wide-eyed with rapt attention. As she was nearing the end of the second dream, Acco, with an increasing sense of their significance and the hairs on the back of his neck rising in accompaniment, was unable to contain himself.

"Sorry, wait," he interrupted. "Are you saying that once the Minotaur left the labyrinth his shape shifted to an eagle?"

"Yes, I think so," replied Eusébie.

"Well," Acco continued, "all the time the procurator was tormenting Quentin a huge eagle was watching from the barracks roof."

"Then when you leapt up and declared the words of Stephen it took flight!" interposed Dunnius.

Eusébie set her violet, faraway eyes on the two messengers.

"Melissa, who you met last night at the slave church said that these are warnings, but more, they are commissions with which to turn back the beast and his empire. Somehow we have to do that."

"All the way from Gaul to here, the dominance of Rome confronted me," replied Acco. "And yet the love that Quentin and Fuscian lived by conquered it. I felt it particularly in the mountains and I said to Dunnius, we are held, safe, in the arms of a different kind of power. I feel it here, now, even although we are in Rome and at the heart of the empire. A greater power by far than Rome's. It's the power of love!"

"Yes," responded Eusébie elatedly, tears streaming down her face, "that's what it is, it is love. Like a river flowing to us and through us. We must make way for the river of love wherever we are and whatever we do!"

Valeria, hearing the dreams now for the third time, shifted uneasily on her couch. Each time she heard the first dream she was the more uncertain of her relationship with her husband. Lucius was an imperial patriarch to the point of a bully. He saw his relationship with his wife as domination not reciprocation and more than once during the past weeks his behaviour and that of the white bull in the dream had come together in her mind and experience. She had been immensely relieved at his departure to the Western front, and her discovery that she was now with child by him disturbed her, although she loved the thought of being a mother. This was not something she could share with her niece but she decided, there and then, that she would attempt a conversation with her sister-in-law Claudia on the subject as soon as possible. In the meantime, she would attend to her extraordinary guests. Abaskantis, emboldened by the love between them all, spoke up.

"If our guests are planning on returning home tomorrow, why don't you show them Rome, Valeria, and I'm sure Eusébie would like to come with you too? In the meantime, I will go down to my mother and Fuscian and suggest a special meeting of the ecclesia for this evening. Love is flowing deeply at the moment and we need to receive as much of it as we can!" They all agreed.

What a day they had! Despite her sadness, Eusébie basked in the aura of her uncle's substance that she perceived between the youth and the big man. For Valeria it was an opportunity for further reflection about Lucius' attitude toward her, deepened by the honour and respect that they showed her. Acco saw and felt acutely the glory of Rome in juxtaposition with the power of loving friendship. He knew what kind of life he would live from the smithy at Augusta Veromanduorum in the years to come. It was a no-brainer. The smithy would be a centre of excellent work and loving friendship. As for Dunnius, he resolved to put it to Fuscian that after seeing Acco safely home to Gaul he would join him and the companions in the work of the mission if he would have him, here in Rome, back to Ambianum or wherever the Spirit blew them. That night, after a sombre but triumphant meeting together with the slave ecclesia, Acco and Dunnius said their farewells. Fuscian received Dunnius' proposal with enthusiasm, agreeing to meet up in Ambianum the following month and discuss the details of their future partnership with Mama Junia and the rest of the companions there.

Later that week, after Acco and Dunnius had departed for Gaul, Valeria invited her sister-in-law to Domus Chlorus for cena, ostensibly to talk about the events of the last few days. "So you have guessed?" began Claudia, once the slave girl had served the repast and withdrawn. "Guessed what?" asked Valeria, nonplussed.

"I'm sorry," responded Claudia, "somehow I assumed, you had sensed that I'm pregnant. I thought that was perhaps what this was about."

"Well," replied her sister-in-law, "so am I, and that's why I invited you!" Claudia beamed. "That's wonderful. Then we can be together in our solitary state without our husbands."

"I would like that, Claudia," answered Valeria and surprised them both by bursting into tears.

"What is it, Valeria? Whatever is the matter?" responded her sister-in-law compassionately, placing an arm around her. Haltingly, Valeria related Eusébie's first dream and explained how the Minotaur's rape of Europa triggered her feeling of invasion by her husband.

"I know what is expected of a patrician's wife, and maybe my faith causes me to expect too much of Roman men. But having the witnesses of Quentin's death here these last few days has demonstrated such a loving alternative to domination."

Claudia remained in silent thought for quite some time before responding.

"I think three things. First, I too have felt the impact of Quentin's life-laying-down loving. Up until now, I have not publicly acknowledged that I too believe, but I do, Valeria, I do, and I will hide it no longer. Second, not all Roman patricians dominate their wives. Julius is the most loving of men, and I truly believe that this is part of the impact of his brother and mother on him. Which is why I feel free now to publicly admit my faith and I will do all I can to support you as you try to stand up to Lucius in the future. Finally, let us commit together to be to our yet-unborn children what your mother and Quentin have been to you and Eusébie. And we will include Eusébie; the three of us will bring up these children in the stream of love that's been flowing here these past few days."

"And will you come with us into the slave ecclesia?" continued Valeria. "We will need their support and guidance. Especially if either of our children are boys. For I'm so glad that Julius is good to you, but he'll be away, and when here, he will still have much of the Roman patriarch about him!"

"Yes," continued Claudia, "He's like your father Zeno. They can see that the Jesus way could one day replace the old gods, but still don't yet understand that love is a different kind of power to the Pax Romana."

Part Two

Interlude

Beyond Hadrian's Wall, Michael watched in trepidation the progress of the four horsemen riding together ahead of the marching legion. As he raised his staff skywards, the geese rose from the firth and flew high above them, wings tipping, as first one and then another took point and led the flock forwards. Yes, there was hope for a Daniel posse here. Faith for a future fullness indwelling these islands and coastlands. The song of hope still resounded across the hills and valleys. Yet much hung in the balance. Here was frailty and strength, agony and victory. Here was self-giving power and self-serving power. He knew that the eagle soaring on ahead was the emissary of the imperial forces, strong, dominating, would-be omnipotent power. He strode down towards the four riders, dispersing wind and hail across their path as he went. He stood astride the debatable lands. "Hear the sound of the earth," he cried out in the voice of the wind. "Love, not hate. Love, not hate".

Chapter Four

Empires to Be

Flavius Valerius Constantine stretched himself on his couch, one hand running through his thick black hair and the other hanging idly at his side. His usually animated face was blank, expressive of his daily routine and probable future. He was seriously fed up. He was thirty-three and had absolutely nothing to do. Since his return to Nicomedia, the Roman Empire's Eastern capital, three months previously after a highly successful engagement with the resurgent Persians, he had expected better. At least a new and honourable assignment fit for a young general. In those times of the tetrarchy, the huge and unwieldy Roman Empire had been divided on East-West lines. Diocletian was Emperor in the East, with Galerius as his Caesar, and Maximian was Emperor in the West, with Constantius as his Caesar. However, the Emperor Diocletian's failing health had played directly into Caesar Galerius' manipulative hands. With Diocletian effectively forced to abdicate in Galerius' favour, his co-Emperor Maximian resigned simultaneously in favour of Constantius. To avoid a power struggle in which both Constantine, who was Constantius' son, and Maxentius, who was Maximian's son, might well have both become Caesars, Galerius, who Constantine regarded as a complete narcissist and a loser who cared about nothing and no one but himself, had placed him under virtual house arrest. So now, his father was Emperor of the West and he was languishing in the East, and Severus, who was another narcissist, was Caesar to his father. Worst of all, here in Nicomedia Galerius had appointed as his Caesar, Maximinus Daza, the infamous persecutor of Christians.

Internally, Constantine was fuming. Truth to tell, so far he had been a compassionate and somewhat self-effacing leader with an eye for the common good. Which was why the appalling self-interest and naked desire for power represented by Galerius was so insufferable to the young general. Nevertheless, he was at present unable to do anything about it. Instead, he brooded over the problem of leadership within the empire, which was so evidently undoing it from the top to the bottom and the inside out. What was particularly galling was that some of the most impressive leadership in the empire was in the nascent Christian community right here in Nicomedia. If there was hope for the empire, it was in just this quality of others-orientated responsible leaders. Yet it was precisely these that Daza was obsessed with jealousy towards, persecuting and killing them mercilessly.

"Are you hungry, sir?" Constantine fairly jumped out of his skin. Cassius, his local adjutant, stood looming over him concernedly.

"Yes, I think I am, very," he responded, swinging his legs off the couch and leaping to his feet.

"Well, Atticus is here to see you and I thought that you might like to take a late cena together." Atticus was a talented architect and builder who Diocletian had employed to design and erect several of his most prodigious palaces. As a result, the emperor and his household benignly overlooked his role as elder in the church although it was well known. The previous year the new church building had been razed to the ground and the respect with which the Christians were held among the populace led to a riot in which part of the imperial palace had itself been burnt. Ironically, Atticus was now employed in the necessary restoration work. He showed a benevolent interest in the young general whose respect for the Christians had come to his ears and they had taken the opportunity for several meals together already. He also hoped that Constantine might be able to avert some of the persecution, having already lost several of their best young men and women.

And so with a more than adequate spread of fish, wine and bread set out before them, Constantine and Atticus embarked on a private and personal conversation that soon revolved as usual around the politics of the Eastern capital, leadership in the empire and the future role of the church.

"You need something useful to occupy your time, Constantine, before you die of boredom. So I've brought you some reading material." Atticus produced a book from beneath his toga. "It's from the Greek version of the Hebrew Scriptures – you do read Greek, don't you?" Constantine nodded.

"It's an intriguing book about Daniel. Have you heard of him?" Constantine said he had, which was only just about true. He thought that he might have heard the name from Lactantius, whose lectures he had attended as a youth in the city. The professor's radical views had helped form his view of leadership. However, he knew little of the story.

Having nothing else to do, Constantine remedied this lack of knowledge thoroughly over the next few days. He spent them buried in the story of Daniel, his effective kidnap from Jerusalem with his young friends while still a youth, their installation in the court of Nebuchadnezzar, and the accompanying apocalyptic material. He struggled to get his head round the statue of empires, the four great beasts and the ram and the he goat. The idea of an indestructible empire given to "the children of the saints of the most high" disturbed his sleep and dreams for the next two nights. He quickly became convinced that the reason Nebuchadnezzar wanted to take the Hebrew youths back to join his wise men in training in Babylon was that there was the same kind of leadership crisis in the late Assyrian empire as he was seeing in the empire of Rome. Nebuchadnezzar must have discerned hope for a different kind of leadership in them.

Daniel's concern for the mental and physical wellbeing of the king despite his threats and actions against his own health, safety, and that of his friends moved Constantine greatly. What was it about the Christians and their Hebrew prophetic forbears which made them care about the good of all? His mind recalled his relatives back in Rome at Villa Metilia. His young cousins Titus and Marcus reminded him of Daniel and his friends. Their fathers had both died in Gaul in the battle to defeat the usurper Carausius in 296, when they were just nine years old. Since then his aunt and her sister-in-law, together with the extraordinary Eusébie, had raised them, backed by Fuscian, Dunnius and the slave ecclesia. While in Rome the year before, negotiating troop deployment for the Persian wars, the wisdom and grace of the teenagers, their guardians and their extraordinary slaves had affected him more than anything in his previous experience. They believed in a new humanity and were already beginning to look like it. He wished that he had found a way of putting the care of his son Crispus into their hands. When news of his young wife Minervina's sudden death from typhoid fever had reached him on the Eastern battlefront the previous year, he had no real option than to send the boy with his nurse to his relatives in Illyria. He knew them to be good people, but not the exceptional characters of Villa Metilia.

Later that night Cassius once again loomed over him, this time shaking him urgently.

"Sir, sir, you must wake up! Messengers are here from your father. You are to leave immediately for the Western front and join him there." Constantine was instantly awake and on his feet.

"Galerius won't like this," he responded.

"Galerius doesn't know and mustn't know," retorted Cassius. "Horses are at the ready. You must leave immediately and put as many stadia as possible between yourself and the emperor's men as you can. A passage is booked on the early morning boat to *Byzantium* not three hours from now. All being well you will be in *Gesoriacum* in six weeks." Fleeing in secret with the messengers from Constantius, Constantine's immediate decision was to head straight for Illyria and collect his young son. He arrived there thirteen days later. At each garrison, they had changed the horses and hamstrung the remainder. Constantine hated doing it, but he knew that Galerius' men would be close behind and would stop at nothing to prevent him from escaping. In the concentrated gallop that it took him to reach his Illyrian family home in Naissus, he had plenty of time to contemplate the implications of his father's summons. He knew that he, too, was not in the best of health. If anything happened to him there was no way that he would want Severus, loser that he was, to succeed him as Emperor of the West.

As this all began to dawn on him, adrenalin was pumping through the young general's veins like never before as he galloped. A chance to have the ultimate rule! For there was no way that could be left to the treacherous Galerius and the failing tetrarchy. A true leadership was required and he needed to prepare for it. Deep down, he recognised that a risky, counterintuitive move was necessary. The plan gradually formed in his mind. Yes, he knew now what he would do. From Illyria he would head to Salona and take the sea crossing to Rome where he would conscript his two young cousins as his special personal *comēs rei militaris*. They would keep him true to their vision of a new humanity and be the perfect role models for Crispus. As he neared Naissus, Constantine was aware that his arrival at his Illyrian family home would be entirely unexpected, and he was concerned that his now nine-year-old son would be uneasy at the prospect of such a journey as awaited them. They had barely been together for more than a few days at a time in the preceding years. However, he need not have worried. Crispus had grown into a tough outdoor child beyond his tender years. As Constantine and the messengers galloped towards the Chlorus villa, the boy was at his favourite post high in the branches of the huge oak that stood at the entrance gate from where he surveyed the passing traffic in and out of Naissus, dreaming of his father's return.

"Pater, Pater, Pater, is it really you!" he cried, half scrambling, half tumbling down through the trees' branches. Leaning from his horse, Constantine swept him up in front of him and they rode the final stadia to the entrance together. "I prayed you'd come and now you are here," was all Crispus could find words for.

Pretty sure by now that they had outridden Galerius' men, Constantine secured an *essedum*, a fast two-horse chariot, and informed his accompanying messengers from Constantius that they were to return directly to his father in *Gesoriacum* with the news that he would not be far behind. Then he and the boy set off at high speed on the ten-day trip to Salona, where they were to board the regular ferry across to the Italian peninsular and so on to Rome a further five days' journey beyond. Crispus' mind was reeling in concert with his body as they sped down the Roman highway on the first leg of their journey. While thrilled at his father's arrival, the tempestuous events that followed had turned the boy's world upside down. Constantine's hasty departure from Nicomedia had meant that he had little in the way of supplies and changes of clothes and although he was sure that they had eluded the threat of being overtaken by Galerius' men, he was loath to stay more than a night in Naissus. He had merely accepted what food and clothes the family villa could spare for the journey and instructed Crispus' nurse to pack supplies for the boy. She had done her best to pack a bag of necessities enough to still her own qualms about his welfare. All told, there had been barely ten hours from Constantine's arrival to his departure with his son.

Hardly surprisingly Crispus was eager to understand what was happening to him.

"Pater, where are we going?" Constantine threw his head back and laughed heartily, putting an arm around the boy, while he continued to hold the reins and the chariot lurched momentarily as a result.

"We are on the journey of a lifetime and it's going to be wonderful! In ten days, all being well, we shall be in Salona, where you and I will board the Rome ferry and five days later we will be at our cousins' villa." Crispus breathed in his father's enthusiasm and stilled his own uncertainties a little. It was a lot to take in, and his mother's death and the years at Naissus had provided little human interaction beyond his nurse and occasional times with his aunt and uncle, whose children had grown up and were about their own lives.

"Pater, what if they don't like me?"

"They will love you, and you will love them! After that we shall see what happens," was his father's unequivocal reply.

***

At the same time that Constantine was racing through Illyria with his nine-year-old son, Eusébie was strolling in the peace of the *peristyle* at Villa Metilia. Unable to see anything physically, the limits of the courtyard provided familiarity and security for her farsighted thoughts and contemplations that travelled way beyond Rome. It was approaching vesperna and her young brother and cousin would be joining her. Maybe Felix too. Eusébie loved Felix dearly. Abaskantis' younger brother had been born the same momentous year as Titus and Marcus, and these days the three were rarely apart. His father Fortunatus was the lead slave and effective steward of the estate and for the last few years had been initiating all three of them into the workings of a farm and estate like theirs. She could hear their cheery voices from the field below as they made their way back to the villa for the evening meal.

"Come on, Felix," Marcus was saying, "You are fully one of us. Stay for vesperna."

"Yes," continued Titus, "Be a sport, you know Eusébie will love to see you." Eusébie made her way happily through the atrium and into the dining area where Abaskantis was spreading a vesperna fit for the appetite of the hungry young males.

"Felix is coming, Abaskantis," she called, "Make sure there's plenty to eat and please join us too, as the others are still busy in the city."

In the eight years since she, Claudia and Titus had inherited the estate on her father's death in the final skirmish with Carausius, much had changed at Villa Metilia. According to Roman law, a woman inherited her husband's estate equally with her children in the event of his death, and so it had been. In the ensuing years, the boundaries between the slaves and their owners on the estate had become increasingly blurred. The majority of the slaves were members of the slave ecclesia and in any case those who were, embraced and loved on those who were not, so generally there was no significant distinction between them. Long before Julius' death, Claudia, Valeria and Eusébie began to take a full part in the ecclesia, Zeno's old heart having failed only a year or so after the death of his eldest son and Julius having been almost continually away on the Western front. In those years, the patrician women and their sons became used to accepting the leadership of the slave ecclesia and the slaves continued to accept their leadership of the Villa Metilia and farm. Eusébie was extremely happy with these developments.

Later, once they had inherited, they had discussed what it would mean if they made all the slaves free men and women, let go those who wanted to leave, and ran the farm as a kind of cooperative, like in the Acts account of the early church. It seemed to recognise the new reality. However, while hoping for that to be the destiny of their children, the older slaves such as Melissa and her husband Fortunatus had advised against it at this point. They said, probably rightly, that it would draw too much attention and possibly bring persecution, particularly towards the unusual patrician household of the three women and two boys and their involvement in the slave ecclesia. Then one day, stumbling on the Hebrew practice of love slavery in the book of Exodus, they had simply declared themselves love slaves like in the biblical account. They held a ceremony where they all, patrician household and slave ecclesia alike, bored one another's ears to the doorpost of the villa with an awl as described in the story, and the villa was increasingly recognised as a centre for the church. What had been Quentin's apartment was now set aside for Fuscian and Dunnius as their base when in Rome and other travelling leaders from among the companions across the empire occupied the guest quarters frequently. However, the church there continued to be known almost universally as the slave ecclesia.

Such was the relationship between the household and the ecclesia as Eusébie, Titus and Marcus sat down at table together with Felix and Abaskantis that evening. As the meal progressed and the diluted wine took positive effect, the sense of camaraderie and friendship was palpable.

"Tell us a Quentin story, Eusébie," requested Titus. The stories of Quentin had embedded themselves deeply in the corporate psyche of the slave ecclesia and tended to surface at moments like this.

Eusébie hesitated, reflecting on Titus' words to Felix that she had overheard earlier that evening. "You are fully one of us." Then she brought to mind one of the first ever incidents of Quentin's life that she could remember.

"I will tell you about my first memory of Quentin. It was when I was barely seven years old and he was caring for his mother, Titus' and my grandmother, in the last days of her life. *Aviae* struggled with the idea of her patrician son doing the practical tasks of caring for her. 'Slaves work', she called it. Quentin simply told us the story of Jesus washing the disciples' feet. 'Taking the lowest place is God's work,' he said. 'That's the difference between the kingdom of God and the empire of Rome!'"

"I think it's time for Felix to be fully one of us," interjected Titus, "and Abaskantis."

"But we are already, to us and to you," responded Abaskantis.

"Yes, but that's the whole point," put in Marcus, "to us, yes, but to the rest of Rome you are still slaves."

"Surely it's time," said Titus, taking Eusébie's hand, "you, Mater, and I, we can do this!" Felix cleared his throat awkwardly.

"It would be amazing," he responded, "but if you do this for us, what about the rest of our generation? My father and mother and the other leaders advised against this before, for your safety and ours. I know they want us to be free, but has anything really changed in the city? Won't it be asking for trouble?"

"I think it would be," Abaskantis spoke up. "We should all be patient a bit longer yet."

"Let's sleep on it, and discuss it again in a few days," ventured Titus. They all agreed, and the conversation moved onto the practicalities of tomorrow's work on the farm before they all mucked in to help Abaskantis clear the remains of the meal away, before heading to their beds there in the villa and down at the slave quarters.

As it turned out, they did not have time to wait for a further discussion before the matter presented itself again with considerable urgency. For late the next afternoon Constantine and Crispus' chariot swept dramatically into the forecourt of the villa. Their arrival was entirely unexpected although the young general himself was no stranger to the household. When he had been in Rome the year or so previously, organising the troops for the Persian engagement, he had stayed at Villa Metilia and been a favourite of everybody. Valeria had let go of Domus Chlorus on her husband's death, and moved back to Villa Metilia with her son Marcus, and so the villa was now Constantine's port of call and they were delighted to see him once again.

Crispus stood by shyly awkward and uncertain as the cousins gave his father their customary bear hug, but once introduced, he was quite literally lifted off his feet in welcome by the whooping Titus and Marcus. Then Valeria greeted her nephew somewhat more decorously and Claudia welcomed him warmly to their home.

"How long can you stay? You and your son are most welcome here."

Eusébie stood a little to one side taking everything in but waiting for her moment, aware of Crispus' eyes on her. "Welcome, Constantine, you have a special place in our hearts here, and now so does Crispus," she said. Abaskantis hovered briefly in the background, assessing the situation before hastening to the guest rooms to prepare towels, robes and bedding for the guests and running to pull together the catering help for the extended vesperna.

That evening, the whole household, Claudia, Titus and Eusébie, Valeria and Marcus, sat down with the general and his son to a vesperna of fish, fowl, bread, sweets and wine that surpassed anything that normally constituted a Roman evening meal at Villa Metilia. Lanterns lit, they similarly prolonged the evening well beyond their usual routine. The sense of a momentous occasion was on them all, even although no one had yet said as much. To begin with, Abaskantis served in deference to their guests, but before long, the whole household were involved, and the slave woman seated herself at the end of the table. Constantine observed the shift in patrician protocols without surprise; it was something already in the air on his previous visit, although it went further now, with a slave seated at table with them. Crispus, however, emboldened by the welcome, piped up, "How come you all eat together and serve one another like this? My uncle would never allow it!"

As was increasingly the case on moments like this, all eyes turned towards Eusébie, although her physical eyes saw none of them.

"Well, you see, Crispus, Villa Metilia is home to the slave ecclesia. When we come together to remember Jesus' suffering and death, we follow what his brother James wrote. He reckoned that if we make distinctions among ourselves about where people sit and who does the serving then it gives place to oppression and domination. However, if we treat the lowly in this world as beloved brothers and sisters then we are all heirs of the kingdom that Jesus promised to those who love him. It's beginning to affect everything we do." Crispus looked questioningly at his father, wide-eyed.

"Pater, is this the way of the empire to be? That you are going to lead?"

"With help, it may be so," Constantine responded, casting his eyes around the table before focusing on Titus and Marcus, "which is exactly why we have come."

As simply and clearly as he could, Constantine explained the events of the last few months in Nicomedia. How the Eastern Empire had fallen into the hands of Galerius and the West to his father. How Galerius was a scheming and selfish manipulator who had displaced Diocletian in his time of need. That he was now the son of the Western emperor and a threat to Galerius' plans. He explained how he had come to recognise the crisis in leadership that had befallen Rome repeatedly. Then how his friend gave him a copy of the book of Daniel, which had helped him to see that a different kind of empire with a different kind of leadership was the focus of a promised future. "The emperor Nebuchadnezzar struggled to be a good leader but was pulled in all manner of directions, and he knew that about himself. Then things began to change with him. The clue was his trust of a posse of young men who belonged to a different way of being, who he had discovered when occupying Jerusalem. I could not get that story out of my head. Then I thought of you."

He told them how only four weeks ago, in the middle of the night, he had received the summons to join his father in defence of the Western Empire in the far reaches of northern Britannia. That his life would be in danger if he did not leave immediately before Galerius found out. "I knew then what I had to do. I would fetch Crispus from his temporary home in Illyria and head for the West via Villa Metilia where I would ask you both to join me." At this, a shocked hush fell on the company. It was as if time stood still. Claudia eventually broke the silence.

"But they are still just lads," she exclaimed. "How old are you? Thirty-three? When you arrive in Britannia, you will take command of legions. What role can they play to a general and son of the emperor?" Constantine regarded her respectfully.

"If they are willing then I will make them my personal comēs rei militaris. They will have charge of all my personal administration and needs. I saw that they are well trained and educated beyond their years when I was here before. To the rest of my men they will appear as servants, but in our inner circle they will be my closest friends and advisers." He turned his attention to Titus and Marcus. "You have already learnt to cross those boundaries here with care and sensitivity. You will know how to do it there."

Silence again descended on the company as the significance of what Constantine was suggesting sank in. Then Titus spoke up.

"We are not two, we are three. Inseparable, complementary. You will need all three of us." Constantine raised his eyebrows.

"Then who is the third?"

"Abaskantis here has a brother, Felix," continued Titus, "he was born at the same time as us and we have grown up together. He is a slave, as she is of course. All the same, just as we are, he is. Even more, because he knows instinctively how to serve without being subservient. That is what you will need us to do, as you have said. Only last night, we were talking about the right time for us to give him his freedom. To be a comēs he will need to be a freeman, won't he? Mater, Eusébie and I have the authority to set him free. We'll not come without him, cousin."

"So be it," responded Constantine, and threw back his head and laughed in his customary manner. Whenever he embraced the unforeseen, he laughed at the obstacles.

Claudia interposed again, "They are young, Constantine, as I have said, but I know that at sixteen, Roman men are ready for enlisting, and they will be twenty before we know it. Yet what of Crispus? He is half their age. Surely you can't mean to take him into the battle?"

"I want him as near me as possible, but you are right, he can't come all the way north to the battle front." Crispus was crestfallen.

"Then what will become of me?"

"It's alright, little cousin," intervened Eusébie. "I have an idea. Our great friends and advisers, Fuscian and Dunnius, have a school in the companions' villa at Ambianum. It would be brilliant for you, Crispus. You will be nearer your father once the border is secured."

"School?" retorted Crispus, pricking his ears up. "I was going to have a tutor next year. What kind of school?"

"One for new humans if I know anything about it," responded Constantine.

Valeria, who had taken a great interest in the school and imported some of the techniques in the education of the two cousins and some of the emerging young slaves on the estate, joined in. "It's for children aged up to eleven or twelve where they learn to read and write and understand mathematics. They have all the latest equipment, a stylus and a wax tablet for writing and an abacus to learn basic mathematics. Mama Junia, who began it with Quentin, is quite old now, but she still mothers the pupils and they have some great young tutors. The most trusted families in the ecclesia take care of all the children in their homes."

Crispus was both excited and overwhelmed by so many new possibilities that he fought hard to hold back the tears, but Valeria's intervention reassured him. The truth was that the events of the last weeks since his father's arrival fulfilled the daydreams that had sustained his childhood since the shock of his mother's death. This extraordinary turn of affairs filled him with hope despite the emotional challenges.

After such a potentially world-changing vesperna, Claudia and Valeria went uneasily to their rooms, as did Abaskantis, who shared the events with her parents, Melissa and Fortunatus, late that night. They were all understandably reluctant for their sons and brother to embark on such a high profile and risky enterprise. Eusébie, on the other hand, was full of anticipation. Of course, she would miss their proximate presence. However, she would travel the roads to Gaul and Britannia with them in her thoughts and prayers within the gardens of the peristyle, just as she did the journeys of Dunnius and Fuscian. Melissa's words in response to her dreams were still fresh in her mind despite the passage of years. Particularly the word "commissions". Her dreams were commissions. Eusébie, although unable to go with her nephews in person, understood that she had a chance now to have a part with them in turning back the beast and his empire.

Titus and Marcus, of course, were thrilled with excitement and talked long into the early hours together of all that it might involve and still awoke bright and early, setting off down to the slave quarters to tell Felix what had transpired. They found Claudia, Valeria and Eusébie already there, having been in deep discussion with Melissa and Fortunatus and were now at the point of waking Felix. He joined them a few minutes later, his open face beaming to see all his favourite people gathered expectantly.

"We have something very important to tell you," began Melissa. Felix knew that if his mother said something was important, then it was extremely so! He listened intently as she related the events of the previous evening.

"If you are willing, you should go with them, Felix," interjected Fortunatus. Felix, as usual, simply took it in his stride and did not appear remotely fazed by any of it.

"Yes, Pater, of course I will go!" was his reply. And so it was agreed.

The rest of that day was given over to all the necessary preparations for the long journey ahead. That evening, at yet another extended vesperna, the household gathered together with Constantine and Crispus, Felix, his parents, and several other leaders and young companions from the slave ecclesia, for a brief legal transaction in which Felix was made a freeman. After that, the three young men were sworn in together as comēs rei militaris to the young general. Eusébie, with complete ease, offered a toast to the newly formed fellowship.

"The lords of the nations, lord it over them; and those who have authority over them are called 'Benefactors'. But it is not this way with you, but the one who is the greatest among you must become like the youngest, and the leader like the servant." At which Constantine once again threw back his head and laughed uproariously. Then the farewells began, for the newly formed fellowship were to be on the road at first light.

Chapter Five

Ways and Means

The stories of the journeys of Fuscian and his companion with the tidings of angelic intervention, together with those of Acco and Dunnius with the news of the martyrdom, had begun to carry almost biblical status for the slave ecclesia. It followed that the Alpine and Colonia route by the Via Solemnis and Via Belgica had become their preferred route between Rome and Ambianum, a route that Fuscian and Dunnius had traversed many times since.

It was, therefore, hardly surprising that Felix announced, "We should take the Colonia route," as they gathered in the early dawn next morning. Constantine was quite taken aback by the forwardness of someone so recently a slave. Then, after a moment's hesitation, and making a mental note of it, he gave his customary laugh.

"Let's take the Reschen Pass at least and on to my father's palace in *Augusta Treverorum*, and then if the Colonia route is still one of the fastest although a bit of a detour these days, of course we will."

"Alright, then," replied Felix, somewhat begrudgingly.

What Constantine had not fully realised yet was quite how the lines of initiative between the slave ecclesia and household aligned. Felix family's descent from the North African mariners who had brought the Jesus testimony to Villa Metilia had given them an unspoken authority, an influence strengthened further by Fortunatus' wisdom and Melissa's prophetic gift. All this meant that the ex-slave was often the lead player in the threesome, especially where things they regarded as spiritually significant were concerned. Actually, Constantine was already contemplating the Alpine route, as it passed through Augusta

Treverorum, and he wanted to see how well his father had improved things since he was last there as a youthful officer in resistance to the Carausian rebellion. He had no knowledge, however, of the state of the roads beyond Treverorum since those times, and was willing to take the longer but probably better road preferred by Felix and his cousins, with the proviso that they must now move quickly as he had already lost some two weeks diverting via Naissus and Rome.

Eager to make as much speed as possible, Constantine had secured another two chariots and four more horses. They made an impressive sight, Constantine and Crispus leading, Titus and Marcus next and Felix bringing up the rear. The three were well used to horse and ox carts, but this was very different and a challenge that partly delighted, partly daunted them. It was extremely tiring, and required far too much concentration for their usual bantering conversation. In any case, the necessary safe distance between them, and the noise of the chariot wheels and horses' hooves on the surface of the road combined to silence them. Only the meal breaks at *mansiones* and the night-time stopovers gave them opportunity to talk, and by then they were usually exhausted. The first stopover was a well-attended mansiones midway to *Clusium*. At Clusium itself, they overnighted at the barracks. Subsequently they stayed at another mansiones after passing through *Arretium*, before reaching the barracks at *Florentia* some four days into their journey. The military base at Florentia was typically located by the river beside the Arno Bridge and reminded Felix and the cousins of the stories of the angel visitation at Ambianum and the martyrdom of Quentin at Augusta Veromanduorum. This resonance added a significant atmosphere to their arrival, which rubbed off on Constantine and Crispus too. It remained with them when their horses were led away to be fed and rested in the stables, and the travellers lounged together in the Tuscan July evening warmth, while they consumed an ample vesperna of pork sausage and bread with diluted wine, rounded off with fruit and honey cakes.

Florentia as a city had a considerable impact on them all. The aqueduct, the forum and the two theatres made it the most impressive conurbation on their journey so far, since Rome. Titus had been especially impressed by the centuriation of the surrounding land as they approached the city. While a comparatively common and obvious means of landscaping throughout the Roman Empire, as they had journeyed towards the city in the late afternoon sunshine the resultant layout of regular squares appeared to him as an enlarged version of the mosaic floor in the atrium of Villa Metilia. The positioning of the city itself in the distance had recalled for him the Minotaur's presence, and reminded him of Eusébie's dreams that had been such a formative part of his inner life. This was probably why, as the wine and the warmth took effect, he began a conversation, which was to become a recurrent theme as the journey progressed and the relationship between the triad of comēs and the likely tetrarch unfolded.

"Constantine," Titus began, "tell me more about why you think we are like Daniel and his friends."

"Oh yes," Marcus joined in, "and what it is that you think we can do to bring a new humanity to the leadership of the empire." Felix fixed his eyes quizzically on Constantine.

"Saying nothing as yet, but clearly willing me to share my heart, if I dare," Constantine reflected silently to himself. Then, his laugh barely concealed below the surface of his words, he glanced across at Crispus now peacefully sleeping with his head lolling against Titus' shoulder, and embarked on the conversation that he had been hoping for all along.

"What are the qualities of a true leader, and how does someone become one?" Constantine asked.

"Humility, like you are showing towards us," responded Felix, immediately. "How come you, a Caesar-in-waiting, ask that of me, an ex-slave of less than a week?"

"I guess because I've learnt first-hand that leadership is not something a person has just because they have power, money and an army," replied the general.

"Fuscian reckons it's a gift," interposed Titus. "You can't insist on it or make someone accept it."

"That's why it can't be over anyone," continued Marcus, "because then it's not a gift but a kind of domination."

"That's why I think slavery is a sign," continued Felix. "As a slave I could see that everyone was a slave to the system, even its so-called leaders."

Constantine's laughter broke surface and he threw back his head and quite literally roared with it.

"Where do you get all this from?"

"It's just the Jesus testimony," rejoined Felix. "It's how he lived among the people once he started his public work."

"Everyone recognised his gift, but they rejected it for a time and killed him, like our Uncle Quentin," added Titus. In the silence that followed, they all became aware that darkness had fallen. Finally, Constantine broke the silence.

"Then I guess there's nothing to be done to guarantee that won't happen to any of us!" he added soberly.

"But Jesus rose again," said Marcus, "and that established his way of love forever. It's how come Uncle Quentin's death still has such an impact on us. Let's not forget that."

"I guess that's lesson one to sleep on then," Constantine concluded.

***

On the third day following the departure of what she had come to call the Daniel posse, Eusébie let her inner sight track with them as she sat musing in the gardens of the peristyle. The arbours and cloisters provided plentiful shade for her to sit and pathways to stroll along as she focused her thoughts on her friends. Suddenly, the pungent aroma of rosemary from the flowerbeds heightened by her lack of visual sense, triggered childhood memories of Quentin's reassuring presence in the days that they would sit here together with her ailing grandmother. She recognised palpably that her fearlessness, her sense that all would be well, stemmed from those days conquering the fear of death with her uncle. She reflected again as she so often did on the two approaches to the fear of death, her father's embrace of violence and warfare and her uncle's confrontation of death with love and life. Now Constantine, an expert in war, had reached out to disciples of love and together they were journeying to the frontiers of violence and war. Her commission, she reflected, was to watch over the consequences.

As the sun dipped towards evening, her heightened senses discerning accurately the northern edge of the peristyle, she ran down the broad gravel pathway to where the gardens opened out into a wide vista across the estate with the city on its seven hills beyond. Then, standing at the balustrade with outstretched arms, she cried at the top of her voice, "Your kingdom come, your will be done, on earth as it is in heaven."

Below on the path back up from the farm, Melissa and Abaskantis caught sight of her as she stretched out her arms and stood watching as she cried out her prayer.

"Amen to that!" they called. They were on their way to prepare a vesperna love feast for the meeting of the ecclesia. For years now, the meetings had moved from the barn to the atrium of the villa. That evening, Eusébie recollected, they would be reading from Matthew's story of the discussion about the coming of the kingdom of God, and her spirit lifted with expectation. A highly relevant topic, given the journey on which their young brothers had embarked. The plan was to start with Jesus' warnings of wars and rumours of wars that would accompany the interaction of kingdoms in Matthew's gospel chapter twenty-four, and then compare it with his promises in Luke's gospel chapter twenty-four and the Book of Acts chapter one that he would be with them by the Spirit to carry the kingdom of love to the ends of the earth.

Claudia and Valeria were both literate and offered lessons in reading and writing to any of the ecclesia who wanted them. These were integrated into the normal working life of the farm and villa as a kind of all-age learning provision, and the majority of the estate's inhabitants embraced the opportunity enthusiastically. As a result, there was an unusually high rate of literacy among them. Nevertheless, some still could not read the stories for themselves and so the practice was for one of the more literate to read the stories aloud. Then someone with the obvious gift to do so would offer several possible interpretations. This would be followed by collaborative discussion in the context of a collective expression of shared gifts and abilities. The particular history of the slave ecclesia meant that they had early on discovered how to make way for each other in love without usurping anyone's place in the Metilia estate community. Ever since they had all constituted themselves love slaves, it was hardly an issue. Due honour was shown to Eusébie, Claudia and Valeria, whose faith and generosity had made way for the kingdom of love among them. There was also a tendency to give place to the descendants of the original leaders from North Africa. However, Melissa, Fortunatus and their family refused to take any power advantage from it, with the result that rank and hierarchy simply did not operate among them.

That evening Melissa read, her mellifluous tones shaping the impact of the story.

"As he was sitting on the Mount of Olives, the disciples came to him privately, saying, 'Tell us, when will these things happen, and what will be the sign of your coming, and of the end of the age?'" She read of the danger of being misled, of wars and rumours of wars, of nations and kingdoms divided, of persecutions, betrayals, false prophets, lovelessness and lawlessness. Culminating with the encouragement that "this good news of the kingdom shall be preached in the whole world as a testimony to all the nations, and then the end will come." "But weren't they advised against even asking the question of when the kingdom would come everywhere?" piped up Junia, a bright young slave girl.

"I think that was because they were still thinking that the kingdom was just for themselves," responded Melissa.

"Yes, that's why the couple on the road home after the crucifixion almost missed the resurrection and what it meant," continued Valeria.

Jonas the stableman interrupted impatiently, "Whatever, doesn't the piece you read sound like a description of life in the empire right now? Surely we want all this to come to an end and the kingdom of love to come everywhere as soon as possible?"

Despite differing views on when they could expect the kingdom of God to come fully, they agreed three things together about the kingdom in the course of the evening. Eusébie summed them up.

"So how about this," she began. "First, it was embodied in the way of Jesus and his cross that both Israel and Rome rejected, so it can't be Israel or the Roman Empire. Those like Quentin who literally laid their lives down, tangibly carried it too. Second, it is still present among us now. We sense it and we live it. But thirdly and importantly it's not us but the love we share in the justice we do, the peace we bring and the delight we take in seeing the world system overcome by it." They went joyfully to their beds in the knowledge that this was the purpose of their brothers' journey, and what they at home were all about too, in their life in the villa, on the farm and everywhere their lives intersected with the wider life of the city.

Meanwhile, the following morning the Daniel posse set out from Florentia north towards the distant Alps. They were a sombre company as they embarked on the next leg of the journey with the previous night's conversation still heavy in their thoughts. However, the bright sunshine and the wind in their hair soon lifted their spirits. Marcus even attempted to engage them all in song, discrete phrases of Paul's hymn to Philippi projecting fitfully forward and backward as they journeyed.

"Be consoled by love, have Jesus' mind,
He showed the highest place,
The divinely human space,
Which is the lowly place,
Cruciform space,
Where the slave is the leader,
And the leader is the slave."

The following few days brought them uneventfully to the foothills of the Alps. From there it was another three days to the Reschen Pass. Once again, the resonances with the stories of Acco and Dunnius' journey leant an expectation of significance to Felix and the cousins. Like their counterparts' journey back and forth through the mountains some eighteen years before, they sensed bodily the underlying authority of the land, preceding the Roman Empire by untold millennia, yet somehow recognising and welcoming them on their journey.

Despite it being midsummer, the cold permeated even their riding cloaks, which they unpacked in defence of the wind that gathered as they surmounted the heights towards the pass. The pass itself now had a small military barracks where they spent the night. The horses once again installed safely in the stables, the company gathered round a brightly burning brazier, as the late evening sun began its descent towards the horizon of the nearby peaks. A palpable sense of camaraderie descended with the dusk, and Constantine recognised and consolidated it by proposing a toast to his comēs rei militaris.

"To a friendship that remains and outlasts the test of time," he declared.

"Amen to that," responded Marcus.

"What about Judas?" Felix interrupted suddenly. "Don't all serious friendship groups risk an Iscariot?"

"Whoa!" interjected Constantine. "That's a bit heavy."

"But surely we must be ready to face that," Felix continued. "If we are moving beyond roles and tasks to an inner core of friendship? If that's to be the hidden strength of our leadership lives together?"

Constantine did not laugh this time. In fact, it was as if time stood still. Marcus was looking across at Titus and both saw how Felix was holding Constantine's gaze.

Titus broke the silence. "Don't let's run ahead of ourselves. We can affirm our friendship together and learn how it relates to leadership one step at a time."

Constantine visibly softened. "I'm with Titus. I have invited you to accept a huge calling. I let my feelings run away with me. Thank you for trusting me this far, and now let's get some sleep; there's still a long way to go before we meet my father."

Somewhat subdued, they all made their way into the main guest rooms of the barracks, recognising that they had engaged deeply both with each other and the unknown challenges yet to face them.

The journey from the Reschen Pass to Augusta Treverorum, their next significant destination, represented twelve days of fast travel ahead of them. Typically, Constantine and Crispus led the way followed by Titus and Marcus, with Felix bringing up the rear. They had already been travelling at pace for ten days and inevitably the discomfort of chariots, the tension of body, reins, and horses, the solid terrain of the Roman Way and the heat of the summer sun combined to blur the days into a soporific tedium of travelling and sleeping. The impact of horses' hooves drumming and chariot wheels rotating still impregnated their subconscious even as they slept in almost identical and unmemorable mansiones and barracks. They barely talked, since it was virtually impossible while they travelled and they had little inclination for anything other than food and bed otherwise. By the time they were in striking distance of the city, arriving there had become the whole focus of their concentrated energies.

Augustus Treverorum was one of the primary cities of the empire in the West and as such it had been subject to intrigue, invasion and attack for many years. It was now thirty years since the Gallic uprising, in which it had been one of the main centres. In the end, the Alemannic tribes had sacked it. Subsequently Diocletian reclaimed it as the main base for the Western tetrarch and his armies, and Maximian and now Constantine's father Constantius had their imperial court there. A city of some one hundred thousand people, it had been an important centre from which to defend the Western Empire from the Carausian revolt in Britannia and Northern Gaul in which both Titus and Marcus' fathers had lost their lives. In the ensuing decade, there had been much rebuilding of the city with massive reconstruction work on the already monumental amphitheatre and circus. A new stadium had also been added, to stage chariot races.

It was mid-afternoon on the twelfth day since their discussions at the Reschen Pass when the posse swept into the ostentatious driveway of the imperial palace.

"Wow, so this is your father's place," Felix announced to Constantine. The two cousins, as well as the general and his son, looked around them with no small sense of entitlement. Two of their fathers had won the victory that one of their uncles was right now consolidating in northern Gaul, who would, with their support, carry it to the furthest borders of the Roman Empire in the north of Britannia. The bemused officers and retainers who came out in response to the commotion had never before met Constantine, and although he was clearly dressed as a general, the young men were not yet in military uniform. However, Constantine soon explained who they were and where they were going and they were ushered into the royal apartments within the court.

Word soon passed through the palace that the emperor's son and grandson were in residence, together with the sons of two famous generals who had lost their lives in the now almost legendary victory over the Carausians. Slaves hastily appeared and, seeing that they were tired and begrimed with the heat and sweat of their journey, quickly supplied them with towels and directions to the adjacent Imperial Baths that Constantius had recently constructed. In the relaxing atmosphere of the steaming water, their tiredness dissipated and was soon replaced by elation.

"Here we are in the imperial court en route to join a probable Caesar to help his emperor father fix the greatest empire in the history of the world!" Titus mused dreamily.

"No, not the greatest empire," interjected Felix. "We already carry an empire that cannot be destroyed."

"Plan is you are here to help me align those empires," responded Constantine cheerily.

"Well, maybe I can help with that," came a voice from the far end of the bathhouse.

Amidst the steam and their eagerness to get into the water, they had failed to notice that they were not alone! Sitting, partially submerged in the water, a late middle-aged man of well-preserved physique was observing them, smiling. Constantine reacted with annoyance, and some shock.

"Listen here; I am Flavius Valerius Constantine, son of the Caesar Augustus Constantius, Emperor of the West. What are you doing in the Imperial Baths without invitation or introduction?"

"Yes, I know who you are," responded the stranger, "and I am here by invitation, although without introduction as I was here before you. As it happens, I am here as guest of your father, albeit in his absence. My name is Lactantius and you may perhaps remember me. I believe you attended my lectures in Nicomedia as a young man."

"Lactantius?" responded Constantine, his features brightening and a huge smile spreading across his face. "Can it really be you? Is it possible? You must join us for vesperna, and tell us how you come to be here!"

"I would like that very much," responded Lactantius. "You too can tell me exactly how you come to be here with these young men and see whether I really can help you all!"

An hour or so later, bathed and freshly dressed, their first pangs of hunger satisfied and thirst slaked, Titus, Marcus and Felix lounged back from the table and looked expectantly at Lactantius and Constantine. They were somewhat abashed by Lactantius' apparent eminence and reputation, but they need not have worried.

"Right then, young men," he began, taking his lead from Constantine's benevolent smile. "You want to know how I come to be here, I suppose? I'll begin, but I'll be brief because I'm equally intrigued by your presence here and impatient to hear your story too." A serving girl refilled their glasses with the traditional diluted wine as Lactantius continued. "In the days when Constantine attended my lectures, I was an official professor of rhetoric in Nicomedia, appointed by the Emperor Diocletian. However, at the same time that the emperor, influenced by Maximus Daza who hated the Christians, began to turn against them, I had become more and more impressed by them. Their lifestyle and compassion towards the poor and neglected drew me powerfully. So, before long, I made it known publicly that I was joining them. To begin with there was no problem, but shortly before Diocletian's first edict against the Christians a year ago last February, I realised that my position was untenable, so I resigned my post."

"What did the emperor make of that?" interposed Constantine, "For it was a high honour and big move to make you his official public speaker."

"I hoped it would be alright at first. I had Daniel in mind, and he seemed to find the balance between speaking truth to power and showing love to the powerful. I honestly thought that Diocletian was a kind of Nebuchadnezzar figure. However, as Galerius and Maximinus Daza began to erode his position, I was becoming a political threat. It did not help that at my last public lecture I was asked what I thought about the Pax Romana. I probably shouldn't have said what I said!"

"So what did you say?" interjected Felix.

"Something like 'Together with the Greeks before them the Romans cannot possibly sustain a just peace, since we have so many levels of disparity in our societies, separating the powerless from powerful,'" Lactantius recalled. "Even that might not have been so bad if someone hadn't asked how the Jesus way was different. My reply was taken as a direct invitation to rebellion."

"Come on!" affirmed Marcus approvingly. "What was your answer then?"

"I said that with him there is no slave or master. Since we all have the same father, so we are all alike his freeborn children. No one is poor in his eyes, except for want of justice; no one is rich, except in moral qualities."

The young men's whoops, claps, and Constantine's laughter briefly woke Crispus who was fast asleep with his head on his father's chest. He looked across at Lactantius and announced, "Pater, I like this man."

"Well, I'm glad you do, young fellow," replied Lactantius.

Crispus, meanwhile, had already fallen fast asleep again. The serving girl who had been waiting on them intervened.

"Let me take the boy to the sleeping quarters," she asked, kindly. Constantine recognised her obviously genuine concern with gratitude, and disentangling himself from Crispus handed him over to the girl who led him gently away, now virtually sleep walking.

"Well, this young lad might like me, but it wasn't a sentiment shared by the Eastern imperial court," continued Lactantius. "By later that evening I had already heard from my contacts in the Praetorium that a warrant was about to be issued for my arrest. I had a strong sense that my time had not yet come so to speak, so I resigned my position and left the city."

"Gosh," said Marcus, generally the most detailed organiser of the three. "Where did you go? Didn't you have a villa or a domus to sort out, or did you just abandon your position and leave?"

"I am single, had no personal slaves, and lived in an official residence set aside for the public rhetorician, with its own imperial staff. I simply returned there that evening, wrote a letter of resignation for the emperor, gathered my personal belongings and secretly visited the leaders of the ecclesia. They furnished me with a horse, some substantially filled panniers and a list of disciples who they knew provided hospitality to pilgrims. I left that very night."

"I made a similar hasty escape, only seven weeks since," said Constantine. "My father sent for me to join him in Gesoriacum and, as I was under house arrest by Galerius, the only thing for it was an immediate night escape. I went via Illyria to pick up Crispus. However, your experience was a year and half ago. Where have you been since?"

"Well to begin with I decided to head to *Vagharshapat*. The king of Armenia has declared the whole kingdom Christian, and is building the most extraordinary worship centre. I thought that I would be safe there and might be of some use to the developing ecclesia. However, it was not long before I felt the same spirit as in the imperial court in Nicomedia. I am sorry to say it, but I fear that they are using the church to consolidate power, not to make space for a new humanity. I saw your mother Helena there, Constantine. Did you know that she was involved in the court of King Tiridates?"

Constantine shook his head. "I've no idea what she's presently up to. Ever since I married Minervina against her will, she seems to have washed her hands of me. When Minervina died, I thought that she might take pity on me for Crispus' sake. However, by then she had fallen out with Diocletian and Galerius and left the city. I'd heard rumours that she had gone east, but no, I didn't know that she was in Armenia."

An uneasy silence ensued. The three comēs were very aware of the hidden currents of emotion underlying Constantine's words. Lactantius gauged that it was not a subject for further discourse just then.

"Well, I didn't stay beyond a month or so. I had heard that there was a growing welcome for the companions of love in the Western Empire, and decided to make my way there via some of the original New Testament churches. So I plotted a journey via Ephesus to Corinth and then via Rome to here. Pretty much wherever I went the companions were thirsty for my ideas and teaching and I invariably stayed for some weeks, and I was several months in Ephesus and Corinth. All the while, I kept hearing of something excitingly new happening in Gaul where Rictiovarus, a Christian procurator, was promoting and protecting the growing movement."

"Well, we can tell you about that," interrupted Titus.

"It's where we're heading next," said Marcus, his face lighting up.

"Then it's high time for your story," Lactantius replied, leaning back onto his couch.

Constantine looked across at Felix, finding comfort in the young man's presence. He was grateful for the ex-slave's confident acceptance of the unfolding events. Nothing fazes you, he thought to himself. No hidden agenda here, simply new humanity in the making.

"You tell the story," he said. Felix took a deep breath and took up the tale.

"We're from Villa Metilia on the Janiculan Hill in Rome," he said. He nodded towards Titus and Marcus. "These two are patricians whose fathers lost their lives winning back Gaul from Carausius. I am Felix, legally a freeman of only three weeks, but actually an equal part of the slave ecclesia of Villa Metilia with these two, their mothers and Titus' sister Eusébie for as long as I can remember. Life was running smoothly along until three weeks ago when Constantine here burst on the scene with Crispus and the news that Titus and Marcus were to be his comēs rei militaris and accompany him to join his father in defending the Western borders. They immediately informed him that there was no way that they were coming without me and he was sensible enough to invite me too!" Felix sent the general a twinkling glance, and continued. "There was the small matter of recognising me officially as a freeman, but Constantine had no problem with that. But he'd better tell you the whys and wherefores!"

"It is partly your fault, Lactantius!" remarked Constantine as he took up the tale. "You had the most compelling and practical ideas about leadership back in those days when I attended your lectures, even before you joined the ecclesia. It was quickly becoming obvious to me that the quality of leadership in the imperial court was fatally flawed. Like you, I was drawn to the Christian companions in Nicomedia. I became great friends with the architect Atticus who was one of them. He introduced me to the book of Daniel where, also like you it seems, I soon became convinced that Nebuchadnezzar chose the young Hebrews because he was desperate to find a way of reframing the failing leadership in the Babylonian Empire. Basically, it made me think of these fellows, and the rest you've heard!"

"Well not quite," interposed Titus. "The best bit is about the procurator Rictiovarus that you mentioned. Actually, he used to be a murderer persecuting Christians just like Saul of Tarsus before he became the apostle Paul. He killed our Uncle Quentin.

However, the way he died had such an impact on the consul that he eventually came to embrace the way of love himself. So then he made it his business to protect and promote Quentin's friends and co-workers at the companions' villa in Ambianum. Our friends Dunnius and Fuscian from our slave ecclesia divide their time between Rome and there. We are heading there now to find a place for Crispus."

"Well then, if you will have me, I'll accompany you to Ambianum. Then if they will have me, I will stay there and help with Crispus' education," concluded Lactantius.

"Come on!" exclaimed Marcus once more, excitedly, barely restraining himself from jumping on him. "Let's do this."

"Yes," added Constantine, "this is all serendipitous indeed! But now to bed!" he announced to them all. "If we are going via Colonia Agrippina to Ambianum then we must leave early tomorrow. It's essential that we get to my father within two weeks more at the latest, and as I calculate, it's another four days to Colonia Agrippina, another six to Ambianum and maybe a further three to Gesoriacum depending on the road."

They were all drooping with tiredness despite the excitement. Well aware that the luxury of the royal apartments would be in marked contrast to most of the accommodation of the previous weeks and the expectation of what was to come, they wanted to make the most of it. Constantine, however, arriving back at the apartment already half-asleep was surprised to discover that there was no immediate sign of his son. Seeing light from an apartment further along the corridor he went to investigate. He was immediately reassured to see Crispus sound asleep, but surprised to discover a second child, a girl of approximately the same age as Crispus, fast asleep on a bed alongside his, and in a chair beside them, the servant girl dozing silently. As he turned, deciding to leave any explanations until the morning, she awoke. "Your Excellency," she called, softly. "This is your half-sister Constantia. Forgive me, but I thought that they would be company for each other, she has been so alone for such a long time."

Constantine stood quietly, looking at the sleeping children. "You've done nothing wrong. Far from it," he concluded. "Get some sleep. We'll speak more of it in the morning." Then, pondering the unexpected turn of events, he headed back to his apartment.

If this young girl was virtually alone here in the imperial court, her father in Britannica and her mother who-knows-where, he reflected as he was drifting off to sleep, then what was to stop them adding her to the party? She could study with Crispus at Ambianum and be company for him there. No one else, except Lactantius, failed to fall immediately to sleep that night. He, on the other hand, had much to contemplate. This was an extraordinary turn of events. In all likelihood, the young general would make Caesar at least, maybe even Emperor of the West in due course. Could a new approach to leadership among the people really conjoin the kingdom of love with the empire of Rome? Would it not be like trying to combine oil and water? Surely, love must rather displace the dominating spirit of empire. What might be his role in achieving such a move? He had offered to tutor Crispus whatever, but the whole experiment attracted and enthused him. He determined to give himself to the posse as far as he was able. It was the early hours of the morning before sleep finally overcame him.

The following morning, Crispus, beginning to stir, opened his eyes and was shocked to find that a girl of around his own age was sitting wrapped in her bedclothes gazing at him. She had long brown hair and matching brown eyes. She felt somehow familiar.

"Di Omnes! Whoever are you?" he asked.

"Well, I think I'm technically your aunt, Constantia," the girl responded, calmly. "And am I glad to meet you! I've been marooned here for months ever since the rest of my family headed back to the East and decided I was too young for the journey and would be safer here until my father came back from the front. Is that where you are going? Can you ask your father to take me with you too?"

"Come on then," exclaimed Crispus impulsively, taking her by the hand. The two of them went looking for the general. He was just emerging from his room to look for them.

"Well, I see you two have met already," he observed.

"So you already know this girl?" asked Crispus. "She says she's my aunt, even though she's obviously only my age," he continued, "and she wants to come to Ambianum with us."

"Does she indeed," replied Constantine. "Then she shall! But first put on some day clothes and come and eat something." At this he headed into the dining area where the three comēs were already setting about ientaculum. Calling one of the attending slaves he instructed him to secure another essedum.

"Can't Lactantius simply ride with me?" interposed Felix.

"Well, here's a thing," replied the emperor, as Crispus and Constantia bounded into the room. "It turns out that my young step-sister here has been left in the imperial palace entirely alone save for the servants. She wants to come with us, and it seems to me that she'll be company for Crispus and can stay with him at the school at Ambianum which will be great for her if it's as good as it sounds."

A light breeze accompanied them as the posse in their now four chariots trotted briskly out through the gates of the imperial palace. Once again, Constantine led the way, with a much-refreshed Crispus, followed by Marcus and a somewhat garrulous Constantia, eager to talk oblivious of whether or not her new companion could even hear her, so long had she been left to her own company. Titus was now joined by Lactantius, and Felix, as usual, brought up the rear. As soon as the city was behind them Constantine set a ferocious pace and before long, they settled into their familiar gruelling routine of travel down the hard Roman roads. Even Constantia eventually gave up her attempt at conversation as the vibrations and concentration occupied their whole bodies, particularly the drivers'. Although they made brief stops to rest themselves and their horses every two hours or so, the driver was never ready for more than a perfunctory conversation. By the nightly stopovers, they were, as usual, ready only to eat and sleep. The first two days and nights thus passed uneventfully, except for Constantia who was thrilled to find herself rescued from her isolated existence and undertaking the very kind of journey of which her family had thought her incapable. Far from nervous, she embraced the experience wholeheartedly and Crispus found himself increasingly under her spell. He had a child aunt, and he liked the idea!

However, the final stopover before Agrippina was different. Unlike the previous two mansiones, which had little to distinguish them from those they had already experienced on the road from the Reschen Pass, this was a much grander affair. On their arrival, it presented an unexpectedly welcoming prospect and they looked forward in anticipation to a more comfortable stopover than usual. However, positioned as it was, only a day's journey from the colonial city, the mansiones at Bonna had become a place of choice for citizens looking for sensual pleasure. While the frontage was set out as a dining area in the usual fashion, here, several large rooms at the rear of the premises were set out with tables for gambling. Although gambling was outlawed in Rome at this time, this by no means meant it did not happen. In the further territories of the empire, any ban was far harder to enforce. Prostitution, on the other hand was legal, and legal prostitutes were known as meretrix, often wearing trademark green slippers. While they were in evidence informally around the more regular mansiones, here several rooms were specifically set aside for their use on either side of the gambling rooms. This situation was not at all obvious at first, but as the group were finishing a more than usually hearty vesperna with good wine, the hubbub from the gambling rooms grew louder, and the atmosphere became increasingly raucous.

Constantine, mindful that his young half-sister had been left at Augusta Treverorum because she was thought to be too young for such vicissitudes of travel, soon excused himself with Crispus and Constantia to see them safely off to bed leaving Lactantius and the young men surveying the scene around them. Before long, they were accosted by the heady perfume of several attractive serving women in green slippers offering bread rolls from their trays. As they set them down on their table, it became obvious that these were in the shape of male genitals!

"No thanks," said Felix peaceably. Undeterred, the women lingered alluringly at the table. "Really, not just now," continued Lactantius politely but firmly. Recognising his natural authority, the women moved reluctantly on.

"Hmm, that was awkward," remarked Titus.

"Well, I hope I didn't dismiss them too prematurely," Lactantius responded. "But those rolls were a direct invitation to sex as I expect you know."

"Yes, we do know," replied Felix. "Thank you for your polite intervention. It was easier from you, apparently, as prostitutes do not always expect senior Romans to accept their services. But young fellows like us are a different matter."

"Well, don't mind me," continued Lactantius. "If you would like to go with them, be free to do so!"

"Thank you, but no," Titus responded. "Almost certainly they are in thrall to the innkeeper, either as slaves or kept women. Whatever, they are certainly not free to choose. But there's something else too. We aim to discover the power of celibacy. Dunnius and Fuscian teach that sexuality is a good gift, but it's a gift to wield, not to wield you. So first, one needs to discover how to be celibate. Then it can be a blessing not a curse."

"You fellows are quite something!" retorted Lactantius.

"It's no small thing," interposed Marcus. "My father was a mess. As a small boy, I would wander into his room and find him copulating with his slaves, both men and women. They belonged to him and he could do whatever he liked with them. He simply couldn't stop. I don't want to be like that. I think that the young male slaves he took to war with him were basically his sex slaves too. To be going to the front with Constantine as a comēs in the purpose of a truly loving kingdom is a big privilege to the son of such a father. I don't want anything to spoil that!" He became aware that the other three were looking at him with appreciation. Titus and Felix knew his story but had never heard it expressed with such feeling.

"We're with you," they said.

"Then count me in as an elder in a mutual commitment to put love first," added the professor.

Chapter Six

Momentous Meetings

Valeria watched as the gnomon-like edge of shadow moved inexorably once more across the mosaic of the Villa Metilia atrium. She was incapable of seeing its progress without recollecting Eusébie's dreams of so long ago. It hardly seemed possible that twenty years had elapsed. She and Claudia had committed to support one another and be an alternative pole to the bullish oppression of the empire's patriarchy. Together with Eusébie, they had loved, worked and prayed for a new humanity to manifest. With a grateful heart, she meditated over her son, her nephew and their much-loved ex-slave companion. How right that he was now a freeman. Nevertheless, their characters would be challenged to the limit in their new role. She wondered how they were faring. Eusébie's urgent call jolted her out of her reverie. "Valeria, where are you?"

"I'm sitting in the atrium," she replied.

Her niece appeared from the peristyle. "I think there are soldiers and some kind of vehicle coming up the driveway. I can hear their voices, the hooves and the rims of the wheels on the flagstones. I do not have a good feeling about this. We need to be ready."

Since inheriting the estate ten years previously, they had been left in peace to make the quietly radical changes to the life of the villa. However, the last eighteen months had been worrying. Galerius had put pressure on Diocletian to accelerate greatly the persecution of Christians throughout the empire and the same edict that had faced Lactantius in Nicomedia shook Rome too. Until now, the slave ecclesia had remained untroubled and Villa Metilia had continued to prosper, but it was becoming a hub of hospitality and safety for fugitives in

Rome, and the concern was that this would bring them to the attention of the increasingly hostile authorities.

"We should find Claudia and go and meet them," responded Valeria.

"We need to be seen to be on the front foot and no easy target to take advantage of," Eusébie agreed. Her uneasiness was not fear. It was rather a sense that something was shifting at a foundational level, like tectonic plates moving beneath the deep structure of their lives. Claudia had heard the commotion emanating from the driveway and was already standing in the entrance of the villa.

"These men are *frumentarii* from *Castra Peregrina* part of Emperor Galerius' secret service, I'm certain," she confided as the *carpentum* and the accompanying riders drew up. "I can tell from their distinctive grey military *sagum* cloaks and pins."

A corpulent official in the same uniform as the riders emerged from the carriage. "Ave, honourable ladies," he greeted them. His voice was silkily sweet, but his eyes belied the amicable tone of his greeting.

"I am officer Flavius Octavius of the Praetorian Guard. Imperator Gaius Galerius Valerius Maximianus has sent me to enquire after your welfare."

"How kind of him," replied Claudia, smiling calmly, "We are all well and in good spirits here at Villa Metilia. To what do we owe the honour of your visit?"

"His excellency the emperor understands that General Constantine has recently visited you," replied Flavius."

"Yes, this is his home in Rome," Claudia replied. "However, he was here some weeks ago and is long gone. How can we help his excellency?"

"Our enquiries have led us to believe that your villa houses a Christian slave ecclesia. His excellency is anxious lest his friend and son of his honourable colleague Emperor Constantius be associated with the enemies of Rome," continued the silky voice.

"Nothing has changed at Villa Metilia that our honoured husbands who gave their lives for the empire were unaware of," Valeria interposed. "Surely you have not come here calling us 'honourable ladies' only to dishonour our husbands' and fathers' memories. We are shocked at your suggestion, aren't we, Claudia?"

"We are a place of peace, and we seek peace," continued Eusébie. "Won't you come in and take some refreshment? We can provide fodder for your horses too."

Flavius was unused to women who were undaunted by the presence of powerful men. He hesitated before stepping back towards the open door of the carpentum.

"You would do well to take my warning most seriously." He stomped his vine staff on the ground for emphasis. "I will inform his excellency Galerius that you fully understand there is no longer any place for the Christian Church in Rome, and that we can expect Villa Metilia to cease all Christian activities. Otherwise we will come back with a cohort of soldiers and arrest the offenders."

He signalled to his men and climbed back into his carriage. The caravan turned around in the driveway and headed back down the Janiculan Hill, the dust billowing behind them. The three women stood briefly in silence, watching as the frumentarii retreated. Then they turned toward each other, smiling with elation and relief.

"Well done, Mater," cried Eusébie. "You handled that perfectly."

"Yes, you did," echoed Valeria.

"We all did," concluded Claudia. "But that might not be the end of them."

"These are precarious times," ventured Eusébie. "Much depends on Constantine and more still on Titus, Marcus and Felix. If they succeed, the West will at least balance the oppression of the East. In the meantime, we must strengthen ourselves in love. There is much to do."

Already the rest of the Metilians, as they had begun to call the whole estate community, were beginning to wend their way from the farm and the now much improved slave houses up to the villa for the meeting of the ecclesia scheduled for that evening. Many had seen the presence of the frumentarii and the news passed among the others, so they had held back from making their way up to the atrium of the villa until now. However, with the departure of the secret service agents they made their way in excitedly, clamouring for news but sobered by the events that had just taken place. As was so often the case when the peace of the community was disturbed, whether by sickness, death, or bad news, it was to Eusébie that the members of the ecclesia turned. To begin with, it was the young men and women who looked to her but with the passage of time, the wisdom of the blind seer carried increasing weight among them all. That evening, among the familiar ingredients of the meeting, the songs, prayers, and discussions over the practicalities and challenges of daily life, everyone was looking for Eusébie's contribution. When it came it was brief and to the point, echoing the words of Jesus' sermon on the plain.

"My advice is to find strength to love our enemies, do good to those who hate us, bless those who curse us, and pray for those who mistreat us."

"So be blessed you frumentarii!" cried Junia and Jonas, in chorus.

***

Constantine was feeling the pressure of time acutely as they rode into Colonia Agrippina. He knew that his father would be awaiting his arrival in Gesoriacum with growing impatience. He wanted to leave enough time in Ambianum to settle Crispus and Constantia so had no desire for more than an overnight stopover here. He also knew that the three young men were eager to explore the city, so he was relieved that their early afternoon arrival allowed time for Felix and the cousins to explore the sites briefly. They felt almost obliged to do so. In the folk history of the slave ecclesia, Colonia Agrippina had come to stand for the dominance of empire mainly because it was where the young Acco had first encountered the Pax Romana in its overbearing fullness. Actually, they were less than impressed when it came to it. Unlike Acco, they were born and raised in the heart of the empire. Nevertheless, it served to remind them how much they took it for granted. They turned over in their minds together this unexpected lack of impression, acknowledging to each other how deeply the empire was embedded in their attitudes and assumptions despite their embrace of the alternative kingdom of love. They determined to hold one another to their commitment to the way and leadership of love in the face of whatever came.

"It's a strange reality that while Constantine wants us to represent the way of love, here we are moving inexorably towards the battle for the way of the empire of Rome!" exclaimed Felix. "We must talk this through with Constantine before we get to Gesoriacum."

"It will for sure have big practical implications for battle!" responded Marcus thoughtfully. "Hopefully Lactantius will help us prepare ourselves," mused Titus.

Their anticipation of Lactantius' input was realised when the posse reached Ambianum six days later. Chariot-sore and dog-tired, they arrived at the companions' villa at nightfall, having pushed themselves to the limit to make it possible to spend a whole day there. It was like coming home for Felix and the cousins, for although they had never been there before, the connection via Fuscian and Dunnius and the historical link with Quentin was huge. Nevertheless, despite the rumbustious welcome during which the comrades plied them with food, drink and endless questions, they were soon in danger of falling asleep on their feet. Fortunately, the older companions were used to welcoming long distance travellers, and the presence of the school meant that Mama Junia and her young assistant were especially aware of the needs of the two children, so they soon intervened on their behalf, promising their eager comrades that there would be opportunity the following day to hear from the posse, and particularly from Lactantius, whose reputation had preceded him. The question of the clash of kingdoms was the topic of the times for the ecclesia and they were agog to hear Lactantius' take on it all.

The main body of companions were unaware of Constantine's identity, as he had decided to keep it hidden for the time being now that he was in Gaul. It was obvious from his dress and demeanour that he was a military general, which was attention enough, but until Crispus and Constantia were safely ensconced and he was well on his way to his father, he thought it better to conceal who he really was from public knowledge. Dunnius had been away in Augusta Veromanduorum visiting Acco, but was due back the following afternoon. The plan was that the posse would spend some time recovering from their prolonged travels during the next morning and then there would be a cena, at which they would share informally with the community of the villa. During the day, the news about the special guests would be spread to the companions throughout the city, and then in the evening, after Dunnius returned, there would be a meeting for everybody. Once Dunnius arrived, Constantine would share with him his future hopes for Crispus and Constantia to join the school and the possibility of Lactantius remaining at Ambianum with them. He would also attempt to give some expression to his own long-term plans. Truth to tell, the closer they came to his father and the Western front, the less clarity he had as to how to bring a new breed of leadership to bear. Like his three comēs and the rest of the companions, he looked forward to hearing what Lactantius had to say.

What Constantine was not expecting was the presence of the young woman who was to have a huge impact on the next twenty years of his life. For from the moment the posse sat down to cena the following day, the raven-haired beauty, not that she saw herself as such, riveted his attention. In the hectic arrival the previous day he had gladly passed the responsibility of Crispus and Constantia to Mama Junia and her, but had hardly noticed her in his concern to make sure that they were taken care of. But now he was embarrassingly aware of having to tell himself not to stare! Instead, he tried to focus his attention on the meal, which in other circumstances would not have been difficult as he was ravenously hungry. While carefully selecting and chewing pieces of succulent pork it was all he could do to keep his eyes from her. He contented himself with swift glances and stilled his inner disturbance by asking himself what it was about her that had so suddenly sent his head spinning! She was young, probably still in her teens. However, here even among the companions, she stood out for her self-possession and ease of demeanour. She portrayed the same feminine ease and confidence that he admired so much in his aunt, her sister-in-law and Eusébie. He determined to find out more about her.

Later that afternoon Constantine sat down together with his son, half-sister and comès. The latter introduced the general enthusiastically to Dunnius, together with Crispus and Constantia. There was something immediately reassuring about the now hoary headed African. The presence of the young general was of no particular surprise to him, he was well aware of his relation to Valeria and his earlier visit to Villa Metilia, and the impression that the women and the young cousins seemed to have made on the general had been relayed to him at the time. However, he had not known about his son, and obviously nor about his half-sister.

"You are so welcome here in Ambianum, General Constantine," he greeted, rising from his couch to embrace him.

"And you, Crispus. And you too, Constantia," he continued, beaming at the youngsters. Constantine could not help but notice that his hair was reminiscent of the halo used to depict the sun God and even Roman emperors in the days of the emperor cult. This sense of presence combined with his remaining military demeanour encouraged the young general that this was a safe place for both Crispus and Constantia as he set out his request for them to join the school and Lactantius to remain with them. Dunnius was delighted at the prospect. "Having Lactantius here is a dream come true, and the school staff will welcome your son and young sister with open arms. Just give me one moment." Dunnius briefly left the anteroom where they had been meeting, and returned a moment later with the young woman that had so engrossed Constantine's attention at cena.

The general fought to retain and maintain his equilibrium as she stood before him. Dunnius introduced her. "This is Fausta," he said. "She is our wonderful teaching assistant." Constantine cleared his throat uneasily.

"Will you take Crispus and my sister under your wing, and help them to settle?" he said.

"I will, gladly," she replied, seating herself next to them on the couch. Constantine gazed across at her. He cleared his throat again; he hoped it didn't sound too much like a nervous cough.

"Tell us about yourself, Fausta," he began. I'd like to know a little if you don't mind, given that I'll be leaving my son and sister partly in your care." The young woman looked first at one, then the other of the three young men, then at Crispus and Constantia and finally back at Constantine. She was entirely at ease.

"I first came here when I was nine years old," she began.

"That's the same age as me!" cried Crispus, tugging at her arm.

"And me," repeated Constantia.

"Did you go to the school here?" Crispus continued. "Did you like it? Will we like it?"

"Hold on, Crispus," interposed his father. "Let Fausta finish!"

"I'm eighteen years old. I'm the daughter of Emperor Maximian," Fausta continued, astounding Constantine completely. This time he could not contain himself! His mouth dropped open and he stared at her uncontrollably. "You're what?"

"Yes, I'm Maximian's daughter," she replied. "You might have heard that my mother Eutropia is a Christian from a Syrian patrician family with a long Christian heritage. She came to Treverorum with my father when he came to lead the fight against the Germanic tribes before I was born. My mother heard of the school here in Ambianum and I came to stay nine years ago. My mother loves it here and often visits."

Constantine could feel his awkwardness giving way to his characteristic laughter, and he threw back his head and gave it full vent.

"Well, I'm Emperor Constantius' son," responded Constantine, "which makes you a kind of cousin or something. Precisely put, you are the step-sister of my step-mother! An emperor's daughter will be teaching an emperor's grandson and an emperor's daughter! I suppose that's one qualification not many have!" Then he added, "Please sit with us in the meeting this evening, it will be a pleasure for us both to get to know you."

Crispus looked at his father quizzically, and then remarked, "That's a good idea."

As for Constantia, she determined that she had definitely fallen on her feet!

That evening the atrium of the companions' quite modest villa was packed with a motley group of men and women, young and old, slave and free. The majority were Gaulish locals but there was a representative sprinkling of the broad plurality of Rome's characteristically pan-European and near-Eastern population.

What drew them to the ecclesia was partly the practical loving hospitality towards the poor and marginalised, either being given or received, sometimes both. However, alongside that was a yearning for a new politics, a new way of living that would renew or replace the tired, frequently strife-torn and uncertain politics of the late Roman Empire. Word had got out that Lactantius, Emperor Diocletian's official professor of rhetoric who had been sacked for embracing the message of love, would be there. The room was pregnant with expectation and bursting with questions, the pre-eminent of which was how the two kingdoms integrated or diverted to bring about the reign of peace. Mama Junia, her wizened features wreathed in smiles, was presiding.

His twinkling eyes roaming benevolently around the sea of faces, Lactantius began his disquisition.

"As I understand it, there are no hierarchical categories in the creator or the creators' intention for human society. With God, there is no slave or master. Since we all have the same father, every one of us are freeborn children. No one is poor in his eyes, except for want of justice; no one is rich, except in moral qualities, so government needs to reflect that. Neither the empire of the Romans nor the Greeks before could do this, since they had so many levels of disparity in their societies, separating powerless from powerful. Because of this, left to its own devices, the empire will fail, indeed is already failing. Our task is to build a truly just society within it where all are rich in love, all are free and all are equal. It will not happen overnight but it is real and it is for now, not simply some future hope. It's about the presence and practice of love, like Jesus who gave place to women and children, advocated for the poor, welcomed strangers, released prisoners, healed the sick and realigned them with creation, washed his disciples' feet, and gave his life for us all. We can do this and more besides. We must embody this way of being in and through all the different parts and expressions of empire; its imperial court, its slaves, its army, its patricians, its plebeians and its peasantry."

A heavily built man, probably a smith by the size of his muscular shoulders, simply could not hold back his question a moment longer.

"So what about the future of the empire as we now have it? What happens to that?" Then it was as if the floodgates had opened. Male and female, young and old all added their voices. "But what if we had a good emperor?"

"And what about the barbarian hordes waiting at the borders to loot and enslave us?"

"What about bandits and thieves?" and so it went on. Mama Junia simply stood, hands raised, and gradually the noisy questions subsided.

"Can you suggest answers, Lactantius?" she asked. "If so, please continue."

The professor thrived on confrontations and questions and was entirely happy with the hubbub. He beamed at the enquiring audience.

"The kingdom of God is the alternative to empire but can be actualised in this world which is made for it and calling for it. This is what the Spirit of Jesus is given to us for. As the apostle Paul put it, 'you are no longer strangers and aliens, but you are fellow citizens with the saints, and are of God's household, being built together into a dwelling of God in the Spirit.' The place we live this out is within the empires of this world. When we have fully inseminated it throughout the earth, the world's empires will ultimately fall; leaving behind the kingdom of love, and then Jesus will return and establish it everywhere."

The likely smith was on his feet again.

"What about those who have already died, like our founder Quentin and all the others who have gone before?" he interrupted.

"Well as I understand it, they will all be part of it," was Lactantius' response.

Throughout all this, Constantine and Fausta sat with Crispus and Constantia between them. This time it was Fausta who kept glancing across at Constantine. What did the likely Caesar make of this? At which point Constantia surprised them all by asking loudly enough for all to hear, "How long will the kingdom of God last?"

"For at least a thousand years as far as I know," continued Lactantius. "At the end of which the earth itself will be renewed, and because God never ultimately forces anyone, those who don't want it will be allowed to go to their own way of destruction."

Constantia shivered, and Fausta, whispering loud enough for Constantine to hear, remarked, "God might not force anyone, but Roman generals often do."

"That's what this one's trying to resolve," responded Constantine quietly.

"Will I be safe here?" asked Constantia, looking up at Fausta.

"Yes, you will," she answered. "I know what it's like to be a sometimes forgotten part of an imperial family. Both you and Crispus will be my special charges, and I promise, you will love it here."

Afterwards Felix, Titus and Marcus talked late into the night.

"What d'you reckon to all that?" began Titus.

"I'm not sure about the final stuff," wondered Marcus.

"You are right," retorted Felix. "No one can know those kinds of future details for sure. However, the question of love versus the power of empire is clear. It will cost, but it's not complicated. Love replaces domination, and above all love displaces hate."

"So this is our task," continued Titus. "Somehow we've to help Constantine substitute love for hate in the battle for the empire, so that before we're done, Rome as we know it will fall and the kingdom of love will prevail."

At that point, they became aware that someone was standing in the doorway of their room. It was Dunnius.

"I heard your conversation as I was passing by to my room," he said. "Can I join you for a little while?"

"Oh yes please," they chorused. "We need a soldier's wisdom right now."

"It will be the wisdom of a changed man," he began. "I take it that none of you have even seen a battle, let alone seen the bodies of the slain. I take my stance from the soldiers that listened to the Baptist John, and his answer to their questions."

"Were they Romans?" asked Marcus.

"Well even if not, they were fighting for them, just like I did," the big man replied.

"He didn't exactly say stop fighting, as I remember," Felix remarked.

"No," continued Dunnius. "He said not to take anything by force, nor accuse anyone falsely and to be content with their wages. What d'you make of that?"

"I guess it was a challenge to take the most loving approach in the face of violence," responded Titus.

"We'd better remember that Quentin got killed in his attempt to do that," interposed Felix. "Eusébie would remind us that we Metilians come from the land where they used to throw the crucified enemies of the state and now we follow the crucified God, so it's a question of how to do that in practice," surmised Marcus. As he stood framed in the moonlight in the doorway, Dunnius lifted his arms in blessing.

"In a nutshell, love, pray, serve. That way we align both heaven and earth where love is rooted." His deep tones underlined his simple statement. "And that's enough to sleep on," he concluded, moving on to his room.

The following morning Constantine greeted the three comēs with four splendid horses saddled ready for the journey, and with the news that they would be riding the rest of the way on horseback.

"I'm sorry," he said, "I know that you've little experience of horse riding, but it is the preferred method of travel for army officers, and I need you up with me from Gesoriacum to the front. So it's best to get used to it now, and have any initial problems sorted before we arrive!"

The three were not entirely unused to riding horseback which they had often done on the estate as youngsters. Then, however, it had been bare-back. There was little question about their horsemanship, it was rather the getting used to saddle and bridle.

"Ouch! It's going to be from chariot-sore to saddle-sore, I guess," commented Titus to the rest. They groaned in anticipation. In the event, they managed to cope with the less than three days' ride to Gesoriacum, and required only two brief stopovers, one at a somewhat run-down mansiones and another at a small barracks. By the time they reached their destination, Constantine was feeling refreshed and relieved at the prospect of meeting his father and taking his place with him at the head of the army. However, a weary and saddle-sore crew accompanied him into the army base. Nonetheless, they were young, strong and generally undaunted at the prospect of the channel crossing and the long ride ahead. What did the government of love look like in the face of a battle? They were excited to find out.

Chapter Seven

Shaping the Future

The security at the gate of Castra Gesoriacum was unexpectedly tight. The reason was that there was only a single cohort permanently stationed there, the main legions being back in Augusta Treverorum and up at *Eboracum*, and the officers in charge were intensely aware of the resultant vulnerability of the Western emperor. Constantine was irritated to find himself having to explain who he was, and that the accompanying men were his comēs rei militaris. However, once he introduced himself it became clear that he was expected, Constantius having been waiting for him with increasing anxiety ever since his messengers had returned two weeks earlier. So, while the comēs were appraised with considerable curiosity by the watch, their horses were quickly led away to the barracks and the four men ushered swiftly to the emperor's quarters. Constantine gave immediate directions that his comēs be fed and shown to their accommodation, while he made his way alone to his father. He was shocked at how he found him. For the emperor was still lying in bed, despite it being the middle of the afternoon.

"At last, Constantine, my son. I thought you would never come," he said.

"What is it, Pater, are you ill?" replied Constantine.

"I'm not exactly ill, Constantine. It is more a case of broken in body. So unless I'm needed to address the troops or engage in anything publicly, I simply conserve my strength."

Constantius' faithful *servus corporis* emerged from the anteroom.

"Unhealed wounds, miss-set bones, collapsed lung, hernias, struggling heart. All the effects of years of combat. Thank the gods you have come, Constantine. I don't know how much longer he can keep going like this."

Erastus had been the emperor's slave since he was a teenager. As his personal body servant, he attended to all his needs and expected no other life. Constantius regarded him with huge affection and gratitude. He knew what he owed him. "Are there no senior officers that you can trust, Pater?" Constantine asked, watching for Erastus' reaction, whose grasp of the situation would be astute, as he was well aware.

"Trust, yes. Rely on to act for me, or one day take my place, is an entirely different matter." The slave nodded sagely and Constantius continued, "Basically, I have two lieutenants that I can trust, in their way. There is Justus, who is the *Legatus Legionis*. He leads my cavalry here and the legions back in Eboracum and Treverorum. He is an excellent soldier and commander, fearless in battle. However, he is an angry and violent man, subject to dark moods and incapable of leading for long in peacetime. Then there is Linus the *Praefectus*. He is a veteran of many battles, third in command and fiercely loyal to me. However, I fear that it is only because I guarantee his position. He can be a terrible manipulator and is no team player. Then there are several good tribunes, but none ready to step up. So that leaves you." Erastus looked long and hard at his master's son all the time the emperor was speaking.

"He's right, you know," he interposed gently. Not many slaves were allowed to give an opinion like this, but he was no ordinary slave.

"When do we make a move, Pater?" Constantine ventured.

"Just as soon as we can line up the transport across the channel," replied his father. "It's technically there, but we were waiting for your arrival before finalising things. Another day or so should be sufficient. However, we cannot afford to leave more time if we are to be at the front before summer runs out. In the meantime, I need to introduce you to the troops."

"There is one more thing," said Constantine. "I've known ever since I received your call to come, that this was big. You have not once mentioned Severus, and I assume he is not functioning as your Caesar. I take it that is my role. At least functionally."

The emperor snorted. "He's a dead loss, and wholly in thrall to Galerius. Frankly, I have no idea where he is and he has shown not the least interest in supporting me so far. So yes, I want you as my Caesar in function."

"Well then," continued Constantine, "Everything you say confirms my thinking about leadership in the empire. It is hopelessly weak in real terms. You are not weak in character, Pater, but even you are weak in body. I believe that we need a new kind of leader, one who leads by love. I aim to discover how to bring love to bear. I have invited three young comēs rei militaris to help me with that. I want you to meet them before we move on towards the front."

His father's face was a mixture of interest and concern. "We'll talk more of this tomorrow. For now, let's eat and drink. I've long anticipated your coming and now you are here I want to celebrate."

The following morning Constantine breakfasted with his father.

"Are we going to be able to make it all the way to the Antonine Wall before winter sets in?" was the young general's first question. Aware as he was that he had held up their move by his detour via Rome and Ambianum, he was eager to make up for it now if at all possible. "Well," responded his father, "the cavalry can cover up to sixty kilometres per day, although that's a punishing pace. Even at that rate, it will be ten or eleven days from here to Eboracum. My thinking is to send a fast messenger ahead and get a legion from Eboracum on the road north in advance of us. We have two currently stationed there and I'd rather leave one of them behind to secure the north in case we don't fare well in our task. It will take the messenger approximately nine days, whereas we will do well to make it in eleven. Which means that at the standard foot infantry speed they can be eighty kilometres ahead by the time we get to Eboracum. At that rate, we can catch them up in just a few days, and then the main band will remain with the marching legion while a smaller contingent, probably one of my elite cavalry *turmae* here, will go ahead to spy out the land, lay plans for the battle and await our arrival."

Constantine nodded approvingly.

"I and my comēs need to be part of that advance party once we reach Eboracum," he interposed.

"For sure you need to be leading that," his father affirmed. "However, we need to talk about these young comēs of yours."

As if on cue, Erastus, who had been lingeringly attentive to the emperor's needs during the preceding conversation, interrupted with the news that the relevant young men were outside enquiring after breakfast. With a cautious glance towards his father, Constantine took the risk of inviting Erastus to ask them to join them. The servus corporis held back, awaiting further instructions from the emperor.

"Oh, alright then," Constantius acquiesced, "let's see what we've got." In point of fact, Erastus had been busy since hearing of Constantine's companions the previous evening and had sent three ceremonial military rig outs for their presentation to the emperor. The result was that Titus, Marcus and Felix made an impressive entrance dressed almost identically in white linen replete with ornamented baldrics across their left shoulders as befitted senior patrician officers. The fact that they refused the swords that a baldric normally held presented no particular alarm as they were only coming for ientaculum. The effect was exactly as Erastus had hoped for, and Constantine sent him a grateful glance as Constantius looked them up and down approvingly.

"Speak up, young men, you certainly look the part. Tell me what makes you think yourselves fit comēs for a coming Caesar?"

Titus in turn glanced across at Felix, who nodded barely perceptibly.

"The two of us are your nephews, Your Excellency, and this is our faithful comrade Felix, a freeman of our family Metilia from the Janiculan Hill in Rome. We have grown up together under the extraordinary care of our Aunt Eusébie and our mothers, the widows of your brother Lucius and his fellow general Julius, our fathers."

"And with the tutelage of the companions of our Uncle Quentin," continued Marcus. Constantius listened carefully but with his eyes most often on Felix, who all the time fixed him with an open-faced gaze, fearlessly appraising the failing emperor.

"And you, freeman of family Metilia, what is your story?" broke in Constantius.

Felix paused for a moment, looked across at Constantine and began.

"I was a slave descendant of North African disciples of Cyprian, the bishop of Carthage, who were rescued from the sea by the late senator Zeno Metilia at the Battle of Tyndaris. Titus, his mother Claudia and his Aunt Eusébie made me a freeman in the presence of your son so that I could join him as one of his comēs reis militaris not five weeks since."

The emperor turned to his son. "Quite some pedigrees, I grant you. However, you said something about a new kind of leadership, one of love. What does that mean for the defeat of Rome's enemies and the protection of its borders?"

Constantine contemplated his father pensively for several moments.

"I don't fully know the answer to that, Pater. Rome's enemies must be dealt with and its borders protected. But not with the self-orientated domination of narcissistic men with no care for anything but their own reputation and advancement. It seems like only the new humans can supply a different kind of leadership, and then only if they genuinely live by faith and do not pay lip service for the same old selfish reasons. I learnt this in Nicomedia, comparing Galerius and his ilk with the companions of the Christ. Then I thought of these cousins from Villa Metilia who had so impressed me last year when I was visiting Rome. When you summoned me, I knew I had to bring them too. They introduced me to Felix, who was part of the package as far as they were concerned. Throughout these five weeks, I've come to understand why. I am deadly serious when I say that whatever the answer to your question is, I can't resolve it without them. But to be clear, they are here as my advisers, and I'm not expecting them to fight in battle unless absolutely necessary."

"Well," replied Constantius. "For sure, I need you. Given that you are adamant, I guess I need them too. However, on one condition. They must receive lessons on defence if they are to travel with the legion, particularly if they are to stay close to you, which I assume is your intention. In any case, I owe it to the memory of Lucius and Julius. I will assign my best swordsman, Commodus Amadeus of *Lindum*, to them and they must give themselves to training for at least an hour a day on top of travel. I will accept no argument." That said, the emperor began to eat his breakfast, and it was obvious the conversation was over. The rest of ientaculum proceeded mainly without conversation, apart from the emperor ordering Erastus to send and have Commodus report to him as soon as possible. However, the silence did not prevent the three young comēs from putting away a prestigious amount of bread, honey and ale! Nonetheless, it was a relief for them when Constantine asked for permission to be dismissed in order to prepare for their imminent departure.

Later that morning Commodus Amadeus came to the guest apartment. He was only two or three years older than the three comēs, but had clearly seen enemy action and carried the marks of battle. Several long, jagged scars cut across his forearms and forehead lending him an authentic authority as he handed them their practice swords and insisted they begin their lessons right away. He also brought a message from Constantius to Constantine that he and his advisers were to be introduced to the troops that afternoon, the transport being ready and the tides favouring an overnight crossing later that day. For the remainder of the morning Commodus put them through their paces, demonstrating the basic strokes and parries necessary to defensive swordplay. To Titus and Marcus' surprise, it soon became obvious that Felix had more than a little expertise already.

"Where did you learn this?" Titus enquired admiringly.

"Dunnius taught me when I was still a boy," he explained. "Back in the days before we all became love slaves together he struggled for a while with the possibility that the Roman secret service would attack Villa Metilia and especially the slave ecclesia. As an ex-soldier, he was still in two minds as to whether we should resist arrest, so he trained a small band of slave men and I found out and begged him to include me too. But in the end Abaskantis insisted that to be true to Quentin we should not violently resist anyone who is evil, but try to negotiate in love and then leave the rest to God."

Commodus' response was equally surprising.

"That's something like John the Baptist's advice to the soldiers who came to him. He said 'take nothing from anyone by violence and be content with your wages.' I've been trying to work that out ever since I became one of the companions of the cross."

"When was that?" responded Titus, attempting an easily obstructed parry and the sword spinning out of his hand.

"In Lindum, where I was brought up." The young soldier reached down, and retrieving the sword, handed it back to him. "Lindo taught the way of peace and my family have welcomed it for three generations," he continued, a mixture of bashful pride and nervous admission. "There are many companions among the legions. But Constantius is in two minds about the way. Sometimes he is sympathetic but then he flares up in anger and refuses all mention of it."

"So where is Lindum?" inquired Felix. "Is it in Britannica?"

"It certainly is," replied Commodus. "We'll be stopping there at the end of our first week or so on the road."

That afternoon the emperor's personal cavalry *centuria* gathered in the courtyard of the barracks with their horses in readiness for the brief ride to the boat. The emperor's *quadriga* was in the middle of the troop, an imposing four-horse chariot more familiarly associated with triumphal processions. This one was specially adapted and extravagantly equipped to provide the maximum impression and comfort for the ailing emperor, while still capable of considerable speed alongside his cavalry. The stable hands led the posse's horses out into the courtyard, as Constantine, Titus, Marcus and Felix stood alongside the emperor by the quadriga. The four horses that Constantine had selected for them were impressive beasts, fit for the imposing young general and his comēs. Constantius raised his hand and the buzz of conversation ceased; all eyes were on the emperor.

"May I introduce my son," the emperor began. "From this time forward he is my acting Caesar and you are to give him your allegiance. He is second only to me and has my utter trust, and if you follow his leadership, you will not regret it."

Justus, the Legatus Legionis, stepped forward. Constantius had already prepared him for this, and knew that his response would seal the cohort's loyalty, and eventually that of the legions. Running his eyes over his men, he raised his voice and turning to Constantius declared,

"I am honoured to follow you and your son, my liege."

A cheer went up from the cohort. Waiting a moment for it to die down, the emperor raised his hand again. "My son has three advisers with him fresh from Rome. Two of them are sons of distinguished generals and the third is the descendant of an African hero. You will give them your respect."

The young men were surprised and somewhat red faced but Constantine was both grateful and relieved. With that hurdle negotiated, he knew that he was ready for the next stage of his strategic journey. A different kind of leadership for a different kind of power. The centuria mounted their steeds and the cavalry moved forward towards the docks, together with their emperor in his quadriga, with the posse bringing up the rear, followed by a long line of packhorses with tents and supplies. As they moved away, a huge eagle rose up soundlessly from the barrack roof behind them, and soared away into the night sky northwards over the channel.

Embarkation onto the array of military transport took place uneventfully under an increasingly starlit sky. Commodus joined the three comēs and Constantine on the emperor's ship for what proved to be a calm but swift crossing assured by a strong southerly breeze. After some two hours, they arrived in the dim celestial light at the port and fort of Richborough. With the help of lanterns and torches the gangplanks were lowered to allow the emperor and his son, accompanied by Erastus, the three comēs and Commodus, to disembark. Their horses and the emperor's quadriga were manoeuvred onto the quayside beside them. The rest of the boats moored alongside and before long, they and the rest of the centuria made their way into the cavalry barracks at the fort where each turma of riders and their horses could rest in the customary ten person barrack double rooms shared between steeds and riders, horses in front and men behind. There were no special stables. The officers' barrack rooms were larger and

Constantius occupied one while Constantine and the comēs another.

"Get as much sleep as you can," Constantine advised. "We'll be away soon after day break."

The next day began with the slaves, of whom there were two in each ten-man turma, providing water more for waking than washing. This was followed by a rapid breakfast of bread and ale, and then they embarked on the first leg of the three-day journey to Londinium. That day they broke for cena and a necessary rest for their horses at midday for an hour or so and then struck camp at around five o'clock, proceeded by vesperna, a rhythm that was to frame their lives for weeks to come. Londinium, when they eventually reached there on the mid-afternoon of the third day, was singularly unimpressive. A crowded river crossing consisting of a wooden bridge on gravel piles knee deep in mud. The fort was more substantial and, although no longer housing a resident legion, was fully equipped for passing reinforcements in transit. So there was plenty of room for the cohort and it provided a solid comfortable night in barracks with proper sleeping pallets not tents, the last before Lindum, five days ahead.

Averaging between fifty and sixty kilometres per day, with the break for cena, was not as punishing for the horses, who were used to it, as it was for the comēs, who most certainly were not. Less fit young men would have been completely exhausted already by the five-week rapid journey they had made from Rome, both physically and mentally. Nevertheless, they were feeling its effects and it was as much as they could do to keep one another's spirits up, let alone strategize together as to how their alternative peacekeeping was going to work out on the battlefront! Ironically, Commodus was the one who eventually insisted on it. His task and their commitment to it as commanded by the emperor meant that, while the slaves struck camp each night, they had to train in swordplay. As they finished an hour of hard training the first evening on the road out from Londinium to Lindum, and were more than ready for vesperna, he plied them with seemingly endless and often unanswerable questions as they ate and drank. To begin with, it was, "So what happens when we meet marauding bands of Picts? They are not going to wait for you to explain that you love your enemies are they?"

"Somehow we either have to approach them first, before fighting, or find ways to hold them back while we talk," Titus had replied.

"Okay, try it on me tomorrow," was Commodus' response.

So began an extraordinary correlation of dialogics and swordplay that took place each evening of the five days it took to reach Lindum. Commodus would come at them on the attack thrusting his sword in accompaniment with a hard question. Whichever of the three comēs' turn it was to train had to parry with a good defensive stroke and a reasonable answer. Questions like "What would stop you Picts from terrorising our farms?" and answers like "Let's agree to divide the land already held between us in return for mutual trade," and so on, flowed to and fro, back and forth. Together with the more difficult "You lot killed my ancestors and took our land, why should we agree anything except fighting to the death?" and "but it wasn't actually us who did that, and we don't want to kill you and your friends today," they attempted to find genuine answers. As the days went by the four of them looked forward to the developing realism as they saw it. And although Constantine was much occupied with his father and discussions about the future beyond a hopefully successful engagement at the frontline, he too would stand watching, often bemused and occasionally joining the action and the conversation on one side or the other.

They arrived at Lindum in time for cena on the fifth day out from Londinium. Commodus was eager for an opportunity to introduce the comēs to his family, and they were intrigued at the prospect. Constantine announced to the cohort that given the availability of proper barracks and the fact that they had been on the road non-stop for a week, they would take half a day's extra rest to attend to the horses' needs as well as their own, before leaving for the final leg of the journey to Eboracum at first light. The four were excited at this news and Commodus immediately asked Constantine for permission to take the comēs to his parents' domus for cena. He agreed, with the proviso that they reported to him when they returned, and that they were not too late. As the place was at the other side of the city near the north gate, they headed off immediately.

"Do you have brothers and sisters at home?" Marcus asked Commodus as they walked.

"I think my sister will be there," he replied. "But my brothers have their own places now, and their own families. But you simply must meet my Uncle Adelphius and hear what he has to say about peace-making. I'm very much hoping he will be there."

Commodus' family domus was the usual Roman merchant's stone-built urban house, fronted by a *tabernae* full of cooking pots and other kitchenware for sale, which was obviously the main trade of the family. Behind this was the *vestibulum*, which led in turn into the atrium with its typical mosaic floor, in the middle of which was an *impluvium* into which rainwater gathered from the opening in the roof above. The atrium was a much smaller affair than at Villa Metilia, but as Commodus led the comēs in from the vestibulum, all three were riveted by a distinctive circular depiction of Theseus killing the Minotaur set in the mosaic floor in front of the pool. What coincidence was this?

"Mater, Pater," called Commodus. "Are you in?" A buxom woman of upright bearing and a face dominated by a beaming smile, followed by her similarly smiling but much thinner husband, emerged from an anteroom.

"Commodus, my dearest, is it really you?" she burst out, running to embrace him. Her husband, however, got there first and the result was a joyful collision of arms and bodies. "Nesta," she cried, "See who's here!"

A young woman of similar age to the comēs came running in from the peristyle. She was undoubtedly pretty but for Titus she was immediately breath-taking. He stood, goggle-eyed, for so long that Marcus had to pull him back to attention by his sleeve. "We were about to have a late cena," continued Commodus' mother, noticing Titus' reaction but taking it in her stride, "so, Nesta, please ask Cosmo and Julia to make enough for four guests. In the meantime, Commodus, introduce us to your friends."

"This is Titus, this is his cousin Marcus and this is their friend Felix," Commodus explained. "They are personal comēs rei militaris to General Constantine. And this is my mater Aurelia and my Pater Cato."

Aurelia led the way into the dining area and invited them to relax on the couches. Almost immediately, food began to appear, as Nesta, helped by a serving girl, piled the table with bread, cheeses, roast chicken, cooked vegetables and dried fish. An older male servant appeared with pitchers and diluted wine that he poured freely, with Cato's help, while the comēs and Commodus ate their fill.

"Thank you, Cosmo," responded Cato. Felix noted the care and respect Commodus' parents showed their slaves, hoping for the opportunity to tell his own story.

"Pater, any chance of Uncle Adelphius coming by?" asked Commodus.

"He'll be here sometime soon," replied his father. "He comes almost without fail these days, now that the ecclesia has grown so much and many look to us elders for a lead. However, he never makes decisions without collaboration so there is plenty to talk and pray about. He generally has cena before he comes.

He is pernickety about timing, and doesn't like to eat late in the afternoon, which it invariably is here."

As if on cue, a white-haired, bushy bearded man strode through the atrium from the vestibulum and across to where they were sitting, his face lighting up at the sight of Commodus.

"What a delight to see you back among us, my boy, and with friends I see." Commodus jumped up and embraced him, clearly moved at the reunion.

"It's only a brief stop-off, Uncle. We're bound for Eboracum and then north to fend off the Picts."

"They're not our enemies, you know, Commodus, just because they paint their faces to scare us. They belong with us in this spacious island."

Commodus nodded respectfully. It was what he expected from his uncle. "Yes, but if I hadn't joined up willingly when being conscripted either I or another of the companions would have been forced to fight them. In any case, I am beginning to see redemption in it since I have met my friends here. They're companions too, and in hope of finding you here and hearing your insight is why I brought them today."

Adelphius cast his eyes around the table at his brother, sister-in-law and niece and then at Commodus and his guests. It was obvious that they were all waiting for him to bring his perspective. He hesitated for just a moment, aware that what he was about to say could be decisive for them all in the days to follow.

"Angels call different kinds of people to places so that they can share them together in harmony, caring for the land, its trees and vegetation, its animal and plant life," he began. "It's all a gift from the Trinity, as I see it, to extend their way of life throughout eternity. We are their image and likeness. Wanting to take it for ourselves alone is death to the earth and in the end to ourselves. Ultimately, it would mean death to God." Again, he looked around at the attentive faces, aware of the grace he carried. "From the very start, the Trinity were ready to embrace that death if it came to it. They would take it full on, identify with it and overcome it. Empire is the opposite of all that. It inflicts death on other humans and lands, in the name of a supposed peace. However, it is a false peace, a deadly virus. At its peak, God came to overcome the universal threat of death and raise up a new humanity. At the core of God's action is the cross of Christ. I call it cruciform peace."

A hush had descended on the diners. Then Titus piped up. "This is exactly what our Uncle Quentin taught. But he died for it."

Felix followed up with the question that had filled the nightly dialogics of the previous four days. "But can it ever work at a battle front, in a place of war?"

"In my experience it can," Adelphius continued. "Although not without human cost, not without readiness to die, even for our enemies."

"So what exactly would you do?" asked Marcus, a little frustratedly. It was all very well having an obviously valid argument, but how practical was it really?

All eyes were back on Adelphius. He continued, "What Jesus did, what Peter did, what Stephen did. Identify with your attackers. Take on their sin. 'Father forgive them, they know not what they do. Lay not this sin to their charge.' That kind of thing."

"But Peter?" interrupted Nesta.

"Yes, especially Peter. Both he and Stephen told the people the truth, in both cases they were cut to the heart. Yet in Peter's case it resulted in a huge crowd embracing and shaping true peace, while in Stephen's case they stoned him to death. You cannot know which it will be for you when the time comes."

"You are right," responded the comēs, almost in chorus. "It is why we are who we are. Why we are here."

For the next two hours, first Felix and then Marcus told the stories of Quentin, of the angel's intervention, of Acco's recognition of the principle of identification. Of how the same principle that worked out for Stephen and Paul had manifest for Quentin and Rictiovarus. Of the contrast between their fathers' peacekeeping and Quentin's. Then Titus drew attention to the mosaic of Theseus and the Minotaur in the entrance to the atrium and told the story of Eusébie's dreams. Of how in the dream it was the Minotaur that had conquered Theseus, but then released him only to dominate and control him.

"Makes all the sense in the world," responded Adelphius. "Aurelius," he continued, "Do you think it's maybe time to replace this imperial mosaic?"

"How about with a cross?" interposed Nesta. Time quickly passed in the conversation that ensued. Felix told the story of his faith-filled ancestors, and explained how he had been a slave at Villa Metilia.

"Much to think about here," said Adelphius, looking again at Aurelius and then at Cosmo, who still lingered at the table with the drinks. It was Commodus that remembered Constantine's instructions not to be too late back and that they were to leave at first light. "Gosh, time's flown. Uncle, Mater, Pater. We must go."

As he and his friends stood up to leave, Nesta stood too. "Would you mind if I walked with you as far as the Western Gate? I promised Paul my brother to sleep over tonight to help take care of their children tomorrow, and I've left it a bit late."

"Well, of course." responded her brother, "We are going that way."

Titus barely concealed his enthusiasm at the prospect of a few minutes more with the mesmerising young woman.

Chapter Eight

Roman or Cruciform

They took their leave of Commodus' parents and uncle with much warmth and Felix made sure to go and thank the slaves too.

"There are gangs of muggers about," warned Aurelius, "our conversation notwithstanding, we take staves at night. A threatened bang on the head warns them off, and if we do have to use them, they are almost wholly defensive, unlike swords." With uncertain glances at each other, they helped themselves cautiously to the proffered sticks, then, promising to return, all being well, on their journey back from the north, they headed out with Nesta into the growing dusk. The path back via the Western Gate led through a wealthier part of the city and then through a somewhat deserted area that had been devastated a year or so earlier by a house fire that had spread across several adjacent villas. Nesta was in the lead as Commodus was less familiar with the route to his brother's domus, and Titus was next to her, Commodus and the others a little way behind out of recognition for the obvious feeling generated between the two of them.

Suddenly, quite without warning, two hooded figures, barely visible save for their extended arms, grabbed Nesta and pulled her through a hidden gap in the undergrowth. As soon as he realised what was happening, Titus wielded his staff and charged through behind her, only to receive a hefty blow to the head from a weaponised lump of masonry and tumble headlong. As soon as the others realised what was happening they saw the gap and pushed their way through, falling over Titus. They were quickly to their feet but Titus was out cold, flat on his back with blood pouring from a substantial cut to his forehead. By the time that they had gathered their wits, neither Nesta nor her attackers were anywhere to be seen.

"Marcus, stay with Titus, and Commodus and I will find Nesta," instructed Felix. The ruins of a burnt-out villa stood darkly before them and they made their way gingerly towards it.

The muffled voice of Nesta was crying out in warning from the inside, "Take care, there are more of them!"

At which point another pair of hooded figures pushed past them, heading back towards Titus and Marcus. Felix and Commodus made the painful snap decision to ignore them and try to rescue Nesta. They entered the burnt-out villa, their staves held out defensively.

Inside a room dimly lit by two oil lanterns, they encountered the original hooded figures holding a still struggling Nesta, but more threateningly, two more men, one of whom had war paint striping his face, unhooded but brandishing swords. There was no time to plan; Commodus, the master swordsman, and Felix his best pupil among the three comēs, simply wielded their staves like swords and proceeded to disarm the swordsmen. In the meantime, the other two hooded men came back through the ruined entrance behind them, now dragging a stumbling Marcus and a semi-conscious Titus. Then everything else happened in a flash. Nesta somehow broke free from the two hooded figures holding her, and kicked the one dragging Titus full on in the genitals. He promptly doubled up and collapsed in a heap crying like a baby. Marcus broke free and got the other in a headlock. Titus threw himself feebly at one of Nesta's captors, while the other jumped on Commodus who had managed to kick the swords away and get one of the swordsmen in a headlock. Felix had the other in a rather precarious arm grip. That left the one original hooded attacker still trying to hold onto Nesta while shaking off Titus. At which point Felix surprised them all.

"I'll give myself up to you on one condition," he said. "You tell us why you are doing this." Without further ado, he then threw off the swordsman, who fell over onto his back, and stood, arms wide open in their midst, his staff laid on the floor in front of him.

Time seemed to stand still, while everyone remained fixed in position. Nesta's remaining captor still held onto her, although their hood had become dislodged revealing her to be a woman too. The other still clutched his groin in agony. Marcus was upright, a hooded head firmly under his arm. Commodus stood like a giant with a hooded man on his shoulders and a swordsman under his arm.

"It's a deal," spoke up the hooded figure on Commodus' shoulders, pulling back his hood to reveal a swarthy young head, "we'll risk it," he said, clambering down as Commodus released the head of the former swordsman and stepped beside Felix, placing his staff next to his. The swarthy youth stood facing them. "I'm Audaios, and these are my friends Aidan and Duccius. This is my sister Nelia. We are military slaves who escaped from the legion when it passed though Lindum several months ago. These two are local runaway slaves who helped us and showed us their hiding place here in this ruined villa." As he introduced each of them, they came and stood by him, Duccius still wobbly with groin ache, while Marcus and Nesta supported Titus. Soon the three comēs, Commodus and Nesta stood facing their would-be captors. "We attacked you because we want revenge – payback for my sister's rape and the abuse we all received from soldiers," Audaios explained.

"And you were going to do that by attacking me? Maybe even raping me?" exclaimed Nesta, shaking with rage and shock. "And what of my brother here and his friends," she continued. "Were you planning to kill them?"

"I'm not fully sure what we were planning," interposed Aidan, his auburn hair glowing burnished bronze and framing his painted face in the lantern light. We simply heard this morning that a cohort of Romans were lodging at the barracks and guessed that some might be exploring the city and hoped to get our own back. You need to understand that if you've been captured as a young Pictish freeman like me and then forced into slavery and degradation, you don't much care what happens to your enemies."

"I too was a slave not seven weeks since," interrupted Felix. "Yet these men here and their relatives set me free. While we may look like soldiers we are working undercover for the prince of peace."

"You're what?" responded Audaios. His fellow outlaws shifted awkwardly, uncertain of what that might mean.

"So what happens now?" asked Nesta. "Will you let us go, or do you still want to rape or kill us?"

"Not now we can see you," replied Nelia.

"I tell you what," interposed Titus, somewhat recovered although still bloodied from his blow and looking pensively at Aidan. "I've an idea. Our cohort is heading for the Antonine Wall. We are due to leave for Eboracum at first light. Aidan, why don't you come with us, not as a slave but as a translator for when we attempt to make peace with your countrymen?"

"Yes, of course," continued Marcus, "That would be perfect, and then when we come back triumphant in a month or two, we can make you all freemen, and you, Nelia, a freewoman!"

"Wait a minute," intervened the older of the two local outlaws. "Who are you to make such promises?"

"The three of us are comēs rei militaris to General Constantine, and Commodus here is sword master to the emperor himself," replied Felix. "If you don't believe us, why don't two of you go with Commodus and my two fellow comēs here together with Aidan to the North Gate by the barracks. The rest of you can hold me hostage securely here while the others hide until Aidan signals that the plan is working. If he doesn't signal you can all escape back here and do what you want with me."

"It's a fair risk," declared Aidan, seeing at last a hope of returning to his people. "Let's do it."

Although the rapid chain of events bemused them, everything happened at once. Aidan fairly herded Commodus, the cousins and Nesta out of the ruined villa and back onto the path. Audaios took immediate charge of the remainder.

"Duccius and Nelia, get after them and don't let them out of your sight. Find somewhere to hide that's close enough for you to see their signal by the lights from the watchmen's guard post." Then taking Felix roughly by his arm he declared, "and you are staying here with us then," and in a somewhat face-saving gesture beckoned for the two locals to join him in a huddle around Felix to make sure he made no attempt to escape.

"No need for this," responded Felix. "I'm going nowhere unless Aidan is safely installed as our interpreter. Until one of the others returns with the news, which they will, let me tell you my story." And so, beginning with his ancestors' rescue from the sea he related once more the extraordinary tale of the slave ecclesia.

Meanwhile Aidan, Commodus and the others made their way to the barracks. Nesta was adamant that she would come with them to see what transpired before they left her at her brother's domus on the way back for Felix. Duccius and Nelia found a hiding place in the entrance to an apparently unoccupied tabernae diagonally across the street from the barracks' entrance. Nesta joined them there, by now feeling connected to Nelia by their shared vulnerability after the experience of the night. Commodus, Titus and Marcus led Aidan towards the entrance to the barracks. Although the latter had done his best to scrub away his face paint, he still presented an unusual sight and they were nervous of the reception he would get from the guards unless they could get past and find Constantine quickly. Titus too had done his best to wipe his bloody visage clean and kept his head down. The majority of the cohort had been out that evening, leaving just a couple, of turmae to attend to the needs of the emperor and prepare for the next day's journey. So although it was getting late and most were back already, the group attracted little attention as everyone knew Commodus and the comēs. They nearly made it through without incident until one of the guards called out.

"Wait a minute. That's not Felix. Who is this guy?"

"It's alright, this man has an important message for General Constantine," answered Commodus. "Felix will be here shortly."

Marcus slipped ahead while the conversation was taking place and dived across to the block they shared with Constantine.

"Please come quickly, we need your help," he called as the general rose to greet him. "What's happening here?" Constantine replied, joining him at the guard post.

"Trust us, please, Constantine," began Titus, "we have found a Pict who is willing to be a translator to help us make peace at the Antonine Wall. But first we have to let Felix know that he can come with us, because he's standing surety for him!"

Constantine looked Titus up and down, taking in his bloodstained face, and then at Aidan with his barely concealed war paint. Then he threw back his head and roared with laughter.

"I'm not sure what's going on here, but you had better come in and tell me all about it," he exclaimed. "But first let Felix know I'll trust this plan of yours." While he stood with Titus and Marcus, Commodus and Aidan went back out of the gate and crossed over to the tabernae. Nesta emerged with Duccius and Nelia.

"All is well, and the plan is working," announced Titus.

"And the rest of us will be set free from slavery?" responded Nelia.

"Yes, if we make it back successfully," he replied, inwardly hoping his promise would not prove empty.

With Commodus in the lead, they set out at a run back along the wall to Nesta's brother's place at the Western Gate.

"Stay the night with me, Nelia," Nesta burst out. "We can't make you a free woman yet, nor your brothers free men, but the Lindum ecclesia treats slaves totally differently to the military or the patrician establishment. We can make a plan and maybe find safe and caring places for you and the others."

Nelia visibly hesitated. "What d'you think, Duccius?" she asked.

"It's a night of new possibilities, for sure," he ventured.

"Then I'll stay," she replied, "if you are sure it is alright."

"I'm sure," Nesta replied.

So Commodus and Duccius headed back to the ruined villa with the news of Aidan's welcome and Nesta's hopeful plans. By the time they got there, anyone might have thought that Felix, Audaios and the remaining outlaws had been friends for some time.

The extraordinary details of his story of the slave ecclesia had so affected them that, when Commodus and Duccius told the remaining outlaws that Nelia had remained with Nesta and that there would be a welcome for them in the Lindum ecclesia, they took it very seriously indeed. Commodus added his affirmation.

"This is no dream," he said, "you won't be free yet, but you will be safe and given meaningful work until we return."

"If you return," interposed Audaios.

"I have faith we will, and if we do, I promise we won't forget you," said Felix, "Let's embrace on it!" The two local outlaws, who didn't know the military slaves well, having only been with them a few weeks, were a mixture of scepticism and hopeful gratitude. However, the corporate experience of the four escapees from the legion meant for a shared hope, just as it had meant originally a shared desire for revenge. Now that Aidan and Nelia had cast in their lot with the comēs and their friends, they were ready to do the same. They too embraced on it, and Felix and Commodus headed back to the barracks.

In the meantime, Titus and Marcus had done their best to put as positive a slant as possible on their experience to Constantine. Aidan was a highly intelligent and expansive individual who was already explaining his scheme to introduce Constantine and the comēs to some of the tribal chiefs related to his family whose farms now included lands on both sides of the Antonine Wall. By the time Commodus and Felix joined them, a completely innovatory approach to the coming military engagement was already emerging!

"I'm not sure what the emperor or his lieutenants will make of this," Constantine declared. "I guess we will have to explain it as both a diplomatic and a military approach, but it gives me great hope of something new emerging."

"The Picts won't respond unless it's both to begin with anyway," added Aidan. "We are an angry lot who have put up with years of being pushed back from our lands by you and your Celtic allies. But in the end what we want is peace and freedom to live our lives and love our lands."

"But now," intervened Constantine, "we have an early start to make. Aidan is going to have to spend the night with us in our block here, and then we'll think about how to make a freeman of him."

***

Eusébie had been increasingly uneasy ever since Dunnius arrived. It was so good to have his reassuring presence and receive news of the posse, but she was aware that if anyone was at risk of the secret service's warnings, he was. She had been delighted to discover that the posse had met up with Lactantius and that he would be remaining in Ambianum tutoring Crispus, and to hear that they were well. She was especially encouraged to hear of Dunnius' own discussions with them about what to do in the face of violence. Nevertheless, she felt the threat that his presence posed, personally. As the family of a respected late senator and renowned generals, it was unlikely that Galerius would make any move against Claudia, Valeria or herself despite the threats of Flavius Octavius and the Praetorian Guard. Nor could she see that they would make any kind of move against the slaves in the ecclesia, as, according to Roman law, they were still their personal possessions. They would have to arrest their owners first, which she remained certain they would not do. Dunnius, however, was a leader among them all, and an ex-soldier and a freeman. They could make a move against him. When on the third day after his arrival Valeria came running out into the peristyle to say that the carriage coming up the drive was the Praetorian Guard once more, she was sure that her fears were about to be realised.

Claudia was visiting friends in the city, so as Eusébie made her way with her aunt to the vestibulum she was expecting that she and Valeria would be left to confront the praetorian tribune alone. However, Dunnius was already there, together with his leather bag of belongings. Before either Valeria or she could intervene, he picked up his bag and approached Flavius, for it was he.

"This is very kind of you," Dunnius remarked, smiling. "Have you come to give me a lift? Visiting prisoners is a central definition of the new humanity I practice. Staying with them will make it so much easier. I take it that it's what you want me to do?" Flavius' face glowed red.

"You think being an enemy of the emperor is a small thing from which you will escape lightly? Do you treat this as a joke?" he barked.

"Which emperor do you refer to?" continued Dunnius. "I take no emperor to be a joke, but I have received great support from the Emperor of the West these last months, via his procurator Rictiovarus, who sends his greetings."

"Well, you are in Rome now, not Gaul, and I am carrying out the edict of the emperor of the East. You will come with me."

To which Dunnius responded by clambering into the carriage. "You will regret this, *caput capitis*," responded the tribune, climbing in behind him and trying to look like the victor. The carriage promptly turned around in the drive and headed back down the Janiculan Hill to the city, leaving the two women in a mixture of concern and amusement.

Dunnius was genuinely unafraid. His seemingly nonchalant attitude had been his strategy towards the established powers ever since he had first heard the stories of Quentin and Fuscian and their response to the threats from Rictiovarus. The approach was simply to disregard their position once it moved beyond the common weal. Following Peter and Paul, they had been willing to submit to established authority as long as it opposed evil and upheld good. Otherwise, the response was to act as free men and women whatever the outcome. He knew that torture and death might await him, although he felt in his guts that it was probably not yet. However, when the carriage pulled up outside the notorious Tullianum prison, he realised that this was serious. He suspected that his arrest was a warning message to the Metilias and the slave ecclesia rather than an attempt to extract information, as in any case their activities were in full view for those who wanted to know. He also knew that Constantine would be by now with the emperor Constantius heading for the Western border. If they were successful, then his Parousia in Rome would bring a wholly different attitude to the companions than this.

As the doors opened to receive Flavius and his prisoner, the praetorian tribune raised his hand in caution to the guards.

"Take care of this one," he instructed. "I want him alive and well for when I need him. Put him in a single cell, we don't want him up to any deceptive tricks with the inmates," he continued. "And no visitors without my permission."

Dunnius found himself propelled down a flight of stairs, worn to a marble-like surface by centuries of repeated use. He knew by repute that the lower he went the worse the conditions would be and so was relieved when the guards led him quickly onto a landing at right angles to the descending flight of stairs below. The cell into which he was ushered was empty, bar a pallet bed, a bare table, a simple chair and a clean slop bucket. However, from his experience of conditions in which petty criminals were confined until their execution, he knew that this was more like superior accommodation for patricians who had fallen foul of the authorities temporarily, and might one day wreak revenge on those responsible if not properly treated.

Claudia returned from the city to Villa Metilia to find the whole place awash with a host of different responses to Dunnius' arrest. Some of the ecclesia had seen the events first hand, and those who had not had soon heard the news. An emergency meeting was planned for that evening to decide how to respond, and food was being prepared, furniture moved, possible agendas being discussed. At first, it seemed to her like some kind of celebration was afoot, but once Valeria and Eusébie told her the news she realised that Valeria's tendency to make an adventure out of everything was still in play and the sense of helplessness was being met with activity.

"Come on," said Claudia, taking Eusébie by the arm, "let's go down and talk to Melissa." Melissa was preparing a huge cauldron of lamb porridge, and at first Claudia thought her to be caught up in the frenetic atmosphere.

"Is this for the meeting of the ecclesia tonight?" she asked in surprise.

"No, this is for Dunnius," she replied. "We've already heard that the praetorian tribune has taken him to the Tullianum, and we can't let them think we are going to ignore this, so my plan is to head right on down there with food to be shared with Dunnius and the guards. You know how it goes: love your enemies, and bless them that curse you, do good to them that hate you, and pray for them which despitefully use you. So here we go."

"Well done," responded Claudia, "I'll come with you."

"Yes," said Eusébie, "And I'll stay with the rest of the ecclesia and pray, while you look after the blessing and doing good!"

So it was that Claudia headed back down the Janiculan Hill to the city, this time with Melissa, clutching the cauldron of lamb porridge wrapped in layers of woollen cloth to keep it hot and herself from getting burnt. There was some competition among the youth about who would drive the carruca. In the end, it was Junia and Jonas together, and even though it was a close fit up front, that was partly why they had wanted to come! That, and their memory of Eusébie's admonition when the praetorian tribune had threatened them previously. The guards were nonplussed at the arrival of the two women and their cauldron of food. It was not uncommon for wealthy prisoners to receive food from outside, and usually there would be a bribe for the guards. However, this felt different. This was not a bribe, but a blessing, and they could feel the difference. Then there was the aroma of Melissa's lamb porridge. She was no mean cook, having been catering for the supposedly great and the good at Villa Metilia her whole life. After all, had not Flavius said to take good care of the prisoner? They did not let the women in, but they gratefully received the cauldron with the promise that they would feed Dunnius amply and enjoy the rest themselves.

"We'll be back tomorrow for the cauldron," promised Melissa, "and with some more food too."

With this began a rhythm of visits that gradually opened up the prison to the villa in the proceeding weeks and months. Some days Melissa and Claudia would come themselves, on others Junia and Jonas would bring the food. Before long, the carruca gave place to the carpentum and the food supplied the needs of some of the poorer prisoners as well as Dunnius and the guards.

"Why are they doing this?" Tullius, one of the older guards, asked Dunnius, some two weeks into the new rhythm.

"Why don't you ask them?" he replied. "Maybe ask the young ones." Later that afternoon Junia and Jonas carried several cauldrons of different porridge varieties, some sweet, others savoury, into the prison. As usual, the aroma was mouth-watering and the sheer quantity meant that the guards were grateful of help in dishing it up for the prisoners.

"Why are you doing this?" Tullius asked them as they spooned the porridge out into the prison bowls.

"Easy answer," replied Jonas. "You know how it goes, love your enemies, bless them that curse you, do good to them that hate you, and pray for them which despitefully use you, and persecute you."

"Who said that?" broke in Gaius, the younger warder.

"Well, our friends Melissa and Eusébie did," responded Jonas.

"But I'm sure I've heard it somewhere else," Gaius continued. "It was Jesus, wasn't it?"

"Yes, it was," said Junia, "and we are not afraid of saying so. But it's why Dunnius is in here."

"You what?" asked Gaius. Tullius looked at him despairingly.

"Hadn't you realised? He's one of the leaders of the slave ecclesia that these kids come from."

"Never heard of it," responded Gaius. "Sounds great. Where is it? Can I come and see?"

"Of course you can," replied Jonas. "When is your next time off?"

"The day after tomorrow," he answered.

***

While the foundations were being laid for a prison ecclesia in the heart of Rome, a new framework for peace was being shaped on the road to Eboracum. Having commandeered a suitable horse for Aidan, and rigged him out in Felix's spare military garb as he was of similar height and build, Constantine's comēs now appeared to have swelled to four. On the first evening out from Lindum as they gathered for their meal, Constantine surveyed the four of them and threw back his head and roared with laughter as was his habit.

"Well, Aidan, given that you were a freeman before being enslaved by the legion, and that I'm commander of the legions and therefore technically your owner, I've decided to give you your freedom back and that's that!"

At which, Felix rose to his feet, wine in one hand, and pulled Aidan to his feet with the other.

"Welcome, comrade!" he cried.

The two cousins, following his lead stood to their feet too.

"A toast to peace-making," announced Titus.

"Come on!" responded Marcus, characteristically.

Aidan hesitated, silent for moment, taking in the significance of what was happening. Then he said, "Thank you, General Constantine, thank you all," he responded, blushing to the roots of his red hair.

When Constantine told the emperor of the development later that night, he was acquiescent to the point of disinterest, providing further evidence that having entrusted Constantine as his acting Caesar, the tight grip he had held on mind and body was slipping away. The official explanation to the cohort was that Aidan was part of an agreed plan to employ a Pictish translator to negotiate reparations and taxes after a successful engagement at the Antonine Wall. The young Pict proved to be an expansive and adaptive character who slipped in alongside the three comēs with ease. Truth was, he had been living by his wits in uncertain times for several years now and was happy to roll with events and wait and see what happened. This development, however, went way beyond any hopes he had entertained previously. It seemed almost too good to be true. If they treated him well he would treat them well, he reflected;

if not, he would act according to his own interests. Time would tell.

The cohort arrived at Eboracum by early afternoon on the following day and found everything in place for their arrival. The express messenger had arrived almost three days earlier as planned, and the legion had left as soon as they could under the leadership of the legate Caius, who was second to Justus and was already two days ahead of them. Constantine was eager to continue immediately in hope of overtaking them and reaching the Antonine Wall before they did. So, leaving the rest of the cohort in the capable leadership of Justus, Constantine, together with the comēs, Aidan and the elite turma of which Commodus was part headed straightaway for the Antonine Wall. They left the emperor in the careful hands of Erastus, and his own centuria. They would all follow in the morning. It would be an understatement to say that the company who headed on towards the legion would have liked the extra half-day's rest. Nevertheless, the young general's energy and enthusiasm was as infectious as ever and the comēs were in eager anticipation of some cruciform peace-making! As for Aidan, he was longing for home, now that it was becoming a real possibility.

They struck camp in flat and marshy lands north of Eboracum with some difficulty that evening and awoke damp and uncomfortable. However, by the morning a warmish wind was blowing from the south and by the time they halted for cena, they were already dry and feeling much more cheerful. That evening they arrived in *Cataractonium* to the encouraging news that the legion were now less than a day ahead of them. Half way through the following day, they could see them in the distance, the six thousand five hundred men looking more like an impressive army of ants! By the evening, they joined them at *Coria* on Hadrian's Wall. Here they struck camp alongside Caius, and Constantine introduced himself and the posse. Caius was somewhat bemused to hear that the posse and their turma planned to move on ahead of them at first light. The news that they would attempt to meet with the Pictish leaders in hope of a diplomatic peace was even more discombobulating. Frankly he had never heard of such a thing taking place before a battle, rather than after an assured victory. He tried at least to send a second turma ahead with them. But Constantine refused, pleading his superiority as the emperor's functional Caesar.

The posse and turma left by Dere Street the following morning. The ancient road was by now overgrown and little used. The Antonine Wall had been virtually abandoned for a century or more, and, despite repeated attempts to reconsolidate the province of Valentia between the two walls, there had been no real Roman military presence since Emperor Septimius Severus had attempted to invade Caledonia in 208. They spent the next night encamped in a deserted Roman fort surrounded on all sides by the Northumbrian fells. As the sun went down behind the pike to the West, a stillness descended on the posse, unbroken until Marcus piped up.

"I can hear the voice of the land. It's the same sound of peace and reassurance we experienced back in the Alps and heard in the stories of Dunnius and Acco. But now it's clearer. These fells are our allies. They welcome us and the peace we bring."

Aidan looked at the young Roman quizzically. "We'll maybe encounter something different to peace here before long. The locals are generally in no doubt that these lands are theirs and regard both Picts and Romans as necessary evils to be played off against each other to maintain their freedom," he explained. "The best approach is to recognise them as the indigenous people of the land and to honour them as such. Make it clear you want to bless them and affirm their belonging and you'll get no hassle from them I think."

Marcus struggled to get to sleep that night as he listened to the land and reflected on Aidan's advice. Maybe they had been premature in embracing him into the posse. But then without

Felix's cruciform response to the attack in Lindum they would not have got this far. And Aidan's advice aligned pretty well with the way of love – not all the way, but some way, and that was perhaps enough to this point. Sometime before dawn, he wriggled out from under his *sagum*, careful not to wake Felix or Titus, who were sleeping on either side of him. Then wrapping his *paenula* around him, hood up, he ventured out, wandering wonderingly upwards along the overgrown street towards the distant pass, spellbound by the starlit sky and the line of light emerging along the ridge of the eastern fells. Such was the synchrony of time, place and space that he barely noticed the figure drawing alongside him and, even when he did, was far from startled for they too seemed encompassed in the same sacred moment.

He felt a hand on his shoulder and stopped to face his accomplice. Similarly cloaked against the cold, but slightly bent with apparent age, the man, for such it was, lowered his hood and, in the golden light of the sun's rays now breaking over the fells' ridge, revealed a kindly face with a high, wrinkled forehead, a bald head, piercing blue eyes and a flowing white beard. "It's good to belong, don't you think?" remarked the man, enigmatically, speaking Latin with a lilting accent.

"What d'you mean?" Marcus responded.

"Well, you do feel you belong here, don't you?" the fellow replied.

"Well, yes, I do," responded Marcus, "but who are you and how do you know that?"

The man looked reassuringly at him and replied

"I'm a druid, and know these things. Walk with me a while, if you will, and tell me your thoughts."

Marcus looked inquisitively back at the man, deliberately meeting his eyes. Then, taking a deep breath, he began, "I hear the voice of these hills," he said. "And they welcome us, and the peace we bring."

"You hear rightly," the druid responded. "Some call these lands debatable, because they are fought over by Picts, Celts and Romans alike. But the real reason for the debate is that they belong to no one – as with all land in actual fact. They are a gift to steward for the good of all, and that all includes these geese, you, me, all humanity and the hills themselves."

As he spoke Marcus became aware of the flock of geese overhead, and the leading goose, neck outstretched along the ridge of the dawn, pointing the way ahead. Even as he watched, a second goose took its place, and then a third, as the flock moved forward, heading north in front of them.

At which point Marcus remembered who and where he was. "I need to be heading back to the fort," he said. "They will be wondering where I am."

As Marcus began to turn, the druid turned with him, his cloak opening to reveal a white tunic and an equal cross around his neck, striking against the whiteness in the bright dawn light. "What's that?" Marcus demanded.

"I'm a renewed druid who has discovered that the new fulfils the old. It's the cruciform sign of the ecclesia together with the Trinity equally engaged in restoring peace and reconciliation to the land."

Marcus looked at him incredulously. "Will you come back with me and meet my friends?" he asked.

"You and these hills were my task this dawn," the druid replied, and once more lightly touching his hand on Marcus' shoulder strode away along the street, the intersection passed. Marcus briefly stood watching his retreating figure against the light of the sun's rays, and then turned and ran back down to the fort, contemplating what to tell the others, and wondering what they would make of it all.

By the time Marcus made it back to the fort, ientaculum was over and the posse and turma were getting ready to depart, wondering where their companion had got to. He simply remarked that he'd gone ahead to enjoy the sunrise and lost the time and so with a "get your things together quickly now," from Constantine, they set out for *Trimontium*, the next destination before the final leg of their journey. The day passed uneventfully with only a handful of ox carts on the road going about their business unfazed by the small battalion of soldiers. As usual they stopped but briefly for cena, a stop that was becoming shorter still with the decreasing daylight hours and Constantine's desire to make it to the wall well in advance of the legion. At Trimontium they encountered their first significant settlement of Celtish Britons, who surveyed the posse and its turma with some trepidation. However, their concerns seemed more the risk of Pictish invasions than any small party of Romans, who at least gave them some sense of security. So they found their way undisturbed to the deserted but substantial cavalry barracks with its typical arrangement for horses and riders and, setting a larger than usual guard, the posse sat down together for vesperna.

Titus looked across at Marcus. Their lives had been so intertwined that not much passed without the other noticing when something was going on.

"Alright, Marcus, what were you really up to this morning?" asked his cousin.

"Honestly, I was just enjoying the dawn to begin with. But it was extraordinary, so much so that time seemed to stand still as I walked. Then, before I knew it, someone drew alongside and touched my shoulder to get my attention."

"What!" interjected Felix, "Who was it?"

"It was a druid," Marcus replied. "Some kind of Celtic priest who understood exactly what I was thinking. He said the land belongs to no one, in fact that no land anywhere belongs to anyone as any kind of possession. But rather that it is a friend and ally to all who pursue peace and the common good. More extraordinary still, he was wearing a special kind of cross, one with four equal stems intersected by a circle which he said was the sign that through the cross, the Trinity and the ecclesia can work with the land to bring peace and reconciliation." The posse reflected in silence on Marcus' story. Then Felix spoke.

"This means it's time to make a proper plan now, I reckon."

"Yes, please!" interposed Constantine. "We'll be in Pictish country before we know it, and I've no experience of pre-battle diplomacy."

Titus spoke up. "If the land and God are on our side as this druid fellow seems to have been sent to remind us, then we can take courage."

"Aidan and I did have one practical idea at least," said Felix. "It seems that white flags mean peace for both Picts and Romans. So we found some discarded white tunics back in Eboracum and packed them with our clothes. We can tear them up and make banners to fly above us as we approach."

"My father is probably a chieftain himself by now," proposed Aidan. "And even if not, some of his cousins will be, as my grandfather's brother was. It all depends who is still alive. In my opinion we should aim to make it to Camelon, just a few kilometres beyond the wall. It was my ancestors' southernmost stronghold before the Romans took it. Once they retreated beyond the wall, we took it back. I suggest that we head tomorrow for Dun Law, which is another old Roman fort about twenty kilometres this side of the wall. I expect it is deserted, as it's pretty remote and not somewhere I would expect Picts to occupy. It's a good vantage point from which to survey the land. Then hopefully we can head directly for the wall. When I last saw it there were plenty of broken-down places where we can make it through unless I'm much mistaken."

Chapter Nine

Culmination and Consummation

The following afternoon, with the posse at the head of the turma and each sporting white banners on staves of wood, they made their way cautiously up to the entrance of the small fort at Dun Law. Just as Aidan supposed, it was deserted and provided a panoramic view of the countryside ahead. There was no sign of any Pictish war parties and, apart from a few smallholdings in the distance, all appeared peaceful. So after a somewhat sparse vesperna they set the watch and settled down for the night. Constantine, however, had difficulty sleeping. Here he was in an alien land, far from his familiar environment of the Roman East. He reflected on the past weeks, and his determination to find a different kind of leadership for the empire. Now that the Antonine Wall and the home of their reputedly barbaric enemies were within sight he felt vulnerable and way beyond his comfort zone. His dependence on the young band of comēs and an unproved Pict fairly took his breath away. He recalled the book of Daniel. At least the young Jewish hero had not chosen his plight. Unlike Constantine he had not deliberately entered the lions' den or put his compatriots into the fiery furnace! Here he was, leading his young cousins and two ex-slaves into the heart of his enemies' stronghold with no defence, bar ten cavalrymen and their crew. Or rather, they were leading him! He remembered their unflinching faith in the God of their uncle, who had experienced both miracle and martyrdom. As he lay in the dank and musty fort, for the first time in his life, he deliberately and consciously prayed.

"Please go with us as we follow your cruciform way."

The next morning Aidan was the first up, eager to get moving.

"Come on, all of you!" he cried. "We need ablutions and proper food. All being well we will find all of that in Camelon before the day is out."

The rest of the posse were more nervous, and ate only a little of the dwindling supplies. Commodus spoke out on behalf of the turma. "We defend ourselves if they ignore the white flags. Then we hope that the legion isn't too far behind?"

"Do nothing without my signal," responded Constantine. "If anything happens to me, you take charge, Commodus. I trust you and know that you understand our desire for peace too." With that the posse took their position in the lead and together they set off on the next stage of their momentous adventure. The wall, when they arrived at it, was a diminutive affair compared with Hadrian's. In the course of the previous century, as Aidan had said, his particular tribe of Picts had spread across both sides of it, which was only ever an earth and turf embankment. It was by now simply an obstacle to normal communication and trade between small holdings, and to occasional marauding parties or would-be migrants searching out fertile prospects for new settlements.

However, their initial reaction to the unimpressive Wall was soon dispelled. For in the middle of the crossing point where Dere Street culminated stood an enormous *aurochs*. Easily six feet high and with a huge head and mane it stood staring angrily at them, pawing the ground. The posse halted and restrained their mounts from bolting with some difficulty. The turma likewise backed up behind them.

"What's this?" enquired Commodus, nervously.

"It's an aurochs," Constantine replied, "I've seen them back home in the Eastern empire, but never one this big."

"I reckon it's the spirit of Zeus, the Minotaur's father," declared Titus.

"Well, whatever, we can't stand off here," continued Constantine, making as if to circumvent it by peering along the side of the wall to find another gap.

"Wait," cautioned Felix, and without more ado stepped forward to within a metre of the beast, eyeballing it unswervingly. The animal lowered its head as if to charge. Commodus' hand was on his sword. But then, suddenly, the aurochs tossed its great head, turned aside, crashed through the turfs of the wall and charged off into the undergrowth. At the same moment there was a noisy honking overhead and a flock of wild geese encircled them before landing tumultuously on the tarn close by.

Shaken, but enlivened again with the correlation of time, place and heavenly purpose, the posse proceeded onward through the wall.

"I know the way now," said Aidan, "follow me," breaking into a canter. Before long they could see the fort of Camelon barely a kilometre in front of them. As they drew closer it became obvious that it had been recently repaired and fortified, with a whole new palisade surrounding it. "I think I know what this means," Aidan declared. "My uncle has died and my father is chieftain. Let's not worry them unnecessarily by the whole troop of us arriving at the gate. Why don't just Felix and I go on ahead and prepare the way?"

This sounded good sense to Constantine and the rest.

"We'll stay put here, but with our banners unfurled and swords at the ready just in case," responded the general. So Aidan and Felix trotted on ahead and soon drew up at the gate of what was now a fortress. The gates were wide open, however, and only a single guard sat at the entrance. When he saw the two soldiers he leapt to his feet, and reached for a well notched club lying on a low table beside him. But then he recognised Aidan.

"Hey, Aid, is that you?" he cried.

"It is indeed, cousin," the young Pict replied, "and I've come home a freeman."

At which point a door to a building to the right inside the gate flung open and a woman burst out and ran towards them, arms open wide and auburn hair streaming out behind her.

"Aidan, is it really you at last?" After a prolonged and tearful greeting while Felix stood happily aside, Aidan's mother recovered herself and tasked the guard, who was in fact her nephew, to go and tell her husband that their son had come home.

While that was happening Aidan introduced Felix as one of those who had rescued him. Wherewith he too was caught up into a Pictish embrace.

"Well, well, what's all this about then?" cried Aidan's father, striding up and likewise embracing his son.

"*Tad*, it's quite a story. But first will you trust me if I tell you that a small troop of Roman cavalry are my friends and come to make peace?"

"The look-out up on the tower just told me about them," responded the chieftain. "They are the ones with the white banners, I take it?"

"Yes, Tad, they are," his son replied. "And the next part you may find hard to believe, but one of them is General Constantine, the emperor's son."

"It's a bit early in the day for a surfeit of ale, boy," replied his father. "Are you having me on?"

"No, Tad, really I'm not, but we need to act swiftly."

At which Aidan turned to Felix, "I'm telling him about Constantine and the others and that we need to act swiftly before the legion arrives." Felix nodded vigorously. Turning back to his father, Aidan continued, "The legion is only a day or two away at the most and we need to make peace and decide what to do, or else we'll be overrun. I take it that the hype about Pictish hordes about to inundate Britannia is still a virtual myth?"

"Aye, it is that, or near enough," his father replied. "If it's all as you say, you'd best be fetching your noble friends and we'll somehow prepare food and drink fit for a parley with a Roman general."

At this, Aidan and Felix remounted and cantered back to the others.

"All's well," announced Felix.

"Yes," continued Aidan. "They are delighted at my return and my father believed me when I said that we are here for peace but need an immediate parley before the legion catches up with us. Be assured, my Tad won't double cross you, Constantine."

Silently appraising his comēs and turma, Constantine reflected that there was not much they could do about it if he did anyway, and so without more ado he threw back his head and laughed, and declared, "Come on then, let's see what cruciform peace looks like here," and led them up the track to the fort. Quite a reception of Aidan's friends, relatives and retainers awaited them. Some ready to lead away the horses, others already carrying trays of pewter vessels filled with ale, the rest simply curious. In the midst, now sporting a Pictish chieftain's goatskin cloak of skins and feathers, stood Aidan's father, fully six inches taller than Constantine, but with hands stretched out in obvious welcome.

"I am Chief Vipoig. You are welcome here, as you come in peace," he announced. Aidan translated this greeting and then, in turn, Constantine's reply, "I thank you, for we do come in peace."

This was followed by his father's, "Come in and eat and drink all of you and let the parley begin right away," and Constantine's "We will be honoured to do so." So began the to and fro of speech and translation, stilted at first but soon gathering pace into a flow of harmony and peace-making that encompassed the challenges that faced them.

By the end of the evening, three things had materialised. The first was that there were no barbarian hordes amassing at the Caledonian border. The Picts were farmers and small holders happy to co-exist with the scattering of Celtic neighbours. The truth was that they were not a single organised military entity but mainly peace-loving agriculturists whose only argument with the Romans was the desire to be left alone. But once riled, they would quickly band together in unexpectedly violent defence of their land and their freedom. There having been little to disturb them for decades, their reputation for rebellious attacks against Rome's northern borders was mainly political hype. Secondly, the only real exception to this was a marauding battalion of revenge-crazy descendants of a Pictish tribe known as the Wid, whose lands and relatives had been decimated by the emperor Severus on the last Roman expansionist initiative almost a century before. So deep had the wounds gone then, that their very identity had been vested ever since in moves against any remnants of Rome's presence or that of any of their erstwhile friends between the walls.

Worryingly, the news was that this battalion were right now only a few kilometres further west along the Antonine Wall. The assumption was that they had heard a rumour that the Roman legion had returned and meant to face them at whatever cost, although it meant their five hundred against six thousand five hundred! So finally, the plan was drawn up that tomorrow morning at first light they would go together, posse and turma, accompanied by a similar troop made up of Chief Vipoig and his men, and attempt to forestall the Pictish battalion before they were overrun by the arrival of the legion. Vipoig was fairly confident that his past positive dealings with the Wid, together with the shock of them seeing a party of Roman and Pictish peacemakers complete with white banners, would protect them from being attacked by them. It was certainly a risk, but both groups accepted it.

The next morning the multifarious band of Pictish and Roman peacemakers rode back out along the Antonine Wall in search of the Wid, bearing high the unfurled white banners. What they found was not at all what they had anticipated. For barely a kilometre along, in a wide moorland below the wall, a pitched battle was already about to begin between the Wid and what appeared to be the frontline of the approaching legion.

Both groups were a mixture of cavalry and infantry and the potential carnage was immediately obvious.

"I think I know what to do," said Constantine, suddenly. "Our two groups should line up with the Wid. That will distract their attention for a moment, while Vipoig and I ride between the two lines."

"That's mad," said Felix.

"But it might work," said Aidan, "I'll explain to Tad."

Within a few minutes the peacemakers had lined up with the Wid and, in the confusion, Constantine and Vipoig, with Aidan as translator, rode between the two lines of engagement. What they found at the heart of the line was even more unexpected. For lined up facing the Wid chieftain's charger was the emperor Constantius standing in his quadriga held up by some kind of contraption of wood and cushioned support that left his arms free to hold both lance and longsword.

"Cease action!" cried the two peacemakers, the one in Latin, the other in Pictish. At the sight of the two commanders standing together white banners aloft, the Wid chief drew up his charger and turned to face his battalion.

"Hold back!" he called, "Let's hear these men."

When Constantius saw his son in front of him, bearing the banners of peace, he was silent for a few moments, seemingly transfixed. Then in a tremulous but piercing voice he cried out, "It is over!" and sank down through the sides of his supports and fainted away in his quadriga.

"As your general and commander, I command you to stand down and remain where you are until further instruction," shouted Constantine at the line of troops. Further instructing the two lieutenants alongside his father to tend to his care, he turned to Vipoig and Aidan. "What do we do now?" he asked.

"Let's suggest an act of reparation right here," suggested Vipoig, "the Wid and this front line of the legion should exchange tunics. Then all can return with the apparent spoils of victory."

The Wid chieftain looked at the apparently dead or dying emperor on the floor of his chariot, and then at Constantine alongside Vipoig still bearing high the banners of peace, while Aidan translated Vipoig's words. Then, calling out across his battalion, "Now do what I do," he began to strip off his tunic.

Pict warriors did not go in to action semi-naked as the hype had it, but nonetheless their tunics were more like string vests, offsetting their tattooed torsos. Their lower body was covered with little more than a loin cloth and a leather pouch covering their genitalia. So they were an impressive site as some five hundred men held their vests aloft! Constantine, having relayed to the frontline that they were to exchange tunics with the Picts, similarly removed his. This was something of a challenge to the legionaries, some of whom were wearing body armour which they first had to remove, before undoing their tunics. The whole place took on the aspect of a playing field! Then, led by Constantine and the Wid chieftain, the combatants selected an appropriate opponent and exchanged tunics with them. Vipoig asked Constantine to do him the honour of having the ailing emperor carried back in his quadriga to Camelon to be cared for as best possible. He then invited the Wid chieftain together with his lieutenants to join him, Aidan, Constantine and his comēs back to Camelon to discuss long-term conditions for peace.

The rest of the troops retreated to their camps wondering quite what had just happened, a mixture of dumbfounded and elated, carrying their enemies' tunics as spoils of a battle that was not a physical one and yet they sensed had changed the future of the land. The day concluded with Constantine decreeing that if they could accept it, the Wid were to receive back all the lands and properties that were their ancestors' when Severus had crossed Hadrian's Wall in 208, including any forts or structures that the Romans built on them. Aidan translated this to the Picts to the amazement of the Wid chieftain. Then in turn, his face streaked with tears, Aidan translated for the Vipoig and Wid Picts as they covenanted with Constantine to live at peace with their neighbours in the lands between the walls. While peace was being made, the emperor remained barely conscious in the Pict chieftain's own bed, still hovering somewhere between life and death, Erastus watching over him tenderly, having by this time made his way up from the support wagons. By the morning, Constantine was eager to get on the road back to Eboracum as soon as possible in hope of finding help for his father, or at least being back at the Roman heart of Britain where there might be a fitting burial place. He knew deep down, his father's life and reign were all but over.

***

The return to Eboracum was characterised by an intense combination of sorrow and jubilation. The death and burial of Constantius was the cause of great grief and mourning but the consequent proclamation of Constantine as the new Emperor of the West was an occasion of great celebration. Despite it all, however, Titus was becoming more and more impatient. The truth was that ever since they left Lindum on their race to the Antonine, Nesta had increasingly occupied his dreams, night and day. Far from fading, as he thought his after all only brief encounter with her might do, it had increased in proportion to the time that elapsed. Now he was compelled by the desire to see whether this near obsession was based in reality or he had allowed his feelings to get the better of him. Starting on the journey back south, and spending time at Lindum as they had promised Aidan's fellow outlaws they would do, became his whole focus. He determined to accomplish three things. Firstly, to discover whether Nesta was as wonderful as he remembered; secondly, to find out if she felt the same about him and then crazily, whether she would agree to marry him and return with him to Rome. How exactly that would fit with his role as comēs he was unclear. But if she was willing, they would find a way.

After only two weeks in Eboracum, Constantine was likewise impatient. But for him it was his quest to become the only Caesar in the empire that consumed his attention. Content to leave the two legions under the overall charge of Justus, his father's trustworthy Legatus Legionis who had been the first of those to proclaim him emperor at Constantius' death, he began to make plans to set out for Rome. Linus, his father's second in command, he would keep alongside, promising him a significant position in the future, on the basis that it was better to have the ambitious praefectus where he could see him.

"We will head for Rome in a few days," he announced to his comēs, as they sat over vesperna together with Commodus several days after the official public proclamation of his emperorship by the legions, the bishop and the townsfolk. "We shouldn't meet any opposition before Treverorum," he said, "and the legions there will almost certainly accept my lead."

The comēs had found themselves with but little to do in the tumultuous events that had unfolded, so they received the news gladly, but none so much as Titus.

"Constantine, would you mind if I went on ahead to Lindum?"

"Affairs of the heart, I wonder?" interposed Felix.

"Come on!" added Marcus.

"I know I can trust you with my sister," said Commodus, fixing Titus in a long serious gaze. "I can, can't I?" he added.

"I'm sure you can, but I hope she'll reassure you of that herself when you get to Lindum in a few days' time," was Titus' answer.

"Hmm, so this explains an increasing preoccupation on your part that I've noticed even with everything that's occupied me!" the emperor said, throwing back his head in laughter. "I guess I can do without you for a few days while you resolve it. But no staying behind in Lindum. I'm going to need the three of you more than ever now if I'm to avoid becoming a Nebuchadnezzar."

Titus had his belongings already packed in a saddlebag on his bunk. So taking leave of his friends, and picking up his bag, he mounted his horse and left straightaway. That night he spent the hours of darkness in a sheltering thicket wrapped in his sagum and was back on the road at first light. On arrival at Lindum, he made first for the barracks where he found the adjutant who had taken care of them when they were there on the journey north, and arranged accommodation for himself and his horse. Then he took time to make himself presentable before heading off to the Amadeus' family domus. He found Nesta stationed pensively in the tabernae at the front of the domus, where she was making and selling pots. Titus stood quietly appraising her for several minutes before she became aware of his presence and looked up at him.

"So, you've come," she said. "I've been stationed here for days. I opted for the job when I'd calculated that enough time had elapsed for you to make it back here if you were going to. To be honest, I've not been able to concentrate on much else since you left!"

On hearing this, Titus remained looking at her with a smile wide enough to split his face.

"I left Eboracum the moment I decently could," he said. "There's lots to tell everybody here which I'm eager to do, maybe tonight, if your folks are happy to invite me."

"Of course they will invite you," she answered, "but what about Commodus and the others, are they not with you?"

"They should be here the day after tomorrow," he replied. "But I begged Constantine's leave to come in advance to spend time with you, if you are willing. There's lots I want to talk about."

"Let's go in and see my parents," Nesta said, similarly smiling. "If they are happy, which I'm sure they will be, then we can have the whole of tomorrow together."

That evening over vesperna, Titus told an attentive Aurelia, Cato and Adelphius the barebones of the posse's story. However, he was careful not to tell them everything. He was well aware that he might be a poor substitute for Commodus and there would be the opportunity for a bigger gathering when the others arrived. But as far as they were concerned Commodus' trust in him and his obvious care for their daughter was more than enough. They plied him enthusiastically with question after question. He answered as well as he could, explaining that they would get a fuller picture from Commodus and he didn't want to leave him out, explaining that he and the others would be there by the day after next.

Finally, Cato spoke up. "Then how come you are here early?" he asked.

"Well, to be honest I couldn't wait any longer before taking the opportunity to see Nesta," he admitted. "So I got permission from the now Emperor Constantine to come on ahead. I'm hoping to spend time with her tomorrow, if you don't mind."

Cato looked at Aurelia and then at Nesta.

"Well, this sounds exciting," broke in Adelphius.

"You are a grown woman, Nesta my dear," declared her father. "If you want to spend time with this young man, I'm sure you will decide!"

"I'll meet you at the southern gate near the barracks first thing in the morning," Nesta responded. "I'll show you the city and its surrounds." Titus made his way back to the barracks full of hopes for tomorrow.

The late November day dawned bright and sparkling, a haw frost thick on the ground and on the bare branches of the trees. The city was situated on a hill above the River Witham and gave a spectacular view across the flatlands below, over which the accordingly huge sky stretched for as far as the eye could see. Nesta was already at the gate wrapped in her winter furs and clutching a basket when Titus arrived, his sagum on top of his military garb to keep out the cold.

"I want to walk with you down beside the river," she said. "I've food for ientaculum and afterwards we will head up through the northern gate back home for a late cena if that's alright with you. If we stay out longer we'll freeze to death! But I wanted this morning outside to take you to my favourite places!"

"I'll not mind the cold," Titus replied. "I've got used to it on the journeys since autumn ended, and in any case I want to be with you, never mind the cold."

As they strolled along by the river, Nesta's arm though his, Titus began to explain his thinking. That these two days were all the time they had before he headed onwards with Constantine on the quest to make him emperor of the whole empire, West and East. Of his prior commitment first to Jesus and the kingdom of love, and second to Constantine and his vision to somehow integrate the two kingdoms. "But now," he said, "there's you. I have fallen for you, as much as I know you. And it feels like you have become the most important person in my life over these last months since we met. Which is a quandary, because I'll not go back on my allegiances, which only leaves one option. That they become yours too." Nesta made as if to interrupt, and then fell silent. "And I'll not insist on that, never. It has to be your choice, your risk with me," Titus declared.

"Wait," said Nesta. "I need to get this right. Your first allegiance is to the messianic kingdom of love. Well, that's no problem because it's mine too. But would your allegiance to Constantine come before me? Surely, if I'm understanding you, you are basically asking me to marry you. But that's for life. Is your commitment to Constantine for life?"

"I'm not sure how long it's for," Titus continued. "I know now that you come before it. But in this present moment I'm committed to seeing it through until Constantine ends it. Which is what is behind the urgency and the risk. I'm asking you to come with me now on this quest. I promise it won't come before you in the final analysis. Ideally, I could ask you to wait until I've seen it through. But I've no idea how long that might be! So my question is, will you take the risk of love and make the choice to come with me in two days' time? To marry me tomorrow, after the others arrive, if your parents will agree, and Adelphius is willing to marry us? Then to come with us as part of the posse until we get to Rome? Then we can make Villa Metilia our home base and we can see what happens next."

"You've given this a lot of thought, haven't you?" Nesta responded. "And I've been thinking and dreaming too. But this is a big ask. I've loads of questions to ask about you as a person. I need to understand about Villa Metilia. And to find out as much as I can about what really motivates you at heart. Now. Today. Then by the time we arrive at the northern gate this afternoon, I will give you my answer."

There followed the most intense personal grilling Titus had ever experienced. Her questions interrogated his earliest memories, his teen years, and his relationship with Claudia, Valeria and Eusébie, his friendship with Marcus and Felix and his life in the slave ecclesia. Finally, they stood breathless at the top of the hill at the northern gate looking at one another. Nesta reached out and took both his hands in hers. "The answer is yes," she said. "And I'm confident that will be Pater and Mater's response too, as it's what I want."

Over cena later that afternoon the pair broke their news to Cato and Aurelia, to whom it was no surprise, despite the speed of events. Adelphius, as usual, joined them soon after and agreed wholeheartedly to marry them the following day. And so it was that Commodus, Marcus, Felix and Constantine arrived at

Lindum to be told that they were guests of honour at a marriage ceremony and supper that very evening. The atrium of Domus Amadeus was filled to overflowing for the celebration. Nothing was quite normal, neither the speed of the arrangements nor the presence of the Emperor of the West. Legally he had the right to marry them, spiritually Adelphius did, so they did it between them, making history together. When the public vows were complete the whole assembly erupted in cheers and laughter, among which the whoops and shouts of Felix and Marcus rang loudest. Later that night as the guests departed, Nesta took Titus by the hand and ushered him into the guest apartment, for that night the bridal suite.

"Stand there, in the light of the lamp," she said, closing the door behind them. "Now take off your clothes. I want to see you, all of you." A mixture of nervousness and elation electrifying his body from head to toe, he did what she asked. He stood there naked in front of her. "So this is male," she said. Then, still facing him, she removed her clothes too. "And this is female. As Jesus said, 'From the beginning God made them male and female. For this cause a man shall leave his father and mother and cleave to his wife, and two shall become one flesh.' You have left father and mother, Titus Metilia, and here I am," she concluded, taking him by the hand and leading him to the bed. "So come and cleave to me, and let's be one flesh."

Part Three

Interlude

Clouds of hooded crows murmured across the Seven Hills as the sun went down, shrouding two spectral beings with wind in their wings. They carried between them a striking Jezebel-like personage seated in a massive measuring container. The birds swarmed in acrobatic accompaniment as the beings slowly but firmly lowered the ephah down onto one side of an enormous set of scales that sat securely on the roof top of the Palatine market. On the opposite scale was a huge leather money bag clearly marked with the Latin letter P. As the balances found their equilibrium, a clear, strong voice cried from the Tiber where the angel of Rome emerged from the Western side of the river, tears pouring down their face. They held a great leaden lid between their hands like a tremendous discus, poised as if in readiness to hurl it onto the Palatine Hill.

"Mammon or Love? Mammon or Love?" their voice resounded, "Which cross will it be? Which cross will it be?"

Chapter Ten

Taking Ground

"It's certainly a complicated position to be in," burst out Fausta, brushing tears from her eyes and glaring in turn at Lactantius, Crispus, Constantia and Marcus. "I believe in Constantine, and he's my husband, and I can't see the kingdom of love inseminating the empire without him becoming sole Augustus. Licinius was the dreadful Galerius' choice and Maximinus Daza is unequivocally awful. Maximian wasn't much better and nor is Maxentius. But the fact remains that they are my father and my brother!" Crispus met her eyes sympathetically. "I still think that secretly executing our opponents is less destructive than fighting them on the battlefield, even if they are our relatives. At least thousands of legionaries are saved from death or injury. And for sure their relatives will be thankful for that."

"I suppose now that Commodus is head of the *Scholae Palatinae* he'll make sure that assassinations are kept to a minimum and conducted as painlessly as possible," Fausta acknowledged.

"But this doesn't seem like the amazing cruciform diplomacy at the Antonine Wall that everybody talked about!" interjected Constantia.

"It's absolutely not!" responded Marcus. "Neither is it the leadership that Constantine was looking for, and nor will it further the kingdom of love, I'm sorry to say."

At this, Lactantius stood to his feet. He had just returned from consulting with Constantine in northern Italy where more and more cities were opening up to him and shifting their allegiance away from Maxentius.

"Milan and the nearby towns opened their gates to Constantine with great rejoicing," he began, "but it would never have happened without his strategic military victory at

Augusta Taurinorum. True, his cavalry skills averted a major bloody battle there, but diplomacy didn't do it. It's hard to live in the in-between." His friends looked at him quizzically. "The kingdom of love hasn't come yet," he continued, "and when it does there will be no more bloody battles. But until then we will sometimes have to make compromises. Otherwise we will lose the opportunity that circumstances have given us."

"Well you know how much I love and respect you, Lactantius," responded Marcus. "But I think that you are wrong about this. Quentin and Eusébie taught us that the kingdom came when the Messiah came and the cross and resurrection secured it forever. It's not everywhere yet, but it is our possession in the Holy Spirit right now. We must hold on to it in faith or lose the ground we gained." Lactantius sat back down.

"Well, if you are right, Marcus, what's to be done? If Fausta's father hadn't been secretly assassinated, Constantine would not be Augustus at this point. And if Maxentius isn't dealt with, he still won't be for long."

Marcus pondered the question from his hitherto wise friend. Then, meeting his gaze, he continued.

"We meet them, face to face, like we did the Wid, and we trust the way of the cross. I realise that you weren't there, but you recognised, I think, when you heard about it, that our experiences in Lindum and Camelon were ground-breaking."

Lactantius smiled. "I agree, it was extraordinary. But the ideal times surely prepare us for the uncertain choices."

Marcus shook his head. "Some of us will die in place of our enemies like I nearly did at the gates of Marseille last year because I insisted on negotiating with Maximian. Nevertheless, if we follow the cruciform way, the companions will grow in strength and numbers and in the end love will win through. For I still think we could have won Maximian over with your help, Fausta."

As she considered Marcus' statement, Fausta, relaxing in the warmth of the room, and the voices of her friends, found herself contemplating inwardly the events that had brought about her life as mistress of the emperor's palace, the home of the Western imperial court in Augusta Treverorum. Six years had elapsed since the death of Constantius after his confrontation with the Wid and the extraordinary reparations that followed. Hanging onto life by a thread, he had finally died in the arms of Erastus on their first night back in Eboracum. Since the legions had declared Constantine Emperor, he had been almost entirely focused on establishing the selfless leadership that he had reached for in the adrenalin soaked days on the road to Naissus at the beginning of his journey, all the way from Eboracum to Rome. After that the ultimate goal was to establish himself as sole emperor everywhere. Unlike Titus, whose primary concern was Nesta, Fausta reflected, Constantine's attention was first of all on his new role and only secondarily her part in it. His declaration of love for her on his arrival at Ambianum on the return journey from Lindum had convinced her of his genuine desire to make her his empress and partner. It had been more than enough to persuade her to accompany him to Augusta Treverorum and marry him just as soon as the formalities could be arranged. But the fact was she was still here, without her husband, whereas Titus and Nesta were together in Rome and already had Amadeus, their now three-year-old son.

Those initial eventful days and weeks had become an unstoppable maelstrom of change throughout the years that followed, Fausta realised. To begin with it had been an exciting challenge to preside over the palace. Her mother and father had come to Augusta Treverorum for the wedding. Having Eutropia alongside her was wonderful, but her father's politicking was impossible. He had declared himself as emperor once more after Constantius' death, which had put him on a collision course with Constantine. At first he had tried to consolidate his power by helping his son, her brother Maxentius, in his attempt to install himself as emperor of the East. However, once this succeeded he then proceeded to try and depose him and take the role himself. This failed dramatically and sent him running to Constantine for help, using their marriage to protect himself and temporarily retire. But he was incorrigible in his thirst for power and in 310 attempted a coup to displace his son-in-law and seize again the emperorship of the West. To prevent this Constantine's legions had pursued him and his army across the Rhine to Lyons and eventually to Marseille where Marcus was wounded in his attempts at diplomacy and had returned to Treverorum to recover. The covert assassination had followed, about which she was both deeply troubled and greatly relieved. Hence her earlier outburst.

She had been delighted when Constantine had asked Crispus, Constantia and Lactantius to remain with her in the palace at Treverorum after the wedding, and now six years later they were still here together. Lactantius' counsel had been a great help in her responsibilities, not just for the palace, but the new construction and reconstruction work that Constantine had left her to oversee for the improvement of the city. Crispus, once her pupil and now her stepson, was sixteen years old and benefitting greatly from the philosopher's tutelage. Constantia had passed from pupil to confidante, mature in ways that belied her sixteen years and already someone she could not conceive of being without. Crispus, likewise, was wise beyond his years and by now both were unswerving in their commitment to the counter-political kingdom of love espoused by his cousins. So while the emperor and his comēs had continued onward with the task of establishing his supremacy as leader of the West, she had joined up with the innovative companions of the ecclesia in Treverorum, together with her mother, stepson, sister-in-law and Lactantius. The palace had soon become a place of virtual freedom for the palace slaves and a centre of welcome and support for the companions in the city. As such it was becoming a beacon of light for other cities with reverberations all the way to Rome itself. It was partly this that was such a threat to Galerius and the other surviving competitors for the tetrarchy, who rightly recognised that Constantine saw himself and the way of life of the companions as the future of the empire.

Fausta re-entered the conversation at the point she had left it, although it had continued for some minutes during her reverie.

"Maximian would not have listened to me, Marcus. Nor will Maxentius. Like his father he has only the twin ambitions of money and power. Peace is but a secondary matter. I have no hope whatsoever for changing that. I'd rather concentrate on Constantine, if only he were here, or we with him, as I have no doubt as to his heart's intention. Money and power is not his desire. Peace and love is what he seeks. But I'm not sure that he doesn't still think money and power to be at least in part a means to the selfless loving end. That's why I fear your talk of compromise, Lactantius, however plausible it may seem."

"You mean that Pater might think money and war could bring peace and love in the end?" chimed in Crispus.

"Yes, that's what she means," interjected Marcus, "and as his comēs, wife, son, sister and counsellor, it's our task to convince him otherwise yet!"

At this, Fausta sighed audibly. "But how are we going to accomplish that if we are here and he is in Rome?"

***

Villa Metilia was awash with rumours and counter rumours of Constantine's advance. Dunnius, Fortunatus, Eusébie, Claudia and Nesta were seated in the peristyle, the city set out before them in the late-October sunshine. In the distance Maxentius' preparations for the expected siege could be seen, as the bridges over the Tiber had all been cut with the exception of the Milvian, where a flotilla of boats were moored together and concealed a series of rafts which provided a temporary way across.

"Maxentius seems determined to preserve an atmosphere of normality while his military preparations are anything but," observed Dunnius. "I heard this morning that some of our friends in the prison ecclesia are among those that Maxentius has released from gaol and compelled to boost the numbers of the forces amassing along the western bank of the Tiber." From their position on the Janiculan Hill they could see the troops spread out on each side of the temporary bridge, facing towards the Via Flaminia down which Constantine and his five legions were expected to appear over the next few days.

"Hardly the time for Maxentius to organise chariot races like he did last night," added Fortunatus.

"Well, it was supposedly his six-year anniversary event to celebrate his emperorship," put in Claudia. "But if it was meant to please the people, it failed by all accounts. And Jonas says that the crowd openly taunted him, shouting that Constantine is invincible."

Then Eusébie broke in. "The problem is that battles and violence only perpetuate the centuries of strife. If this is to be Constantine's way of doing things, he'll not arrive at the home fit for a new humanity that he is so eagerly seeking. What do you think Felix and Titus make of it all?"

Her question hung between them in the autumn air, and for some time they all remained silent. Finally, Dunnius spoke up.

"They won't be for battle, they will be for peace-making, just as they were at the gates of Marseille, where Marcus was so nearly killed when they tried to do so there."

"That's an understatement I should say," responded Nesta. "Titus is adamant that they will oppose any form of deliberate conflict and that violence can only be justified in defence and then proportionally and as an absolutely last resort! He was extremely uneasy about the events at Augusta Taurinorum, and the last thing he said to me before we left him in *Mediolanum* was 'Watch how diplomacy will now open the cities to us.'"

"Well, it's hard to see how advancing on the capital is any kind of defence," continued Claudia, "so hopefully diplomacy is the plan here too."

At which point Abaskantis appeared from the atrium with a three-year-old in tow.

"Here's a progress report from Felix and Titus," she informed them, as Amadeus went running first to his mother Nesta and then clambered onto Eusébie, who he clearly adored. Fortunatus began to read aloud from the report. "We've set up camp at Villa *Volusii Saturnini* in *Fiano* alongside the Tiber River about a day's march away. Most of the cities since Mediolanum have been wide open to us. Apart from Verona that is. Ruricius Pompeianus, general of the Veronese forces and Maxentius' praetorian prefect, was having none of it. He had no interest in negotiating and relied on the fact that the town is surrounded on three sides by the Adige River, so is easy to defend. But once again Constantine contrived to minimise the conflict by evading and defeating the large detachment Ruricius sent out to attack us. Then we successfully surrounded the town and laid siege. Ideally Constantine wanted to pick off and kill only Ruricius, but his personal guard defended him to the hilt and there was considerably more loss of life than intended. However, as with Augusta Taurinorum, the news was enough for the rest of the cities en route here to simply open their gates and welcome us in. Now, the big question is whether Maxentius will deal or fight. We need you all to pray like there's no tomorrow!"

"Then that's what we'll do!" cried Eusébie, gently disentangling herself from Amadeus, who was still clinging to her, and getting up from her chair. "We need a future fit for you, little one."

"Let's call an emergency meeting of the ecclesia this very evening," responded Claudia. "Fortunatus and I will spread the news," offered Dunnius, stretching out his hand to Fortunatus and pulling him to his feet.

Together they headed down the steps from the peristyle towards the farm, the Tiber glimmering below them in the near distance. "What's your reading of the likely outcome of the next few days' events, Fortunatus?" his friend enquired, as they proceeded down the familiar path.

"I honestly don't know what I think the outcome will be, but I do sense a pivotal moment, one on which all our futures hang in the balance," responded the now ex-slave, sagely. Below them a crow took flight, soon joined by many more for the autumn nightly ritual, before descending among the trees along the banks of the river, and adding a menacing mien to the enveloping dusk.

Later that evening the gathered ecclesia struggled for prayers of faith that would elevate them beyond superficial platitudes on the one hand or desperate longings on the other. But gradually a palpable sense of the Spirit's presence fell on the assembled companions. For quite some time they luxuriated in the immanent comfort.

Then eventually Melissa rose to her feet and began to read Jesus' words in the final days before the cross from Luke's testimony. "When he approached Jerusalem, he saw the city and wept over it, saying, 'If you had known in this day, even you, the things which make for peace! But now they have been hidden from your eyes.' For the days will come upon you when your enemies will throw up a barricade against you, and surround you and hem you in on every side, and they will level you to the ground and your children within you, and they will not leave in you one stone upon another, because you did not recognise the time of your visitation."

A great hush followed Melissa's familiar tones. Then Jonas spoke up. "So what do we do with that? Say 'Amen,' or 'please not?'"

Then gradually, without any obvious lead, the whole company began to pour out their hearts aloud together, that whatever took place, they would have courage, the river of love would flow and redemption would follow. Long after the companions had dispersed, Eusébie and Dunnius remained in the atrium under the stars.

"Are they bright yet?" asked Eusébie, taking the big man's hand.

"Not yet," he replied, "But ours is the morning star, and nothing can ultimately dim that!"

***

Helena sat back among the cushions of the carruca, tired and in some trepidation at the thought of being reunited with her son. Donna, her companion and effective lady-in-waiting, sat dozing fitfully beside her. They had been on the road for the best part of five weeks including several days at sea. Helena knew that she was now nearing the end of one of the most portentous journeys of her life. Before tomorrow evening they would be in Fiano with Constantine's legions. In the eight years that she had lived in Armenia she had contrived to hold onto her title and install herself as an accepted, if unofficial, Roman dignitary in the court of King Tiridates the Great, the first monarch ever to make Christianity the official state religion. From there she had formed a rapid overview of the lines of power and the role of the church in the politics of the city and had soon become a prominent member of the cathedral worship centre. There her exceptional administrative skills together with her penchant for behind-the-scenes manipulation had placed her at the forefront of the lay worshippers. Always ambitious, the news that Constantine was Emperor of the West with pretensions for the consolidation of power across the whole empire had galvanised her into action. What if the partnership of church and state being experienced in Armenia could be established throughout the whole Roman Empire? What if Constantine would formally reinstate her as dowager empress to help achieve it? And who better to help than Eusebius, the young prelate and would-be bishop of Caesarea who she had met and befriended at court the previous year, now travelling in the carruca behind hers?

Having lived through the Diocletian persecution and seen the martyrdom of many of his companions, Eusebius found the idea of a Christian monarchy a very attractive one. Highly educated and hugely knowledgeable, he had long pondered the future of church and empire. His one-to-one tuition in the school of Pamphilus the disciple of Origen, in whose famous library at Caesarea Maritima the school was based, and where he had read extensively, gave him a strong sense of the critical importance of the moment. He also recognised that the calling of the church was to the whole family of humanity and not just itself. The church in Armenia was technically under the bishopric of Caesarea, and the bishop had been keen on getting a first-hand report on what was happening there. So as soon as Eusebius heard of this he had volunteered as delegate to the Vagharshapat court, despite the distances involved. On arrival he had been impressed by the stately dowager empress and spent several memorable extended cena exchanging insights into the relations of church and court in the capital. He was delighted when the following year he received her request for him to meet up with her in the port of Caesarea and travel together to Italy as a potential adviser to Constantine. Hence here he was together with his novitiate, travelling separately as befitted celibate clerics, in a second and slightly less luxurious carruca behind Helena and her lady-in-waiting.

That night the two vehicles pulled up the steep hill into the fortress of Riano. Helena had connections with the Scipio family who had lived there for generations.

"The empress," observed Eusebius drolly to his novitiate, Aristarchus, "seems to have connections everywhere!"

Drusilla, the current matriarch, now a widow, had been a confidant of Helena's back in the days when Constantius had been a military tribune under the emperor Probus and had remained a firm friend in her years as empress. Helena had always found her to be an abundant source of inside information on what was going on in the political machinations of the empire. Now she was agog with the impending confrontation between Constantine and Maxentius and once she had overcome her surprise at her unannounced guests was eager to know Helena's plans. As soon as she had set in motion the necessary hospitality and given instructions for a suitable vesperna to be prepared, she steered them into the atrium where her woman friend and her son who was visiting overnight from Constantine's forces in Fiano, were already seated. They stood to their feet as the visitors entered, sensing immediately the aura of authority that emanated from the empress without yet knowing who she was.

"This is the Dowager Empress Helena," Drusilla announced. "And this is Cornelia, a friend and confidante, and my son Brutus, an officer in Constantine's *Scholai Palatinae*."

Helena, shaking hands with each of them, visibly brightened on hearing of the role of Brutus, and then presented Eusebius and his novitiate.

"This is Eusebius, one of the most learned and well-placed Christian leaders in the empire and Aristarchus his most fortunate novice," she announced, and then almost as an afterthought, "Oh, and of course, this is Donna, my faithful lady-in-waiting."

"Come across to the dining area," Drusilla requested, "the slaves will bring the food presently."

Seating herself on one of the comfortable couches, and hardly giving time for the rest of the party to be seated, Helena immediately addressed Brutus.

"So, how well prepared is my son for the final advance on Rome? When will it be? Hardly tomorrow or you would not have been granted leave to visit your mother and grandmother. But is it imminent?"

"I'm not exactly on leave," responded Brutus. "We are scouting out the lie of the land. It's what the Scholai do. I have already been across the Milvian Bridge and back disguised as an ordinary plebeian before heading back via here. And Mater is a great source of information," he continued, realising that Helena's presence and the revelation that she was Constantine's mother was already extracting more information from him than he intended.

"He is bold then," responded Helena, "establishing a new intelligence service and naming it the Palatinae before he is in possession of the real Palatine!"

"He's rightly confident, Helena," interposed Drusilla. "By all accounts the masses jeered Maxentius at the games held the day before yesterday to celebrate his six years in power in Rome, and were all chanting '*Constantinus Invictus*! Constantinus Invictus!'"

Having let out more than he had intended, Brutus now decided to utilise the intimacy of the moment to find out what the empress and prelate were up to. It had to be more than maternal or domestic interest that brought Helena and her influential confidant to the vicinity of Fiano at such a time as this.

"You have chosen a strategic occasion to reconnect with your son," he observed, "and accompanied by an apparently impressive cleric."

Helena was unfazed by the young officer's directness. Already she sensed the opportunity to manoeuvre the converging connections to her own ends. "I have heard of the emperor's desire to align heaven and earth via a Christian empire, and I share it. So does Eusebius here. We have seen how this has brought great peace and prosperity to Armenia and we hope for the same alignment here."

Brutus, typical of the mainstream among Constantine's officers, was pragmatic in his attitude to war and diplomacy, religion and politics, so he merely listened in silence. Like many of his fellows he was a career soldier who simply recognised in Constantine an inspiring leader through whom his own ambitions might find fulfilment. However, the difference with Brutus was that his military competence successfully concealed a brooding capacity for violence that bordered on the psychopathic.

The slaves spread the food and poured the wine as the conversation continued.

"Please eat," Drusilla encouraged. Helping herself to a portion of olives and some honeyed wine, Helena smiled benevolently at her host and then, addressing Brutus again, enquired, "Are you planning on returning to Fiano tomorrow? And if so, then, if you don't mind, perhaps you could ask your commanding officer to inform the emperor that his mother is about to arrive and would welcome an audience with him tomorrow evening?" She was aware of her lengthy and complete estrangement from her son and thought that some advance warning and an official request for a formal meeting had the best chance of securing Constantine's sympathetic attention.

"Certainly, Your Excellency," responded Brutus. "I will be honoured to pave the way for your arrival. And please, if I can be of further help, don't hesitate to let me know. I am General Commodus' first lieutenant so it won't be difficult to contact me if you wish."

Eusebius, who had been following this attentively, joined in the conversation at this point. "I would love to know how the emperor is arriving at his strategic decisions so far. He seems to be having exceptional success. I hear that he is receiving counsel from the Christian convert Professor Lactantius, and that he and the Empress Fausta are strongly involved with the ecclesia in Augusta Treverorum. Indeed, I am given to understand that the imperial court there is something of a hub of Christian influence in Gaul and the farther west generally."

Brutus made a mental note that the personable prelate shared the empress' air of entitlement that drew out information while giving the informant a sense of being part of a highly trusted inner circle. This did not prevent the allure from working on him nonetheless.

"Your information is quite right, reverend, as far as it goes." He was not sure how to address the prelate and hoped this nomenclature would suffice. "But the real strategy lies with his comēs rei militaris."

Both Helena and Eusebius started noticeably at this.

"Surely that's highly unusual?" interjected Helena.

"You've been away a long time," put in Drusilla. "Have you not heard by now of the influence of the Metilias and the Janiculan slave ecclesia on Constantine these past seven years? He made the two young Christian heirs of his brother-in-law Quentin his comēs on his journey from Nicomedia to answer his father's summons to the defence of Britannia. He made their slave companion a freeman and included him too."

"Well, this is interesting," observed Helena, looking at Eusebius. "This adds an extra dimension to our thinking."

"You will certainly need to win their support if you are to gain the emperor's," put in Brutus. When he saw Helena's momentary facial expression he knew that his remark was unwelcome. The empress did not appreciate anyone giving her unasked-for advice. Certainly not if it suggested somebody else had more insight than she. The moment for serious conversation was clearly over, and the rest of the meal passed without further consequence. Discussion focused on the weather, the excellent food and wine and a few polite inquiries into the memorable aspects of the empress' and prelates' journey, particular the sea crossing. "Well, this has all been most satisfying," eventually concluded Drusilla calmly, signalling for the slaves to clear the table. "We will make sure there is an adequate ientaculum first thing tomorrow so that you can be ready for your important travels."

At which she signalled for the slaves to conduct her guests to their rooms.

***

That same night Constantine sat at vesperna in Villa Volusii Saturnini with Felix, Titus and Commodus.

"So what's happening?" Titus asked.

"Tomorrow we'll survey the troops, and as soon as we have definitive news on what to expect, we'll head for Rome," the emperor replied, and turning to Commodus asked, "When do we expect the Scholai to return, Commodus?"

"The majority returned today," he replied, "but I would prefer to hear from Brutus before forming a clear picture of what to expect. He is the most astute of the seven and almost certainly he will have dropped by his mater's place at Riano. He reckons that she always knows the inside story. I'm pretty certain he will be back tomorrow."

"How about you survey the troops first thing in the morning, at dawn?" suggested Felix. "Why do you suggest that?" Commodus asked. "Because if we are going to do that we'll need to get the word out across the legions to be ready. It's not fair to catch them out while they are still about their ablutions. It puts them at a disadvantage."

Felix was quiet for a moment. "I just have a sense of something very significant pending that we need to be up and ready for."

"We'll do as Felix suggests," said Constantine. "So, Commodus, can you put the word out to the tribunes as soon as you have finished here?"

"Of course," he replied, rising from the table, "I've eaten and drunk plenty enough already, so I'll go right away and get on with it."

Titus and Felix remained at the table with Constantine.

"I miss Marcus," volunteered the emperor. The two remaining comēs concurred.

"It was the right move though," reflected Felix, firmly. "Even when it cost him dearly and lost us his companionship and wisdom at a crucial time."

"Lactantius thinks we need to be prepared for more compromises you know," Constantine continued. "And I don't want to risk you two with any more dangerous attempts at diplomacy unless I'm confident there's more than a chance of success. Otherwise, I'm for feinting an attack while sending the Scholai to separate off Maxentius and assassinate him like we did his father."

"I admit it is a better compromise than a full-scale battle," granted Titus, "but the cruciform way is surely still the best way if we can find it. After all, while we've lost hundreds in battle, thousands, counting our opponents, we've lost no one in face-to-face peace-making so far." Constantine threw back his head and laughed, something he had done each time cities had opened their gates without bloodshed.

"I love you, *amici*. Where would I be without you? But if Maxentius is anything like his praetorian prefect, Ruricius, he'll not be for talking. More likely for vengeance, giving what became of the prefect."

The following morning dawned with a stunning sun rise. Constantine and Commodus stood with the two comēs at the entrance to the villa and looked out over the assembled legions as the sun's globe emerged from behind them. Slowly, clearly and breathtakingly the clouds formed beneath it into the unmistakeable shape of a cross. Streams of sunlight flooded from behind and around its four equal arms and encompassed the whole army and the surrounding countryside.

"That's your 'something significant impending' we needed to be ready for," observed Titus quietly. Constantine stood between the three of them, Commodus on one side and two comēs on the other. Tears streamed down his face and his body shook uncontrollably.

"What does it mean?" he asked, as much to heaven as to his companions. For fully ten minutes the sign of the cross loomed over them until the sun burst through the clouds in the full glory of dawn and the sign was gone. "I'll never forget this," said Constantine.

"Nor I," echoed Commodus.

"It's not so much the phenomenon or manifestation that is important," interposed Felix. "But we have to understand what it means and why it was here."

"Yes, and find and fulfil its purpose and significance in the days that come," added Titus.

Constantine went about the business of reviewing the troops in a daze. He acted and spoke without conscious thought, drawing on his extensive reservoir of military experience as required, the impact of the vision heavy upon him. Seeing such a sign was a completely new experience for him and it burnt itself onto the retina of his eyes and deep into the cortex of his brain. By cena he was still in a semi-stupor and had retired to take a long siesta in his room when Commodus came to him with the astonishing news that his mother was due to arrive later that afternoon and wanted a formal meeting that very evening. He knew without further thought that this and the dawn vision were somehow connected. He needed to be ready for her arrival, and at that precise moment, the most pressing preparation seemed to be sleep! So tasking Commodus with organising a private reception for vesperna, he wrapped himself in his toga and was soon fast sleep and dreaming.

In his dream he was in the peristyle of Villa Metilia on the Janiculan Hill. Rome was set out before him. He could see the Milvian Bridge and alongside it his legions and Maxentius' battalions preparing to engage. Behind the battleground lay the Tiber and the city on its seven hills. As he looked, a murder of crows rose up from the trees along the river, obscuring the city from view. But then the dawn vision of the cross which still filled his mind, extended out from him, encompassing everything. The light of the sun behind the cross outshone it all, dispersing the hooded birds, the legions and battalions until it transfigured the city, its hills and beyond, as far as the eye could see. Then he heard a voice cry out "In this sign you will conquer!" As he continued watch, the vision of the cross with its four equal arms reconfigured like the components of a kaleidoscope and the crows began to reassemble. The top arm of the cross was obscured, forming a huge letter T. After that the top arm reappeared but curled around to make the shape of a P. Finally, the four equal arms once again embraced everyone and everything and the crows were gone. Then he awoke.

Hardly was he awake when Commodus appeared.

"Your mother's party has arrived and are waiting in the atrium," he said, leaning over him anxiously. "Are you well?"

"I've been fast asleep and having an extraordinary dream," Constantine responded. "I think I'm well enough physically, but the dawn vision and the dream are still really heavy on me. It's as if I'm still partly in them. Tell my mother that I'm briefly indisposed and will join her later, after vesperna. Then have her party seated in the dining area and have the meal served. Is it a large group?"

"No, just her, her lady-in-waiting and some kind of prelate or other with his assistant. But she's some impressive lady!" replied Commodus. "Can I do anything else for you?" he asked.

"Yes," responded the emperor. "After you have informed my mother that I'll join her later, have Felix and Titus come here to my room as quickly as they can. Tell them to come around the side way, not through the atrium."

"Consider it done," concluded Commodus and was gone. Constantine got up from his bed and made his way over to the washstand where a jug for drinking and a basin of water for washing remained from the previous night. He drank thirstily from the jug and washed his face from the basin. Then in an attempt to revive himself properly he scooped several cupsful of water over his head and ran his hands through his hair. Then, at last, he threw back his head and laughed.

He was seated expectantly on the side of his bed when the two comēs entered the room. They were not in the general habit of meeting together in Constantine's bedroom since he had become emperor. They stood awkwardly for a moment but then the emperor swung his legs up and sat cross-legged on the bed and motioned them to join him facing each other in a kind of impromptu pow-wow.

"I've just had an extraordinary dream which clearly follows on from this morning's vision," he began. "I need to share it before I forget the details, and in any case I'm going to be entirely unable to face my mother until I've some idea of what it all means. On past experience I'll need all my wits about me before I discover why she has reappeared after all these years!"

"Right," said Felix, "so what did you dream?" Constantine took a deep breath and began.

"I was in the peristyle at Villa Metilia looking out over the city. Both our forces and Maxentius' troops were facing each other below me at the Milvian Bridge, with the Tiber and the city on the Seven Hills behind. As I looked, hooded crows rose up from the trees by the river and overshadowed the view. But then this morning's vision of the cross, which has been burning inside my skull all day, spread out from my head and encompassed everything, dispelling the crows and the troops. I heard a voice cry 'in this sign you will conquer!' But then the vision of the cross started changing shape and the crows returned. Instead of the four equal arms it was without the top arm so it looked like a huge letter T, until the top arm came back again but this time curled round to make a huge P shape. In the end it went back to being the four equal arms embracing everyone and everything, and the crows were gone."

"Was that the whole of it?" asked Titus.

"Yes, that was it," Constantine replied. "Then I woke up. What do you think it means?"

Titus and Felix looked at each other.

"It's significant that it was located at Villa Metilia," said Felix.

"Yes," continued Titus. "We sent a report to the slave ecclesia only the day before yesterday. And we asked them to pray particularly with our advance on the city in view. So I think we need to interpret all this in the context of their prayers, and our common vision of the kingdom of love."

"Something else is important," put in Felix. "Do you remember when Marcus met the druid on the road to the Antonine Wall? The cross that he wore had the four equal arms that your dream began and ended with."

"Oh yes," continued Titus, "the druid said that it's the cruciform sign of the ecclesia together with the Trinity restoring peace and reconciliation to the land."

"So what of the T and the P shapes?" Felix wondered.

"I don't think we can understand the whole of this without what's coming," considered Titus. "That sounds wise," Felix responded. "Melissa reckons that visions and dreams are never ends in themselves. They belong in life. They give us starting points, but then they only make sense as the future unfolds. They are warnings or reminders so it's vital not to forget them, especially when they are as strong as this."

"Well then," concluded Constantine. "That's what we'll do. We'll head onwards into what's coming, but we'll be sure to remember what has been shown us. Help me not to forget."

Chapter Eleven

Rights and Wrongs

Helena sat with increasing impatience in the luxurious dining room. It was growing dark and the palace slaves were lighting lamps which cast shadows onto the spectacular wall paintings to dramatic effect. Eusebius had been pointing out the battles that they depicted and the identities of the imperial celebrities that they displayed. The meal was of only mediocre quality for her taste, and the wine not much better. It contrasted badly with the vesperna of the previous evening at Riano. And she had precious little interest in the old battles. Her focus was on the opportunity for her own present advancement. She sensed strongly that this was her moment. The past demagogues had rejected her, among which she included Constantius, maybe unfairly. She had perhaps overplayed her hand those many years ago. But that was simply not going to happen this time, she determined. This time she would use the insight gained in exile to full effect.

All the same, she held her breath as Constantine strode into the room. It was fully ten years since she had seen him. Then he was thirty, now he was forty. Then, to her mind he had been wilful and ill-advised. Now he carried himself with a compelling mixture of confidence and sensitivity. She rose to her feet and took a step towards him. He halted, standing a metre or so away from her, taking in for a moment what she knew to be her dignified bearing and mature beauty.

"General Commodus was right when he remarked to me earlier this afternoon that you are an impressive woman, Mater. Like a good wine that matures with age!" Then he threw back his head and laughed. Helena remained standing before him. "By God, I've missed you," he said, and drew her to him in a great bear hug.

She yielded gratefully to this warmth of acceptance on his part. But internally she was in full control of her emotions.

"So am I forgiven for staying away so long, Constantine?" she asked. But it was not so much a question as a position statement. She had been away ten years and now she was back and meant to behave and be treated as his mother irrespective of the intervening years.

She has not changed then, reflected her son. "Take me or leave me," that was always her demeanour. And he would take her, of course! Quite how she would handle his wife, her grandson, his comēs, time would tell. She would have to work that out if she was back for good. He would remain independent from her if he could. He knew her manipulative abilities well! But she had a strength and determination that he needed, if she used it wisely and he could channel it while keeping her at arm's length when necessary.

"Of course," he said in response to her question. "Who is it that you have brought with you?" he continued. Eusebius had remained seated deferentially together with Donna and Aristarchus, watching the unfolding reunion. Now he rose too and came and stood beside the empress.

"Now this," Helena began grandiosely, with a wave of her hand, "is the prelate Eusebius of Caesarea, one of the most impressive theologians in the empire today."

"Well, it's very kind of you to say so, Your Excellency," he responded, the colour rising along his high cheek bones.

"And how would you describe yourself?" asked Constantine.

"Well, it is for others to assess my skills and gifts," acknowledged the prelate. "But I can say what my motives and desires are. I desire a just and godly leadership to be shared between the empire of Rome and the Christian church under a noble emperor such as yourself, and I commit here and now to do all in my ability to see this happen." He knelt right then and there, at Constantine's feet. Constantine swallowed his characteristic urge to laugh.

"I thank you, Eusebius. Please get up and take your seat back at the table. And you too, Mater, please be likewise seated." He joined them at the table. "I trust you have found the vesperna adequate? And the wine too?" He reached out for the jug on the low table and poured out more for his guests and filled a goblet for himself. "So Eusebius, how do you, a scholar with an eye to the alignment of church and empire, advise me on my progress to Rome where another would-be emperor has had the support of the Senate these past six years and even now is preparing to oppose me at the very gates of the city?"

Eusebius barely blinked.

"There can only be one emperor, Your Excellency, and God is with you. So advance in that knowledge and you will be victorious in battle. No question about it."

"Well, you seem very sure about this," Constantine replied, and turning to his mother asked, "Am I to take it that you would give the same advice? You see, my own advisers, who I trust, favour diplomacy and peace-making even in the face of violent resistance. They hope that once we arrive at the Milvian Bridge, and before engaging the troops in battle, we will first send a delegation to offer Maxentius his freedom on condition that he defers to my superiority and recognises me as the legitimate Augustus. And in case he does not, I will instruct the Scholai to penetrate his guard somehow and assassinate him with minimum loss of life. What is your response to that?"

Both empress and prelate observed him silently for a moment.

"What do you say on this, Eusebius?" she asked, apparently deferring to him, although he was well aware that it was to her that Constantine had deliberately addressed the question. He realised that he needed to answer with care therefore.

"As I understand it," he began, "lordship is God's and he gives it to whom he will. We must be careful not to impose it by our own might, but if God is with us then he will impose it, whether by force or diplomacy. Both are in his gift. If he advances with our troops then the victory is his to grant. God is with you, Constantine, and so he will give victory."

The emperor stood to his feet.

"And the cross, Eusebius," he asked. "Where does that come into it?" For a moment the prelate appeared at a loss. Helena waited, expectantly.

"Well, the cross, of course," he continued, "is where God's anger at our failure to accept his authority was appeased. So now it is a powerful sign of his blessing."

Constantine looked thoughtful.

"Hmm, that's a new one on me. I thought it rather the sign of all that's opposite to the current empire, and signified a new humanity with an entirely different kind of authority. The authority of love. And that it's now our task to bring that new form of authority into the deep structural workings of the empire."

"We need to speak further about this," announced Helena, "this is very important." Despite her apparent composure, and the passage of the years, Constantine still recognised from her demeanour precisely how important she thought it was.

About to take leave of his mother and the rest of his guests, he hesitated pensively and sat back down instead.

"I had a dream of the cross, this very day," he confided. "It began with outstretched arms equidistant and all encompassing. But then it was overshadowed by two other alternative forms. One was the shape of a T, and the other extended above into the shape of a P. Then the original shape resurged and overwhelmed them both. I heard a voice say 'in this sign you will conquer.' What do you think it means, Eusebius?"

The prelate folded his hands and leant back on the couch, apparently deep in thought. Then he looked inscrutably at Constantine.

"Have a *Tau* shaped cross constructed and hang from it a banner with the *Rho* shaped cross painted on it. Carry it before you into battle with Maxentius. It will be your *labarum*."

The emperor met his gaze with the same impenetrable look. He stood to his feet.

"Thank you for your opinion," he replied, "I'll sleep on it. You will stay tonight, Mater, of course," concluded Constantine, turning his attention to his mother. "The villa is pretty full, but I will make sure that there is a room set aside for you and Donna. Eusebius and Aristarchus, you had better take my room, and I will join my comēs for the night, something that is no new thing for me on our many lengthy journeys."

"Thank you very much," Helena responded gratefully, surprised at his generosity, not least to Eusebius, who didn't know what to make of it, feeling flattered yet displaced both at the same time.

"Thank you, Your Excellency," he intoned.

"No problem, Mater, no problem, my friends. I'll have the house steward prepare the rooms and then come for you. What are your plans for tomorrow? We will be moving first thing down to the city to confront Maxentius."

"As for us, we will head back to my friends, the Scipios," Helena replied, improvising once more. They could wait out the results of the confrontation and all being well head down and join Constantine in the imperial court at the Palatine if the advance was successful. Yes, she thought, that was a good plan. She would settle herself there right at the heart of the imperial court in Rome from the very start when everything was reconfiguring and before the lines of power were otherwise set. Then she thought of something else, she must get a message to Brutus. So as Constantine got up to leave she took his arm.

"Constantine, my son, I have a personal message for Brutus, General Commodus' first lieutenant, from his mother and grandmother. I promised to give it in person myself if I could."

"That's easy, Mater, wait here and I'll have him come to you right away. Good night then." Kissing her on the cheek, he took his leave.

Half an hour later, the steward came to take them to their rooms. Duly installed with Donna in hers, and leaving instructions for her to ready the room for the night and to lay out clothes for the morning, she headed back into the now empty dining area. Not long afterwards, Brutus appeared, having received the emperor's message while in the midst of a strategic planning meeting of the Scholai Palatinae in preparation for the next day's action. Excusing himself as soon as he reasonably could and intrigued as to what the assignment with the empress might be about, he had made his way back to the villa.

"What can I do for you, Your Excellency?" he inquired.

"What I am about to ask is of strategic importance and requires the greatest secrecy," she began. "The emperor is concerned that nobody besides you and me should know of this." She looked at him unfalteringly. "By the end of tomorrow it is highly likely that Maxentius will be dead, in battle or by assassination. Either way you will be closely involved as one of the seven. In order to consolidate your role we need you to locate Maxentius' body and hide it somewhere safe. Tell no one, not even the emperor at that stage, as it is most important you are not overheard. Then come to me at the Palatine Palace. Can you manage that? I will explain what to do next then."

Brutus shuddered internally at the implications of this request. But he remained outwardly calm and resolved to fulfil it if he could. He sensed honour and possible future promotion in this commission.

"Yes, My Lady, I will do all in my power to fulfil your request," he replied. She stretched out her hand for him to kiss, which he did.

"Then hopefully by the day after tomorrow if not before, or at the very least soon after, it will be done. I, or Donna, will be waiting in the atrium of the palace to hear from you."

Having brought together the five tribunes and Commodus, with the comēs as usual present but not engaged in the military strategising, the emperor set out his plan for the next day. They would simply march towards the city, and by late afternoon set up their field camp opposite but at a reasonable distance from Maxentius' troops. As this was the accepted military practice of the time it was most unlikely that his battalions would attempt to rush on them. Battle would be engaged by the protocols of common agreement once the troops were in place and at the ready. An attempt would first be made to get Maxentius to make peace by submitting to Constantine's leadership in return for a subordinate role. If this was unsuccessful, then they would move ahead and begin to engage in battle. However, simultaneously, the Scholai hidden within the cavalry immediately behind Constantine would spring out and charge directly at Maxentius in an attempt to assassinate him before anyone realised what was happening. The hope would be that with their emperor dead, his troops would surrender quickly. So, the strategy being agreed, the tribunes and Commodus departed for their beds and Constantine, explaining that he had given his room to the prelate and his novitiate, headed back with his two comēs for the night.

Felix and Titus, being cramped in the latter's bed in order to give the emperor the other, were in no immediate mood for sleep, and Constantine soon revealed that it was not simply respect and hospitality that had moved him to give up his room.

"What a day," he exclaimed. "I most surely need your help in reflecting over it, and what it all means for tomorrow."

"So where do we start?" interjected Titus, sitting up and dangling his feet over the side of the bed. "Do we assume that you have had some more light on the vision and the dream?" Constantine got back out of bed and stood facing them, concern marking the creased corners of the now familiar eyes in the flickering candlelight.

"It's the cross that I'm still trying to get my head around," he confided. "I'd like to think, and yes, am beginning to be sure, that the cross in the vision and at the beginning and end of the dream, represents the arms of Jesus wrapped around our whole venture. That the druid that spoke with Marcus is right, it is the cruciform sign of the ecclesia and the Trinity together restoring peace and reconciliation to the land."

"Then how about the other crosses that it merged in and out of in your dream?" interposed Titus.

"It didn't exactly merge into them," Constantine observed. "When I try to recall it clearly, it seems to me more like it revealed them. Do either of you know anything about those second two signs of the cross?"

"I've been thinking about this all day," Felix replied, "and I've heard of them both from Lactantius. As for the Tau shape, apparently some of the early fathers of the faith like Tertullian saw the similarity between the letter T in Latin and Greek and the shape of the crucifixion gibbet. Others took Jesus' words that everything in the Hebrew Scriptures was about him so seriously that they even hunted there for numbers that represented him symbolically. It so happens that Tau in Greek also represents the numeral 300, so in turn any scripture accounts containing the number 300 were reckoned to prefigure Jesus' death on the cross. For example, it would work for the 300 who Gideon routed the Midianites with. In this way, as well as being a straightforward depiction of the cross it was loaded with other meanings too. So it could be taken to mean that God was ready to go with us into battle. Something that at the time Lactantius regarded as a mistake."

"Is it or isn't it a mistake, I wonder though?" interjected Constantine. "And what about the P shaped cross that followed the T? What do you know about that?"

"Well, Lactantius talked about that too," responded Felix. "And rather like with the Tau, there's a twist to it. The Chi 'X' and the Rho 'P' are the first two letters of CHRISTOS in Greek, and were used as a code for Jesus in the early persecutions.

It dates from ancient pagan times as a marker for something thought to be a good thing. Obviously, the X is also a cross on its side, so some people used it as a code for Jesus' cross. Problem is, though, like Tau also represented the number 300, the Rho 'P' is also the initial letter of money in Latin; *pecunia*. So while the T and the P signs are legitimate signs of the cross, they are signs that can also be interpreted in terms of military power and money. I think that your dream is a warning. Beware twisting the true cross towards war and money."

Constantine was silent. Was that what Eusebius' proposal of going into battle against Maxentius under a banner bearing a Rho shaped cross, draped over a Tau shaped cross was about? Would the labarum bend the cross and his leadership of the empire towards war and money? And in any case was it a good idea to allow the prelate to intervene so directly into his operations?

"Very interesting," he observed. "Thank you. I am so glad of your counsel." But he would sleep on it nonetheless, and said no more that night. Felix and Titus eventually settled down uneasily to sleep. There was little room in the bed, and for the first time they sensed a hesitation in Constantine's reception of their advice, less room in Constantine's deliberations. He had certainly not dismissed out of hand Felix's suggestion of the dream carrying a warning, but they sensed that he was holding something back. In his turn, the emperor, waiting for sleep to come, rather hoped that he would dream again. However, although the original vision remained imprinted on his cortex, and he was well able to remember and reflect on the contents of the dream, he could find no further interpretative light as he turned it all over in his mind. In the process of which he fell soundly asleep.

The following morning Helena was at the stables by dawn, instructing that the two carruca be ready and waiting immediately after their early ientaculum. Her plans had grown exponentially in the night and she was anxious to be at Riano as soon as possible. It was only a little after midday when the two vehicles pulled once more up the steep ascent to the Scipios' castle. Hurrying from the carriage she quickly found Drusilla. Hardly waiting for Eusebius to catch up with her, she began to explain her plan to Drusilla and enlist her immediate cooperation.

"Last night Eusebius had a strong sense that Constantine needs to go into battle against Maxentius – who most certainly isn't about to make any kind of deal – with a special banner to invoke the divine blessing. I want us to make a collection of six of these before tonight is out. One to go before Constantine and his cavalry, and one each for the five legions. We need wood to make six Tau crosses, we need material for banners to hang on them and we need paint to draw the Chi Rho on the banners. Can you have your slaves begin to do this immediately?"

"Well, you have got the bit between your teeth," Drusilla retorted. "But yes, we should be able to achieve this by nightfall." "Olipor," she called, summoning her head slave. "There's important work to be done."

"Aristarchus and I will oversee this, Your Excellency," Eusebius announced to Helena. And then turning to Drusilla, continued, "That is if you are happy for us to do so, My Lady?" "Gladly, do whatever you wish," she replied, "You can be sure that Olipor will make it happen if at all possible."

By nightfall the six crosses and banners were all completed and lashed to a horse-drawn plaustrum in readiness to be taken to Constantine's field camp at dawn the following morning. Eusebius had watched over their construction with avid attention and Helena had instructed Olipor himself to convey them without fail to the tribunes of each legion with a message that she repeated to him several times over.

"Say that the emperor instructs that the banner is to be carried in front of them when the command has been given to go into battle." The final banner was to be given to Lieutenant Brutus with the instruction that he should present it to Constantine as a gift from the empress. "He will know what to do with it," she said, with typically unshaken confidence in her own powers of manipulation. Instructions which Olipor, leaving the following morning with two fellow slaves before the sun was even up, had carried out to the letter by midday. His habitual subservience, coupled with a smooth expectation that any instructions he gave would likewise be carried out to the letter, meant that the tribunes received the impressive banners with interest, but entirely without suspicion. Constantine received Brutus and the sixth banner, moments before he was about to give the command to his cavalry to advance, with the five legions beside them. He sensed his mother's hand immediately, and after a moment's hesitation threw back his head and laughed. Handing the banner to his commandant he gave the call to proceed.

Maxentius was on the Milvian Bridge waiting for any movement from his enemy. When he had ordered the other bridges to be removed he had ordered the main structure of the Milvian to be dismantled as well. Then he had instructed that several rafts be constructed utilising the wooden planks and supports from the other bridges to be lashed together to make a temporary bridge. This had then been concealed between the flotillas of ships that he had lined up across the Tiber where the original bridge had been. His plan was to move forward with his troops once the moment for engagement came. But if they were in any danger of being overwhelmed he would immediately withdraw back across the bridge and into the city with as many of his men who could follow as possible. As soon as the enemy converged towards the bridge, then the temporary rafts would be rapidly untied and pulled across to the city side leaving the enemy legions marooned.

As soon as Constantine began to lead his cavalry forward, Maxentius, surrounded by his elite riders, rode towards him.

Halting a matter of only ten metres apart, Constantine, the labarum held high beside him by his commandant, addressed Maxentius clearly and calmly.

"I desire you no harm, Maxentius. I would gladly make you my second in command. The court in Rome can remain your home. What say you?" Maxentius cleared his throat. Then slowly and deliberately he leant forward, his steed pawing the ground. Then, projecting his head forward, he spat on Constantine's horse's hooves.

"I am already the recognised emperor in this city, and I submit to no one!" he cried. Immediately, casting aside the accepted protocols, according to plan, the Scholai Palatinae emerged from either side of Constantine and charged at Maxentius. He barely had time to shout "Engage the enemy!" to his assembled battalions before he found himself driven backwards onto the first raft of the bridge, pulled from his horse, and suspended between Commodus and Brutus.

Then everything happened at once. Maxentius' throat was slashed wide open by Brutus' sword and Commodus was speared through the heart by the dying would-be emperor's elite commandant while all along the banks of the Tiber on either side of the bridge, a bloodbath was taking place. Seeing the success of the plan to assassinate Maxentius, and anxious to prevent as much further loss of life as possible, Constantine urged his cavalry forward onto the bridge where he turned and faced the erupting carnage, the labarum held high beside him. "Maxentius is dead, spread the news and head for the bridge!" he called. Swiftly and surely the news spread along the banks of the river where Maxentius' vastly outnumbered troops were already being forced back towards the water and surrendering in preference to drowning. As the ferocious battle gradually stilled, the remains of Constantine's legions made their way behind the cavalry over the still functioning raft bridge and up the Via Flaminia into the city, the other five labarum held boldly above them. As the chants from the crowds at the chariot race had forewarned several days before, the people of Rome, plebeians and patricians alike, were mainly delighted at the sight of the victorious emperor's Parousia. Those who were not, kept well out of the way as Constantine and his cavalry, followed by the surviving legionaries, made their way up the Palatine Hill into the imperial palace. There was no resistance as they entered. Far from it, the palace guard welcomed them as if they were the returning emperor and his armies, which indeed they now were.

Meanwhile, having eventually heard the news that the advance on the city had been successful, Titus and Felix, with troubled hearts and mixed feelings, made their way from the field station down towards the bridge, guiding their horses past the many bodies of the dead and wounded, and with tears pouring down their cheeks, determined as they went to make absolutely sure that help was sent back as rapidly as possible to tend the injured and dying and give the already dead an honourable burial, whichever side they had been on. Then, as they stepped onto the bridge, they encountered Commodus' lifeless body, lying dead in a pool of blood. Desperately desiring to attend to him immediately, they tore themselves away nonetheless, concerned first to get help for everyone, but promising each other that once they'd secured help for the others they would come back without delay for Commodus.

Once inside the city they made their way quickly up the Palatine Hill where the crowds were by now dispersing. In the courtyard of the palace a temporary camp was being set up and the surviving tribunes, two of whom had fallen, were reassembling what remained of the legions, preparatory to despatching units to recover the injured and bury the dead. The two comēs continued to be held in great respect by the tribunes who stopped and listened intently as Felix and Titus pleaded for all the wounded and dead to be shown equal respect, no prisoners to be enslaved nor the bodies of Maxentius' men dishonoured. Their task completed, they commandeered a plaustrum and made their way back down the hill with the first units who had been organised to take care of the fallen.

"We should take Commodus to Villa Metilia," Titus said, suddenly.

"Of course," responded Felix, "that's exactly what we must do."

"Nesta will be devastated," Titus continued, "but I think she will want to bury him here on the Janiculan Hill, and not attempt to take his body all the way back home to Lindum."

"Maybe her parents will come and pay their respects some future day," Felix ventured. "And the ecclesia will give him a great send off, for sure."

Commodus still lay where he had fallen, although some officers making their way from the battlefield up to the imperial palace had done the honour of placing a *sagum* over his bloodied body. The two comēs lifted his body as gently as they could up onto the plaustrum. He was no lightweight, his years of soldiering and swordsmanship having packed his limbs and torso with highly developed muscle. They were both sweating profusely by the time he lay on his back on the cart, his glazed eyes fixed on the sky, and they took the reins and led the oxen forward off the bridge and out onto the road to the Janiculan Hill.

Up at Villa Metilia a paradoxical atmosphere of jubilation and sadness had prevailed ever since it became obvious by distant sight and then from returning youths who had gone charging down to the silent battlefield for news, that Constantine and his legions had overwhelmed Maxentius' battalions. Now the steady progress of Titus and Felix and their ox-drawn bier up the Janiculan Hill to Villa Metilia attracted the attention of Claudia and Melissa. They had been keeping a prayer vigil with Eusébie while Dunnius and Fortunatus had been attempting to maintain some kind of normality in the community for the benefit of the farm and its livestock. Dusk was approaching and Nesta was busy settling Amadeus into bed, never a straightforward business with the lively boy, when she became aware of Eusébie standing behind her.

"I'll tell him a story, Nesta, he loves that, and it will soon settle him," she began, placing her arm gently around her sister-in-law. Nesta reflected, as she often did, that Eusébie had an amazing ability to know exactly where someone was.

"I think you will be needed out in the driveway," Eusébie continued. "I will pray for you."

"Why, what's happening?" Nesta asked.

"I don't know for sure," Eusébie said, "except that Titus and Felix are coming up the hill and they are bringing something or someone on a plaustrum." Nesta's heart fell, and touching Eusébie lightly on the cheek she hurried to the driveway where the comēs and their load had by now come to a standstill. Melissa and Claudia stood with their arms around their sons, looking sadly at the outstretched figure on the plaustrum. As Nesta approached they reached out their arms signalling her to halt.

"Wait a moment, Nesta. You need to prepare yourself," said Claudia.

Nesta had sensed something of the loss she was about to face from the moment Eusébie had placed her arm around her.

"It's Commodus, isn't it!" she exclaimed, stepping around her friends and gazing down at her brother. Leaning over the low edge of the cart, she brushed aside the blood-soaked fringe of his hair and gently closed his still staring eyes. "Be at peace, my lovely brother," she said, tears pouring down her cheeks.

The others stood by, amazed by her composure and fortitude.

"He was a soldier who well knew what might await him," she continued. "but at the same time he was first and foremost a disciple of the prince of peace and he is with him now." Then she stood quietly alongside the make-shift bier, her shoulders convulsed with grief. After a few moments she allowed herself to be enfolded in Titus' arms.

"We were thinking to bury him here at Villa Metilia," he said.

"Oh yes," affirmed his wife, "Lindum is so far away, and this is our home now. Let him share it with us, and all being well my pater and mater can visit us now that the West is secured."

The following morning, just before midday, the whole ecclesia gathered on the Janiculan Hill at the edge of the Metilia orange grove where a carefully constructed gazebo had been erected over a freshly dug grave. As an ex-Roman soldier, Dunnius was especially glad to have been asked to preside at Commodus' burial. In any case he was the obvious person to do so, as he was one of the only companions on the hill to have known him personally. Everyone approved Nesta's desire to eulogise her brother's attempts to prioritise the peaceful kingdom of God in his work as a young officer and then as a general and director of the Scholai Palatinae. This clash of priorities between the kingdom of God and the empire of Rome was uppermost in all their minds. Although many of them had heard the story before, they all paid solemn attention as Nesta, faltering at first, but gaining in boldness despite her tears, recounted the story of her attempted kidnap in Lindum. She described how Commodus stood like a giant with a hooded man on his shoulders and a swordsman under his arm, bravery soon surpassed by his willingness to follow Felix's daring example of reconciliatory peace-making. Then when she retold the story of how Constantine had appointed him commander at the Antonine Wall if their peace-making failed and how he was ready to kill the aurochs, everyone understood why Constantine had made the brave young general the leader of the Scholai. They knew that the man they were laying to rest had courageously represented the conflicting kingdoms of love and domination.

As she concluded her eulogy, tears still streaming down her face, with the words "Well done good and faithful brother, enter now the joy of your Lord!" the whole assembly broke out in shouts of "Yes and Amen!" and "Come on the kingdom of peace!"

Then Titus and Felix, this time assisted by Jonas and Junia, lay Commodus to rest as Dunnius began to lead them all in the companions' prayer. At the statement "Your kingdom come, your will be done on earth as it is in heaven," shouts and cheers accompanied the prayers of the veteran soldier even more loudly.

***

In the meantime, in parallel to all this, Brutus, having seen Commodus speared through the heart at the same moment that he himself ripped open Maxentius' throat, decided that his first act as the commander of the Scholai Palatinae would be to fulfil his promise to Helena. Quickly pulling the dying emperor behind him in the melee, he manoeuvred them both over the stern of one of the small ships of the flotilla beside him. Then extricating a knife from his belt he proceeded to make sure the would-be emperor was dead by severing his head from his body. Seizing a sack from the ship's hold he placed the head and body inside and concealed it in the storage space in the stern. By this time he could see that Constantine and his cavalry were assembling on the city side of the bridge, the momentum of the charge having carried them quite across it, and were gathering there in preparation for their Parousia. The surviving tribunes were already beginning to make their way from the defeat of their enemies to join them. He quietly clambered unseen down into the water without letting go of the side of the ship and then pulled himself back onto bridge and made his way across and slipped among them.

"Is Maxentius definitely dead?" asked Constantine as Brutus emerged from among the cavalry, clearly soaking wet.

"Most certainly, Your Excellency, by my own hand. I slit his throat irrevocably and he fell between the rafts and the flotilla. I have been looking for him there with no success so far and the river is deep. But have no fear, I will send men to dive and search until they find him." "Be sure to make haste to do so," the emperor replied. "It is important to find him and give him an honourable burial. But what of Commodus? Did he survive the attack?"

"Sadly not," replied Brutus, careful to appear appropriately subdued although inwardly exalting. "He fell by an elite bodyguard's sword, even as I cut Maxentius' throat."

"We must recover his body too, Brutus, he was my friend as well as my trusted general," Constantine responded sadly.

"I believe he also may have slipped down between the raft and the ships," Brutus replied, "but on my word, sir, I will do all possible to recover both bodies and bring them to the palace before daybreak tomorrow."

"Thank you, Brutus," the emperor responded, "you have done well on a tragic but victorious day. You must take charge of the Scholai immediately and use your authority to get this done. And use your intelligence skills to root out any opposing influences remaining in the palace when we get there shortly."

Turning to the rest of his elite turma and about to set out up the Via Flaminia to the imperial palace, he saw the surviving tribunes making their way across the bridge towards him. "Well done, friends," he cried. "Now I think we can expect a triumphant Parousia up the Via Flaminia and into the palace!"

***

Later that evening, as soon as Helena received confirmation of Constantine's victory and the death of Maxentius, she summoned her carruca and leaving instructions for Eusebius and Aristarchus to join her at the imperial palace the following day, set out with Donna through the gathering dusk to the city. It was dark as they made the ascent up the Palatine Hill, and she observed the many lights and sounds of victory celebrations coming through the open gates of the palace with rising anticipation. Leaving the driver to deal with the vehicle and horses, she made her way directly towards the source of the commotion which was the massive atrium of the imperial palace. The vestibulum was guarded by several retainers who had seemingly exchanged the care of one emperor for another as all in a day's work. Although Helena was unknown to them, her inimitable bearing as she bore down on them registered her immediately as a dowager empress or suchlike. So when she introduced herself as Emperor Constantine's mother the Empress Helena, the retainers welcomed her with due deference and without question. They were about to usher her into the atrium where Constantine was sitting with the tribunes and officers of his elite turma, when she startled them by insisting that they take her immediately to the kitchens and their own superiors. She was almost certain. Maxentius' chamberlain, secretary, chief of staff, and their respective staffs would have by now beaten a hasty retreat, but rightly surmised that the domestic staff would still be in place.

Aware that whoever this woman was, she expected to be obeyed, the retainers did what she asked. Taken aback at the unexpected arrival of an apparent empress so soon in the change of regime, but already uneasy as to what would happen next, the imperial domestic staff gathered before her.

"I am the Empress Helena," she announced, "and I will be taking charge of the food and hospitality arrangements for the emperor, his family and his entourage. What has been arranged for this evening's celebrations, baths, and sleeping arrangements? Are there sufficient supplies for tomorrow's ientaculum, cena and vesperna? Please set about providing all that is necessary forthwith. Right now, please, open up the wine cellars and bring the best of wine and food for a late vesperna. Check that all the necessary oil is provided for the torches and lanterns. We will be sitting up late no doubt, but rooms and baths must be perfectly ready when required! I will wait here for you to fetch the wine and appropriate food and oversee the setting of it out in the dining area. Please make haste."

The gathered palace staff hesitated for just a moment, meeting one another's glances, and then in an unspoken acknowledgement of Helena's irresistible authority immediately set about their tasks. Within barely half an hour, a procession of slaves appeared bearing the best of wines, honey cakes, fruit and cold meats for a lavish vesperna. The dining area being to one side of the atrium, as Helena had anticipated, she instructed the head servants to follow on behind her leading the laden slaves as she made a grand entry into the atrium. Although Constantine was seated with his tribunes and officers with a few somewhat haphazard supplies of uninspiring food and drink he was paying scant attention to either the company or the provision. As the afternoon had lapsed into evening he had become increasingly preoccupied with growing anxiety for news of Titus and Felix and was about to send for Brutus to find them when his mother strode majestically across the atrium towards him, followed by the extraordinary procession of slaves and supplies.

"Constantine, my son and liege," she announced imperiously. "I had to be here as one of the first to congratulate you. You have done marvellously, under the sign of the cross! But I also needed to be here to take charge of the day-to-day running of the palace, given that the Empress Fausta is still in Augusta Treverorum. And as you can see, I have already done so." Constantine looked languidly at his mother, temporarily setting aside his concern for his comēs, while the slave entourage set out the food and drink and the palace servants began to distribute it among the tribunes and officers.

"Mater Empress," he cried. "There is no repressing you. What a woman!" Then turning to his tribunes and the officers of his turma he announced, "This is my mother the Empress Helena, for any of you who don't know. She is the one who had the labarum made and presented to us in readiness for our victorious battle. And this sumptuous spread is the true beginning of our victory celebration. Set to!"

Then signalling to one of his officers he instructed him privately to find Titus and Felix as a matter of urgency and bring them post haste to the palace.

Chapter Twelve

Shifting Powers

Decurio Anthony, the officer assigned to find Felix and Titus, was entirely unfamiliar with the city of Rome. He was a brilliant soldier and swordsman, and had proved himself an invaluable cavalryman, but he was less than adept at self-organisation. In any case he was dog-tired. So having hunted the immediate environs of the imperial palace for the two comēs he remembered that they were from Villa Metilia and concluded that they had probably gone there. He knew it was on a hill in Rome, but unfortunately assumed that it was one of the Seven Hills and that he could easily walk there. He thought it might be the Esquiline Hill, but rightly rated his chances of finding his way anywhere in the dark that night as slim and decided to find somewhere to sleep in the rambling palace buildings and wait until dawn. As the sun rose it was the ridges of the Capitoline and Aventine Hills to the East of the Palatine that presented themselves, and telling himself that he must ask someone the way, got it into his head that it was the Aventine Hill instead. Being of the particular mindset that waits for the last possible moment before asking directions, he was at the summit of the Aventine Hill before admitting to himself that he had no idea what he was doing and wondered why he had not stopped to ask. Finally, he accosted a friendly looking passer-by and asked him if he had heard of Villa Metilia.

"Oh, you mean the slave ecclesia! It's over on the Janiculan Hill at the other side of the river. You can see the hill from here, and probably that's the outline of the villa just there," he gesticulated, shading his eyes and squinting away into the rising sunlight.

"I need my horse," Anthony responded, thinking out loud and thanking the stranger. Then he headed frustratedly back to the

Palatine Hill. By the time he had recovered his horse and made his way down over the Milvian Bridge across to the Janiculan Hill, it was mid-afternoon and the burial of Commodus was just concluding. He was standing with his horse at the back of the gathered companions in the orange grove when Felix spotted him and drew Titus' attention. It was not until that moment that it dawned on either of them that they had just buried the emperor's friend and chief-of-staff without consulting him. They looked at each other, crestfallen, by now fully aware that the officer was Anthony from the emperor's turma come looking for them.

"Come on, we've got some explaining to do," said Felix. Titus turned to Nesta. "I'm going to have to go, I'm so sorry. Constantine's officer is here looking for us. He will need us, and we will need to explain why we did this without him."

"Oh no!" Nesta responded. "He should have been here, but he couldn't have been, not easily, not as emperor. He would have wanted to bury him with full military honours at the Palatine or somewhere. And it simply wouldn't have been the same."

"It's alright, we'll explain," retorted Titus. "Knowing him, he'll definitely want to come and pay his respects here, once he's got over the shock and annoyance of being left out. So let the others know we'll be back soon enough with the emperor himself in tow. But right now, we must go."

Earlier that morning, while Decurio Anthony was wending his way up onto the Aventine Hill, Brutus helped himself to a small horse-drawn plaustrum from the palace stables, headed down from the Palatine and made his way across the rafts of the Milvian Bridge to the far side. There he halted the plaustrum close to the ship where he had secured Maxentius' body and, as stealthily as possible, climbed back over the stern of the ship to pull the sack containing Maxentius' body parts onto the raft bridge. Brutus was extremely fit and, with a confident look around at the several small traders, scavengers and the like scurrying by, he picked up the sack for all the world as if it was a bag of sail sheets, and deposited it onto the cart. He looked carefully round once more, and as far as he could tell attracted no unusual attention. Nevertheless, he waited a few moments to ascertain that all the passers-by had proceeded without suspicion before heading back across the bridge and up the Via Flaminia to the palace. There he found an empty stall in the stable yard where he deposited his burden and covered it with straw. Content that it would be safe there for a few hours at least, he headed across to the vestibulum of the palace, and looked into the atrium. Although there was no sign of Helena, her lady-in-waiting was doing exactly that, waiting, just as the empress had promised. She looked up as he appeared, and setting down a garment which she was sewing, came across to him.

"Please wait here, Brutus," she said, "and I will fetch the empress."

Helena soon appeared and led him into one of several anterooms. "Thank you for coming. It will be more private here," she began. "Have you done as I asked?"

"The body is right here in the stables, in a sack hidden under straw in an empty stall," Brutus replied.

"That's wonderful," responded Helena. "Now for the next phase of our plan." Brutus noticed the "our" but remained expressionless, waiting for what followed. "We need a show of power. Not just to Rome, who seem pretty supportive of Constantine. But throughout those parts of Italy and the empire where Maxentius held sway. What I want to do is publicly display Maxentius' head, first of all through the streets of Rome, and then all the way back up to Mediolanum and particularly in Verona. After that across to Carthage."

If Brutus was at all taken aback by this, he didn't show it. Instead, he remarked, "Well, I've already severed the head, so that helps."

Helena looked at him appreciatively. "Well done," she replied. "We need to begin this quickly, if possible this very day. But there is one more aspect to it. I want to display one of the labarum I had made for the battle alongside it."

"How exactly are you planning to do this?" Brutus asked.

"Well, I'd like your advice and help of course," continued the empress, "but I was thinking that a chariot would be best. It would carry the sense of spectacle, as well as being able to move relatively quickly in a small defensive caravan of other chariots."

"We would need some method of securing a stake to display the head and the labarum alongside, but it should be relatively easy to achieve," Brutus responded.

"Then how soon can it all be ready?" Helena enquired.

"It can be ready in an hour or two," Brutus continued, "but won't this need to be run past the emperor?"

"He fully supports it," the empress retorted, looking shocked. "Do you think I'd do such a thing without his agreement?"

"In which case, consider it done, Your Excellency," he replied.

"Then be sure to have it ready by the middle of the afternoon. I will join you for the first display. Make sure that there is a chariot suitable for me. I will see you in the stable courtyard at the third hour this afternoon."

***

Titus and Felix selected two horses from the Metilia stables, theirs having been left at the imperial palace when they borrowed the plaustrum. Then, without taking time to explain themselves further to anyone, they left with Anthony for the palace. On their arrival, leaving Anthony to see to the horses, they made their way immediately to the atrium where they found Constantine pacing up and down in considerable distress, anxious for their welfare. Seeing them, his countenance lifted and broke into his characteristic broad smile.

"Am I glad to see you? What a relief! I was beginning to think you might be injured or killed right at the time I need you most. Commodus is dead you know and I'm desperate to find his body and give him a hero's burial. After that I need to consult with you on the way ahead."

"Commodus is found," said Titus. "We found him yesterday lying dead where he fell at the foot of the raft bridge."

"What, you found him yesterday? Then why was I not informed?"

"This won't please you, Constantine," Felix responded, "and we are very sorry, but we both felt strongly to take his body to his sister up at the Villa Metilia. Then events rather overtook us."

"What events?" asked Constantine, colouring angrily.

"You are our very dear friend and emperor, please forgive us," Felix replied. "We buried him without you."

For a few moments Constantine looked as if he would be overwhelmed with rage and emotion. But then, passing his hand over his forehead as tears rolled down his cheeks, he reached out his arms and embraced them both.

"No, forgive *me*," he replied. "You did what love motivated you to do, and it was wisdom too. I'm Emperor of the West, the possessor of Rome's throne. I could not have simply buried my most trusted general over at Villa Metilia. I would have given him full honours here on the Palatine. But he's better resting there."

The two comēs heaved sighs of relief in the emperor's embrace.

"Will you come with us now to pay your respects, or are their immediate actions you must take here to consolidate power?"

"It's the kingdom of peace that comes first still," Constantine retorted. "What better place to consolidate that than over on the

Janiculan Hill with my family and friends of the slave ecclesia? Come on, let's go."

Hardly had the horse-borne trio left the Palatine before Brutus led the promised caravan of four chariots into the entrance square of the palace. Helena, silently and unseen, had observed the conversation and departure of her son and his comēs. She rightly discerned that this was not the time to reveal her plan to the emperor and was on tenterhooks lest the caravan appeared before he had left. Now she swept out of the vestibulum without the least sign of her concern.

"Well done, praefectus! Show me how you have secured the head and the labarum." She was quite confident that Brutus would have organised this perfectly, but was looking to delay their exit in time for Constantine and the comēs to be well on their way. She rightly expected, and indeed wanted, a huge commotion to be stirred as the chariots made their way around the Palatine and down the Via Flaminia. But she wanted to ensure that there would be no preventing her plan until it was beyond curtailment. She remained confident that she could justify it to her son, but she knew it would be no easy task. If they encountered each other prematurely, he would probably resist her.

In the event, he had long crossed the bridge and was heading up the Janiculan Hill before the caravan made its way into the busy city centre. News of the display spread quickly through the surrounding streets and before long the Via Flaminia was thronged with spectators. At first the ghastly head and the strange ensign were greeted with uncertainty, but then some among the crowds recognised the head's identity. Before long the news that it was Maxentius' head and the banner that had heralded Constantine's victory spread throughout the growing crowd. Soon the silence gave way to cheers, and chants of "Emperor Constantine Victor" and "*in hoc signo vinces*" accompanied their progress throughout the city.

***

Titus' and Felix's parting words to Nesta in expectation that they would soon return with the emperor were taken very seriously by the Metilians. Nesta had immediately informed Claudia and Valeria and the intended funeral feast was temporarily halted while it was expanded in content and quantity in expectation of the emperor's arrival. So it was that the trio entered the courtyard to a welcoming reception of Claudia, Valeria, Melissa, and Nesta. Dismounting, they were ushered into the vestibulum where Dunnius, the ageing Fortunatus, a maturing Junia and Jonas and others who led among the ecclesia joined them. Then, as they entered the atrium, what seemed to be the whole of the rest of the residents of the villa – few remained slaves except for several newcomers fleeing from violent masters and mistresses – broke into song, and the certainties of the twenty-third psalm filled the villa:

"In death's dark vale, I fear no ill, with you O Lord beside me, your rod and staff my comfort still, your cross before to guide me."

While recognising the honour being shown for his position as Emperor of the West, Constantine drank gratefully in the deeper glory of the ecclesia's commitment to the kingdom of love. He knew that another than he was lord here, and that his honoured chief of the Scholai Palatinae was lauded for his embodiment of the deeper glory of peace-making and not the dubious compromise of war and assassination. As the assembled crowd began to serve each other from the laden tables, he turned to Titus and Nesta who were by now hand in hand beside him.

"First take me to Commodus' grave, before I eat or drink anything," he asked, his voice breaking. So they led him out into the peristyle from where a path led across to the orange grove. On her favourite seat in the peristyle sat Eusébie, seemingly waiting for them. "Welcome, dear Constantine," she said, rising to her feet. "Please forgive me for not being with the others to welcome you. I wanted to keep my head clear for what I'm beginning to see. I thought you would probably come this way to the grave. May I join you?"

"It is a great joy to see you again," Eusébie," replied the emperor. "Yes, please accompany us, and after I have mourned my friend, please tell us what it is that you are seeing."

The late October sunshine silhouetted the whole city as the five fellow mourners stood at the grave. After a few moments Constantine knelt and, gathering a handful of the fresh soil, ran it through his fingers. Then, quite without embarrassment, he wept uncontrollably. When his tears subsided he spoke from the heart: "You understood my dilemma, dear friend. You lived it with me. How will I manage without you?" They remained together in the deep stillness for a long time.

Then Eusébie spoke. "Constantine, may I tell you now, what I see?" she asked.

"Please, please do. I need to hear this, I know."

"It's about the cross," she said. "It doesn't belong on a chain, on a vestment or on a banner. It belongs in the heart and it beams out love from there. John of Patmos knew all about it when he wrote the words he heard from the risen Christ. 'He who conquers and who keeps my works until the end, I will give him authority over the nations, and he shall rule them with a rod of iron, as when earthen pots are broken in pieces, even as I myself have received authority from my Father.' The kind of conquering authority he speaks of here is the overcoming love which breaks through all the dominance and violence of empire, its power and its money, its cruelty and disregard for humankind. On the cross, the Trinity soaked up all of it in uncontrolling love. You know this. With the help of your brothers and sisters, you can do this."

Constantine looked at her blind eyes but sensed her deeply seeing heart. "As Constantine with my friends I can. As Emperor of Rome, it's much harder. But you are right, I want it, and it's why I came here six years ago to ask the help of you, dear friends."

Later that evening, after the funeral feast, Constantine sat in the now almost deserted atrium with Titus, Felix, Claudia, Valeria, Melissa, Fortunatus and Dunnius, gathered together around the fire that burnt brightly in the centre of the room and staunched the chill of the autumn evening. Dunnius still felt awkward with Constantine, especially now he was undisputed emperor of the whole Western Empire. Old military sensitivities die slowly. But Constantine deliberately reached out and took his hand. "I need your wisdom," he said, "especially now Commodus is no longer at my side." And turning to the rest, "I need to know what you think I should do next," he said. "I can't promise to do it, but I do agree to take all that you say very seriously."

It was his sister-in-law Valeria who spoke up first.

"You should bring Fausta and Crispus here to Rome to join you. She loves you and I know you love her. Crispus must miss you hugely too. At the same time you can bring Marcus back. He must be quite recovered by now, and he is my only son!"

Dunnius surprised himself by speaking up next.

"I've been thinking about Licinius. He remains a threat. Would it be possible to arrange some kind of diarchy, with you the senior of course? That way you can extend your authority across the whole empire without further bloodshed."

Constantine smiled benevolently at them all.

"This makes good sense to me. Of course Fausta must come, and the last thing I want is to pick a fight with Licinius. But I do want to establish my position as sole emperor, so I can give space for the true authority that Eusébie has been talking to me about."

The others all looked at Eusébie. "I was speaking about the true cross being the ultimate loving heart of God," she said, "when we were together at Commodus' grave."

Melissa cleared her throat. "I am going to raise something that is very sensitive," she said. "It's about your mother." Constantine shifted his legs, and a frown passed across his face. "I hear that the labarum was her idea."

"I won't ask where you heard that from," the emperor retorted.

It was Felix's turn to shuffle his feet. Melissa continued, "It's right to honour your mother, but fortunately once we're adults we are no longer expected to obey them."

Felix nodded gratefully.

A tangible silence fell. Constantine was inscrutable, and everyone, not least Melissa, wondered if she had gone too far. Then, exactly as the comēs had experienced so many times in the past six years together, he threw back his head and laughed uproariously.

"You've got some courage taking her on," he replied, "so you'd better pray for me on that account!"

It was now late, and Claudia asked whether the emperor would like to stay the night.

"I'm sorry," he replied. "I must get back." And looking apologetically at Titus, he continued, "And I'm going to need the help of my comēs."

"Then you are going to need torches to light your way," interposed Fortunatus. "I'll find a couple of reliable fellows to accompany you with them."

Titus slipped away to take his leave of Nesta and Amadeus, promising to be back and forth between the palace and villa just as often as possible. Felix took reluctant leave of his ageing parents. While this was going on Claudia quizzed Constantine caringly about Crispus, promising that he would always be welcome at Villa Metilia once he was back in Rome. Finally, the torch-lit trio headed back for the city.

Back at the palace, Constantine was greeted by Brutus with the news that the display through the streets had gone very well indeed. The emperor, of course, had no idea what he was talking about. Brutus, on the other hand, having been informed from the start by Helena that Constantine knew all about and supported the plan, was nonplussed that he didn't understand him right way. After all, he had surely been wondering all day how it was going and wanting a report. Indeed Brutus, tired out by organising and leading the whole initiative all the time under the imperious authority of Helena, had deliberately stayed up late in order to reassure the emperor that it had gone well.

"I'm sorry, Brutus, have I forgotten something?" the emperor asked. As the awkward possibility dawned on the praefectus that the empress had lied to him and engaged the Scholai Palatinae in an unapproved venture that was entirely her own initiative, Brutus tried to improvise.

"I think I possibly misunderstood the empress, Your Excellency," he began. "She has an ambitious plan to advertise and affirm the authority you have gained in battle by demonstrating it throughout the city and particularly back to Verona and maybe across to Carthage."

"And what exactly is this plan?" Constantine asked ominously.

"She has managed to retrieve the head of Maxentius and create an awesome display of it on a stake alongside the labarum on a chariot which forms the centrepiece of a caravan that has been displayed this afternoon and evening throughout the streets of the city."

"She has, has she? And where is she now?" enquired Constantine.

"She has retired to her apartments, my lord. She played a central role in the procession and I think she was quite worn out."

"Yes," the emperor replied. "I imagine she is, quite. Nevertheless, I would like you to fetch her now."

Helena had half-expected Constantine's summons and was well prepared for it. She had put on a soft and comfortable evening gown in which she looked less imperious and more homely than in her usual attire, and entered the room deferentially, as if coming to enquire after any needs he might have.

"Eho, Mater," Constantine began. "Since when are you the main authority in the empire?"

"Whatever is the matter, dear, have I done something you disapprove of?" she replied.

"Done something I disapprove of? Now don't go pretending that you don't know full well what I'm talking about! Displaying Maxentius' head around the city, and with the labarum you had made without my authority in the first place?"

"I'm sorry, Constantine," continued Helena, her voice strengthening and her look becoming much more challenging. "In both instances it was something that needed doing, and I wasn't sure that you would do it."

"Vah!" responded the emperor angrily. "For sure you didn't think I would do it. The labarum, probably not; Maxentius' head, definitely not. But in any case, you can't go taking authoritative initiatives into your own hands. I am the emperor and any authority you may have derives from me and only me."

Helena met his gaze unflinchingly.

"What's done is done. You will be grateful in the end."

"This horrible dishonour of Maxentius must stop now," her son replied.

"No, Constantine," she continued, "You would only appear weak. The majority of the city have already seen it or know of it and are glad. They also know that the caravan is going to Verona and after that across to Carthage. If you go back on it now it will have the opposite effect of affirming your authority. Instead you will appear irresolute and indecisive".

The emperor hesitated. She pressed on immediately. "Furthermore, I want you to promise me something. I know that you value the advice of your Metilian comēs rei militaris. Of course, you will continue to listen to and receive their wisdom when it is of benefit. But will you please make time and space for Eusebius of Caesarea? He is a highly reputable fellow believer and scholar and as you know he also has committed himself to your noble cause."

Constantine stood silently contemplating his mother for some time. She in turn continued to meet his gaze, undaunted.

"Three things, Mater," he then responded. "Get this gruesome business finished quickly. Have the display despatched to Verona first thing tomorrow. Then get it back here and shipped to Carthage permanently. And do or say nothing else about it. Secondly, I am sending for the Empress Fausta to join me here as soon as possible. You will say nothing to her of this ill treatment of her brother's body. She will take responsibility for all court domestic matters. You will be honoured as dowager empress but you will respect her wishes. Finally, thank you for securing the services of the prelate Eusebius. He will be helpful to me. Please go ahead and let him know I will appreciate regular audiences with him. That will be all, Mater."

And with that he turned on his heel and left for bed. Helena stood for a moment, considering what had transpired. Then she made her own way to bed, concluding that things had gone well, considering. And she would deal with Fausta in her own inimitable way.

The following morning Dunnius was surprised by the return of Decurio Anthony to Villa Metilia. He was more surprised still to discover that he carried a formal request from the emperor that he should return with the cavalryman to the Palatine. Eliciting nothing from the decurio, who in fact had no idea what the summons was about, he left a message with Jonas to let Eusébie, Melissa, Fuscian and the other informal leaders among the Metilians know what had transpired, and headed off immediately to the city. On arriving at the imperial palace,

Anthony left him briefly in the vestibulum but within a few minutes the emperor himself appeared.

"Thank you so much for coming," Constantine greeted him warmly, leading the way into the royal apartment where an informal cena was awaiting them, and where Anthony was already seated. "I have a favour to ask," began the emperor, "but first eat, and I will explain the thinking behind my request." Dunnius and Anthony helped themselves to the steaming savoury porridge as Constantine continued, smiling at the veteran soldier-come-disciple. "I have long held you in great respect, and observed your labour of love among the companions from Ambianum to Rome." Dunnius listened respectfully. "I am in need of a personal legate who understands the empire but at the same time is committed to the kingdom of love. There are not many such, and you are by now a veteran of both."

"Surely your comēs rei militaris are exactly that?" Dunnius replied.

"That is true," agreed Constantine, "but I need Titus and Felix with me, and Marcus is still in Augusta Treverorum. Which is why I need you on board too. I need someone I can trust fully, and who understands our mission, to go to the Western imperial court there and bring Marcus, together with Crispus, Constantia and the Empress Fausta, back here to Rome. If Commodus were still alive I would have sent him, as he understood everything we face. I need you to explain to them why I need them urgently to help me establish a court where the companions of the way are fully represented. Anthony here will travel with you, and you can return with such of their courtiers as they choose. You will need to leave behind a trustworthy praefectus, maybe Rictiovarus, if he's not too old for it by now. And see if you can persuade Lactantius to return with you too."

Dunnius leant back on the luxurious couch, contemplating the arduous journey to and fro between Rome and Gaul, a trip he had undertaken many times. He remembered the childhood trips with his military family, the military marches with the legions, and his many excursions as emissary between the slave ecclesia and the companions and their school in Ambianum. But most vividly of all he recalled the journey with the young Acco to Villa Metilia bearing the news of Quentin's martyrdom. But now he was sixty-nine years old, and had begun to assume that his travelling days were coming to an end. Nevertheless, the request elated him, and Fuscian, while too old and feeble in body to make the journey in his stead, was well large enough in spirit to fill his space in the ecclesia. It seemed a satisfying culmination of all those journeys, an opportunity to bring together the two halves of his life as Roman veteran and leader among the new humanity.

The emperor surveyed him appreciatively, waiting patiently for his response. He thought back to their first meeting at the companions' villa in Ambianum and how the veteran's hair had glowed like a halo in the moments before he had introduced Fausta to him for the first time. "So that's why I want him for this task," he mused silently to himself. He was the obvious protector for his wife and son. Maybe there was a specific ongoing role for him as their own personal comēs and pastor. "Jesus, help him decide to do this," he prayed. They sat silently musing to themselves for quite some time, now entirely at ease in one another's company, while Anthony continued to devour the remains of the *cena*. Then the emperor emerged from his reverie with a start. "There's some urgency, Dunnius. I need to get them here as soon as possible. So will you do this for me?"

"It will be an honour," he replied. "Give me a day to organise a few things with the slave and prison ecclesiae and I'll head out tomorrow. But there is one more thing. I will need to take a couple of younger companions with me, to assist me on the journey alongside Anthony here and to be ready to head on to Ambianum to seek out Rictiovarus if required."

"Do you have anyone particular in mind?" asked the emperor.

"Yes, I do," Dunnius replied. "Jonas and Junia will be ideal."

"A young woman?" Constantine responded, nonplussed.

"Yes, definitely," the veteran continued. "They are a couple and a perfect team. And this is the way of life in the kingdom of love. Neither rich nor poor, bond nor free, male nor female."

The emperor threw back his head and laughed delightedly. "It is indeed," he replied.

Dunnius headed excitedly back across the Tiber and up the Janiculan Hill. Gathering together the nucleus of informal leaders he told them of his commission from Constantine.

"He's doing it then," said Valeria. "Bringing them back to help form a company of friends and advisers at the court."

"I would like you two, Junia and Jonas, to accompany me alongside Decurio Anthony from the Scholai Palatinae," Dunnius asked. "Will you come?" They looked at each other, enquiringly. They had been trying for some time to conceive a child. Would such a trip help or hinder? Junia took Jonas' hand.

"We'll come, and gladly," she replied.

"When do we leave?" Jonas asked.

"Tomorrow morning," Dunnius replied. "Anthony will be here with supplies and horses first thing."

Then Eusébie spoke up. "This is momentous," she said. "Let's call a special meeting of the ecclesia for this evening. We need to commission you for this. It is the coming together of two streams, two authorities that can't yet be fully separated or fully united. So special grace needs must encompass them until times of resolution come."

That evening as the ecclesia gathered in the atrium, Dunnius remembered his first encounter with the slave ecclesia, as he and Acco brought the news of Quentin's extraordinary death. Then they were seated on logs and bales in the barn down at the farm. But the same unmistakeable presence of the Spirit that had been with them then was among them now. Eusébie too remembered that day, and despite the passage of the years, the dreams and interpretations were as real to her now as then. And although for most of that time the labyrinth beneath her feet had been obscured by her blind eyes, she saw it still in her spirit, and knew that the feet that walked on it were the bearers of the good news of the Minotaur's ultimate defeat. As the songs and prayers came to a crescendo proceeded by a familiar weighty stillness, she stood to her feet and began to recite the words of Isaiah the prophet. "How beautiful upon the mountains are the feet of him who brings good tidings, who publishes peace, who brings good tidings of good, who publishes salvation, who says to Zion, 'Your God reigns.'" Reaching out her arms to Dunnius and calling Junia and Jonas to join them, she began to pray. "Let this journey be filled with fruitfulness. The Trinity be your portion, the emperor's call be heard and received with faith, hope and love, and may a new phase of peace for the empire begin."

***

A late autumnal lull in a period of strong winds and rains brought a soporific sense of peace to Augusta Treverorum. A welcoming fire was burning in the centre of the atrium where Fausta, Crispus and Constantia were seated, exchanging stories of their extraordinary childhoods. They found great comfort in each other's company, discovering that the very adversities that marked and separated them from the lives of their friends and acquaintances in court and ecclesia drew them together in an inseparable bond. On the other side of the atrium, Marcus, Lactantius and Rictiovarus were busily debating the practical realities of loving diplomacy in the surviving institutions and customs of the changing empire. The three imperial heirs had just descended into laughter at Crispus' exaggerated account of tumbling out of the tree at the sight of his father's chariot entering the gate to the Chlorus family villa in Naissus, when

Dunnius and his companions entered through the vestibulum. The laughter, the discussion and the brightness of the fire combined together into an overarching embrace of welcome. It had been a demanding three-week journey through the autumn winds and rain. Almost immediately the embrace became a literal human one as the occupants of the court recognised Dunnius and rose to meet him and his three comrades.

Dunnius stood tall with his arms open wide in introduction.

"This is Decurio Anthony of the Scholai Palatinae, and these are Junia and her husband Jonas from Villa Metilia on the Janiculan Hill. We come with greetings and an important request from Emperor Constantine."

"You are most welcome here," responded Fausta. "I have been longing for news of Constantine, who I miss unbearably! But first, let me see, who doesn't know who? Or is it only me that doesn't know everyone already?"

"Well, I don't know Decurio Anthony," responded Crispus. "Although it's been a long time since I met you, Jonas, and you, Junia, as a boy at Villa Metilia. But you stood out to me!"

"It's an honour to be here, Your Excellences," Jonas and Junia responded.

"Well, I'm Fausta and it is first names only from now on," responded Fausta. "We are all companions here, and that includes you, Anthony, if you don't mind." The decurio had begun to understand something of the nature of the way on his journey from Rome with Dunnius and the two ex-slaves, now free citizens.

"Well, thank you, Fausta," he replied awkwardly. In point of fact, apart from Dunnius, who passed through twice en route to Ambianum in the years since Constantine became emperor and established them there, the other three were unknown to the rest, apart from Crispus. So Constantia, Lactantius and Rictiovarus stepped forward and held out their hands to them. Then Marcus, who had been holding back while Fausta had led the welcomes, flung his arms around Junia and Jonas, tears flowing openly down his face.

"It's been too, too, long," he cried. "How I've missed you and all the slave ecclesia!" They remained in an extended embrace until Fausta interrupted.

"But you must all be quite exhausted and probably starving. Let me call Theodoricus the chamberlain and he will find you rooms and water while we let the kitchens know that we are an extra four for cena. Then after you are refreshed and we have eaten, you can tell us the reason for this wonderful surprise visit!"

Later that evening, refreshed and fed, with talk of the journey, the recent events at Milvian Bridge and the taking of the city having filled their dinner conversation, they relaxed back on their couches. "So, tell us, Dunnius," Fausta began. "Are we to come back with you to Rome? Is that the request?"

"Yes," replied Dunnius, looking enquiringly around the table. "What do you think about that?"

There was silence for a few moments.

"All of us?" interposed Crispus. "What will happen to this city, the court and the surrounding Western Empire?"

"Well, that's one reason why I have been so pleased to see Rictiovarus already here," Dunnius continued, meeting the procurator's eyes. "Constantine would like you to remain here as praefectus."

"I'm your age, Dunnius, and while I'm willing to do it for a year or so, it needs a Caesar here in the long term and several fresh legions to keep the empire from breaking up in Gaul and beyond. And I'm not sure I want to give my last years to Rome. The kingdom of love is what I'm focused on these days, as you certainly know. But hopefully Lactantius can help me with that!"

"I'm sorry, old friend," Dunnius continued, "But Constantine is eager for Lactantius to join him together with Fausta, Crispus and his daughter. And as for you, Marcus, he and your fellow comēs are desperate to have you back with them, not to forget your mater!"

"Well, I'm excited," exclaimed Constantia. "I love you all, but I have become restless here. I'm ready for the next stage of my life now I'm sixteen! When do we leave?"

"Constantine is keen to have you with him as soon as possible," Dunnius responded. "He says to bring any special courtiers you require, but to be honest, I think we need to leave before the month is out."

"That's but three days," said Marcus. Fausta stood up, her face wreathed in smiles.

"Well in which case let's head for bed and get organising in the morning. If Constantine wants us, he shall have us!" she declared.

That night Junia and Jonas lay in bed reflecting on the day's events. Here they were among the patrician heirs to the Pax Romana, but carrying a different peace. A way of love that had brought them, slave girl and stable hand, to free and open companionship with the emperor's son and heir and his wife and empress.

"Wow, here we are then," observed Jonas, gently brushing Junia's hair away from her face, luxuriant in the candle light. "Quite literally ambassadors of the Emperor of the West, making love together in the guest apartments of his imperial palace!"

"That's not what's brought us here though," she responded. "We are bearers of a deeper peace. The representatives of the Prince of Peace!" Taking Jonas' hand in hers she began quietly to recite the words of Isaiah the prophet. "For unto us a child is born, unto us a son is given."

Jonas joined in, tears flowing down his cheeks. "And the government shall be upon his shoulder. And his name shall be called Wonderful, Counsellor, Almighty God, Everlasting Father and Prince of Peace. Eusébie's prayer for our fruitfulness will be fulfilled tonight," he said.

"And may our child, boy or girl, play their part in the new phase of peace for the empire that she prayed for," added Junia, enfolding him in her arms.

Chapter Thirteen

Governing Bodies

On the first day after their arrival in Rome, the whole party from Augusta Treverorum were seated for cena with the emperor in the imperial palace's dining plaza on the Palatine Hill. Dunnius and Anthony were with them still, together with Junia and Jonas, and Constantine had made sure that Titus and Felix were there too, together with Helena, Brutus and Eusebius. This would be his court of advisers for the coming years. He was well aware that it would be a challenging consortium to hold together, but he was determined to make it work. Helena's strength of purpose, Brutus' intelligence network and Eusebius' political theology would be the foil for the comēs' ingenuous idealism, Dunnius' peace-making and Lactantius' loving counter-politics. For the time being at least, he and his two heirs would embody imperial authority and Fausta would manage the domestic arrangements of the court. Hopefully, she would lovingly extend his reach with more heirs to imperial power. It would all take time, but in due course the empires of love and sovereignty would intertwine to form a new, true Pax Romana. That was the plan anyway.

The meal passed pleasantly enough. Helena's skills at holding and facilitating space were at their height, as he knew they would be. And Eusebius was at his obsequious best, genuinely honouring Lactantius and Dunnius, respecting their wisdom while preferring his own. He was going to have to handle his mother and the prelate carefully, Constantine reflected to himself, but if he did so then they would hold a wide space for his plans which the loving grace of his more radical friends would fill and in which his imperial authority would sit. While the conversation ebbed and flowed he took time to survey his court. There were fourteen in all, not counting Theodoricus and Calvia, the two courtiers who had come from Treverorum, or Donna, Helena's lady-in-waiting, and Aristarchus, Eusebius' novitiate. He would make plain that they were welcome as apprentices and observers. He was in two minds about Junia and Jonas. Should he regard them similarly? He was aware, however, that while Donna and Aristarchus and the two courtiers from Augusta Treverorum were from a culture in which they would regard this as an honour, the two young Metilians were of the counter-political mindset of the freed citizens of the slave ecclesia where the protocols were more egalitarian. They would be twelve without them. He decided to take the risk of recognising them as part of the fourteen. The senate would need calming, of course, but to begin with he would look after that and in due course appoint a consul.

"Replenish the glasses," he requested. Helena snapped her fingers at the chamberlain. Not something Fausta would do once she was in position, Constantine observed to himself. He wanted a staff that served gladly, like Erastus had done for his father. The chamberlain, in turn, barked instructions to the wine waiter, who approached the table with a flagon.

"Can I do it?" interrupted Junia, politely, rising to her feet. The man hesitated at first. Helena looked imperiously across the table at the young woman.

"Thank you," he said, handing it to her. She began to pour the wine around the table.

"This is the way we do things in the slave ecclesia," she said, holding the empress' gaze. Maybe you can do it yourself another time."

"Thank you, young lady," she replied, presenting her most magnanimous smile. "I would be delighted to take your lead." She's not even lying, Constantine reflected. She means it. But not out of any inner change. She views it as ridiculous, but regards her position as benevolent dowager and *proavia* as more important for her to establish.

Rising to his feet he addressed them all.

"You may be wondering quite why you are here. But to me the reason is simple. You are those who I wish to advise me in the work of consolidating my rule across the whole empire, West to East. There are fourteen of you; my Empress Fausta and you my son Crispus, and you Mater, as dowager empress, and you Constantia, my dear sister. And how could I be without my three honoured comēs, Felix, Titus, and Marcus? Then you, Lactantius, my teacher from my youth, now supplemented by the venerable Eusebius. Keeping a wise and pastoral eye on us all, and particularly as comēs to my wife and royal heirs is Dunnius here, while guarding us from the political wiles of our opponents is brave Brutus, leader of the Scholai Palatinae and his lieutenant, Decurio Anthony. Finally, and perhaps most surprisingly to some of you, here are Junia and Jonas, greatly respected young leaders among the ecclesia in Rome. Their task is to help multiply companions throughout the city and beyond. The other four of us present, Aristarchus, novitiate to Eusebius, Donna, lady-in-waiting to Empress Helena, Theodoricus, Fausta's doughty chamberlain, and Calvia her assistant, are most welcome as our apprentices, to observe and serve in confidence and faithfulness. He raised his glass. "A toast!" he cried. "To my imperial court!" The whole company rose to their feet and lifted their glasses.

"To the imperial court!" they echoed in unison.

"I would like us to meet for cena every day this week," Constantine explained. "We need a long-term plan to work towards, and I want us to formulate it together."

The following afternoon they all gathered again for cena, as asked. In the intervening hours the members of the emperor's new court had made no attempt to discuss the momentous development with each other. Frankly, all were in a measure of shock. None of them had expected Constantine's complex and inclusive initiative, and they had enough to do to process it internally as they retired late to their beds. The only exceptions were the three comēs, who were perhaps the least surprised, being well used to the emperor's bold and unpredictable moves. After all, it had all begun with his unforeseeable decision to choose them as his key advisers six years before. Ever since that portentous event they were in the habit of spending the last minutes of everyday catching up with each other as and when it was possible, and with Marcus' injury they had missed being together for many weeks. With his return it was particularly important as they had so much to share, not least about Constantine's visions of the cross, and the central part played by the cross worn by the druid that Marcus had encountered in the debatable lands.

"We are going to have to learn the way of the equal cross," Marcus exclaimed, once he had absorbed Felix' and Titus' account of the visions, implications and actions that had ensued, "for if this court is to survive and function, the Trinity and the body of companions living out the cruciform way of love will need to be at its heart."

"Maybe not everyone will see or want that," Titus replied.

"I suspect probably neither the dowager nor the prelate will," surmised Felix, forebodingly. "But love bears all things, believes all things, hopes all things, endures all things, and so shall we if we remain true to one another and our humble heavenly three."

"Come on!" affirmed Marcus.

"Amen to that," concluded Titus. As a result, the three comēs came best prepared for the next day's discussions.

"Eat and drink, dear friends," Constantine cried, throwing back his head and laughing. "I can't tell you how excited I am with you all. I hope you won't mind if I begin right away while we are all still eating. I want to draw the broad outline of what I am seeing, and then together we can begin to fill it in. It won't be a theoretical strategy, either," he continued. "What you help me to plan will be your practical charge too, and so think carefully before you speak! This court is going to be an intensively applied one! As I pointed out last night, there are fourteen of us. What I emphasise now is that fourteen is a significant number in the Hebrew Scriptures. Daniel, in his visions, saw that there would be several fourteen-year periods before the kingdom came in its fullness. So we fourteen will plan our next fourteen years." He looked around at them all. "In fourteen years it will be my vicennial! By then I want to be firmly and finally established as sole emperor."

They sat quietly on their couches, munching and gulping, glad that they were having a working meal. It gave them something to do while they contemplated what was for them all a lengthy period of time. For the youngest like Crispus and Constantia, it was nearly as long as they had lived. For Dunnius, Lactantius and Helena it would see them into old age, if they survived it. For the three comēs, Jonas and Junia it would occupy the deciding part of life. As for the celibate Eusebius and the wily Brutus, they reflected contentedly that if they played their part right, this could make their careers.

"Right, my splendid confidants," the emperor continued, "Who would like to begin?"

"I'll go first," announced Crispus. "I reckon we need three bases from which to govern the empire effectively, even once you are the sole emperor, Pater. So we need to consolidate and establish them in the coming years, starting as soon as possible. Augusta Treverorum needs consolidating, Rome here is obvious, but where should the Eastern base be? It seems to me that Nicomedia is too far east, and in any case it has been too long in the hands of our enemies. So what about Byzantium?"

"Wise words, wise words, young man," declared Helena. "I have been thinking about this too. And I like the idea of a glorious new Rome for the East, based in Byzantium and radiating the splendour of the empire throughout the whole region."

Eusebius nodded, sagely. "His young excellency is quite right about enemy influence in Nicomedia. Maximinus Daza remains a threat to the cause of Christ there. But there is a good chance Licinius will defeat him, which bodes well. Can we make peace with Licinius, maybe as a Caesar under you, Emperor?"

"Good thinking, Eusebius," Constantine acknowledged, meeting the prelate's eyes. "I already have some thoughts about that. I'm thinking of making both Crispus and Licinius co-Caesar under me. Would you be up for that, Crispus?"

"But are you sure we can trust him?" his son replied uncertainly, unsure of whether the suggestion was a mark of trust or recognition of his own youthful inexperience.

"I've been thinking about that," said Constantia. "How about I marry him? I'm sure that I could win him round!" They all looked at her in wonderment. "I'm serious," she continued. "I might be only sixteen, but this is Rome and there's nothing unusual about that. It's what children and siblings of emperors do. It's a better way of peace than war. And my status will protect me. In point of fact I deliberately met with him in Mediolanum on the journey back here, just to check him out. Actually, I quite like him."

"Hang on," interposed Marcus, who had drawn increasingly close to the young princess during his stay at the court in Treverorum. "I know something about dominating patriarchs, and the visionary warnings some of us have had about them. Are you sure you know what this might mean for you?"

"We'll make no final decisions yet," declared Constantine. "You can be certain that I will sound Licinius out carefully before making a move on any of this. But thanks for being ready for it, Constantia."

"You can trust my advice and protection too," Helena added. "I was your age when I married Constantine's father and I learnt a great deal that I wouldn't put myself or you through again."

In the brief lull that followed this discussion, Felix stood to his feet and began to replenish everyone's glasses. They all felt his reassuring presence.

"Well, the emperor can guess my thoughts," he remarked as he served Constantine. "We need an undergirding commitment to maintain and strengthen peace through love and not through war and domination. It's easier said than done, but it is expressly for this purpose that you chose us Metilians in the first place, these six years since. So am I right that it remains the bedrock for our plans? It is the bar to which we must bring everything, and I for one will keep on being your conscience for it."

"Thank you, Felix," Constantine replied, laughing. "You are forever my conscience!"

"Come on!" affirmed Marcus, "But in very practical terms this means that we need to prepare an edict that guarantees freedom of religion throughout the empire as well as draw up a list of diplomatic negotiations that we will have to succeed in if we are to avoid war."

"Then please do exactly as you suggest, Marcus," the emperor continued. Eusebius listened appreciatively.

"It is a great gift that Marcus brings us," he declared. "For my part I recommend church councils, so that we avoid misunderstandings and misrepresentation of doctrine and practice that might test the fault lines of culture and peoples."

"Then we need to strengthen and multiply the companions in the stream of love that poured from the cross," Titus observed. "That's the antidote for acrimonious disagreement. So well done, Constantine, for including Junia and Jonas in our fourteen, for multiplying the stream of love is what they do!"

"As soon as the week is over, we'll be back out there in the prison and on the streets, just as Jesus showed us," agreed Jonas, happily.

"If the poor are with you," continued Junia, "you'll have nothing to fear."

Brutus scowled inwardly, but did his best to contrive an outward expression of acquiescence. It was not that he had no feelings for the poor, but knew from experience that they could be vulnerable to rabble-rousing opportunists. To be honest he had not been beyond stirring them up himself in the complicated years of Maxentius' tenuous hold on Rome before he had made his decision for Constantine.

"I have three recommendations to make alongside these laudable suggestions," he said. "Then let's hear them, Brutus," declared Constantine, "and don't hold back."

"As well as the poor, we need the rich!" he said. "Beginning with the senate. While they no longer have executive power, they do have influence, and they did more or less support Maxentius because he protected their interests. So we must fill the senate with our supporters. My mother and her friends will help with that. She still has much influence despite my father's death."

"That's your task then," responded the emperor. "Enquire who the appropriate candidates are and bring their names to me. Come to think of it, we can begin with Titus here. The House of Metilia has a noble record in the senate. We will hold a celebratory feast and invite them and the existing senators that support me. We won't invite the others, and hopefully they will get the message and drop away. But what of any who persist in opposing me, if any do?"

"That's where my second recommendation comes in," Brutus continued. "We must continue with our policy of covert assassination. None of us likes it, but it is far better than the horrendous wastage of life that is open warfare."

Dunnius contemplated the warrior silently. He has a point, he thought, his eyes meeting Lactantius. But nonetheless he doubted the warrior's genuine loyalty.

"Point accepted," responded Constantine, "but we'll do all we can by love and diplomacy first. And your third recommendation?"

"We must regroup and repair the legions," Brutus continued. "They must be on hand if we need them, at all three bases that Crispus has so sensibly proposed. Here in Rome, back at Treverorum and particularly in the East in the new capital. Indeed, that will need to be a military base before anything else. Wholly new legions utterly loyal to you must be located there."

"Do it all, Brutus," the emperor responded. "You have my full authority."

Helena welcomed Brutus' recommendations wholeheartedly. "I got that right," she reflected to herself, recollecting her rapidly contrived stratagem from the moment they met at Riano. Then she spoke up. "Yes," she said, "I have been thinking about that. About authority and whence it comes. And how it impacts the people from poor to rich, plebeian to patrician. We need symbols and metaphors that carry power in themselves. We have the *labarum* which already carries God's presence on the side of our imperial authority. But I'm thinking of more, much more. I wish to find the true cross, its actual remains. Relics that we can enshrine in these three bases of government. I propose to send an excavation party to Jerusalem to find it and bring it back. I may even go myself, which will also strengthen our authority. Such relics will help establish power if we want to minimise war and violence. Don't you agree?" She looked penetratingly around the rest of the fourteen.

"For sure the cross is most important, Mater," the emperor answered. "And I think by now you all know of my vision and dream before the battle of Milvian Bridge."

The comēs looked at each other. Then Felix spoke up. "The cross certainly matters, Helena." She winced imperceptibly, uncomfortable at his direct address and his use of her name without title. Felix went on. "But what matters is its meaning, not just its mystical power. It's why we need love for friends and enemies alike to undergird everything, because that is what the cross is truly about. Otherwise, the symbols can justify anything, including violence and domination."

Helena sat smiling magnanimously at them all.

"Well, of course, Felix is right," she said, looking at Eusebius. "That's why I want to find the true cross. True and truth go together, and so the true cross will undergird the truth about the cross."

She waited for her words to sink in. Then seamlessly, apparently unaware of the impact of what he was about to say, Eusebius took up the theme.

"But love for authority is where all love begins. Is it not true that we love God because he first loved us? And God is the ultimate authority. Our failure to love him is why everyone is condemned to eternal death. This is why the cross was necessary. Jesus appeased God's offended authority and we need to demonstrate our respect for it too. Which is why I propose that we acknowledge the presence of God's reflected authority on earth, in you, Your Excellency Emperor Constantine. We should kneel when we enter your presence."

And so saying he prostrated himself at Constantine's feet. Titus smothered the temptation to laugh. And looking at the other comēs, and Fausta, Crispus and Constantia, he realised that they all struggled similarly. Constantine looked down at Eusebius, spread-eagled before him, then at the other members of his court. Then he threw back his head and laughed uproariously.

"Do get up, Eusebius," he said. But then, to the now rather red-faced prelate he remarked, "Don't mind us, you actually have a point. When delegations from opposing groups, foreign dignitaries or representatives of potential enemies enter my presence, yes, good idea, let them do me obeisance, but not you, my friends."

In the silence that ensued, Lactantius considered the best way to insert his more egalitarian vision. Thus far he felt he understood Constantine's inclusive approach and supported it.

But he foresaw problems ahead where compromise and nuance might give way to conflict and confusion among them. He remembered the famous companion Tertullian, who he knew that Eusebius respected.

"While there might be situations where imperial authority may be insisted on, Eusebius, and while I admire your own willing humility, we need to recognise the freedom of all to express their discipleship according to their own understanding of the gospel. As I'm sure you remember, Tertullian stated it really clearly to Scapula the Roman magistrate a century ago. 'It is a fundamental right,' he said, 'A power bestowed by nature, that each person should worship according to his own convictions, free from compulsion.'"

"Well said," agreed Dunnius. "You may remember that our friend and mentor Quentin died for that conviction."

At the mention of Quentin, the three comēs looked at Constantine, willing him to further qualify his partial affirmation of the prelate, which he seemed about to do. They knew that he recognised Quentin unequivocally as the source of their quality of life, and an exemplar of the new humanity that he was seeking to inseminate into the new Rome.

"All very good, all very true," intervened Eusebius, before Constantine could speak. "But we must also remember the words of King David, the Psalmist. He well understood the issues here. He recognised the king's two bodies and the need for due honour. He distinguished between himself as David, and David as the king worthy of obeisance, when he said 'The lord said to my lord, sit at my right hand until I make your enemies a footstool for your feet.' He goes on to say that this is what will attract youth to him, and here you are," he said, indicating the three comēs, the two heirs and Jonas and Junia, with a triumphant wave of his hand.

The whole court contemplated the masterful prelate soberly. He certainly knew how to apply his knowledge. And so the day's strategy concluded with an uneasy agreement that in certain formal situations obeisance would be the protocol, but not for the ordinary day-to-day life of the court.

***

Snow was falling in Mediolanum the following February as Licinius and Constantia promised life-long devotion to God and each other before bishop Merocles and the emperor. The palace, with its massive sixteen-metre towers and the surrounding twenty smaller four-sided ones, framed the atrium at the centre of the palace. Huge braziers held back the cold and melted the snow around the dais where the wedding party stood to make their vows. With Marcus' diplomacy in the previous weeks it had finally been agreed that the tetrarchy would be replaced by a diarchy, with Constantine and Licinius as joint emperors. But all knew that Constantine was the superior of the two, and what his ultimate ambitions were. As long as Licinius accepted that and supported him in it, Constantine reflected, all would be well. Whether these sentiments were actually shared by Licinius was unclear. But that very morning the plans for the transition from tetrarchy to diarchy had been finalised and Licinius had agreed to head west and hopefully depose Maximinus Daza as peaceably as possible. He would carry with him a copy of the edict prepared by Marcus, signed by the two emperors and guaranteeing tolerance of all religions throughout the empire. Constantine surveyed Licinius as he stood resplendent in his imperial regalia complete with orb and sceptre beside his beautiful young bride. Although in truth he was easily old enough to be her father, Constantine observed to himself that despite being some seven years his senior, Licinius was an undeniably handsome man and still in the prime of life. The two certainly made an impressive pair. In fact, the whole ceremony had taken on a fairy-tale aspect. He hoped it had not been a mistake to add to his rival's attractiveness as a leader by marrying him to his sister in such a splendid environment.

Afterwards at the wedding feast, Constantine sat back on his couch and observed the dignitaries and family members that surrounded him. Yes, he concluded, his court's strategy was well underway. He squeezed Fausta's hand and turned to speak to her privately.

"You must be tired, my love, travelling all this way and you with child!" he said.

"I'm fine," Fausta replied, "I'd not have missed this for worlds. Constantia is extraordinary, and Licinius seems a good man. But she needs to know that she has my support, and Helena's. And speaking of Helena," she whispered, glancing across at where the empress was deep in conversation with the bishop, "I never know what to make of her, it's as if she is following some unseen strategy all of her own, but so far I must say she has been very kind and supportive of me."

"It's the way she's always been, my darling," Constantine responded. "She weaves a web of complex commitments and stratagems all together without any regard for contradictions. I'm just glad she's being supportive of you."

Fausta turned back to Crispus, who was on the other side of her with Lactantius. The two of them were heading straight on after the feast en route to Augusta Treverorum, taking with them some of the staff from Mediolanum. They would help strengthen the team there which would now permanently replace it as the Western imperial court.

"I half wish I could come with you back to Treverorum. I miss it. Be sure to remember me to Rictiovarus."

Constantine turned to Marcus who he had insisted on having next to him so that they could discuss the necessary further diplomacy.

"Is there anything more we can do to strengthen Licinius' hand in the East without overplaying his role? I'm concerned to establish my own influence rather than his."

Marcus pondered this for a moment. "Brutus will be in Byzantium by the time he arrives or soon after. I'm confident that he is loyal to you. I think we must hope that the show of military might and the edicts of diarchy and religious freedom will be the writing on the wall and Maximinus will go quietly. If not, Brutus' second line of approach will kick in, I suspect. But I will pray for the better outcome."

Constantine put his hand on Marcus' shoulder. "Can you go and join with them as well, Marcus? I would feel better if you did."

Something attracted them both to look up at the towers. An eagle swooped between them.

"This is no ordinary task we have set ourselves, Constantine," Marcus concluded. "We are going to need more than diplomacy, the machinations of the Palatinae or the strength of the legions. I was hoping to spend a few days back at Villa Metilia on our return, and even now that you've asked me to take my team of diplomats to the eastern empire, I will still stop by briefly. We are going to need their prayers."

For the first time, Constantine was aware of some ambiguity in his response to this proposition from Marcus. Was there a possible divergence between what prayer might achieve and what he might be willing to accept? Truth to tell he knew that the Janiculan folk would clearly be supporting him in only one direction. Somehow, he was attempting a middle ground. Yet he also knew that his comēs and Felix in particular were his strength, and that he could hardly continue without them or the prayers of the slave ecclesia.

"Thank you, Marcus," he replied after the briefest of pauses. "You are right. We need their help."

Ineluctably, the ensuing years were about to indicate just how great that help would need to be.

Licinius insisted on heading for Byzantium with his young bride immediately after the wedding. This delighted Constantia. For despite their age difference and a shared recognition of the political terms of their marriage, neither of them felt the arrangement to be problematic. Licinius on the one hand could hardly believe his good fortune. While Constantia both furthered and limited his political prospects, she fired his bodily senses unquenchably. Although his vision to establish himself as emperor of the East remained undimmed, his accompanying desire was to have her beside him in his sight and in his arms as often as possible. For her part, getting to know this man presented itself as the next adventure of her life. It seemed to follow naturally from her rescue out of lonely childhood confinement in the imperial court in Augusta Treverorum into the lively relationships of the posse, then the years in the companions' school with Crispus and Fausta, and life back in the newly constituted imperial court in Treverorum with which she had begun to be so bored. So to go with Licinius to Byzantium was exactly what she wanted, and to be left behind in Mediolanum or Rome would have been insufferable, notwithstanding her role at court.

The journey to Byzantium was more than three weeks long, but once they left the harbour in Ravenna on Licinius' friend Senator Bassianas' personal ship, the weather became unseasonably warm with clear skies and calm seas. Other ships were few, it being the time of the *mare clausum*, and the passage through the Greek islands was utterly memorable. Throughout the ten days at sea the newlyweds divided their time between the wealthy senator's cabin in the stern and drinking in the sparkling beauty of the scenery from the prow of the ship, away from the sail hands and oarsmen. The retainers responsible for preparing food and an elite turma for their protection all lived and slept on the deck with the crew. Constantia's education at Ambianum with Lactantius and Fausta, and the subsequent time at court with them in Augusta Treverorum, had given her an astute political interest in all that was happening. This was something recognised by her brother who had included her in his court not only because she was his half-sister and it was confirmed immediately by her offer to marry Licinius. Now her mind constantly weighed up and turned over the obvious tension between her husband's role as Constantine's brother-in-law and co-emperor and both their pretensions to power. She was as yet unclear as to whether Licinius' desire for leadership included the ultimate goal to displace Constantine. Was he genuinely satisfied with the diarchy, or would he take any opportunity that came along to become sole emperor himself? She had no such question about Constantine. He would support and respect her husband only if he supported his primary role. If he contested him for the leadership their lives would be at risk, and if they had a child, which clearly was Licinius' wish and hope, it would be in great danger in such circumstances. But for now the need for both emperors was the removal of Maximinus Daza, who had established himself in Nicomedia and intended to be emperor of the East, not Licinius, and whose pretensions for power would not stop there.

"You will love Byzantium," Licinius remarked on the second day out from Ravenna as they lay together in their cabin. "The great palace that Severus repaired is dazzlingly beautiful and I am determined that we shall have a splendid apartment there overlooking the hippodrome." "But we'll not be truly safe unless Daza is beaten, will we?" Constantia replied.

"There is a legion encamped around the city, my dear," replied Licinius.

"Yes, but are you sure that they will accept allegiance to you rather than Daza?" she answered.

The emperor was somewhat perplexed at his young wife's engagement with the political reality. "You should not worry your pretty young head about such things," he suggested. Constantia, however, was having none of it.

"I may have a pretty young head, but I'm married to you for more than my body," she answered forthrightly. "And if you want me with you, I will be watching out for our safety just as you will be. And I know that you are hoping for an heir, and if that's to be, that's even more reason to have both our heads attuned to future strategy."

Licinius looked her up and down with a new appreciation.

"Alright," he said. "I grant that you are clearly more than just your outward attractions. But Brutus will soon join us with a full intelligence briefing and his own two newly convened legions. Maximinus is ageing and has always been a dolt in my view. Although he has plenty of troops with him in Nicomedia, by all accounts they are ageing and unwieldy, like him. He will attack, but we will overcome. Mark my words!"

And so it turned out to be. That spring, an ageing and now ailing Maximinus Daza approached Byzantium with no less than 70,000 militia. Marcus, along with his diplomatic team, met with him and his advisers in an attempt to make peace in return for an honourable subordinate role for him under the diarchy, but, despite lengthy deliberations, they got nowhere. Daza and his legions proceeded to surround and lay claim to the city, but not for long and without any lasting victory. Constantia watched them from the balcony of their apartment, by now pregnant with Licinius' child. But at no time did she feel that she or the city were in any real danger. In the end the ill-equipped and weary militia were no match for the legion defending the city, now supplemented by Brutus' newly assembled legions that arrived spoiling for battle. After pushing the massively unwieldy battalions back, they soon routed them. Daza retreated to Nicomedia disguised as a slave and died there the following August. In the weeks that followed, Licinius established his court at Byzantium and between spring and that summer of 313, he, Constantia, Marcus, Brutus, Senator Bassianas and the three legionary tribunes together formed the imperial court of the Eastern Empire. Constantine was delighted to receive the news of the victory over Daza, but determined that the only real imperial court must be his. Having already yielded over his wise young sister, he summoned Marcus and Brutus back to Rome.

Chapter Fourteen

Tension and Conflict

And so began a decade of uneasy tension and occasional outright conflict between the two emperors, which played out in Constantia's own relationships with the two of them, particularly when she visited Rome with Licinius. Once their son Valerius Licinius II was born, such visits became longer for her but shorter for Licinius who was increasingly away battling against the empire's enemies. He enjoyed war and was a master at it. In 314 and 315 the battles initiated by the two emperors to quell uprisings and border incursions entangled into direct conflict between them. But on both occasions Constantia and Marcus intervened to keep the peace and they were reconciled around the greater quest to secure a truly loving Pax Romana. This continued uneasily until 321, when, as a result of Constantine's initiatives to quell threats from the Samartians and the Goths, Licinius complained that he was deliberately breaking the treaty of diarchy between them.

"This can't keep happening," Constantine remarked to Felix at what had become a routine weekly cena meeting between the two of them, Marcus being almost permanently away engaged in diplomacy and Titus occupied with his responsibilities as a senator.

"It won't," responded Felix, "not while Brutus remains chief of the Scholai Palatinae. His option two will kick in sooner rather than later I suspect, unless he senses you are firmly against it."

The emperor lounged back on his couch without speaking for several minutes. "We need a meeting of the whole court to thrash this out," he responded eventually. The court now met only sporadically as and when Constantine felt the need. "I need you all to help me with this. I'm almost sure of what

Helena, Eusebius and Brutus will say, and they may be right. But I want to balance it with the way of love."

"Yes, Constantine, I know you do," retorted Felix. "But I think we may be coming to a wall more insurmountable than the Antonine and an opponent greater than an aurochs!"

"It's why we need the whole court," continued Constantine.

"We'll need the complementary wisdom from the Janiculan Hill too," added Felix. Constantine was silent for a moment, then, somewhat to Felix's relief, threw back his head and laughed.

"Yes, my friend, we certainly will!" he acknowledged.

***

The sun burnt down relentlessly on the orange groves and you could smell, almost taste, their ripening skins in the sultry air.

"They will soon need harvesting," Eusébie reflected inwardly from her shady seat in the peristyle.

Like the Scriptures put it, "While the earth remains, seedtime and harvest, cold and heat, summer and winter, day and night, shall not cease."

"Heia!" she breathed out softly to herself. Thirty-five harvests since she sat here with Quentin after the death of her grandmother, and fifteen since Constantine disturbed their peace that momentous summer's day in 306. "Which peace had he disturbed?" she wondered. "And what peace would come?"

It was now already nine years since she had sat here with Dunnius, Fortunatus, Claudia and Nesta on the eve of the battle of Milvian Bridge, praying for true peace to replace the bloodstained peace of the imperial Pax Romana. On the face of it, maybe some measure of peace for a new humanity had followed that fateful day. From where she sat, she knew, as if she could see it, Commodus' grave lay surrounded by flowers, a reminder of the cost of the supposedly winning strategy.

But despite everything, how much was the peace loving new humanity being harnessed to the cause of the same old imperial power? The murderous murmurations across the Seven Hills were still a regular event as if to remind them that living in "peace as far as it depends on you," as the apostle Paul had advised his followers, was still to be fully grasped.

Most Saturdays Fausta and the children joined the companions on the Janiculan Hill. Constantia and Valerius came too if they were in Rome. The younger children adored Amadeus and he enjoyed inventing imagination games for them to play. And now that Titus was a senator he had been able to join Nesta and his son and make Villa Metilia his permanent home once more. Eusébie loved his optimism and hope for a permanently love-based politics to infiltrate and emanate from the Palatine. The three comēs were still her Daniel posse she reflected, even although they were less often able to be together physically. Marcus was unstinting in his efforts to strengthen the peace throughout the empire's trouble spots. She knew that he was uneasy at the way the threat of assassination and war brought into question the substance and depth of the peace for which he strove. The truth was that Brutus saw diplomacy only as a weapon with which to subdue opposition, rather than the spirit of the messianic peace which was their long-term objective. Overshadowing everything was the increasingly volatile relationship between Licinius and Constantine. It would not end well without a deeper change within the emperor himself, she concluded. As James had written in his famous letter, so foundational to the slave ecclesia, "the harvest of righteousness is sown in peace by those who make peace." And it was this for which she had prayed so diligently throughout the years of the posse's original journeys, and persevered with still.

She heard Titus' feet on the gravel path. He had cut across the grove from the stables hoping to find his aunt at her near permanent post. He was light footed, unlike Lactantius and

Dunnius who would soon follow. Valeria, Melissa and Claudia would not be far behind, hopefully Felix too, she mused. Then she heard Felix calling out a greeting.

"Hey, Titus, how goes the senate's affairs?"

"Unendingly slow and dull, my friend," he replied, "but invariably supportive of Constantine, and I think, hopefully, in pursuit of a loving politics."

"Your influence then!" responded his fellow comēs. They approached with their familiar jocularity, embracing their aunt as she rose to meet them.

"How is the empress of Metilia?" asked Titus. Eusébie gently brushed this aside.

"In which case what do the senate make of the seemingly unresolvable threat of open conflict between Constantine and Licinius? How do they suggest that will end in a truly love-based Pax Romana?"

"Whoa, Aunt," responded Titus. "Straight for the jugular!"

"Straight for the jugular in more ways than one, I fear, if Brutus has anything to do with it," added Felix.

"What's Brutus up to now?" interposed Lactantius, arriving at the tail end of their conversation.

"Something I really want to talk about, so that we can continue to pray more intelligently," Eusébie replied.

Dunnius, Melissa, Valeria and Claudia having by this time also arrived, they pulled the available chairs into a circle around Eusébie.

"What do you see as the heart of the matter?" Felix asked her.

"Well, if we are talking of heart, then you, Felix," she replied. "He loves you and listens to you now more than ever. But I fear that he is trying to hold together two irreconcilables."

"Which are?" Felix enquired.

"Achieving and maintaining supreme power by any means beginning with the least violent, and using the God-given leadership opportunity to make the greatest possible room for love." "I believe you are right, Eusébie," interposed Lactantius, "they can't both stand."

"Is the second one really achievable, anyway?" asked Valeria.

"Yes, I think that the second one is doable," broke in Melissa. "But the two can't mix in the end, and we are coming to a crunch point. Don't forget those childhood dreams, Valeria, that you and I helped Eusébie interpret all those years ago. There is a toxic power at work here, and we have yet to overcome it."

"Brutus represents the bloodiest of approaches," interjected Dunnius, "and is the most susceptible to the shape shifts of the Minotaur."

"Well, with you all behind me, I'm not afraid of the Minotaur!" Felix exclaimed.

"Only the equal cross can deliberate between the two pathways," declared Titus.

"Then that's where I'll be positioned," Felix replied.

***

While their friends were meeting up on the Janiculan Hill, in the city below, Jonas looked on contentedly with his daughter Lucia, now eight years old, as the gathering of the prison ecclesia dispersed. The current inmates were heading back into the prison building while those now free spilled out into the street.

"Tell me how this all began, Pater," she asked, noting how the ecclesia separated in their different directions. So he related yet again the stories she loved to hear of the early days of the ecclesia's formation when he and Junia had come with food for Dunnius, the warders and then eventually for his fellow inmates.

"When Constantine was recognised as Emperor of the West, Flavius Octavius and a Praetorian Guard, aware of the probable fall of Maximian and Maxentius, came and set Dunnius free. That was a day of rejoicing!"

Other times she would demand stories of the subsequent years when the Metilians had continued to engage with the prisoners and the majority of inmates had become members of the prison ecclesia and continued to be so. Then she would recount her own memories of the inmates who she had come to love, gradually emerging as they invariably did from lives of violence and oppression into the freedom and light represented by the young girl.

As with the slave ecclesia, Jonas reflected, those who were part of it embraced and loved on those who were not. So except for just a few who vehemently objected, there was no significant distinction between them all. And as these few were regarded as particular objects of enemy love, even they had become evidence of an alternative rhythm of life. It was hardly surprising, he reflected gladly, that the prison ecclesia had taken on the responsibility for the surrounding city, just as the term ecclesia implied from the beginning. Dunnius had taught them from the start that this word chosen by Jesus to describe his companions derived from the name of the body of citizens called to take responsibility for the wellbeing of a Greek city. He looked forward to the meeting with civic leaders that was about to take place. For, as with the slave ecclesia, an informal leadership eschewing any form of hierarchy had emerged among them, and over the last two years or so their sense of responsibility for the city had motivated them to meet and engage relationally with those civic leaders who were willing to explore initiatives that could inseminate a loving counter-politics. Not unexpectedly, given their practical role in the early stages of the ecclesia, Claudia and Valeria had remained an ongoing part of this, as were Decurio Anthony and Titus, who had joined in more recently together with a number of leading merchants and senators.

This growth of the prison ecclesia had meant that there was need of a meeting place outside the gates but close by where prisoners could come under escort and continue to build with ex-prisoners and their families, friends and newcomers. Many people who had never been prisoners themselves had joined them over the years and swelled their numbers considerably. They had eventually found a disused warehouse adjacent to the prison and it was here that Jonas and the wider group were now assembling.

"It's a kind of alternative court!" exclaimed Junia, joining her husband and daughter and watching the civic leaders beginning to relate quite naturally with some of the existing prisoners and their guards together with others who were now free.

"Not sure how widely or loudly you should say that," he responded.

Junia looked at him inquisitively. "You are thinking that Constantine might not like it?" she asked. "Surely the whole purpose of his job is to make way for this kind of politics?"

"Hopefully," Jonas continued. "But I'm not sure whether he would describe it quite that way."

"Then don't we need to be bold and raise the question when we meet for cena tomorrow with the imperial court? We need to know!" Junia replied.

Crestus, formerly an alcoholic and violent robber who had completed his sentence and was now part of the informal leadership of the ecclesia, welcomed everyone and reminded them of the agenda items from their previous meeting.

"We all agreed last time we were together, that despite whatever is happening on the political main stage, caring for the poor, the homeless, strangers and particularly widows and orphans must be our priority. So can we have a report on the progress of our initiatives to establish shelters at key points throughout the city for food and clothing distribution? And then let's draw up some proposals for long-term changes that we can put to the senate and the imperial court."

There followed a time of exciting reports of the success of the shelters as places of resource and mutual empowerment. Emboldened by this news, the proposal was put forward that the senate should officially fund and staff several such shelters and that the imperial court should be encouraged to pursue the same policy in the three capitals as a prelude to an empire-wide initiative.

"This is the opportunity we need," whispered Junia to Jonas. "We can raise these proposals tomorrow."

Jonas nodded his agreement, while wondering uneasily what the response might be.

Dawn was only just breaking when Constantine rose the following morning. He had slept fitfully, his night broken by a mixture of dreams, memories of dreams, and obstacles encountered on the journeys of the previous fifteen years. These ranged from the moment Cassius awoke him with his father's summons and his impulsive decision to include Crispus and his Metilian cousins in his response, to the initial days of the Daniel posse and the messianic breakthroughs at Lindum, the debatable lands and the Antonine Wall. They culminated in the visions, dreams and brutalities surrounding the battle of Milvian Bridge. Felix's stark remark of the day before yesterday rang continually through it all.

"I think we may be coming to a wall more insurmountable than the Antonine and an opponent greater than an aurochs!"

The problem of Licinius was surely exactly that. While Constantine had only ever partly applied Eusébie's childhood dream of the Minotaur to his own situation, a shadowy recollection of the encounter between the princely knight and the shape-shifting Minotaur now featured in his reveries, recalling the presence of the eagles and the aurochs along the way. The Minotaur had promised to track with the prince and secure him an empire forever if he would lead him out of the labyrinth. But didn't the knight represent the kind of leadership Galerius and Maximian, Maxentius and Maximinus Daza had embodied and that he held in contempt? "In this sign you conquer." The labarum dominated his dreams, its shape increasingly interchangeable with the shape-shifting Minotaur. Surely it was Licinius that the Minotaur tracked with? Or could it actually be him, the great Emperor Constantine?

"I need to escape this cloud of confusion," he exclaimed aloud.

"What confusion, my love?" Fausta asked, emerging dishevelled from the bed and standing rather unsteadily beside him.

"What to do about Licinius," he replied. "We need to resolve it at the meeting of the court today."

"I believe that love will prevail, Constantine, not hate. I fear that he has come to hate you, but you don't hate him. You will prevail in the opposite spirit."

He looked at her, remembering the first time they had met those fifteen years before in the companions' villa at Ambianum. After a moment's hesitation, he threw back his head and laughed.

"You are a pure heart, Fausta, my darling. Where would I be without you?"

That afternoon, after a sumptuous cena of deer roasted in onion sauce followed by stoned dates stuffed with honey-fried pine kernels, they sat back on their couches, waiting for Constantine to introduce the subject of the meeting. They were all fairly certain that it would be what to do about Licinius. Then Helena stood up, still stately and erect despite her seventy-some years, and with her eyes on Junia picked up the wine flagon and beginning with her, proceeded to serve the wine around the table.

"Still at it," her son reflected to himself, recalling the first meeting of the court nine years previously. "What is she really up to?" Then he looked around at the others. The fourteen were all present except for Constantia, who was in Byzantium with her husband and son. Dunnius and Lactantius were now the epitome of venerable elders he had hoped for, and the comēs had matured into the treasured friends and advisers he had expected them to be. Brutus was as brutally committed to the covert work of the emperor's personal military guard as his name implied, his unremitting focus ameliorated by the gentler Anthony. Junia and Jonas were impossible not to love, but he had to admit that their applied idealism left him increasingly uncomfortable. And then there was Eusebius. What to say about the now Bishop of Caesarea Maritima? A theologian and politician if ever there was a combination of the two! For sure his theology gave Constantine's vision to be sole emperor great legitimacy, and his determination to secure the unity of the churches was undaunted. Aristarchus was now appointed as his archdeacon and busied himself in collecting and distributing information, a kind of clerical version of Brutus, but no longer functioning as the bishop's personal assistant, so not present at the court. Donna continued faithfully but silently in her role alongside Helena, and Fausta's two assistants continued to play a senior role in the running of things. They were a veritable hive of information no doubt, for anyone who could get it from them, but thus far had certainly proved themselves reliable.

"Licinius is the primary reason I have called you all together," Constantine began, "but I expect you guessed that already."

Helena was the first to speak up. "I think diplomacy is failing despite Marcus' and Constantia's best efforts," she said. "We surely must find a decisive solution. What do you think, Brutus?"

The emperor shifted uneasily in his seat. He didn't welcome it when his mother intervened directly with her opinions and he knew it was because he did not find it easy to contradict her, especially when others were present. She only acted this way when the influence of the Metilian cohort, as she regarded them, might divert significantly from her own covert plans.

"So what do you think, Brutus?" he repeated, deciding that it was better to have the initiative back in his own hands.

"We should confront his legions now and wait no longer," Brutus replied immediately. "My intelligence is that he is strengthening his ground and naval forces by the day. There may be as many as twenty Eastern legions, and the Eastern fleet has three hundred and fifty ships. Licinius is good at war, no question about that. But we are better Constantine, and we can beat him."

Then Marcus spoke.

"With all respect, Empress Helena," he said, addressing her directly, "diplomacy never fails, even when war appears to be unavoidable. If Brutus is right and Licinius is determined to engage Constantine in battle, there will still be the occasion for diplomacy both before and after any confrontations take place."

"Marcus is right, as ever," interposed Eusebius. "Both Licinius and Constantine have faith in God, although I doubt the depth of Licinius' testimony. But it gives some basis to pursue peace, and to understand that if Constantine is God's chosen representative, which he clearly is, then Licinius should find his subordinate place beside him in the end."

Constantine brightened at this.

"And you, Lactantius, what do you have to say?" he asked.

"Dunnius and I were talking together earlier this morning," he replied. "We feel that at our age and stage we will simply listen and not interfere, but offer our advice and support once the decisions are made, rather than present our opinions beforehand."

Dunnius nodded in agreement.

"Thank you," Constantine replied, "but be sure to let us know what that advice is! We respect it."

"Well here's what I think we should do, Pater," Crispus announced. "I will go to Byzantium with Decurio Anthony and three legions, together with Marcus and his team, and seek peace with Licinius. His legions are dissipated throughout the whole of the Eastern Empire by all accounts, so our three should be enough to overcome him if necessary. In the meantime, you should instruct the Western fleet to make its way to the Bosphorus ready to provide extra support if we need it. If he won't agree to submit to your role as supreme emperor of both East and West we will engage his troops, but only with the aim to capture him, not assassinate him. After all, he is your brother-in-law and the father of your nephew! We will try to persuade him to agree to be a peaceful but subordinate member of this court as Eusebius hopes. At worst he must remain under house arrest for as long as necessary."

"I'll take another two legions to Byzantium, in case of unexpected eventualities," put in Brutus. "The legions we put in place there after we removed Daza may prove loyal to Licinius rather than you, Constantine, and we'll need to be able to overcome them."

The emperor screwed up his face.

"So we will go with this plan of Crispus' although it is all going to take time, given Licinius' expertise and determination, and Marcus' commitment to diplomacy," he concluded, acquiescing irritably. "But my patience is running thin."

Dunnius smiled sympathetically at him. "Relax, Constantine," he said. "You can be sure that our companions on the Janiculan Hill and in the prison ecclesia will be praying for you."

Dunnius' intervention provided the opening Junia was waiting for. "Yes, they certainly will," she exclaimed, "and you will be excited to hear that the prison ecclesia has been growing by leaps and bounds in numbers and influence. In fact, we had a positively messianic meeting yesterday with a group of prisoners and ex-prisoners together with some senators and leading merchants.

They asked us to bring a suggestion to the court when they heard we were meeting today. Is this a good time to raise it?"

"Yes, of course," Constantine responded. "Let's hear it. But first explain what you mean by 'positively messianic'."

This time it was Helena who shifted uneasily in her seat. Junia continued. "Messianic time is when the kingdom of the equal cross emerges in the here and now. When hierarchical distinctions fall away and there is no more male and female, bond and free, Jew or Roman but all work together as one. This is what your reign as emperor has been making room for! Last time the group met they agreed to establish shelters for food and clothing distribution at key points throughout the city. Yesterday there were exciting reports of the success of the shelters as places of resource and mutual empowerment. So we agreed to propose to the senate that they should fund several such shelters and to ask the imperial court to pursue the same policy in the three capital bases of the empire."

"Be encouraged, everyone," added Jonas. "This is the river of love that we have been working together to make way for. And it's beginning to flow! It proves that Constantine's reign has been a success in real terms in these nine years since Milvian Bridge, whatever happens with Licinius!"

Silence descended for quite some minutes.

"So what do you make of this Lactantius?" Constantine asked.

"It's as Jonas has said," he replied sagely. The emperor looked across at Felix.

"And you, my friend, what do you think?"

"That wall I warned about may be closer than we thought," he replied, crystal clear for Constantine but enigmatic for the rest.

"What wall?" asked Titus.

"Just something Constantine and I were chatting about," he replied peaceably, "but that's for a future day."

"We need to conclude our discussions," Constantine declared, moving the conversation quickly on. Crispus and I will head off for Byzantium immediately, while you organise the back-up support, Brutus."

Junia and Jonas hesitated, unsure what to do about the swift movement on from their proposals.

Junia, however, spoke up.

"But can we initiate the proposals of the ecclesia?"

Constantine hesitated, frowning.

"Of course. But it's not something I really have time to think about right now."

"Don't worry, Junia," intervened Titus. "I'll raise it with the senate immediately. And I'll talk to Marcus about making the connections with the companions and their friends in Augusta Treverorum. It's exactly Rictiovarus' heart these days. Ultimately we will see to it in Byzantium, I expect. But that will depend on the success of Crispus' strategy!"

***

Crispus leant back in his saddle, the archers and cavalry of the *auxilia* at his back, and viewed the city of Byzantium spread out before them. Their legions now semi-circled it on the western side. He reflected proudly on his defeat of Licinius' fleet just a few weeks before. Licinius now had nowhere to go but further east to Nicomedia. He had not expected his strategy to take a full two years to complete, but it had worked in the end. Throughout that time, they had been occupied with pitched battles and lesser skirmishes between Constantine's and Licinius' legions, interspersed with unsuccessful attempts to make peace and culminating with the rout of Licinius despite his superior numbers, which now left him holed up in Byzantium.

"I so love you, Marcus," Crispus remarked suddenly. Marcus' horse was alongside his, accompanied by several of his negotiating team. "You are always ready to make peace and never mind the risk to yourself, even if it takes you right to the front line."

"The feeling is mutual, Crispus. Your ever-readiness for the way of love to open up is truly wonderful."

"Yes, but it's not just your heart for peace-making," Crispus continued, turning his face towards his companion. "I have loved you from the moment you whisked me off my feet and swung me round whooping that day at Villa Metilia when I was just a nine-year-old. Ever since you came wounded to Augusta Treverorum, and then afterwards when we were together in Rome, just being around you makes me feel that life's worth living. I love my Pater, but he is so focused on being the emperor that he never makes me feel that he loves me just for who I am. But you do Marcus, and I want to thank you for that, whatever happens."

Marcus smiled back at the now battle-scarred twenty-seven year old.

"You won my heart that first day, and you will always have a home there," he replied, his voice charged with emotion. "But right now I'll go on down to the city and see if we can get an audience with Licinius." Crispus suddenly straightened up in the saddle and tightened his grip on the bridle. A ripple of awareness ran through the whole auxilia.

"It may be too late for that," he said, pointing to the city below. For even as he spoke, Licinius' remaining cavalry turmae could be seen charging away to the east of the city, the Eastern emperor himself undoubtedly among them. At that same moment a turma of their own joined them on the hill, having come up from among Constantine's legions to the west of the city. It was a small band of Scholai Palatinae, led by Anthony. Drawing alongside, he shared his news.

"Intelligence is that Licinius is heading to Chrysopolis where his remaining legions are gathering for a final battle. Brutus is heading there with your father and their legions right now."

"Well then we need to be there too," responded Crispus. "And Marcus, your best diplomacy will be required if it truly is to be his final defeat. Tempers will be running high and it will be hard to avoid the Brutus remedy. But there's Constantia and Valerius to think about."

"Intelligence is that they are remaining in Byzantium to await his return," Anthony interposed.

"Even more important for us to be there to help decide his fate then," affirmed Marcus. Crispus turned towards the auxilia.

"We need to return immediately to the camp. We will be leaving with the legion for Chrysopolis as soon as possible." They turned and began the descent down the hill to where their legion remained waiting at the western walls of the city.

"You will be in my heart whatever happens," cried Marcus to Crispus, as the auxilia gathered pace.

Chapter Fifteen

Murder and Heartbreak

The Battle of Chrysopolis, near Chalcedon, took place on 18 September 324. Constantine's thin patience had by this point completely given way to an unstoppable determination to end the competition between the two emperors once and for all. Barely waiting for Marcus to finish his by now almost routine attempt to make peace on condition of Licinius' surrender, he brought Crispus' and Brutus' legions together with his own and launched a single massive frontal assault on Licinius' troops, carrying the labarum banners on Tau crosses boldly before each legion. This had been his practice at every major conflict since Milvian Bridge, and he had rarely lost a battle. However, since his dream-filled night three years earlier he couldn't dismiss the shadowy awareness of a shape-shifting aspect between the labarum and the Minotaur. But he told no one. Once again he won a decisive victory in what was a very bloody and violent battle. Licinius lost 25,000 to 30,000 men, with thousands more breaking away and running in flight. Licinius himself managed to escape along the coastal road to Nicomedia, to where Constantine's elite turma accompanied by Crispus, Marcus, Brutus and Anthony followed him.

"I have come full circle these nearly twenty years," Constantine declared as they approached the city. I fled from Galerius through these very gates to find you Crispus, and it was on this road that I began to realise that I might one day be emperor, and then and there determined to do differently to the self-preserving heisters that preceded me. It was then that the idea began to germinate to come via Rome to you fellows, Marcus, and make you my comēs reis militaris and help me find a different way."

"In the light of which, what are we going to do with Licinius, Constantine?" Marcus replied. "You can't treat him like you expected Galerius to treat you!"

Constantine brought his horse to a standstill and signalled the turma and the accompanying auxilia to pause.

"We will treat him rightly, Marcus. We can't bring him back to Rome on condition that he submits to me, like you once suggested. He will refuse to do so. And I don't want a risky competitor at the heart of things."

"We can't keep giving him chances to scheme and regroup, which we all know he will, given half a chance," said Brutus. "We should assassinate him now, tonight."

"No, Brutus, we will not kill him tonight," retorted Constantine. "But you are right that he is dangerous and he may well have troops here that fled the battle with him. Let's find him and bring him back to Byzantium, immediately if possible."

Giving the order to proceed, he led them through the open gates of the city, where they found that the guard were ready to welcome them as victors. Seeing that it was Constantine himself who was entering, they quickly prostrated themselves, knowing what was required by the emperor.

"Thank you, but please get to your feet," he cried. "Where is my defeated foe?"

Licinius had intended to make his way to the imperial palace and secure himself and his remaining imperial turma there. But the city security forces had already received intelligence of his utter defeat. So while they had allowed him access to the palace, it was only under sufferance and a large security detail held him in check.

"They are secure in the imperial palace, and the city security are awaiting instructions, Your Excellency," replied the leader of the guard.

"Take us there then," Constantine instructed, dismounting. "Anthony, please prepare the auxilia for our return to Byzantium at dawn tomorrow. And send someone to organise a ship to be ready and waiting."

Then together with Marcus, Crispus, Brutus and the rest of the turma, he made his way to the palace. Licinius and his personal guard were sitting in the atrium, but when they saw them coming, scrambled to their feet. Then seeing who it was, they followed their defeated emperor's lead and prostrated themselves.

"Please get up, friend," said Constantine, addressing Licinius. "I have defeated you, but I wish you no ill. You will return with us to Byzantium at dawn, without your guard, and we will discuss your fate."

The party docked in Byzantium the following midday. With Licinius safely under guard, the members of the imperial court present in Byzantium assembled for a celebratory cena. As it happened, six of the original fourteen were present, for as well as Crispus, Marcus, Brutus and Anthony, Helena was there, en route from Jerusalem with a relic of the cross that she was eager to deposit in Byzantium in preparation for its inauguration as the new Eastern capital. In her usual enigmatic fashion, she had brought along Constantia who, throughout the recent months of war, had remained in her imperial apartment overlooking the hippodrome with Valerius, who was now a bright lad of twelve. Constantine could not decide whether having Licinius' wife present at their deliberations was going to help or hinder. Crispus and Marcus, however, were delighted to see her.

"Wow, Constantia, it's wonderful to see you. How long has it been since we were last together in Rome?" cried Crispus.

"Nearly three years," she replied, smiling. "But Marcus and I keep meeting on occasions like this, trying to make peace between Licinius and Constantine."

"It is going to have to be different this time, Constantia," interposed her brother. "There's no going back to the diarchy now. I'm sole emperor and that's the way it's going to be."

"That's what we set out to achieve in time for your vicennial, which will soon be here, and why I suggested marrying Licinius in the first place. So I'm scarcely about to complain!" Constantia retorted. "But I would like you to show him mercy."

"Well said, my dear," broke in Helena.

Brutus coughed exasperatedly. "So what are we going to do with him?"

"I took the opportunity of talking with him on the journey," interposed Marcus. "He would like to be exiled to Thessalonica."

"Why?" asked Constantine.

"I'm not fully sure," Marcus replied. "But it is a beautiful city, and somewhat off the beaten track. Less of an embarrassing place than Rome or here to be under house arrest, which he realises he will be."

"Maybe he's hoping for an angel to set him free, like happened to the apostle Paul there," wondered Crispus, half joking.

"Well, if Mater and Eusebius are right, then angels are on my side," said his father, "so there's no danger of that."

"As it happens Thessalonica has a good security detail that is loyal to you," said Brutus, glancing meaningfully at Helena. "A fellow trained by myself when he was part of the Scholai. So I say, let's give Licinius what he asks. He'll be safe there."

"Sounds good to me," interjected Constantia. "But I've no intention of going with him. I will come with Valerius back to Rome. I want him to see more of his Aunt Fausta and his cousins."

"It's decided then," said Constantine. "Brutus, have Licinius taken to Thessalonica, while you secure the city here. The rest of us will head back to Rome. This is because I have decided to make you, Crispus, together with Fausta, both Augustae. That way the pair of you can represent me fully. You, my son, in Augusta Treverorum and my empress in Rome. I can trust no one else to do this. We'll have a big public ceremony and I'll mint new coinage and memorials to commemorate it. Then, before the year is out, I will return here and make Byzantium my new capital. It shall be called Constantinople!"

Helena took careful note of the words "no one else". Whispering to Brutus, who was seated beside her, to hang back with her and Constantine as the rest of them began to make their way to their rooms for the night, she took her son's arm.

"A word, Constantine," she said. "Good thinking to make Crispus and Fausta Augustae. But, of course, you can completely trust me to represent you too. So I will stay here with Brutus and represent you in Byzantium until you return. I will organise a shrine for the relic of the cross and begin to make plans for the founding of Constantinople."

"Thank you, Mater," he replied, inwardly aware of a raft of motives her proposal might be influenced by. He reflected to himself that she probably didn't know for sure which of a whole bunch of actions she would select when the time came. But she would be forever true to herself as the dowager empress to Constantine the Great, and at least that meant loyalty to her concept of himself, whatever that was exactly! He embraced her, kissing her on both cheeks.

"One more thing," she said. "If there's so much of a hint that Licinius is stirring up trouble in Thessalonica, then Brutus here must have him immediately assassinated. And awkward though you might find it, then his son Valerius must die too."

"She is right, Your Excellency," ventured Brutus.

"Of course, she is," he replied. "You have my authority. If occasion arises, have them killed." Then with an abrupt "Goodnight", he turned on his heel and left the atrium. Helena watched him wonderingly as he strode out of the room. She simply did not know what he would ultimately decide when it came to the conflict of the two visions for the Pax Romana.

"I don't think he knows himself," she thought to herself. "He's more like me than I realised. He makes it up as he goes along." Then turning to Brutus, "I'm glad to see that you have not lost your stomach for peace by assassination," she said, smiling. "Meet me tomorrow morning and we'll make a plan of action for the coming days."

***

The Palatine was decked with palm leaves and all the regalia of Parousia. Licinius was defeated, Constantine was sole emperor and his wife and eldest son were his Augustae! A great banner stretched across the entrance to the courtyard declaring "Flavius Valerius Constantine the Great, Emperor of all Rome!" As yet another sumptuous celebratory meal of the imperial court joined by senators and other patrician dignitaries drew to a close, the now twelve-year-old Valerius, son of Licinius and Constantia, tugged at his mother's sleeve.

"Can we please go and see the street celebrations now?" he enquired. "I'm bored! Everyone takes so long to eat and drink at these formal affairs!"

Constantia leant across to Crispus who was sitting opposite her. "I'm going to go with Val and watch the acrobats," she said. "He's bored and has done well to sit this long!"

"I'm not surprised he's bored. So am I," responded Crispus. "I'll come with you. But my young half-brothers will want to come too, you can be sure. Wait a moment and I'll find out." He stood up and went over to where Fausta, her daughter Helena Junior and the two oldest boys, Constantine Junior and Constantius, were sitting.

"Thank you for putting up with official speeches in your mother's and my honour," he said. "But they are over now. So who wants to come with me, Constantia and Val to see the street acrobats?"

Their enthusiasm was immediate. "Oh yes," they chorused.

"Well only for an hour," interposed their mother. "And stay close to Crispus and Constantia and make sure to do what they tell you!"

Young Helena and the three lads ran excitedly out into the vestibulum, glad to be free from the tedium of the lengthy speeches and attracted by the noise and hilarity from the main square and its adjacent streets. Crispus and Constantia were accompanied as usual by their personal assistants, but even so, despite their efforts to catch them up, the four youngsters quickly disappeared among the crowd. At first the adults were unconcerned, as they were able to see or hear signs of them among the folk just ahead. Then Helena Junior could be seen waving back at them and calling for the boys to wait. It was only a matter of moments before they caught her up, and the boys came running back enthusiastically.

"Come and see," they shouted. "The acrobats are amazing and really funny too."

The crowd encircled the troop of performers who were separated from them by a circle of plaited ropes. They certainly were amazing and for several moments everyone's attention was taken up with their extraordinary antics. But then Constantia became suddenly aware of the absence of Valerius.

"Wait everybody," she cried. "Where is Val?"

Crispus immediately gathered the party together.

"Did any of you see where Valerius went?" he asked.

"One minute he was with us, and the next he was not," said Constantine Junior.

"Yes, he was just a little way ahead and had me by the arm pulling me ahead to see the players," said Constantius.

"Quickly," said Crispus, his military skills kicking in, and addressing his assistant, "You go back to the palace and fetch the elite turma and organise an intensive search. In the meantime, I and the lads will scout out the immediate vicinity. Constantia," he said, "please stay right here with your assistant and Helena Junior. Val quite probably doesn't even know he is lost and may well find his way back to the point he left." The next hours were spent searching for the lad. Then came devastating news from the turma. His lifeless body had been found floating in the Milvian. At first it was thought to be an accident, for who would want to kill an unknown twelve-year-old with nothing valuable on him besides a patrician toga? An utterly distraught Constantia and three greatly shocked youngsters were gathered up by Fausta and Calvia and supported back to the palace, where Dunnius, by now too old to have joined the search, had heard the dreadful news and was waiting to comfort them. He had the turma bring Val's body and lay it on his own bed, remembering the story of Elisha and the young boy. Watched over by a weeping Constantia he laid himself gently over the lad in hope of reviving him, but to no avail.

"How can this have happened?" Fausta asked Crispus.

While they were all discussing possible explanations, a truly dire reality began to dawn. For Marcus and Brutus arrived, having intended to be back from Byzantium in time for the celebration, but delayed by news from Thessalonica. Licinius had been assassinated!

All suggestion of accident faded. There was no way this inexplicable disappearance and drowning could possibly be a coincidence. On receiving the news Constantia collapsed into a catatonic state of shock. Fausta immediately went to her, having previously left her alone with her son's body out of deference for her grief. But now she simply took her in her arms. "I know something of this pain," she declared. "Nothing as terrible as losing a husband and a son. But a father and a brother nonetheless."

Crispus stayed to comfort the three youngsters. Helena Junior and Constantius were full of astonishment and incredulity, but questions blurted out of them nonetheless.

"Who did it, Crispus, and why did they do it?" Helena asked, "Was it father?"

Constantius was dumbfounded. "He would never do such a thing," he declared. Constantine Junior, however, remained silent. Inwardly, he suspected that his father was behind it, and he felt that maybe he understood why. After all, while Licinius remained, his father's position was threatened and, while his heir remained, so did the threat.

It had been arranged that the day after the Parousia, the emperor and his two Augustae would visit Villa Metilia. There the informal leadership of the slave ecclesia would pray a blessing on them in their combined role as the emperor's three bodies in the empire's three capitals. Hardly surprisingly, the events of the previous evening overshadowed everything else as they now made their way up the Janiculan Hill together with Felix and Marcus, leaving Constantia behind at the Palatine with her grief.

So it was a subdued posse that made their way up the familiar road, absorbed in their own complexity of thoughts. What had happened exactly? Who had given the instructions for these murders? Constantine was well aware that it was his authority that lay behind the actions even though it had not been his hands that literally carried them out. Despite their preoccupation, as they entered the courtyard of the villa, the covering love of the slave ecclesia was palpable. Constantine felt it deeply and struggled to quench its unspoken challenge to his determination to be sole emperor at whatever price. Crispus and Fausta, on the other hand, knew that whoever was behind the devastating events had transgressed a possibly irrecoverable boundary between peace through sovereign power and peace through love.

Eusébie and Claudia welcomed them into the atrium where the informal leadership were standing talking among themselves.

"Please come and sit down," invited Melissa, and they all sank gratefully onto the couches that had been arranged in a circle for them.

It was Eusébie who spoke first. "We are saddened by the terrible events of these last few days," she said. "Constantia must be beside herself with grief."

Marcus was the first to respond. "We must face the fact that whoever is behind this, the murder of a twelve-year-old child is not and never can be the way of the equal cross," he said. There was silence after this for some moments. Then Melissa spoke. "Constantine," she began, "this is a crucial moment for us all. Can I be as bold as to ask you a direct question?"

"Well, of course you can," he replied, regarding her seemingly peaceably.

"Thank you," she continued. "Then can you promise me that the messianic kingdom of Jesus and his companions comes first for you?"

In the slight hesitation that followed, Fausta intervened ingenuously.

"You don't even need to ask him, Melissa. Of course he believes that," she said. At which Eusébie, Valeria, Melissa, Dunnius, Junia and Jonas gathered round and proceeded to go ahead and pray the blessing of the Trinity over them.

Then Melissa produced a small equal cross, which she presented to Constantine. "I hope you don't mind my doing this, Constantine, but I have real reservations about the labarum, as I think you know. Please accept this instead, with our love."

Constantine struggled hugely at this, darkly angry at the implicit criticism but yet managing to conceal it from his family and friends.

Later that night he returned to the Palatine with his two Augustae. As they entered the courtyard and stepped down from the carpentum he called them both aside into the anteroom between the vestibulum and the atrium.

"Fausta," he said, "you shocked me just now. Can I be sure that you will stand by me and agree with me whatever happens?"

"Don't be silly, darling!" she replied. "Not whatever happens! The way of love must prevail – but you know that and will surely always want it?"

"And you, Crispus," Constantine asked. "Can I trust you to stand by me and agree with me, come what may?"

"Here now, Pater," his son replied. "What are you playing at? You know that you can trust us implicitly. We love you and seek the true messianic peace of the kingdom for Rome together with you. Of course we won't agree with you if you act against that. You wouldn't want us to. It wouldn't be loving you!"

They half expected his characteristic laugh to resound reassuringly at this point. But instead, with a face like thunder and a voice trembling with anger he exclaimed, "Never contradict me in such a way again, either of you," and turning his back, stormed from the room.

Crispus and Faustus stood looking at each other in a state of shock.

"What's happening, Crispus?" said Fausta.

"I'm not sure," he replied. "But it feels like a line has been crossed somehow, and I'm unsure how to get it back."

On leaving the room, Constantine sent immediately for Brutus.

"Do what we once discussed but I never imagined we would do," he instructed.

Brutus hesitated momentarily. "This is huge, Your Excellency. Are you sure?"

"Everything is changed," Constantine replied. "Do it. And never question me again. I am leaving now for Byzantium with the turma. Have the deed done and wait until you have confirmation. Then follow me. I will wait with the ship at Portus until you arrive with the news. Then we will leave immediately for Byzantium and confer with Helena and Eusebius as to what to do next."

It had already been the plan that the next day the emperor's three bodies would be distributed, with Constantine heading back to Byzantium, Crispus leaving for Augusta Treverorum and Fausta remaining in Rome. Now, following Constantine's instructions without delay, Brutus called to him his personal lieutenant, who he trusted implicitly and had already briefed for such a moment.

"When Crispus leaves tonight with his elite turma, you will be among them," he instructed.

Later that night, Crispus set out for Augusta Treverorum with his turma in order to represent Constantine's imperial body there as agreed. On their second night out from Rome they stayed as usual in the barracks at Clusium. There, as Crispus slept, Brutus' lieutenant softly entered the young Augusta's room and, unseen and unheard, slid his executioner's knife beneath his shoulder blades. Crispus barely stirred as it pierced his heart. Having checked that it had reached its mark, his killer simply slipped away into the night. When dawn broke and Crispus' adjutant attempted to wake him, he was dead.

That same evening Fausta returned to her apartment deeply troubled in spirit.

"Calvia," she called, "could you prepare a bath for me? I have something disturbing on my mind and I think a good long soak might calm me."

While her mistress lay relaxing, Calvia sat sewing. She was so engrossed in the intricate tapestry that she failed to notice the masked intruder who sidled past her. Creeping unobserved into the bathing area they came silently up behind Fausta, and leaning swiftly over, slit her throat from ear to ear. It happened so fast that, apart from a barely audible gasp, she simply sank down under the water, drowning in her own blood.

Calvia found her body there an hour later.

Stunned and walking as if in a dream, Calvia left the apartment and crossed the atrium to where a young slave was straightening the furniture ready for the next day.

"Run quickly and fetch Theodoricus the chamberlain. Tell him it's urgent." Then she sank down on the nearest couch and contemplated the implications of what had happened. A few moments later Theodoricus appeared, somewhat dishevelled as he had been preparing for bed. Rising to her feet she put a finger to her lips.

"Come with me," she said. Nonplussed, the chamberlain followed her into the empress' apartment. "Prepare yourself for a desperate sight," she said, leading on into the bathing area. Fausta's body lay virtually submerged in the blooded water, only her forehead visible, her long black hair sprawled around it. Confronted by the shocking scene, Theodoricus stepped back in horror.

"Who has done this?" he asked. "What did you see?"

"I saw nothing," she replied. "The empress came back from the visit to the Janiculan Hill preoccupied and somewhat disturbed in spirit. She said that something was troubling her and that a long soak in the bath might help. I thought nothing of it as she often took a bath if she was anxious about something. Then I went back to my sewing."

"Whoever did this knew how to operate undetected," surmised Theodoricus. "Getting past you unnoticed is no easy thing. And killing her excellency without rousing her suspicion or giving any opportunity for her to alert you is the work of a professional. Either Licinius' supporters remain more powerful than we thought, or else this comes from much closer to home."

"Surely that's impossible," Calvia replied, her tears now beginning to flow freely. "All the imperial court love her, and from this very day, she was to represent Constantine here in Rome as his most trusted relative next only to Crispus."

"We must tell his excellency immediately," concluded the chamberlain. "Stay in the apartment and if anyone comes, tell them that the empress is indisposed and do not let them in. In the meantime I will get a message to the emperor. Hopefully he has not yet boarded ship for Byzantium."

On reaching the barracks he was surprised to find Brutus still there, sitting nonchalantly in the mess drinking and playing *Latrunculi* with Felix and Anthony.

"Your honours, please come quickly. There has been a terrible attack on her excellency the empress."

Brutus stood up instantly, apparently shocked. Anthony went white as a sheet. Felix, however, shot past them both across to the palace and arrived at the apartment just before them.

"Where is Fausta?" he demanded, seeing Calvia's tear-stained face.

"She is dead, Felix," she cried, as Brutus and Anthony entered the room behind them. "She has been assassinated, drowned in her own blood."

For a moment they stood in silence, then Theodoricus, ever the unflappable chief of staff and who had now recovered his equilibrium, arrived with a team of helpers ready to remove Fausta's body onto a bier and prepare her for burial.

Then Brutus spoke. "We must let Constantine know what has happened immediately," he said. "He will be at Portus by now, preparing for the voyage to Byzantium. I was to join him tomorrow once reinforcements for the turmae had arrived from Mediolanum. But I will go immediately with this dreadful news, and leave you, Anthony, to wait for the reinforcements and then catch us up."

"I will come with you," said Felix.

Later that day as Felix and Brutus were approaching Portus, a solitary rider drew alongside. At first Felix assumed that he was bringing news of the expected reinforcements. However, reining in his horse Brutus remarked, "Just give me a moment to find out what this is about, Felix."

Felix rode several metres ahead and waited at the roadside, not unduly concerned. But then Brutus caught him up, apparently deeply troubled by the news he received.

"Crispus is dead too, Felix. This is greatly disturbing. Licinius' supporters must be stronger than we thought and be avenging his death. Come, we must let Constantine know immediately. He will surely be devastated."

The news shook Felix to the core, and in so doing alerted him to what he could still not believe, and yet was beginning to realise must be true. Without another word he urged his horse to a gallop and charged ahead of Brutus down the road to the port, where Constantine's ship lay at the ready with the labarum flying from its mast. Without waiting for Brutus to catch him up, he left his horse at the quayside and strode up the gang plank and across to the emperor's cabin. With a brusque rap on the door, he opened it and stepped inside. Constantine was reclining on his bunk but immediately stood, startled by Felix's peremptory entrance.

"Constantine, whatever have you done?" he asked, his voice breaking with emotion.

The emperor stood, his eyes lowered. Then stepping forward and looking into his comēs' eyes, he spoke.

"I came down on the wrong side of the wall, Felix. I've damned my good self with Crispus and Fausta and erased them from history. Thank you for your faithful friendship, but you are now released from your commission. Please let the others know. You are free to follow the equal cross, Felix. I'm going with the labarum."

Felix was again struck to the core by what he heard and which further revealed what he still barely believed. But he sensed its finality.

"So it has come to this after everything," he stated. "But know this, Constantine, I do not need your authority to follow the equal cross. It is what I have always followed and will continue to do. The time may come when you need it yet. And if possible I will be there. My love for you remains if you ever turn again to find it."

So saying he left the cabin, silently passing Brutus as he stooped to enter. Wracked with emotion he descended the gang plank and retrieved and mounted his horse. Breaking immediately into a canter, he headed back for Rome and the Janiculan Hill.

***

It took more than the usual three weeks for Constantine and Brutus to reach Constantinople, the weather being appalling and their ship constantly encountering adverse winds. Nevertheless they were greeted with another Parousia of welcome on their arrival. For Helena had wasted no time in their absence, expanding the imperial palace and laying the groundworks for an impressive worship centre alongside the hippodrome to house the relic of the cross. In the absence of opposing claims to the emperorship, the legions were settled and established and well able to deal with any local disaffections. All in all, Helena had seemingly fulfilled Constantine's desire for Augustae who carried his imperial presence where Crispus and Fausta had not. Byzantium was at peace and ready to become the mighty new Rome fit for a regnant human counterpart to the supposed divine sovereignty. Determined not to be surprised by her son's imminent return, Helena had set messengers to watch day and night for his ship and so was informed immediately of its appearance before ever it had docked. So when he eventually arrived there was a reception committee waiting to attend his every need, and locals had been pressed by the legions to line the streets chanting "Constantine the Great, Emperor of Rome; Constantine the Great, Emperor of Rome" over and over again.

Later that night after the multifarious guests at the welcome cena in the ancient imperial palace had all left, Constantine, Brutus, Helena and Eusebius met in a sumptuous anteroom. "The deed I hoped never to do is done, Mater," began

Constantine. "Fausta and Crispus are both dead at the hands of Brutus' trusted deputies. And I regret how it makes me feel now that I'm no longer so angry. But there is no way back. Therefore, we have urgent need to know how to present it. Three weeks have already past so it will be six weeks before we can publish our version of events in Rome."

"Don't worry too much about that," Helena retorted. "Things will have settled down by then and there is no one left to oppose you."

"I have some ideas," said Eusebius. "But I need to think this through carefully. Let's sleep on it and meet again in the morning."

"In the meantime," continued Helena, "let me fill you in on everything I've been doing here. I'm sure you will be pleased with it all. And Brutus can go and confer with the Legatus Legionis and bring you an up-to-date report on the current state of the Pax Romana throughout the East."

The same four formed the core of the imperial court at ientaculum the following morning. "So what have you come up with, Bishop?" Constantine asked when the slaves had cleared the table and left them on their own.

"Well, it is something Severus utilised more than a century ago after Caracalla murdered his brother Geta. It's a legal device known as *damnatio memoriae*. It's a way of justifying having a person or persons removed from the historical record because they have done something so terrible it reflects badly on their successors."

"But that's my problem," the emperor replied. "Their only sin was to refuse to support me even if I was the one doing something bad."

Helena reached out and took his hand. "They were very close to one another," she remarked. "Why not leave open the possibility that they had been sexually involved with each other?" The emperor looked at her quizzically. "Perhaps they had," she added quietly. "And everyone would understand that such a relationship would reflect devastatingly on their father and husband. This damnatio memoriae would make perfect sense in such circumstances."

"Exactly how would it work?" Constantine asked Eusebius.

"There would be a public decree that their images be removed from every memorial, all coinage bearing their image would be recalled and destroyed and any public mention of them would be forbidden," the prelate replied.

From Constantine's perspective it was the perfect device to conceal his own emotions and regrets. He turned to Brutus. "Announce it and do it right away, Brutus," he said. "Send legates to Rome and Augusta Treverorum to decree it, and if anyone asks why, say that you've heard that they were executed for incest. Don't make any official allegation, just leave it hanging out there and let that be the end of it."

Part Four

Coda

In partial darkness, the heralding currents of the gathering storm carried the cries of the wounded and the groans of the bloodied earth that sustained the Pax Romana. Similar wounds and blood had undergirded the Egyptian, Assyrian and Greek empires before them and would continue to uphold the imperial sovereignties of the future. Yet overhead, stars still shone brightly and beneath the same winds deeper harmonies continued to resound. Beatrice sat, tears flowing down the marred visage she shared with her Trinitarian partner. Then, staff in hand, she reached out across the pool and made the sign of the equal cross on the surface of the water.

Afterward, resting back once more on her haunches, she began to sing. "Where were you when I laid the foundation of the earth? Tell me, if you have understanding, who set its measurements? Or who stretched the line on it? On what were its bases sunk? Or who laid its cornerstone, when the morning stars sang together and all the sons of God shouted for joy?" The waters troubled, stirred and gathered into a circle where the sign had been made. Then the angel of the Somme emerged once more. "It's time," Beatrice declared. The angel held her gaze.

"I was here," they answered, "ever ready for such a time as this." And shaking the droplets from their wings, mounted gently upwards and soared away over the horizon.

Chapter Sixteen

Depression and Death

The sun was setting over the city as Marcus and Constantia sat together on the upper terrace of the peristyle on the Janiculan Hill. Since their marriage it had become their chosen place to relax once the day's work was done. Eusébie's favourite arbour was further down below, close to the orange groves and the expanding memorial garden where the bones of Dunnius, Fuscian and Lactantius now lay alongside Fausta, Crispus, Valerius and Commodus. On Saturday evenings whoever from the informal leadership was at home still gathered there, although they were more subdued occasions than when the posse had been in place.

"Days have passed into weeks, weeks to months, months to years, and years to a decade," declared Marcus, "but it is as if messianic time has stood still, paralysed."

"Can time be paralysed?" asked Constantia. "Let alone the time of the kingdom. Surely it's people that are overcome by events so that their faith falters?"

"And you think that is what's happening to us?" responded Marcus.

"I think we have done better than most," she answered. "I thought I'd never recover from the loss of Val, but we discovered our love for each other in the wake of his death and the devastating events that followed, and our marriage has brought some hope to the hill. Then when Paola was born, there was such an outburst of joy. But while it's transformed us, I fear it has still been an uncertain season for the others."

"No one has been more changed by the terrible events of 326 than the companions here on the hill," ventured Marcus. "Ever since Constantine's arrival that fateful summer's day twenty years before, the possibility of a transformed empire shaped the hopes and expectations of our common life together. The three of us, and the posse we formed with Constantine, represented the continual positive progress of the kingdom of love within the empire of Rome in all our lifetimes, and no one seriously doubted it. It wasn't that there was a common certainty that the synergy of empire and kingdom could ever be fully realised. But the interface of our desire and the Pax Romana was at the heart of their rhythm of life. The informal leadership in general and Eusébie in particular kept their faith alive and their prayers strong."

"I know that to be true," affirmed Constantia. "I sensed it whenever the Metilian companions visited us in Ambianum and at the court in Treverorum. Then when I visited Villa Metilia for myself as part of the imperial fourteen it was obvious that love, faith and hope were emanating from the slave ecclesia. But no one embodied the interplay of the two ways to peace more than Crispus and Fausta. And so their deaths killed hope like nothing else could."

"There aren't two ways to peace," said Marcus. "I think I've known that ever since encountering the druid in the debatable lands. But erased from public life, Crispus' and Fausta's unmarked graves, alongside Commodus at the edge of the orange grove, seem to rub out our hope of the kingdom of love as well. This is what paralyses us."

"Not only that," added Constantia. "In the years that immediately followed the murders, the fracture of the relationship between Constantine and the three of you was a constant reminder to them all of the apparent failure of their vision. This was particularly so when Rome was ablaze with the celebrations of Constantine's vicentennial. The fourteenth year of the court of fourteen was to have been consummated! But, instead, it was eradicated. Consequently, it was the pall of the damnatio memoriae that hung over the hill."

Marcus nodded and continued, "And the deaths of Dunnius and Lactantius within a few months of each other that same year only added to the gloom. I know they died of natural causes associated with old age, but I'm sure that the shock and disappointment of their beloved friends' assassinations were contributing causes. Now disappointment bordering on depression threatens to paralyse the slave ecclesia."

"Don't you think a stronger lead is needed?" Constantia asked.

"I think that the passing of Fuscian last year brought a further sense of dislocation from Quentin's original vision among the leadership," Marcus continued. "Apart from Eusébie, only Melissa, Fortunatus, Claudia and Valeria really remember those extraordinary days of the miracles and martyrdom, and the tangible presence of love. Now they are in their seventies and eighties and won't be with us much longer."

"Hang on, wait, Marcus," his wife interrupted, reaching out and taking his hands. "It's the three of you who carried that love into the places of greatest test and won. I know that the abandonment and severance by the emperor has cut very deeply. But the three of you need to step up and not let this set back stop you."

"Set back, is that what you call it?" exploded Marcus, momentarily angry. But then seeing the reaction and the tears rolling down Constantia's cheeks he was immediately sorry. "Forgive me," he said. "You lost your husband and your son. How can I even begin to question your understanding of the heartbreak involved?"

Constantia, still holding his hands, and looking into his eyes, continued.

"I know how shattering it has been, and even Eusébie who is so important to you was strangely silent in the initial months and years that followed the murders. If it hadn't been for Nesta, Junia and Jonas and the prison ecclesia's grasp of the centrality of the poor then the flow of love represented by Quentin might well have given way completely to the imperial ecclesiastical structures favoured by Eusebius and Helena. Those hierarchies of bishops and priests threaten to strangle the life of the Spirit, whether intended or not."

***

It was a typical Saturday evening the following week when the informal leadership cohort of companions on the hill met with Eusébie on the lower veranda of the peristyle. Their usually sober demeanour was lifted somewhat by the news which Junia and Jonas brought from the slave ecclesia. With help from Anthony, a significant network of food distribution shelters had been established in Constantinople at last, to add to the others already in place in Augusta Treverorum and the continuing success of those in Rome.

"They are too important for the future of social care for the authorities to oppose them," declared Jonas.

"But we still have to watch out," added Junia, "Eusebius is determined to bring it all under the monarchical bishops and their ecclesiastical courts."

"And Constantine is determined to make sure that the senate here in Rome is utterly loyal to him, and in no way weakened by the radicals of the equal cross," added Jonas. "He has appointed Senator Bassianas from his imperial court in Constantinople as his consul here."

"I had hoped that the findings of the Council at Nicaea would correct the hierarchical positioning of the bishops and clergy," ventured Melissa.

"If only Lactantius had not been dying, he would have seen through the way that the idea of the *homoousios* seemed to strengthen our understanding of the equalities of the Trinity represented by the equal cross," Marcus replied. "But instead it smuggled in the subordination ideas about Father and Son gods from the Egyptian empire!"

There was a pregnant silence for several moments before Melissa continued.

"Then our legacy must be to embody the difference between that and the loving Trinity of the equal cross, and to pray and teach it while we have breath left to do so," she declared.

Hardly had they finished speaking than their attention was distracted by a rider on the driveway up the hill from the city.

"It's Anthony," cried Titus.

"That's wonderful," responded Nesta. "But what can be bringing him here in such haste? Surely he is still based in Constantinople?"

As he spurred his horse forward up the final stadia of the hill, it was clear that he was drenched with sweat and had come much farther than the city below. Felix rose and together with Marcus and Titus headed out to the vestibulum with Nesta. Amadeus was already there ahead of them, helping the general down from his horse and leading it away to the stables. He could barely stand, so while Marcus and Felix attended to him, Nesta and Titus hurried to prepare the guest room and clear the way for him to head to the baths.

"Whatever has brought you here in such haste?" inquired Felix.

"The emperor's dying," responded Anthony. "And he's calling for you. He sent me to ask you to come to him. I've no idea whether he will last out these weeks, but I have made record time and have a ship waiting in Portus to take us back."

"So exactly who is it that he is asking for?" enquired Felix.

"You at least," responded Anthony. "He said he was fairly sure you would come, being that the last time he spoke to you ten years since, you implied that he might have need of you and you would come if so."

"I'm coming too," interposed Marcus.

"And me," added Titus, returning with the news that the bath was ready and catching the end of the conversation. And so it was that, before the sun was up the following morning, a reconvened posse of comēs headed with Anthony down the Via Portuensis from Rome to the waiting ship.

***

Constantine tossed and turned on his bed and, despite the perspiration standing out on his brow and dripping in rivulets down his chest, he was shivering with cold. He had been awake and wracked with coughing since the early hours. This was the third bout of fever that had dogged his last months, but this was far worse than before and had persisted for weeks on end. It was at the beginning of this latest bout that he had known at last what he must do. Whatever its cause, he was increasingly sure it was the sickness that would curtail his life and reign. He would send for Felix to shrive him. It was close to six weeks now since he had sent Anthony with a message for Felix, and it was in these early morning hours between five and six o'clock that he found it the most difficult to fend off the growing panic and control his thoughts.

"Would Felix come before the end? Might Titus and Marcus even come too? And what would be their attitude to him?"

There was no just cause why any of them should come, he reflected, although his final meeting with Felix played over and over in his head.

"Know this Constantine, I do not need your authority to follow the equal cross. It is what I have always followed and will continue to do. The time may come when you need it yet. And if possible I will be there. My love for you remains if you ever turn again to find it."

"Yes," mused Constantine, "Felix will come, perhaps even all three of them will."

274

Despite his genuine attempt to pursue the kingdom of love in his early years with the posse, Constantine had never been baptised. And since killing the two purist souls he had ever known, he was glad he had not. Submerged in the back of his mind, he had been keeping it for his final act before death. He would repent then, at last. Now he longed for Felix to hear his confession, and it was that which kept him alive through the fever, pain and delirium that increasingly overwhelmed his days. It was late spring, and the warmth of the Bithynian summer was already beginning to dispel the lingering chill of what had been a severe winter. But the emperor's internal temperature followed a law of its own. When his attendants brought him water to cool him it was too cold, but by the time it had been heated it was too hot. It was the same if he ventured outside the palace into the peristyle. When he was outside he wanted to be back in and when he was inside he wanted to be back out. His appetite was all but gone too and his household was at its wits end. Helena would have known what to do, he reflected to himself. But she had passed away seven years before. Eusebius of Caesarea was currently resident in the city, but he was no use to him now, although he supposed it was good that he occupied himself with advising his son Constantine II in statecraft. Although of what use that would be for the future of the empire he was now unsure. He found it increasingly difficult to tolerate the presence of all five of his remaining children. They all reminded him of their mother, and it seemed to him that none understood or loved him like Crispus had. Damnatio memoriae had worked as a political device, he granted Eusebius that. But its practical constraint on his deeper feelings was less and less help. Far from it in fact. Crispus and Fausta's love, their words and their faces increasingly haunted his dreams and intruded on his frequent episodes of daytime delirium. "I miss them!" he would cry.

"Who, Your Excellency?" his servants would answer. "Tell us and we'll bring them," only to leave him the more distraught with guilt and remorse.

It was the Saturday of the third week following Anthony's arrival on the Janiculan Hill that the galleon carrying the posse to Constantinople passed through the Dardanelles and entered the Sea of Marmara. It had been an easy if chilly voyage and had given the three comēs ample time to reminisce together, wrapped in their *paenulae* and sheltered against the side timbers of the stern deck. They all agreed in retrospect that the culmination of their partnership with Constantine had been the extraordinary resolution to their encounter with the Wid at the Antonine Wall.

"What was the key to it?" wondered Titus.

"Constantine's humility, his readiness to submit to the collective wisdom," Felix tendered. "I recognised at the time that the Trinity themselves were with us," he continued, "rejoicing at the unity of love that we had together chosen. Everyone involved was yielding to the good of the other at the cost of their own pride and sovereignty. But it was Constantine who was choosing the greatest submission. He had the most potential power and he laid it down."

"The equal cross then," Marcus concluded. "But when did the rot set in?"

"Perhaps right back in Eboracum," ventured Felix, "when he became emperor."

"No, that surely can't be right," declared Anthony, entering the conversation for the first time. "I know I wasn't there, but surely it's not having power, but what you do with the power that is the deciding factor."

"Helena and Eusebius have much to answer for then," proposed Titus. "They saw Christianity as the means to strengthen power in the hands of the would-be powerful, whereas the kingdom of love is about pouring out what power you have for the peace of the many. That's what was happening in the early days of the posse, what we experienced in Lindum and culminated with the Wid."

"It's hard to do your own inner work," said Marcus. "But I remember Eusébie gently remarking that was what Constantine needed to do."

"It's especially hard when you think that you are the one in charge and everything depends on you," interposed Felix. "Eusébie and my mater saw that struggle in Constantine and tried to help. You can be sure their prayers backed their challenges to him along the way."

Titus nodded his agreement, then pondered, "Was it inevitable that he would embrace the wrong cross, the one that empowered him and his armies? A Minotaur shape not a Jesus' one?"

"Not if he did the inner work," responded Felix. "I think that unless we constantly expose what's going on inside us to the Spirit and each other, everything can crash down in a moment."

"That's why I'm so grateful for the way we have held together," added Marcus, "And I guess at least we owe that to Constantine for taking the crazy step of calling us to be his comēs."

"I'm forever grateful for that," responded Felix. "And it may be that in the years since he came down on the wrong side of the wall, as he put it to me that last day we spoke, that he has been continually holding off that inner work. But now that his body and mind are weakened, his spirit is strengthening and he wants help from us again. We owe him nothing but love, so we must give him that."

Quite suddenly, while they were still deep in conversation, a wind blasted across the waves ahead of them and they became aware of storm clouds gathering rapidly where only moments before there had been clear weather. As the wind quite literally howled through the sails, sheets of lightening began intersecting the rapidly darkening sky. The oarsman pulled hard and the mariners hauled on the sails but huge waves mounted up and began to strike the galleon across the bows raising the whole craft semi-vertically so that the comēs and Anthony found themselves pushed back hard against the stern. There was clearly great risk that the whole galleon might be swamped or even overturned. At this point, Felix, like a man stirred out of a dream, stood to his feet and balancing with his legs planted firmly apart, rebuked the storm with a demeanour reminiscent of the Messiah in the boat on Galilee. "Peace be still," he cried. For a moment there was an expectant lull, and then, without warning, a lightning bolt struck the labarum which flew from the upper bow in front of them and ripped it in two from top to bottom. Immediately the waves subsided, the wind ceased, the clouds dispersed and the sun shone once more.

"Come on!" cried Marcus. "We will surely prosper on this visit, make no mistake. The kingdom of love will yet prevail over the Minotaur!"

***

Since the bouts of sickness had begun to take hold, Constantine had taken up residence in the imperial apartment adjacent to the hippodrome and which now overlooked the worship centre Helena had built to house the supposed relic of the cross. It was where Constantia and Valerius had lived during Licinius' final years. It was more private than Constantine's official rooms in the imperial palace and he did not wish to advertise just how ill he was becoming. But it was not only that. Somehow the atmosphere of the apartment gave him a sense of proximity to his half-sister and the days of the posse back before his father's death and his declaration as emperor. And the memory of his nephew's presence there brought his guilt to the fore and began to enable the inner unravelling of the damnatio memoriae. While he had had little opportunity to get to know the lad, he had spent a memorable evening with him and Constantia there the year before the boy's assassination. He had been a bright intelligent youth, full of questions about the political tension between his uncle and father, who was even then amassing his troops in Chrysopolis.

"Why can't you be friends, Uncle?" he had asked.

"Well, I'd like to be," he had replied, "but only one person can be emperor if the Pax Romana is to survive."

Now again and again he imagined the boy's terror as unknown hands dragged him from the Parousia celebrations and down through the side streets to the Tiber. "Futuo!" he thought. "Some peace, if that was the price paid for the Pax Romana."

"Anthony has returned with several guests," announced his adjutant. "And they have sent word that they would like to see you later this afternoon."

At this news he sat up in his bed. Despite his extreme weakness he managed to revive sufficiently to allow his courtiers to wash and dress him and make him as presentable as possible.

"Fetch the other Eusebius, the *sacerdos* from Nicomedia who is currently living in the city here, and tell him the emperor says it's the time. He'll know what I mean," he said.

And so when the comēs arrived he was seated with the sacerdos in the balcony of the apartment overlooking the buildings of the great capital city that he had built with Helena's help, the worship centre with its presumed relic dominating the scene.

As his sometime comēs entered the room he rose shakily to his feet, making no attempt to conceal how ill he was. "You have all come, and I'm utterly unworthy of it," he said, and immediately broke down, his whole body wracked with sobbing and his tears flowing uncontrollably.

Felix, flouting all protocol, simply took the emperor in his arms.

"Can you forgive me, Felix?" he said. "Can anyone forgive me? I'm the Emperor Constantine the Great, I have my capital, a deadly Pax Romana, a wicked damnatio memoriae but I have no peace. None."

"There is peace," said Marcus, gently helping Felix sit the emperor back on his couch. "The equal cross brings it."

Eusebius the sacerdos cleared his throat, as if to remind them of his presence.

But Marcus continued undeterred. "Everything any of us have ever done, even the Trinity's decision to create, to risk love, it all resolves at the cross. No one is damned if they come to the equal cross. We forgive you, Valerius forgives you, Fausta and Crispus forgive you. They are now with those whose cross it is. They all forgive you."

Felix intervened at this point.

"Yes, it's true," he said, "but let Constantine confess everything he wants to. Then forgiveness will flow and we can baptise him. Is this alright with you, sacerdos?" He looked across at Eusebius.

"All's well my friend," he replied. "His excellency has told me all about you. I'm here with water for baptism and the bread and wine for forgiveness. But he wants you to do it, with your friends' help. I'm just here with my Amen at the ready!"

Constantine struggled down from the couch and onto his knees while his comēs knelt around him, Marcus and Titus supporting him on each side. Then faltering in speech but firm in intent, Constantine began his confession.

"I failed God and I failed you, my faithful comēs. I repent of my self-importance and self-sufficiency. I especially repent for making assassination a tool for peace and love when it was only ever a tool of war and hate towards my potential rivals. I repent for justifying to myself in my anger that Valerius, even Crispus," here he faltered and let out a heart-rending cry – the utter reverse of his old typical laugh, thought Marcus – "were worthy of death."

Marcus was right at that, for then he did throw his head back in the old manner, but now he wailed and wailed. "Even Fausta," he said, "even Fausta."

Felix took the huge water jug from Eusebius.

"Do you believe that Jesus died for all this and more, Constantine?" he asked.

"I do," came the reply.

"And do you now turn to his way of peace and repudiate all else?"

"Oh yes, oh yes," he replied. Felix stood while Marcus and Titus removed Constantine's outer garments. Then with a huge smile he began to pour the water over Constantine's head, where it mixed with his tears and soaked through his underclothes. Then he reached out for the bread and wine that Titus and Marcus held for him. Finally, with a huge effort, Constantine threw back his head and laughed and laughed. Then sinking back against the couch he breathed his last. At first they thought he was just tired out with the effort of their meeting, the confession and the baptism. But as they checked his pulse and the sacerdos felt for a heartbeat, there was no doubt about it. His attendant spoke up.

"I'm amazed he lasted this long. I thought it was over weeks' ago. But he was determined to wait for you."

"We are so glad he did," Felix replied. "And thank you and your comrades for caring for him so tenderly. We are very grateful. Now we leave him in your care. There will be much for you to do to let his advisers know, to prepare for his burial and for his son Constantine II to take his place. But we have done what we came to do."

Turning to Eusebius of Nicomedia he continued, "We thank you for the grace and kindness you have shown, dear sacerdos, but now we will take our leave."

So saying they headed back for the ship and the voyage home.

Chapter Seventeen

Angels and Pilgrims

Eusébie sat quietly on her couch in the atrium. All the time that the erstwhile comēs were journeying to and from Constantine's deathbed in Constantinople, she was doing her best to travel with them in prayer as she had done in former days. When the weather was unfavourable, instead of the arbour in the peristyle, this couch on the labyrinth beneath the palm tree was her permanent post. She could no longer discern the sharpness of the sunlight, the precise line cast by the tree's trunk nor the distinction between the white and black tiles of the mosaic, as she could as a child. But the memory of it was still etched indelibly in her hippocampus. She knew from others' remarks that the tree was by now twice as tall and the trunk vastly thicker than she remembered. It meant that the Minotaur's prison was darkened sooner and for longer. Rather than freeing the beast, might it crush it? Eusébie endeavoured to draw encouragement from this possibility. Her childish hope had been that the empire's armies led by men like her father would overcome the Minotaur's oppressive intentions and destroy it. She had thought that the Minotaur represented the old religion which sustained the wars. Yet, with her uncle's death, she had realised that this was the deeper malignancy also lying behind the Pax Romana's dominance, and which only the kingdom of love could dispel. Her dreams and Melissa's interpretation of them had convinced her that she had a crucial part to play in this, and the arrival of Constantine thirty years ago, with his vision for the posse, had revealed what it was. She was to tend the spiritual space for the kingdom of love to prosper through the posse's journeys to and from the empire's frontier.

Truth to tell, she did not find it so easy now. Hope had been a particularly significant motivation for her ever since she started going blind as a child. True, as the physician had projected, she had developed many different ways of seeing other than physical sight. Nevertheless, it was the hope of success for the posse that had lifted her out of her otherwise shrinking world and placed her into the heart of the journey to a new humanity. Finding the way to permanently inseminate the empire with the transformative seed of messianic love had become her life's objective, so, with what she regarded as Constantine's fall and the consequent dissolution of the posse, the potential of her life's calling had diminished virtually overnight. Of course, she knew that the Metilians and the slave ecclesia were stewards of a great inheritance of love and service to the city that spread right out to Gaul and back to Africa. But her dreams and Melissa's interpretation of them had given her a specific personal objective to bring about the defeat of the Minotaur's imperial power and replace it by life-laying-down loving. It had been hard to persevere with that in the face of Crispus' and Fausta's death. They had seemed to embody her hope and now they had been murdered by Constantine himself as really as if by his literal hands.

Suddenly, she was startled by the sense that someone else was in the atrium with her. Her sensitivity went so far beyond that of any normally sighted person that she recognised her friends and relatives by footfall, smell, and personal presence. So she knew almost beyond doubt that this was no one familiar to her. Yet she was not aware of any fear or even caution. It was a friend who she didn't yet know.

"Welcome," she said. "I am glad you have come. But who are you?"

"I'm the angel of the Somme," came the reply. "I've come to tell you that it's your time."

"That's encouraging," she replied. "I've wondered if it would ever come again. It's felt like time has been paralysed for more than ten years. But please tell me what you mean."

"It's time for you to come with me to the Somme," replied the angel.

"But how and what for?" Eusébie asked.

"I will guide you," replied the angel. "You will need to form a new posse. It won't be hard to find its members because once they hear of your intent they will offer voluntarily and you will know which of them to choose."

"But you still haven't told me why you want us to return to the Somme with you," Eusébie ventured.

"I think that deep down you know," replied the angel. "What is it that you would have wanted to do if you were able?"

"Find Quentin and give him an honourable burial," she said, almost without thinking. "Exactly," the angel continued. "You shall travel to the Somme, to the wharf where Acco and the others searched. But this time, when you step out into the river, you will see with your own eyes Quentin's body emerge to the surface of the water."

"I will see with my own eyes?" responded Eusébie incredulously.

"Yes, your eyesight will be perfectly restored," declared the angel.

"And what then?" Eusébie enquired.

"Then with the help of your companions, you will gently lift your uncle's remains out of the river and place them on an ox-drawn plaustrum. Together you will follow the oxen up the hill. When they come to a halt, there you shall bury his body and new far sight will be added to your restored physical sight. There you shall build a shelter for the poor and needy where his life will be honoured and his messianic love will be manifest and shared throughout the years to come."

"Now I'm going to disappear and hide myself," said the angel. "I will reappear if you need me. But know in any case that I am quite literally at your beck and call for the days ahead. And not only me. There are others of us on the journey, some that companions of yours have sensed before although not seen." At this Eusébie found herself overwhelmed with the tangible presence of love in a way that she'd not felt since the days of Quentin's martyrdom. A surge of faith and hope permeated to the depth of her being, even as she sensed the angel's physical retreat from the atrium. I'll announce this to the ecclesia as soon as Felix, Titus and Marcus return, she decided. In the meantime, I'll begin to make plans. We'll need a fellowship of at least nine, one for each year of my life that passed before I knew my calling. Two good horse-drawn carpenta and maybe three or four extra horses in case of need. Already she had some idea of who her companions might be, but remembering the angel's words, "they will offer voluntarily and you will know which of them to choose," she restrained herself from over planning until she knew who was coming.

***

"What happens now?" mused Titus, as they occupied their familiar positions again with their backs to the stern of the ship. They had been unusually taciturn during the first few days of the return voyage, their conversation mainly concerned with the food, the weather and the uncomfortable sleeping arrangements. They all knew that they would get to the subject of Constantine's deathbed and its implications in due course. There were nearly three weeks of voyage ahead of them and plenty of time for their hearts to open to one another. Now they were ready to talk.

"Constantine Junior will become the sole emperor like his father," Marcus responded. "How old is he now, twenty-two or so? And he's not a bad fellow by all accounts and carries a lot of his mother's grace, and something of Dunnius' influence from his early years."

"But probably now seriously messed up by Eusebius of Caesarea's toxic elitism," posited Felix.

"Do you think the bishop is really that bad?" asked Marcus.

"Frankly yes, if you think about it," Felix replied. "While he might not be directly to blame for the murder of Crispus and Fausta, his hierarchical sovereignty perspective on power justified it."

"I meant something other than what happens next politically in the leadership of the empire," Titus interposed. "I was thinking about us, and the kingdom of love. What just happened has surely resolved something. Constantine's confession seems to me to have accomplished more than allowing him to die forgiven and at peace. It has removed the block of Crispus' and Fausta's murder from our future pathway. Over these last few days I've started to feel like we are the posse again, as if Constantine is somehow restored to it, although no longer physically with us. Like its purpose has been reinstated."

"But what was its purpose?" asked Felix. "If it was to synergise the two ways to peace, surely it didn't work and can't ever work?"

"I'm not so sure," intervened Marcus. "If you mean that the Pax Romana is ultimately dependent on violent domination, Minotaur style, then of course I agree with you. But what if the indestructible kingdom of love has a grace aspect? That while it will one day come forever everywhere, in the meantime it provides the salt and light to the darkened peace to make life bearable for those who live under it?"

"And ultimately provide the chance for people to step out from under it, even on their death beds? Like the thief on the cross you mean?" said Titus.

"Yes, just that," Marcus replied. "That's the power of the equal cross. It extends to any and every person and thing, from the Trinity to the worse sinner and stills the earth's storms and crises too. Jesus' resurrection is surely the proof."

The remainder of the voyage was hardly time enough for the outpouring of ideas, plans and visions that erupted from the three of them at this point. Ideas for elucidating, embodying and expanding the implications of love-based life and activity.

"It can't just be on the Janiculan Hill among the companions," observed Marcus. "It must be inseminated throughout all the classes and people groups of the entire empire."

"And beyond," added Titus. "It's what Nesta, Junia, Jonas, Lucia and the prison ecclesia have already been doing with their food and empowerment shelters."

"They've been the ones that kept the messianic kingdom present this last decade," said Felix. "They've been truly faithful. We need to get behind them more."

"I still have my question of what's next though," continued Titus. "There's something more waiting for us. Something new. When the labarum ripped from the top to the bottom I felt it. As you said, Marcus, it was certainly a sign of success for our meeting with Constantine. But I'm certain that's not the end of it. Something is opening up, some new way ahead for us, for the posse!"

"We are no starry-eyed youngsters now, Titus," responded Marcus. "We are fifty years old, cousin, and you and I have our wives and children to think about. Maybe Felix here can start out anew, be another Quentin, but probably not us."

"We shall see," Titus replied, "and for a fact neither Nesta nor Constantia will appreciate being categorised as wives who hold us back in any way! You should know that, Marcus, given Constantia's unbelievable courage from childhood until now!"

"Come on!" bellowed Marcus. "Put me in my place please, before she does!"

***

Eusébie hardly gave the three companions time to arrive back to Villa Metilia before, on excuse of having the whole ecclesia hear the outcome of their visit to Constantine, she called an extraordinary meeting for the following evening. She extended the invitation to any from the prison ecclesia who were free to come. So it was a packed atrium who heard their account of the emperor's confession, baptism and death. As they listened a palpable sense of relief filled the room. It was not simply that the three had returned safely having fulfilled Constantine's request. Rather the same sense of season change that Titus had felt greeted their news. For the first time in years what Junia had once described as something "positively messianic" lifted the companions' spirits. The very fabric of the hill and villa was once again infused with the presence of love. The decade of gloom and depression had lifted. Their beloved friends' murders had been atoned for. Melissa stood to her feet, helped by a sturdy stick these days. But her voice was as steady as ever.

"I've been thinking," she said. "The news of Quentin's murder fifty years ago was accompanied by the presence of substantial love. But the murder of Crispus and Fausta ten years ago brought no such gift. And now I know why. Their murders were carried out in the chosen cause of our ecclesia and by our beloved adopted brother and leader. It wasn't martyrdom; it was betrayal and heartbreak! It has been hard to rise above that. But now the betrayal is confessed and forgiven and we are back on track. Thank you, Trinity, thank you, brothers and yes, thank you, Constantine."

Silence fell on the company. And then, quietly at first but with the plainsong swelling to a crescendo they began to sing Mary's song.

"My soul exalts the Lord, and my spirit rejoices in God my Saviour.

He has regarded the humble state of his bond slave; behold, from this time on all generations will count me blessed.

For the Mighty One has done great things for me; holy is his name.

His mercy is on generation after generation toward those who run to him.

He has done mighty deeds with his arm; he has scattered those who were proud in the imaginations of their heart.

He has brought down rulers from their thrones, and exalted those who were humble.

He has filled the hungry with good things; and sent the rich empty-handed away."

As the final notes of the refrain ended, Eusébie remained standing.

"I've another story to tell," she began. All eyes were immediately on her. They understood, just by the tone of that brief statement that, their beloved companion was back. Her years of struggle under the pall of the damnatio memoriae were over. Without leaving anything out, she related her meeting with the angel of the Somme.

"I need nine people including me," she announced. "Who will it be?"

"Can I come?" piped up a child's voice. And without waiting for an answer, Paola, the nine-year-old daughter of Constantia and Marcus, pushed her way through the gathered ecclesia and stood beside her. In the moment of surprise that followed, Constantia joined her.

"I suppose you are coming too, Marcus," Constantia said.

Marcus came and stood beside them. Then came Amadeus.

"I'm coming, Aunt, if you'll have me."

There was a sudden movement among some members of the prison ecclesia who were at the back of the atrium by the entrance to the vestibulum. A young woman with a look of great determination made her way forward. It was Lucia, the daughter of Junia and Jonas.

"You will need someone from the prison ecclesia, I'm thinking," she declared.

"That's six already," announced Paola, "If you'll have us, that is. So who's next?"

Titus and Nesta ventured forward.

"We'll be coming too, if Amadeus doesn't think we'll cramp his style," said Nesta.

"Well then I guess that leaves me," said Felix, smiling.

Eusébie stood weeping before them. "Thank you, thank you, she said. It's beyond my expectations. I welcome you all! Not a Daniel posse this time, but a Mary posse!"

Then Valeria came forward.

"I'm willing to come too," she said. "I realise that I'm seventy years old and not as strong as I used to be. But I so wanted to be on Quentin's team to Gaul when I was a girl."

Eusébie met her eyes.

"Without your spirit of adventure, I'd not be who I am," she said. "I would be going nowhere in the spirit let alone in the body!" Then she paused. "I have the nine," she said. "But there is still a crucial part for you. My part, the one I played all those years here on this hill, travelling in prayer and keeping the spiritual space for the journey. Now that shall be your privilege and I know you will do it wonderfully!"

"Thank you, thank you," Valeria replied, her words clearly heartfelt and without regret. "Then that is what I will do, and while I know that Melissa, Fortunatus and Claudia will back me up, it shall be my whole task from this day forward."

It was decided that the nine of them would meet for ientaculum the following morning. Eusébie arranged for Claudia, Fortunatus, Melissa and Valeria to help prepare it for them all in the warmth of the June morning on the balcony of the peristyle so that they too could be part of their plans.

"When do we go?" asked Paola, hardly had they sat down.

"Hold fire, young lady," responded Felix, laughing. "Let your Aunt Eusébie take her time!"

"It's alright, Felix," retorted Eusébie immediately. "I sense an urgency, a precision, in the timing of the angel's visit. I think Paola has been connecting with that from the moment she ran forward yesterday."

"If we go ahead soon, it will mean travelling through the heat of the summer," said Marcus.

"But if we leave it until the autumn we will have wind and rain to contend with," responded Constantia. "And I have memories of some difficult autumn journeys!"

"I'm in no hurry as far as the promise of restored sight goes," said Eusébie. "I've had years of physical blindness as my norm in life. But I think that this journey is somehow about the alignment of times. Even small adjustments are important at times like these."

"In which case why don't we discuss any preparations that we know will be necessary, and after that we can put a date to it," suggested Amadeus.

"Well, that makes sense," said Felix. "So exactly what preparations will we need?"

"I've been hoping for as much comfort as is practical," began Eusébie. "So at least two carpenta, maybe plus a carruca? And enough horses in case of eventualities to begin with, although I realise that we will need to replace at least some of them in the course of the journey. And rather than be too dependent on mansiones or barracks, for occasional nights, while some can sleep in the carpenta I think we are going to need tents too. But you three have plenty of experience of all this of course!" she concluded, stretching her arms towards the former comēs. "Beyond this, can I leave the rest to you?"

"Of course you can, Eusébie," responded Marcus, "but I'm thinking of a different kind of preparation. Have you any idea what the journey is about beyond the messianic promise of its destination?"

"That's a good question, Marcus," she replied. "I think it's why we are together right now. The angel told me that the posse would all be volunteers and I would know they were the ones when it happened. So my thinking is that we plan this together, and each of us brings ourselves with our strengths and, yes, our weaknesses too, as a gift, and we discover the way between us."

"How about we begin by checking as to whether anyone is already carrying a particular sense of what the journey is about?" suggested Titus. "Nesta was beginning to have some thoughts last night when we were preparing for bed."

"It was more about the eventual destination for Titus and me," Nesta said. "We have never been back to my home in Lindum, even after all these years, and it seems likely that this is an opportunity for us to continue on to there. That we should be expecting the journey to prepare us for that."

"Maybe there are some special things we should take with us, you mean?" asked Amadeus. "Well, you for a start!" Nesta replied. "But I didn't mean to make this about us, rather I'm thinking that there may be a definite purpose for each of the posse beyond simply supporting Eusébie in her pilgrimage. And that these personal specifics will combine together to make it all the fruitful adventure that it's meant to be."

"Can I say something?" asked Lucia. "From the moment Eusébie shared about this I knew deep down that I was to volunteer so as to carry the substance of the prison ecclesia. That it was about the shelters for the poor, encouraging them in Augusta Treverorum if we go that way, but maybe inspiring others to start them in places like Colonia Agrippa, and in Gaul when we get there."

"Come on!" cried Paola. "What d'you reckon to that, Pater?"

At which point Valeria spoke up. "When Nesta mentioned that this is an adventure, it made me think of what Eusébie said yesterday about my effect on her over the years. And I may be getting old now but I'm not forgetting her dreams, nor Melissa's interpretation of them. This Mary posse is surely still in the flow of the original posse of nearly thirty years ago? So I'm thinking we should maybe hear from Melissa, and see if she has any more understanding of its purpose?"

"As it happens, I do," Melissa responded. "And it's quite big and maybe rather dangerous."

"Well, we'd better hear it, Mater," Felix replied. "If that's alright with you, Eusébie, of course."

"I know without doubt that this is the restoration of our original calling to defeat the Minotaur's imperial power and replace it by life-laying-down loving," Eusébie responded, "and Melissa remains at the heart of that!"

"Then this is what I am seeing," Melissa began. "I may find it quite difficult to share, as it goes to the depths of my disappointment and personal questioning of my own gift and calling. But I will try and explain it as well as I can."

"It's about the dead," she began, tears welling up in her eyes. "It's what I was feeling for at the meeting of the ecclesia yesterday. The difference between Quentin's martyrdom and the love it released, and the murders of Crispus and Fausta and the pall of depression that followed the edict of damnatio memoriae. It appears that the angel knows that even more love will be released from Quentin's life by properly honouring his martyred body. Now that the betrayal and heartbreak of our beloved friends' murders has been lifted by Constantine's confession and baptism, is there something we can do to release love and blessing from their bodies?"

"But we have honoured both their bodies and Val's," interposed Eusébie.

"Well, yes, we have," Melissa continued. "We have buried them here in the memorial garden alongside Commodus. And now with the graves of Lactantius and Dunnius alongside them it is a place with some degree of peace. But, for me at least, it is more a place of hope deferred and grief that remains. What if we were to go to the actual places of their murders, and do something to apply Constantine's confession to the very ground on which their blood was spilt?"

"Are you thinking that somehow this calling to go and further honour Quentin's willing martyrdom is flowing from that confession too?" asked Felix. "That even more than, say, Rictiovarus' repentance and conversion, the repentance of the emperor himself has shifted something? What do you think, Pater?"

"Well, I did hear that some attempt was made back then to find Quentin's bones, but to no avail," replied Fortunatus. "But maybe it is all a question of the alignment of times."

"I begin to understand why you said that this might be dangerous," declared Eusébie. "You are suggesting that we visit the bathroom where Fausta was murdered and the barracks where Crispus died?"

"Yes," Melissa replied. "And the wharf where Val was drowned in the Milvian."

"Wow," said Amadeus. "Then how and when are we going to do all this?"

"It may not be as hard as it sounds," said Constantia. "After all, I was the emperor's sister and I am still the aunt of Constantine II. I think Helena Junior is currently living in the Palatine and almost certainly will be supportive of an action reinstating her mother."

"And then there's the imperturbable Anthony," interposed Marcus, "He's still a general in the Scholae Palatinae. If anyone can provide the cover for us to visit the Clusium barracks, he can."

"Then this is what I suggest we do," said Eusébie. "We will take the next few days for Constantia to approach Helena Junior and Marcus to approach Anthony. We will get our own stonemasons here on the hill to make discreet plaques for each of our beloved three friends and relatives. We will think more about what to put on them. In the meantime, we will obtain the carpenta, carruca, tents and horses and put together the basic provisions for the journey. Then we will begin our pilgrimage with these acts of loving memory at the Palatine, the Milvian and Clusium. All being well we will leave before the week is out."

***

The following afternoon Constantia presented herself at the royal apartments of the Palatine together with Paola. She had had no close contact with her nephews or niece since the murder of their cousin, mother and uncle and the imposition of the damnatio memoriae. So, in hope that news of her father's deathbed repentance had reached Helena Junior and lifted any remaining awkwardness towards her aunt and cousin, Constantia had asked Paola to come too. Her daughter's openhearted ingenuousness invariably warmed people to her and she hoped that Helena would prove to be no exception. As it transpired Constantia had no need to worry on any account. As the attendants showed them into Helena's personal apartment she leapt to her feet in delighted surprise.

"Constantia, how wonderful that you have come. And Paola too! I suppose you have heard the bittersweet news of Pater's death? Now we can speak again of Mater. It's such a pressure off of my heart!"

"Well, I thought you would have heard and this would be your response," said Constantia. "But it's a relief to hear it none the less."

"We've something very important to ask you," broke in Paola. Constantia caught her breath momentarily, as if to interrupt, but her daughter chattered on. "It could be dangerous if the wrong people found out," she continued. "But we want to bring some friends to pray in the room that Aunt Fausta was murdered in."

Helena sat down quite suddenly on her couch, clearly startled by her niece's announcement. "You had better explain what this is about, Constantia," she said.

As simply as she could, Constantia explained the difference between the impact of an unrighteous death and a willing martyrdom, and the sense that she and some of Fausta's friends at Villa Metilia had, that to pray and take bread and wine at the very site would lift the sense of heartbreak and betrayal left by her murder and the damnatio memoriae. "We believe that if we do this then tangible love and blessing will be released throughout the family and beyond," she concluded. She said nothing yet about Eusébie's encounter with the angel of the Somme or the intended pilgrimage to Gaul.

However, Helena was not the least daunted by her aunt's attempt to explain matters. Instead she stood back up, excitement written all over her face.

"There needs to be a plaque," she said. "Nothing too elaborate. But something like 'In memory of the love-giving life of Empress Augusta Fausta, who filled this palace with the presence of the future!'"

"Gosh," said Paola. "Was she really as wonderful as that?"

"Yes, she was!" chorused her mother and aunt, laughing.

"Then we're agreed," declared Helena. "So when are we doing it?"

"In a few days' time," Constantia replied. "I'll be back in touch with more details shortly."

***

Meanwhile Marcus had made his way to the Scholai Palatinae's quarters at the imperial barracks. He was in some trepidation at the possibility of encountering Brutus, who, as far as he knew, still held the position of their chief of staff. He was unsure of how he would be received by his erstwhile comrade, especially if he had heard of the late emperor's confession. While Constantine had not accused Brutus of the murders, he had certainly exposed him to the accusation of having assassinated the two Augustae and supported both the damnatio memoriae and the wicked lie of their suggested incestuous relationship. However, he very much hoped that Brutus was still in Constantinople where he had been based with Constantine for the last decade. Fortunately, the first person Marcus encountered on entering the Scholai's quarters was Anthony himself, who, on seeing his friend, immediately came and seized him in a bear-like embrace.

"Am I glad to see you, Marcus," he cried. "What a time this is!"

"How do you mean?" Marcus replied.

"Well, it is such a difficult time to judge which way the wind is facing," he said. "With part of me I suspect that the young emperor would like to reinstate his mother's memory. But the likes of Eusebius of Caesarea and Brutus want him to ignore his father's confession and maintain the status quo. Otherwise, they will likely lose their own credibility."

"And you?" inquired Marcus. "Will you stay in place whatever happens?"

"Well, I know that I have a reputation as a peacekeeper who tries to hold together irreconcilable ends," Anthony responded. "But it was one thing to do that under Constantine's leadership, quite another in service of a young emperor if he is under thrall to the likes of Brutus. For Brutus is no public servant. He's only ever been a self-servant. Constantine, however, from my perspective, made a terrible decision to maintain what he saw as the peace, but was ever the servant of the Pax Romana and not himself."

"So if Brutus and the Bishop hold sway, you will leave your position?" asked Marcus.

"I certainly will this time," Anthony replied.

"Well then, maybe you will feel able to help me with what is a somewhat dangerous request, in the circumstances, which is why I have come," continued Marcus.

"Then tell me what it is and I will see what I can do," was the reply. So Marcus set about trying to explain Eusébie's proposed pilgrimage to the Somme, and the possible impact of Constantine's deathbed confession on multiplying the impact of Quentin's martyrdom. And then how they had come to believe that their commitment to the angel's summons also indicated a way to completely lift the pall of the damnatio memoriae and release the love and blessing of Fausta and Crispus' lives. Of how they planned to begin their journey first at the Palatine, followed by the Milvian and then Clusium and wanted his help to access the site of Crispus' death there.

Anthony remained silent for a while.

"So what do you think?" interposed Marcus.

"I think I get it," Anthony replied. "But it's not a question of understanding the purpose of these plans so much as the actual potential danger. Brutus is due to arrive in Portus over the next few days, maybe today. In fact, he may be on the way here now. And I won't know until he gets here whether he is planning his exit or taking back control. If it's the latter, then I suspect that violence will be right out in the open this time. I'm not afraid of him, but I'm concerned at what his reaction might be to the news or discovery of plans to reinstate Fausta and Crispus in the public memory, however discreetly."

"Well then, I think it's probably best if I bid a hasty retreat," Marcus replied. "But can you come yourself to the Janiculan Hill tomorrow, or at least get a message to us as to what is happening? Then we can either count on your help or know we need to make other plans."

"Have no fear," said Anthony. "I know who my friends are and where my loyalty will always be. I will find a way to help you somehow. You can be sure of that."

"Thank you, dear friend," responded Marcus. This time he was the one initiating the bear hug. "I will await your response tomorrow."

***

Brutus had plenty of time to think on the voyage back to Rome. True, the young emperor was going to need some strong legates around him, and his role in the imperial court in Constantinople throughout these last ten years made him an ideal chief of staff going forward for the new reign. But he also knew that Constantine II did not like him, and deep down he was fairly certain this was because he held him responsible for his mother's death. With Helena gone and Constantine's deathbed confession, he was far less secure in his role now. Indeed, he had seriously considered that he might even be under threat for his life. So the reason for his return to Rome was to consolidate support for his position, or else to lay it down altogether. The further he got away from Constantinople the more disinclined he was to attempt to hold on, in fact he planned not to return. But he needed an overview of the situation in Rome, and concluded that the best person to get that from would be Anthony. He resolved to head straight for the Scholai Palatinae headquarters at the Palatine as soon as they docked in Portus. Then he would listen carefully to Anthony's overview before heading for his family home to evaluate it. His mother was still alive, just, and he would lie low there. If his position in Rome was still reasonably secure, it might be that he could eventually persuade the emperor to give him a consul role in the West where his experience could help strengthen the youngster's position while keeping him out of his sight semi-permanently.

Hardly had Marcus left the Palatine than Brutus rode into the entrance of the Scholai's headquarters. Anthony was still standing thoughtfully in the yard, and seeing Brutus, wondered for a moment whether he might have seen Marcus leaving. But clearly not, for he dismounted and greeted his second in command with some warmth and no sign of suspicion of any kind.

"Am I glad to see you, Anthony," he declared. "These are tumultuous times and I could do with the latest intelligence."

"How is the Pax Romana fairing in Constantinople these days?" Anthony asked in reply. "Uncertainly, when I left," said Brutus. "The young emperor is facing a multitude of challenges, and isn't clear who he can trust yet. But it was obvious to me that his position is strong enough in Constantinople for the time being and he needs to know that he can trust his influence in the other capitals, especially here in Rome. So please have someone fetch me ale and you can let me know the state of play. I plan to head on to Riano tonight and decide how best to maintain the Pax Romana throughout the West."

The two generals made their way into the shade of the Scholai's inner rooms and sat down together. Anthony noticed that Brutus was less than comfortable and looked round nervously. "He is unsure of his position and even his safety," he observed inwardly.

"Nothing has changed here since the emperor's recent death," he said, "Have no fear. Everything continues as normal. The only shift is a lightness in the air since the news of the emperor's deathbed confession. The damnatio memoriae is still in place in theory but already the names of the Empress Fausta and Caesar Crispus are back on people's lips. They were much loved and hardly anyone believed the tales of incest. But it won't undermine the young emperor's role, I think. Quite the reverse."

"How do you mean?" asked Brutus uneasily.

"Well surely the love felt by older Romans for his mother will reflect on him, don't you think?" Anthony replied.

"Yes, but maybe not so well on those who stood by his father's decree," Brutus continued, looking searchingly at Anthony. "I'm thinking of lying low in Riano for the time being," he said. "Can you continue to take charge here until I know what's what?"

"Certainly," responded Anthony, breathing an inward sigh of satisfaction. "You can rely on me, you know that."

"Thank you," Brutus said, downing the last draft of his ale and getting to his feet. "I'll be off then."

Anthony waited until he was well on his way and then set out for the Janiculan Hill. There would be no problem for the posse's planned visit to Clusium he concluded, and he intended to travel out there before them to facilitate it.

Chapter Eighteen

Love and Memory

Eusébie was delighted with Helena Junior's and Antonio's responses to their proposals to visit the assassination sites, and particularly Helena's suggestions for the memorial plaque for Fausta. The stonemasons were already working on it and a similar one for Crispus. The one for Valerius simply said "In memory of Valerius, son of Constantia and Licinius. His twelve brief years released the messianic kingdom and always will."

The posse met over cena the day before they planned to leave and Claudia, Melissa, Valeria and Fortunatus joined them. As they discussed the possible actions at the sites of their companions' murders, Melissa suddenly came up with the statement

"A cleansed memory brings the loving substance of well lived lives."

"Did that come to you newly, Mater, or have you heard it before?" Felix asked.

"I'm not sure," she replied, "sometimes expressions like this do simply come to me. But it's possible that it is something Fuscian said. He was prone to pithy summaries, and this could well have been one of them."

"Do you think that is what the Messiah meant when he gave us the bread and wine to eat and said 'do this in memory of me'?" Lucia asked. "That he knew that his life laid down was an utterly pure memory that would literally keep bringing his kingdom of love into the world?" "At least that," Melissa replied.

Marcus then referred them to the statement from the book of Genesis when Cain killed his brother.

"Like with God's words to Cain, 'the voice of your brother's blood is crying to me from the ground,'" he said, "our loved ones' blood has been crying out and speaking a curse against our own beloved friend and leader, and therefore against us too. But now that Constantine has confessed, the curse can be broken by the memory of Jesus' shed blood. So I'm thinking that if we take bread and wine together at the sites of our loved ones' murders then the memory power of his life laid down will bring rest to them and release the loving substance of their lives to us and those we touch. What do you all reckon?"

At which point Eusébie felt the presence of the angel of the Somme so strongly that she could barely stand.

"Are you alright, Auntie?" asked Paola, who was standing by her at the time and felt the heat of her hand as she steadied herself against her.

"Yes," she said, "I am a very alright, and think Marcus has seen clearly what we need to do!" They all agreed.

The following day they set out from the courtyard of Villa Metilia. The whole caucus of Metilians were there to send them off. Titus looked at his blind sister, just eight years his senior, as she boarded the carpentum and his heart went out to her.

"What a woman," he observed to Marcus. "She's hardly ever left this hill, and now she is leading a delegation to the Palatine, the Milvian and Clusium to push back the curse of empire before leading us all to Gaul to honour our uncle. Who would have imagined it?" As they entered the imperial palace, Helena Junior strode out to meet them, making absolutely no attempt to conceal her joy.

"Come on, all of you," she invited, "there's no way I am going to hide what we are doing here!"

The nine of them crammed into the fortunately roomy bathroom of the empress' quarters with Helena. The simple task took only a matter of minutes. Marcus had brought a basket containing bread, a flagon of wine and a pottery cup. Constantia broke the bread and Marcus poured the wine. After they had all participated Felix deliberately spread the crumbs and poured the remaining wine on the flagstone floor. As he did so Helena threw back her head and began to laugh. Before long they all laughed until they cried. Then Eusébie declared the words on the plaque as Amadeus fixed it securely to the wall adjacent to the bath.

"In memory of the love-giving life of Empress Augusta Fausta, who filled this palace with the presence of the future!"

Then Felix cried out, "Instead of the damnatio memoriae the memory of Fausta and the substance of her loving life are released into this room, the creation, and the family of humanity!"

As they left the apartment Helena asked if she could accompany them to the Milvian.

"That would be lovely," affirmed Eusébie.

"Come in the carpentum with Paola, Constantia and me," invited Nesta.

"I loved Val," Helena said as she settled herself among them. "And I remember that fateful day as if it were yesterday."

"What exactly happened?" Paola asked.

Helena proceeded to tell the story of her cousin's kidnap and the discovery of his body in the Tiber.

"It haunts me still," she said as she came to the end of her account. "What was it Jesus said?" she reflected. "Better to have a millstone hung round your neck and drowned in the depth of the sea than cause one of these little ones of mine to stumble?"

"Yes," replied Nesta, "And that is some serious curse to turn back when we get to the river, quite apart from all the other blood that has been shed there over centuries."

"My hope is that by covering Val's murder with the memory of Jesus' lovingly shed blood we will somehow extend to all that too!" declared Constantia.

"Well, the apostle Paul said 'love covers a multitude of sins', so may it be so," Nesta responded.

Despite being the familiar crossing place between the Janiculan Hill and the city, in the shadow of Valerius' murder, the Milvian held a melancholy prospect as they drew up beside the bridge. Titus and Felix were riding together at the head of the posse and recalled their encounter with Commodus' bloodied body after the assassination of Maxentius.

"Was Commodus' death a betrayal or a martyrdom do you think?" asked Titus. "Is there still something to be done to release blessing from his slaughter too?"

"If so, do you think that our response to the robbery of young Val's life might encompass it as well?" Felix replied.

"I would like to think so," Titus answered. "And Maxentius' death too. He may have been our enemy, but retribution never brings life." By this point the whole party had piled out of their vehicles.

"You should take the lead on this, Constantia, if you are able," said Eusébie as Constantia helped her down from the carpentum. And without more ado, taking Eusébie by the arm she strode down to the riverside, plaque in hand. Constantia halted by a tree overhanging the river.

"This is a perfect spot," she said. "Let's free Val's soul and fix the memorial plaque here." They stood in a circle together by the tree and Constantia boldly declared the words from the plaque in the midst of them. "In memory of Valerius, son of Constantia and Licinius. His twelve brief years released the messianic kingdom and always will!"

Then they ate the bread which Marcus once again handed round, and shared the cup. As soon as they had finished an entirely unexpected wind disturbed the surface of the river and blew powerfully through the leaves of the tree.

"Job done!" Amadeus announced.

***

While the Mary posse were completing their messianic task at the Milvian, Brutus sat down to cena with his mother Drusilla in Riano. Now in her eighties and frail in body, she was still thoroughly engaged with the political power plays that had been her life-long occupation. She watched her son as he set about his meal. "He looks more bullish than ever," she reflected inwardly to herself. "He has always had a wide forehead, and now with his receding hair and thickening torso, he is a brutish animal of a man."

"Laying low is never the way," she said to him. "You must get ahead of the curve! If you are right that this young emperor may hold his mother's death against you but also recognises the significance of your ongoing reputation, then the idea of his granting you the consul's role in the West is a good one. Don't wait for him. You are still director of the Scholai Palatinae. You should go immediately to Augusta Treverorum and announce yourself as consul. It won't really be a lie, just a wise move that he may well thank you for in retrospect."

"I'll think about it," he said.

"Don't do anything of the sort," his mother replied. "Learn from Empress Helena, even though she is dead. Remember when you first met her here. She acted instantly whenever she could see a way through the potential obstacles to her power and influence. Go now while you can and before the emperor has further time to act. We have the fastest of horses here in the stables. You can cover forty miles by nightfall." Brutus stood up from the table.

"You were always the decisive activist, Mater," he said. He stooped and kissed her forehead, well aware that he would be unwelcome there for another moment. "I'd best be off then."

By nightfall he was racing north up the coastal road towards Pisa. "She's right," he reflected to himself. "I've never been one to lie low."

***

It was a three-day journey from Rome to Clusium and the posse planned to spend both nights in the available mansiones on the route, arriving at the barracks in Clusium on the third day out from Rome. As it happened it was already late in the afternoon when they set out across the Milvian Bridge and up the Via Flaminia, and it was necessary to spend a third night on the road in a less than comfortable mansiones. This delayed their arrival at the barracks in Clusium until cena on the fourth day, which worked well as it meant that Anthony, having left Rome ahead of them, had time to prepare the guarding turma for their arrival. He needed the time, as it happened! For just as he had remarked to Marcus the week before, these were uncertain days and those in authority everywhere were waiting to see how the lines fell. Had Brutus been the one to warn them of the expected posse's intentions they might well have been at risk of their lives, the decurio in charge being of a dominating and violent disposition. However, Anthony's arrival with his news of the late emperor's deathbed confession, and his slant on the young emperor's stance convinced him, if somewhat unwillingly, to allow the companions' plans. As a result he had a palatable enough meal of bread, fish porridge, wine and ale waiting for them when they arrived. Anthony was eager to hear news of their actions to lift the damnatio memoriae thus far, and made no effort to hide it from the decurio. He had decided that there was no halfway position and gladly invested his future with theirs, and news of Helena Junior's support had strengthened his resolve, convinced as he was of her potential influence on the young emperor. As a result he had gone so far as to concoct a covering letter of protection from the Scholai Palatinae that the posse could use throughout their pilgrimage if they needed it.

That evening, after an extended cena where the posse recounted their experiences thus far, he led them to the barrack room where he had established that Crispus had been sleeping when the assassin's knife penetrated his heart. The beds were fixed structures organised around the side of the room and the posse followed him to the bunk where the Augusta had been sleeping. Titus carried the plaque and this time Felix carried the basket with the bread and wine.

"My sense is that Marcus should give a lead this time," Eusébie said. "Crispus loved him greatly, as I think was obvious to us all." As the posse stood in a semicircle around the bed, Marcus declared the words from the plaque. Then one by one they ate the bread and drank the wine as Felix handed it to them. As Eusébie received and drank the last drop of wine there was a clatter followed by a commotion behind them. The labarum that had been propped against the wall at the end of the room had fallen to the floor and startled the decurio who had been observing them from outside the door.

"Are you alright?" Paola asked him. White as a sheet, he attempted to look as if everything that had taken place was an everyday event.

"Nothing wrong with me, young lady," he replied, "But there's a power here that's obviously stronger than the labarum!"

"It's called the equal cross," she said. "It brings a loving peace, not war."

Satisfied that they had successfully completed the first stage of their pilgrimage, the posse headed gratefully to the guest barracks set aside for them by Anthony and the decurio. The great difference between this journey and the previous trips made by the former comēs was the absence of hurry. The carpenta and carruca were a very different affair to the chariots which had born them post haste to Gesoriacum, or the rapid canters through Britannia to the Antonine Wall. This time there was plenty of opportunity to take in the terrain, reflect on their experiences and pray or discuss as they proceeded. The Reschen Pass was six days' journey ahead and everyone was aware of the significance of the Alps, either from their personal experience or from the accounts of their friends over the years. In particular the story of Dunnius and Acco and their description of how the land itself seemed to carry the substance of the kingdom of love was often in their minds and conversations. The desire to connect more fully with the land meant that everyone happily acquiesced with Lucia's suggestion that they spend the nights in their tents rather than in the mansiones along the way. In any case it was hot, and spending them indoors was uncomfortable. In the tents the heat was less unbearable, although by the fifth night as they began to make their way into the foothills of the Alps, the temperature was anyway decidedly cooler.

On the sixth day, having broken camp and set about their ascent of the Reschen Pass, Felix seated himself beside Eusébie in the front carpentum, eager to discover whether her inner sight would encounter the same sense of belonging that the Daniel posse and Acco and Dunnius before them had experienced on their passage through the mountains.

"Eusébie," he asked, "When we were still children you told us the story of Dunnius' and Acco's journey and how in the Alps especially they felt the welcome of the land and its resonance with the substance of love that they carried from Quentin's poured out life."

She nodded, smiling.

"Yes, and how you and the rest of the posse sensed the same connection with the mountains as you passed through on the way to Gaul and Britannia," she replied.

Felix looked searchingly at her radiant face and her striking yet unseeing violet eyes.

"Well, I'm intrigued to discover how it is for you, who can't physically see their splendour." Paola, who was sitting opposite, immediately clapped her hands.

"O yes please, Eusébie," she responded, "what can you see on the inside of you?"

Eusébie was silent for some time, radiance emanating from her to such an extent that her two companions were rendered speechless. It simply filled the vehicle.

Finally, she spoke. "For the last hour I have had the same sense of someone with me that I felt in the atrium back at Villa Metilia when the angel of the Somme came and called me to this pilgrimage," she said.

"I think that what you all encountered here in the past was the presence of the angel of the land. I see and feel them here with us right now."

By this point her two companions were encompassed by the presence of a love so great that their hearts literally overflowed with compassion and they began to weep.

"I can't see anyone but they are somehow flowing in and through me!" cried Paola.

"I can feel the caress of the mountains, just as I did thirty years ago," said Felix. "But there's something more now. This is not simply the reassurance and affirmation we felt then. This time I feel huge compassion, a gift for someone or some situation."

Hardly were the words out of his mouth before a shout rang out.

"Hang on, everybody," cried Titus, who was riding alongside the carpentum, taking his turn at leading the way. The caravan came to a shuddering halt and the occupants of the two carpenta and the carruca clambered down onto the road alongside the horses. A young man, barely out of his teens, lay spread-eagled at the roadside motionless, his face and naked upper torso bruised and blooded.

Nesta knelt down beside him and gently felt his neck for signs of life.

"He is still alive," she announced.

At this he groaned and moved slightly. Then pushing himself up on the paving stones with the palms of his hands he began to sit.

"Take care," Nesta said, as Titus placed an arm around his back. "He might be badly hurt."

"Please help us," he asked in Latin with a heavy accent.

"Us?" asked Felix. "Who else is there?"

"The rest of my companions," he said. "We were attacked and captured by a Roman turma, but I played dead. They will have taken the others up to the barracks at the head of the pass. We are tribal people living our own life in the mountains outside their reach, and they don't like it."

"We are heading up to the pass," Felix replied. "I think that the angel of the Alps knew of your plight and has brought us by at this moment to help you. But first please let us tend to your wounds and find you a clean shirt."

By this time Lucia had already fetched a flagon of water and another of wine.

"Here," she said, "Let me clean your wounds."

So with Titus continuing to support his back, she gently washed the blood and mud from his face, arms and chest.

"The angel of the Alps?" asked Amadeus. "What's that about?"

"Aunt Eusébie saw them just now," responded Paola, "and Felix and I felt their presence ready for this moment!"

All eyes were on Eusébie.

"They are still here," she said. "We must make haste to the pass and intercede for this young man's friends. They are friends of the kingdom of love and wish their captors no harm. Please tell us your name," she asked the young stranger. "We are blessed to meet you."

"My name is Sean," he replied. "After the apostle. We are companions of the equal cross." "So are we," said Marcus. "I have met companions of yours before, but a long way from here in the north of Britannia."

"We Celts are tribal people found in many parts of Europe. Particularly from here to the islands of Britannia and Eire. The messengers of the Messiah travel often among us and many of us are his companions now."

Sean was by now much revived by their care, and helping him cautiously up the step into the second carpentum they all climbed back into their vehicles and onto their horses, and made their way once more towards the pass high ahead of them.

"It will be interesting to see whether Anthony's cover note of the Scholai Palatinae's formal protection will go so far as to incline the decurio to allow us to intercede for these Celtic tribes folk," observed Marcus to Titus, who was now riding in the carruca with him and bringing up the rear of the caravan.

"I'm inclined to think that the angel of the Alps will tend to that," surmised Titus.

By late that afternoon the barracks loomed ahead of them at the summit of the pass. As they drew off the road and into the courtyard of the barracks, several guards stepped out in front of them, their arms raised in clear indication that they should stop right where they were.

"We can't provide hospitality for casual callers today," declared one of them, obviously the senior.

"We are no casual callers," responded Felix, who was riding the leading horse. "We come with official papers from General Anthony of the Scholai Palatinae."

He pulled the document out from under his sagum and offered it to the soldier.

"Remain here with my fellow guards," he said, and strode across to the barracks. A few moments later he emerged with the decurio, a decidedly portly and benevolent looking character.

"What can I do for you?" he asked. "This is a rather inconvenient moment for entertaining guests," he continued. "We are already stretched in the attempt to contain an unruly bunch of outlaws we arrested earlier as they made their way about their rascally enterprises."

"We may be able to help with that," replied Felix, by now joined by Titus and Marcus. The others remained in the vehicles for a moment, not wanting to alarm the decurio by their numbers until it was safe to show themselves.

"How might you propose to do that?" he replied.

"We are former comēs of the late Emperor Constantine," explained Marcus, reaching out his hand. "We have experience of these tribespeople and already met one of their number who we found beaten unconscious at the side of the road in the midday sun. We have him here with us now. He is somewhat recovered and eager for us to intercede for his companions, who wish the empire no harm."

"Well, it's not what it looked like to us," the officer replied. "By the food and products they were carrying they were clearly bent on illegal trade without any intention of paying the taxes due."

"If there are taxes due, we will pay them," responded Titus. "Please let us speak with their leaders."

The portly Decurion smiled, his chins wobbling in appreciation.

"If you can help us calm the situation it might well earn you a night's sleep," he replied. "Frankly, if you can give me a good reason to send them on their way, all the better. We've more than enough to do with the daily task of patrolling the pass without keeping unhappy prisoners."

"We have some experience of peace-making," Marcus replied. "If you can take us to the group, we will see what we can do."

"Well, I'd be very grateful," responded the decurio. "My men here will help you park your vehicles and settle the horses."

At this point the other six clambered out of the two carpentum followed by Sean. "You had better come with me, young fellow," the decurio said, taking the young Celt by the arm, quite friendlily. Then addressing himself to the rest he remarked, "I can see that you are going to need food, drink and a barrack or two for yourselves." Then turning to the guards he instructed them to "sort something out" and taking Felix by the other arm and beckoning to Marcus and Titus barked, "You three, please come with me."

They followed him into a fortified part of the barracks obviously reserved for prisoners, and where the Celtic outlaws were barricaded.

As soon as the occupants saw Sean, a middle-aged couple, clearly his parents, scrambled to their feet.

"You are alive!" they cried, running to embrace him. At the same time the rest of their company, about twelve in all, broke into a cheer. Sean was definitely much loved!

"These men are companions of the equal cross," he said, addressing them all. "They found me unconscious at the roadside and rescued me. Their other friends tended my wounds and cleaned me up. They are on a pilgrimage to Gaul in the service of the Messiah."

"Now wait a moment," interrupted the decurio. "You can converse as long as you like in your own time. These men have offered to pay your taxes. Your goods are forfeit, but as far as I'm concerned you are free to go."

Several of the Celtic band seemed uncomfortable at this, but looked for a lead towards the couple who appeared to be Sean's parents.

"We will go on these terms if these men and their party are prepared to accompany us on our way," responded his probable mother.

"This is an odd turn of events," retorted Felix. "We simply thought we would be making peace between you and the decurio here. Now we seem to be the price of the peace!"

"Well, will you go with them?" interposed the decurio, delighted at the prospect of a peaceful evening without prisoners or unexpected guests.

The three comēs looked at one another. "Yes, we will, gladly," responded Marcus.

And so it was that later that evening, the caravan found themselves heading up a barely passable track that left the Via Solemnis some two or three miles down the far side of the pass, and following the ponies and ox-drawn plaustrum of the Celtic companions.

Before nightfall they came to a settlement of cottages arranged around a greensward in the lea of the mountainside. A welcome party appeared from the doors of several homesteads as both expected and unexpected travellers drew up onto the grass. Led by Sean and his parents, for such the posse now definitely knew them to be, the Celtic companions embraced the welcomers.

"We were taken by the barrack turma, but these friends rescued us," Sean announced. "They have paid our taxes, which was very kind even though we don't believe in such things," declared his father. "They are companions of the equal cross, like us," he continued. "And now a celebration is due. Come let's prepare a love feast this very night!"

There was a fire pit in the middle of the greensward, so while the returning Celts began to make their way to various cottages, others began loading the fire pit with wood. Soon a substantial fire was burning and a boar was roasting on a spit above it. Barrels of ale were then rolled beside it and benches and trestles dragged from several cottages for the guests to sit on. Before long all the ingredients for a substantial feast were in place and their new found friends had seated the members of the posse around it.

"Is the angel still with us?" piped up Paola as she led Eusébie to a seat.

"Yes," she replied, tears of joy streaking her face and sparkling in the firelight. "It's time for us to get to know our friends and discover what the Trinity has in view for this stage of our adventure!"

"Can I begin?" asked Sean's mother. "I am Maglo, and this is my husband Brennus. We are part of a Celtic tribe known as the Alpinae. Some ten summers ago we were visited by a travelling band of Celtic companions who explained to us how Yeshua embraced the equal cross. In our history it stood for our corporate life together in territory centred by the compass points of north, south, east and west where we steward the four elements of earth, fire, air and water. But in Roman tradition the cross was the gibbet where those who refused to accept Roman sovereignty were executed. However, Yeshua made it the sign of his life-laying-down way of loving your enemies even when they utterly reject you. The problem with our cross was that it excluded non-Celts and made us violent and aggressive at times, particularly towards our enemies, as if the earth was exclusively ours. So when the Trinity were lifted up by the Messiah on the Roman cross to embrace everyone and everything, we realised that our cross was lifted up there too, including us in the new loving humanity that will inherit the earth and steward its elements together. The resurrection affirmed this way of loving as the rule of life forever."

"So why do you stay separate from the Romans?" Felix asked. "Isn't the equal cross the sign that we all belong together in messianic life?"

"Well of course it is," Maglo replied. "But it's easier said than done. We are trying to work out how to do it without losing our unique God-given culture!"

"That's how the Messiah's embrace of the Roman cross works," replied Felix. "It makes even the worse that can happen redeemable. When martyrdom is embraced out of love for God and our fellows, even our enemies, then a stream of restorative love is released for the whole of humanity. This is why we are going to Gaul to honour our Uncle Quentin who poured out his life there like Jesus did his. We believe the angel of the Somme has told us that if we find and honour his body in the place where he died then great blessing will flow."

At the mention of the angel of the Somme a ripple of recognition spread among the Alpinae.

"You have experienced angels too, I think," interposed Eusébie.

"Yes, my pater and mater encountered the angel of the Alps many summers ago when I was just a child, and they called us to this place," replied Maglo.

"It was the angel of the Alps that also brought us to Sean and so here," continued Eusébie. "The angels are calling all peoples to live together in loving harmony and mutual respect, and connecting them through the way of life-laying-down loving."

At this, an excited hubbub of conversation among the hosts in their own language consumed the rest of the feast, while Sean showed the posse where they could erect their tents at the edge of the greensward.

The following morning Maglo, Brennus and Sean woke their guests with steaming mugs of ale and bowls of mushroom porridge.

"We are so grateful for your visit and how we were able to share our stories last night," they said. "We have decided that a few of us should make a return visit to the decurio. He seemed a good man just trying to do his job. We are going to offer to make our village a place of hospitality where he can send passing guests who need safe accommodation for whatever reason, and relieve some of the pressure on the turma. Maybe they can reciprocate with a reduced rate of tax. Anyway, we'll see what he says."

"It's something like our prison ecclesia has been offering back in Rome and is beginning to happen in many other cities," responded Lucia. "The special emphasis is on the poor and homeless. It sounds like yours can be a rural version."

"And with ale like yours," added Amadeus, "I reckon the news will spread like wildfire and you will do a roaring trade. Probably the turma will be heading out here on their days off too!"

The Celtic companions insisted on loading them with supplies for the ongoing journey, including a barrel of ale. They would have given them more, but their vehicles and paniers were already full of tents and belongings and other basic supplies. However, it meant that they were well provided for and could spend the next few nights in their tents in the mountains, which they all wanted to do. Then they could load up with further supplies at the various mansiones that lay before them in the two weeks it would take to reach Augusta Treverorum. Despite the July heat which increased greatly after they left the Alps behind, the journey progressed uneventfully. Apart from the not altogether unexpected need to exchange two of their horses and refit two carpentum wheels at a well-equipped mansiones at the beginning of the second week, the worst that happened was that Amadeus managed to fall off his horse and sprain his wrist while entertaining Lucia and Paola, who were riding in the carruca.

Just two weeks to the day after they left the Celtic village, the mile stones indicated that Augusta Treverorum was only a day away. Constantia was riding alongside the caravan with Marcus.

"I am sure that we will be welcome at the palace," she said. "I realise it is twenty-five years since we were there, but Theodoricus returned after Fausta's murder and, if I know him, he will have secured his old job as chamberlain. He will be absolutely delighted to see us, and it would be wonderful to luxuriate in the imperial guest rooms and the bath house!"

"Well, it makes sense to me," her husband replied, "as long as we approach carefully and are ready to beat a hasty retreat if it turns out that he's not there and we are no longer welcome." "Well let's tell the others when we stop for the night and see what they think," she replied.

As they enjoyed a more than usually hearty vesperna in the knowledge that they could replenish their supplies in Treverorum, Constantia explained her thinking about making for the palace and Marcus added his proviso. Everyone was in agreement, especially with the prospect of a bath and comfortable beds.

"Just one thing, though," interposed Lucia. "I'm eager to head for the shelter and see what's going on before experiencing fine food and a luxurious bed for the night. Is it okay if I do that as soon as we get there? Amadeus is up for coming with me."

"Well, I guess you are capable of looking after yourselves," responded Titus. "What do you think, Eusébie?"

"I've been sensing the presence of the angel of the Somme strongly again," she replied. "I think something momentous is afoot. But no reason for Lucia and Amadeus not to visit the shelter. The kingdom of God is there, and that's the safest place to be."

Chapter Nineteen

Minotaur and Martyr

Two weeks after their meeting with the Alpinae, the Mary posse arrived at the city gates of Augusta Treverorum in the early afternoon. According to plan, Lucia took directions from the wardens at the gate and she and Amadeus set off for the shelter, promising to join the others later. The rest of the posse headed for the palace. It was not difficult for Lucia and Amadeus to find what they were looking for. Even if they had inadequate directions, which they did not, the hubbub coming from the shelter, and the queues outside, made its whereabouts unmissable. Making their way past the clamouring crowd they entered to find the building packed with people jostling around trestle tables laden with food.

"Heia!" cried Lucia, "someone has been providing an abundance of supplies."

"They certainly have," responded a skinny young plebeian who was doing his best to bring some order to the clamouring queue of eager recipients. "The consul is providing a seemingly endless supply of food and drink as long as we support his position in return. He's recently arrived apparently representing the young emperor and not everyone is sure of him."

At this, Thaddeus looked across the atrium of the somewhat decaying domus that housed the shelter and at the opposite side of the room could see a bullish looking soldier, clearly of high rank. It was more than ten years since Brutus had been in Rome, and back then Amadeus had only been in his late teens and Lucia several years younger. But Brutus was a distinctive figure, once seen, hard to forget. Both knew they recognised him, but were as yet uncertain who he was. For their part, although they had been weeks on the road, they stood out among the crowd, and while Brutus had no idea who they were, on seeing them, he beckoned them over.

Reaching instinctively for Lucia's hand, Amadeus crossed the room to where Brutus was standing.

"I'm Consul General Brutus of the Scholai Palatinae," he said, eyeing them up and down with particular focus on Lucia. "We are doing a great work here. I've not seen you before, are you new to the city?"

"We are pilgrims, on the way to Gaul," Lucia answered, boldly.

"I'm thinking that there is something familiar about you," he said. "Have I seen you before?" "Well, you certainly know our parents," Amadeus answered, "they were with you in Constantine's first imperial court."

Brutus beamed externally while rapidly gathering his wits internally.

"You are Titus and Nesta's boy," he said. "And yes, you must be the daughter of Junia and Jonas. What a serendipitous meeting! Where are you staying? You must certainly come and stay with me at the palace."

"Well, my parents are also with us," said Amadeus, "together with my Uncle Marcus, and his wife Constantia, their daughter and two other Metilians, Felix and Eusébie. Actually, they have already headed for the palace."

"Heia!" retorted Brutus, "this is a fortunate set of circumstances. You must come with me at once so that I can make sure the guest rooms and baths are ready and a welcome feast is prepared for you all!"

"That is most kind," responded Lucia. "We will gladly come with you. I didn't know that you were so supportive of the ecclesia, as I assume that this shelter is at least partly their initiative?"

"Yes, it is," he said, "but there is much you don't know about me which you will discover before the evening is over."

While Lucia and Amadeus were encountering Brutus, the rest of the posse arrived at the imperial palace. To their delight, Theodoricus came out to discover whose caravan of horses and vehicles had drawn up into the palace courtyard. Constantia was already out of the carpentum hoping to find him, and here he was. Their years of friendship since she was a child before the Daniel posse came, then as a teenager at Fausta's court and finally as part of Constantine's court in Rome meant that there were no airs between them and he drew her immediately into a great bear hug. Then seeing Marcus, he stood back, momentarily embarrassed, before Marcus similarly embraced him. By this time, Titus, Nesta and Felix were all waiting their turn! And Paola and Eusébie stood by waiting introduction.

"Come in, come in," he invited, "But before you do, there is something you need to know." The posse all stood, hesitatingly waiting for him to continue. "Brutus is here," he said. "He arrived several days ago and has instated himself here in the palace as consul for the new emperor."

"*Quid mirum!*" exploded Felix. "Now what do we do?"

"Well, he's not present right now," Theodoricus replied. "He is down at the shelter currying favour with the plebeians in return for their support."

"At the shelter?" interposed Nesta. "This is even more complicated!"

"All will yet be well," Eusébie declared, "I'm sure of it."

"Thank you, Theodoricus, we will come in," said Constantia. "We will wait and see what Brutus makes of this!"

And so they followed the chamberlain into the vestibulum.

"Let me get drinks for you all," said Theodoricus, and meanwhile I will get the guest rooms prepared. Hopefully Brutus will be back before that's done to avoid any embarrassment."

As it happened, barely an hour passed before Brutus arrived with Lucia and Amadeus.

"This is all such a wonderful surprise," he announced, entering the vestibulum and finding the rest of the posse seated there. "I expect Theodoricus is busy preparing rooms and a celebratory late cena," he continued, striding on into the atrium and calling for the chamberlain.

"Here I am, Your Excellency," Theodoricus replied, coming back from giving instructions to prepare the bedrooms and the bath house for their guests.

"Well done, Theodoricus, I knew I could rely on you to offer the hospitality that these dear friends so deserve. Is cena on the way?"

"I've decided that this late in the afternoon it's best to merge cena with vesperna. I hope that meets with your approval," responded the chamberlain.

"Perfect," Brutus replied. "So now my guests, please follow the servants to your quarters and avail yourself of the baths. I will greatly look forward to hearing all your news over our feast tonight."

Later, relaxing in the lantern light at a table overflowing with food and drink, the posse wondered what the evening would bring. They did not have to wait long to find out. Brutus was outwardly on fine form, and immediately asked them to tell him the story of their pilgrimage.

"Who will begin?" he asked.

"I will," said Eusébie, "As it is originally my pilgrimage which the rest have graciously volunteered to share."

And rather to everyone's surprise she dived straight into the detail of the angel's visit, its synchrony with Constantine's deathbed confession and Melissa's understanding of the difference between willing martyrdom and involuntary death at the hands of betrayal and murder. Then she told of how they had applied the memory of Jesus' shed blood to each murder site, and were heading now to release further blessing across the West from Quentin's martyrdom.

Brutus could hardly believe his ears. "The gall of the woman," he said to himself. Yet he continued to beam benevolently at them all, despite the burning anger conflagrating deep inside him.

Then Lucia spoke. "General," she said, respectfully, "Might I express an opinion?"

"Of course," he answered.

"I am so glad that you are providing provisions for the shelter," she continued. "But it's most important that our help for the poor is a genuine love gift and not a transaction in return for something. Otherwise, it fails to build the society of love but only the power of empire in the end."

Once again he could hardly believe his ears. Not only were they blatantly overturning the damnatio memoriae, they were challenging the whole partnership of church and empire! By this point unmitigated rage was encroaching on his every faculty. He could barely contain it a moment longer.

"This has been very informative," he said, "And I am inordinately grateful to you all for coming. But I have had a heavy day, and I am sure you will need to be on the road early tomorrow. So I hope you will excuse me if I head to my bed."

Brutus left the dining area and crossed the atrium towards the imperial suite. But on the way he checked the bedrooms. If anyone interrupted, he would say that he was looking to see that they were properly prepared for his guests. Actually, he was looking to see if he could identify Lucia's room. It was soon obvious, as she had left her distinctive travelling sagum draped over the bed. Then he returned to his suite.

Once he had left the dining area and was safely out of earshot, Felix looked around at the posse.

"What do you make of that?" he asked quietly.

"I suspect he is seething inside," said Nesta.

"I felt that I was to let the truth confront him," explained Eusébie, "which is why I held nothing back."

"Me too," said Lucia, "which is why I spoke the truth like I did."

The posse remained pensively where they were for a few minutes longer, and then themselves headed for bed. It was an hour later that Brutus, unable to sleep or contain himself a moment longer, his now unquenchable rage combined with uncontrollable lust, left the imperial suite and headed back down the corridor to Lucia's room. The night lanterns were burning in the corridor and he could see where she lay. As he adjusted his toga and began to lean down and take her in his embrace, she awoke and leapt out of the far side of the bed in alarm, temporarily speechless with shock. He came swiftly around the bed and placed his great palms on her shoulders intending to push her back down. In a flash the story Nesta had told of her kidnapping in Lindum came to Lucia's mind and without hesitation she brought her knee up into her attacker's groin with every ounce of energy she possessed. Brutus staggered back, clutching his genitals and screaming with pain. Then tottering forward, he stumbled out of the room, up along the corridor and out onto the balcony overlooking the city. Suddenly a lifetime of vain ambition and violent impulse combined with his seething anger at the evening's conversation and exploded inside him. Without a moment's consideration he threw himself headfirst off the balcony. There was a loud crack as his head broke open on the flagstones beneath, followed by a dull thud as his dying body caught up with it.

Meanwhile, Lucia ran from the room heading the opposite way along the corridor and out into the atrium shouting "help me, help me!"

Almost immediately the rest of the posse appeared from their rooms.

"Whatever has happened?" cried Nesta.

"He tried to rape me, the bully tried to rape me," she replied, falling into her outstretched arms.

"We must leave, now," declared Eusébie, and at once they all set about gathering up their belongings and headed out to the courtyard where their vehicles were parked. Felix and Marcus ran towards the stables holding lanterns that they took from the vestibulum. They almost fell over Brutus' contorted body. It took Marcus no time to establish that he was very dead indeed. Felix turned back towards the others.

"He's killed himself," he said, "Brutus has thrown himself from the balcony and is lying here dead."

They stood motionless in shock. Then Titus spoke up.

"We must bid Theodoricus give him an honourable burial, he is a fellow human after all," he said, "but we should leave right away."

By this time the chamberlain had joined them, having been woken by the commotion and as usual was ready to take charge of all things practical.

"Of course," he said," and although I'm unsure whether the general had any real friends or even support here, and there is no imperial night watch at present, the day watch will be up shortly and it will be best if you are gone by then." Morning was breaking as the caravan set out from Augusta Treverorum. A flock of geese flew high above them.

"I suspect no Minotaur will be troubling us for some while," said Eusébie. "But nevertheless, it's high time we were on our way to the Somme."

Although the longer but more substantial Via Belgicus route via Colonia had been better in the past, being more suitable for chariots, the more direct route was fine for the slower, bulkier carpenta. In the three days and two nights it took them to reach Ambianum, they decided to take turns and vary their travelling companions as they went, as they had so much to process together from the events in Treverorum.

"Was it my fault he killed himself?" asked Lucia of Marcus and Constantia as they rode together. Paola was with Eusébie and Felix in the other carpentum, Nesta and Titus were in the carruca and Amadeus was riding alongside.

"It's not surprising that you ask the question," responded Marcus. "But you mustn't blame yourself. Brutus' attempted attack on you was already the sign that he was beyond help, I think."

"Marcus is right, Lucia," Constantia said. "Brutus made fatal choices at many key moments in his life, some of which we were present for. Ultimately, they summated in an ugly death, and its eventual arrival was inevitable. I'm just sorry you had to be caught up in it."

"But I did confront him," she said.

"Sometimes it is loving to confront lies," replied Marcus. "You gave him one more opportunity to think about what he was about. It was he that made it the last one, not you."

As the posse drew near to Ambianum a tangible peace descended on them all. Throughout the last fifty years the bond between the school in Ambianum and the slave ecclesia at Villa Metilia had stabilised their lives. For all of them except Nesta and Constantia it had endured since birth, and with their marriages to Titus and Marcus it had embraced them too. As the final staging post of their pilgrimage, they were confident that the posse would be received with delight and excitement. They were not disappointed! For while their arrival was entirely unexpected, the companions' school in Ambianum existed in a constant state of living hospitality. There was always a welcome, always provision, always a truly listening ear. The constant choice to love had been at its root ever since Quentin and Fuscian had begun their mission there, but since Quentin's martyrdom a space had opened up that invited constant life and growth, and thus far the new generation of companions had remained true to it. As a result each new intake of youngsters was marked by life-laying-down love. They had hospitable hearts as well as habits. This was particularly true of Acco's grandchildren, the twins Pius and Prisca. They had been in the school for five years, since they were ten years old, when their mother, who had been poorly since their births, had died, as had their grandmother some years earlier. Their father now worked the forge, Acco being nearly seventy and arthritic from his years as a blacksmith, although his presence and influence on his son guaranteed that the smithy continued as a centre of excellent work and loving friendship.

Pius and Prisca could hardly wait to introduce themselves to Eusébie once they had discovered who the unexpected visitors were. Their lives had been framed by Acco's stories of his youth, the impact of Quentin's love and martyrdom, his journey to Rome through the Alps with Dunnius and the reception they received from Eusébie and her friends in the slave ecclesia. That evening the school and its ecclesia met to hear from their guests. As Eusébie related the story of the angel of the Somme's visit and the promised events in Augusta Veromanduorum, the twins determined that they would not miss being part of this whatever happened!

So immediately the meeting was over they bounded up to the posse. "We are Pius and Prisca," they announced. "Acco is our *Avus*." "You know, the one who jumped on the shoulders of the soldiers!" "Can we come with you to Veromanduorum? Please?"

The question of whether to take any companions from Ambianum along with them to witness the promised happenings had been part of their processing on the journey from Augusta Treverorum. Some would want to come, they were sure. Eusébie felt strongly that this wasn't to be some kind of show, or any sort of proof that they were in the right and the procurator in the wrong. After all, he had eventually become a follower of the Messiah as a result. Rather the posse's calling was simply to honour Quentin's remains and release even greater blessing from his life that would continue to flow throughout the West long after the empire of Rome ceased to be.

Nevertheless, Eusébie had always sensed that Acco would have a part to play, and when she heard his grandchildren's request, her immediate response was more than simply pragmatic. She felt once again the powerful presence of the angel of the Somme.

"There's to be no general gathering of spectators at the river either from Ambianum or Veromanduorum," she said. "But my sense all along is that Acco would be there. So I think we need the pair of you to come along with us and help provide our posse with any necessary help we need when we get there."

And so it was that the following morning the carpenta had one more passenger in each as they set out on the final two-day leg of their pilgrimage. Up until this point in the journey, Eusébie had been content to live in the moment. She was having such a wonderful time, despite the challenges of the journey, and now the shock of Brutus' suicide. After all, she reflected inwardly, who could possibly want more than being together with their favourite people and serious angels to cap it! The issue of her blindness had long ceased to be a major obstacle and she hardly ever thought about it. But now it came to her that in a matter of a few days at the most she would step into the Somme and physically see Quentin's remains come to the surface. She would be able to see the faces of the twins who were pressed beside her in the carpentum with Constantia and Paola. See what her brother, cousin and Felix looked like as fifty-year-olds rather than babes in arms. See Nesta, Amadeus, Paola and Lucia in the flesh for the first time! See Acco again! Excitement rose to the surface and tears poured down her face.

"What is it, Eusebie?" cried Prisca.

"Only excitement," she replied. "I am going to be able to see you all!"

They camped that night in their tents. Although there was a mansiones along the way, the sense of expectation and angelic presence was so great they wanted nothing to interrupt it. Once their task was done then would be the time to ground the blessing among the people of the region. It was late afternoon on a bright Gaulish summer's day as the posse drew up outside the smithy in Veromanduorum. Prisca was the first down from the carpentum with Prius hot on her heels.

"Avus, Pater," she called. "See who is here!" A benevolent looking older man with a head of tousled white hair appeared in the doorway of the domus.

"What's all this, then?" he asked, laughing, running his hands through his hair. "Have they thrown you out of school at last, you mischievous pair? And sent a deputation from the court to see you safely received?" But then as the posse disembarked and dismounted he put his hands to his face. "Heia," he cried. "At last! Can this really be? Is it you, Eusébie? And are these Constantine's former comēs that I've heard so much about?"

"Yes, it is," she replied. "And others that I so want to introduce you to. But right now, I need your help. Do you have a plaustrum? And a pair of oxen to pull it?"

"Of course, we do," replied Acco's son, who had joined them. He was a younger mirror image of his father.

"I think from what I've seen in a dream that this is my task, Johannes," Acco retorted. "I'll get them now."

Felix stood with the rest of the posse watching and listening to the conversation.

"You are going to do this right away, Eusébie, aren't you?" he said.

"Yes, I suppose I am," she answered. Acco reappeared with the oxen and plaustrum.

"I take it we are heading for the river?" he observed.

"Yes, as near as possible to the barracks on the wharf where Quentin was martyred," she replied. And so the posse headed off on foot, following Acco and the plaustrum that Prisca and Pius had by now clambered onto. When they reached the Somme and the oxen and plaustrum had halted by the wharf, the twins climbed off.

"Come on, you two," said Eusébie, "this is where I need your help. Can you lead me down to the water's edge?" Together they guided her down over the side of the wharf and onto the river bank. "Now I need to go on alone," she said, and without any more ado simply stepped into the water. She had only taken three or four steps, the water midway between her ankle and her knees, when there was a sudden stirring of the river several feet in front of her. And seemingly unremarkably, the sack containing Quentin's body parts floated to the surface.

"That's it," cried Acco. "That's the sack we saw them put Quentin's head and body in. The one I dived in and searched for I don't know how many times to no avail!"

"Yes, I can see it," said Eusébie, stepping further into the river and reaching out towards it. "They certainly used a strong sack! A good advert for Gaulish workmanship!" she declared. Then she simply manoeuvred it towards her and made her way back to the river bank with it in tow. "Well look at you all," she said, her sight perfectly restored. "Anyone would think you'd never seen a miracle before!"

Acco's son reappeared at this point and together he and his father lifted the sack onto the plaustrum. "This is where the next part happens," said Eusébie, and hardly had they laid the sack on the plaustrum than the oxen set off away from the Somme and up the nearby hill followed by Acco, his son, the twins, Eusébie and the rest of the posse. By this time it was early evening and the sun was beginning to set as the oxen pulled their burden up towards the summit of the hill. Then they stopped. "This is the place then," Eusébie announced.

"What, right here?" asked Paola.

"That's what the angel said, apparently," responded Marcus. "Isn't that right, Eusébie?"

"Yes," she replied. "This is where we will bury Quentin's remains and build a shelter for the poor, the sick, strangers, and runaway slaves escaping imprisonment," she replied, words shaped by the implications of her vision tumbling from her mouth. "And it will be led by women with the help of the men in reverse of the empire way. It will be a place for children to play and grow up in love and friendship. I want to create a labyrinth here like the one I grew up with at Villa Metilia," she continued. "Can you help me with that please, Paola? I was nine when I first began to realise what the Minotaur in the middle meant. But this one will have no Minotaur. Instead, there will be a special space at the centre where love dwells and the angel of the Somme can visit those who stand there! But wait a minute, my words are running away with me. The land is important too. My sense is that the Somme and its surrounding territory is the place this blessing will flow from when we give Quentin an honourable burial here. But first, who does this hill belong to?"

"Well, I wondered when you would ask," said Acco. "Rictiovarus and I bought it from the landowner the day after his baptism in the Somme forty years since. Just in case there was a day like today! And now it is yours to do whatever you want with!" he said.

"Thank you, thank you!" Eusébie responded. "It is to be a gift for all who come, like the whole earth was originally given to be!"

Acco reached under the plaustrum where a spade, a pick and a shovel were slotted.

"I thought we might need these," he said. Then he produced a sheath knife from under his tunic. "Don't misunderstand," he said. "I wear this for practical purposes only. Like this one now. We can cut open the sack neatly and spread out his bones on it properly, then dig a grave that we can place them in. But it's up to all of you, of course," he said. "You are the ones who've come to honour him."

"What does everyone think?" asked Eusébie, addressing the rest of the posse. "I always felt we should keep it simple. There are three tools here, and a knife. Titus, Marcus and Felix, can you dig the grave? Make it really deep so that wild animals can't reach Quentin's bones once we've laid them in it. Amadeus, can you please use Johannes' knife to carefully cut open the sack so that Nesta, Constantia, Lucia and I can retrieve the bones and lay them out on it? Then Paola and I will arrange the skeleton in the grave, feet facing the East ready for the coming day of resurrection! Finally, each member of the posse should have the opportunity to say a few words."

They all acquiesced gladly.

"But there is one more thing," interposed Acco. "Won't we need bread and wine?"

"Why, of course," Eusébie replied, "and you should be the one to share it with us. This is your land. And you are the only remaining witness. The very one who declared, 'Father forgive them,' and 'Jesus, lay not this sin to their charge.' And here we all are to declare again with you that all the empire's sin is covered and the power of resurrection stored up in advance in this place!"

At which point the twins set off racing away down the hill to the smithy for the necessary supplies.

By the time Prisca and Pius returned with a loaf of bread and a flagon of wine, the freshly dug grave lay open and the bones of Quentin had been set in place in it. "Let's begin to share what we are feeling now," said Eusébie.

After a moment or two Paola spoke up.

"I thought it would be a really gruesome thing to do, handling the bones," she said, as the twins leaned over to see the skeleton, the feet pointing eastwards, as planned. "But it wasn't at all, once I took a deep breath. It was a wonder. And the presence of the angel was with us all the time."

Constantia stood beside her with Marcus. "I felt all the wasted deaths swallowed up in his willing sacrifice," she said. "For me each bone represented the devastated bodies of Licinius and Valerius, Crispus and Fausta."

"You are so right," said Nesta. "The bones I held similarly represented my brother Commodus, and his life lost at Milvian Bridge."

"I know exactly what you all mean," said Lucia. "Even Brutus' corrupt and ruined body seemed swallowed up into these bones, and I forgave him."

"As we dug this grave I felt that all the potential of the kingdom of love that grew up among us on the Janiculan Hill and gave Constantine hope of a new kind of humanity was sown by Quentin's life laid down here, even though we never knew him personally," said Felix. "Unless a grain of wheat falls into the ground and dies it remains alone," quoted Titus. "But if it dies it bears much fruit."

"What we are doing here today is confirming the fruit that has already come and releasing a greater crop yet," added Marcus.

"And you Amadeus?" asked Eusébie.

"As I cut open the sack, I felt somehow that Quentin's death had cut through the age of empire. Sovereign power stopped the way of love, but instead Quentin's free decision to give himself like his Messiah severed the shroud of empire, and we are cutting it away again today."

"And you, Eusébie," asked Felix. "What do you see, now that you can see both internally and externally?" She looked around at each one of the posse and then at Acco, Johannes and the twins, Prisca and Pius.

"I am still seeing and hearing it," she said. "As we finished placing Quentin's bones with his feet facing East, I saw into the apostle John's vision of the martyrs beneath the altar crying 'How long, O Lord, holy and true, will You refrain from judging and avenging our blood on those who dwell on the earth?' I see far, far down the years." Tears poured down her face and as they watched and listened to her words, they all began to weep profusely. "I see so much death, fratricide and suicide," she continued. "But I know beyond doubt that it is the martyrs' life-laying-down loving and that of the lamb of the equal cross that is the answer to all judgement and revenge." They stood together with incisive agreement.

Then Eusébie declared, "It's time to fill in the grave now." Taking it in turns, the three comēs passed the shovel between them and covered Quentin's remains with the fresh earth. After they had finished, Marcus took four large stones that they had set aside while digging the grave, and placed them in the shape of the equal cross in line with the four points of the compass.

At this point Acco stepped forward with the loaf of bread.

"In the words of the Messiah, this is my body, given for you," he said, tearing the loaf in pieces and handing it around the posse and then to his son and grandchildren before taking some himself. "Do this in remembrance of me."

After they had all eaten he poured wine from the flagon into the mug that had been attached to its handle and passed that around to them all. "This cup is the new rule of life in my blood," he said.

As they passed round the mug of wine, a living stillness settled on the hillside. The presence of the angel was tangible and Eusébie found that she could indeed see both internally and externally. Then she became aware of another person present among them with the angel of the Somme.

"It's me, Beatrice," said a voice, "together with the spirits of the just made perfect."

As they all turned to see the voice that was speaking to them, Beatrice began to sing Mary's song. When it came to the words "his mercy is on generation after generation toward those who run to him", other voices could be heard, myriad tongues and languages from the depth of the earth beneath and the multitude of stars overhead as the love song of the land filled the evening air. Extemporaneously, after a few moments, they all joined in. Tenderly, then harmonising together in clarion refrain, their song resounded out over the verdant meadows, calling for tribes of humanity to come in unity and make their home in joyful partnership with the coastlands and islands of Gaul and Britannia.

Epilogue

Beatrice stood at the centre of the labyrinth on the hill of Saint Quentin watching the years unfolding like a kineograph before her. She leant back into the transcendent relationship of the three in one, remembering the divine moment when they first contemplated extending love to the point of no return. The angel of the Somme drew alongside as she considered the joys and devastations of the coming generations. Together they watched the progress of the centuries until Eleanor of Vermandois appeared, standing right there in the centre of the labyrinth, wondering over the cosmic insights of Joachim of Fiore and what she could do to help implement a shift from the age of the church to the age of the spirit. Beatrice smiled and took the angel's hand.

"She will need to draw on the heritage of Quentin and Eusébie," declared the angel, "and know that love is stronger than death."

"Yes, love is the substance of the resurrection of all things," Beatrice replied, "and it is people that find the faith to embody it who carry it through to the end."

TOP HAT
BOOKS

Top Hat Books

Historical fiction that lives

We publish fiction that captures the contrasts, the achievements, the optimism and the radicalism of ordinary and extraordinary times across the world.

We're open to all time periods and we strive to go beyond the narrow, foggy slums of Victorian London. Where are the tales of the people of fifteenth century Australasia? The stories of eighth century India? The voices from Africa, Arabia, cities and forests, deserts and towns? Our books thrill, excite, delight and inspire.

The genres will be broad but clear. Whether we're publishing romance, thrillers, crime, or something else entirely, the unifying themes are timescale and enthusiasm. These books will be a celebration of the chaotic power of the human spirit in difficult times. The reader, when they finish, will snap the book closed with a satisfied smile.
If you have enjoyed this book, why not tell other readers by posting a review on your preferred book site.

Destiny Between Two Worlds
A Novel about Okinawa
Jacques L. Fuqua, Jr.
A fateful October 1944 morning offered no inkling that
the lives of thousands of Okinawans would be profoundly
changed—forever.
Paperback: 978-1-78279-892-7 ebook: 978-1-78279-893-4

Cowards
Trent Portigal
A family's life falls into turmoil when the parents' timid
political dissidence is discovered by their far more enterprising
children.
Paperback: 978-1-78535-070-2 ebook: 978-1-78535-071-9

Godwine Kingmaker
Part One of The Last Great Saxon Earls
Mercedes Rochelle
The life of Earl Godwine is one of the enduring enigmas of
English history. Who was this Godwine, first Earl of Wessex;
unscrupulous schemer or protector of the English? The answer
depends on whom you ask...
Paperback: 978-1-78279-801-9 ebook: 978-1-78279-800-2

The Last Stork Summer
Mary Brigid Surber
Eva, a young Polish child, battles to survive the designation of
"racially worthless" under Hitler's Germanization Program.
Paperback: 978-1-78279-934-4 ebook: 978-1-78279-935-1